Five absolu[...]
Christmas [...]

Five gorgeous, [...]
the holidays.

Merry
Christmas!

Love Mills & Boon xx

INTERNATIONAL BESTSELLING AUTHORS

Penny Jordan
Diana Hamilton
Margaret Way
Sandra Marton
Jane Porter

Travel all over the world this holiday season
from the comfort of your own armchair

Merry Christmas!

Love Mills & Boon xx

PENNY JORDAN

DIANA HAMILTON

MARGARET WAY

SANDRA MARTON

JANE PORTER

M&B

All the characters in this book have no existence outside the imagination of the author, and have no relation whatsoever to anyone bearing the same name or names. They are not even distantly inspired by any individual known or unknown to the author, and all the incidents are pure invention.

M&B™ and M&B™ with the Rose Device
are trademarks of the publisher.
Harlequin Mills & Boon Limited, Eton House,
18-24 Paradise Road, Richmond, Surrey TW9 1SR

MERRY CHRISTMAS! LOVE MILLS & BOON
© by Harlequin Enterprises II B.V./S.à.r.l. 2009

A Spanish Christmas © Penny Jordan 2001
A Seasonal Secret © Diana Hamilton 2002
Outback Christmas © Margaret Way 1999
Miracle on Christmas Eve © Sandra Myles 1998
The Italian's Blackmailed Bride © Jane Porter 2004

ISBN: 978 0 263 87714 4

25-1109

Harlequin Mills & Boon policy is to use papers that are natural, renewable and recyclable products and made from wood grown in sustainable forests. The logging and manufacturing processes conform to the legal environmental regulations of the country of origin.

Printed and bound in Spain
by Litografia Rosés S.A., Barcelona

A Spanish Christmas

PENNY JORDAN

Penny Jordan has been writing for more than twenty years and has an outstanding record: over one hundred and seventy novels published, including the phenomenally successful *A Perfect Family, To Love, Honour & Betray, The Perfect Sinner* and *Power Play*, which hit the *Sunday Times* and *New York Times* bestseller lists. Penny Jordan was born in Preston, Lancashire, and now lives in rural Cheshire.

Look out for *The Wealthy Greek's Contract Wife*, coming from Penny Jordan and Modern™ romance in February 2010.

Dear Reader,

I have always been fascinated by my fellow human beings and the way they live. And this fascination becomes even stronger when it involves people from another country and culture.

It was a chance remark by a friend of mine concerning a certain New Year's Eve custom in her home city of Madrid in Spain which led me to write this particular story.

I don't want to give away just what the custom is here and now, but I'm sure when you come to it in the story you will recognise it and understand why, as a lover of love and romantic gestures, I just had to use it.

Spain itself has always seemed to me to be a very romantic country – the first romance books I myself read often had a Spanish hero – and I hope that today you will find my particular 'Spanish hero' as compelling as I did those other writers' over three decades ago.

Happy reading,

Penny Jordan

CHAPTER ONE

'OH, THIS must be our car.'

Carefully parking her patient's wheelchair amongst the throng of people besieging the all too few taxis pulling up to collect the departing airport passengers, Meg hurried towards the sleek chauffeur-driven limousine which was just in sight and which, after the long wait they had had, just *had* to be the hire car they had pre-booked in London before leaving for Seville.

Her patient, Elena Salvadores, was an elderly sixty-something and still very frail following the accident whilst she had been on holiday in London, which had resulted in the operation to her knee. This in turn had necessitated her hiring a private Spanish-speaking nurse from the agency for which Meg worked, to accompany her back to Seville and to remain there with her until after the Christmas holiday. Meg had taken to the Señora as soon as they had met and the Señora on her part had been almost embarrassingly grateful to Meg for the care she had given her.

Perhaps it was because of her own accident that she was so easily able to empathise with the anxiety and pain suffered by her patient, Meg acknowledged. As a busy young theatre sister who loved her job, the last thing she had been prepared for was to be attacked late at night in Casualty by a knife-wielding drunk who had inflicted such serious injuries on her unprotected hand and arm that they would never again be strong enough for theatre work.

The pain of losing her career as well as the complications and physical suffering her injuries had caused might have daunted someone less strongly grounded than Meg, even embittered them, but Meg had firmly told herself and everyone else who asked that working for an agency as a private nurse was helping her to become multi-functional. It had been the fact that she was fluent in Spanish which had gained her her present job.

When she had been growing up her father had managed an exclusive marina in Spain and she had spent her holidays there with her parents, quickly learning the language. Her parents were retired now and living in Portugal, where her father could indulge his twin passions of sailing and golf.

The limousine had pulled into the kerb now, a huge highly polished black beast of a car which was attracting the discreetly awed attention of the crowd on the pavement—and no wonder. Personally Meg would have thought that her request for a car suitable to take a wheelchair-bound patient and her luggage might have resulted in something rather more modest, but as she already knew Elena Salvadores was an extremely wealthy woman.

They had flown out from Heathrow first class, and the Señora had insisted that there was no way she wanted to have Meg wearing a uniform, which was why now, as she hurried to speak to the driver of their car, she was wearing a pair of warm trousers along with a toning butter-soft leather jacket. The trousers, with their fine blending of wool and cashmere, like the leather jacket, had been a birthday present from her parents.

She had reached the car now, and was just about to lean forward to speak to the driver when— 'Excuse me!'

A note of icy warning entered Meg's voice as she drew herself up to her full height of almost but not quite five feet four inches—six if you included the heels of her boots—and confronted the arrogantly imperious Spaniard who had appeared out of nowhere to try to lay claim to 'their' car.

Tall, he dwarfed *her*, Meg recognised, and had to be a good two inches over six foot, and broad-shouldered—he was practically blocking out what little winter light there was. Everything about him commanded—*demanded*—that Meg give way to him, to his maleness, his *arrogance*—and that she allowed him to take 'their' hire car.

Thoroughly infuriated by him, as well as concerned

for her patient, who she had sensed had not enjoyed the flight and who was now looking tired and unwell, she opened her mouth to tell him what she thought of his bad manners. But before she could say a word the Spaniard was addressing *her*.

'*Madre de Dios,*' he stormed. 'Are you a *thief*, that you *dare* to try to steal *my* car?'

His car?

Pink-faced with anger and disbelief, Meg turned to face him. His eyes were the colour of obsidian and as cold as ice, his hair thick and black, and as for his face! Meg could all too easily imagine that hawkish, far too good-looking profile impressing *some* women, but fortunately *she* was not one of them, she congratulated herself as she exclaimed in righteous indignation, '*Me* steal *your* car. *I* was here *first*.'

It was ridiculous, Meg knew. She was not normally given to making impulsive judgements about people on first sight, but there was just something about this particular man that infuriated and antagonised her. Her heart was jumping with emotion, thudding almost painfully against her chest wall—not because he was too good-looking but simply because he was too arrogant, she assured herself.

'First?' He stopped her, scanning her smooth pale skin and wide-spaced turquoise-blue eyes, speaking to her in English, Meg suddenly realised, as she had done to him, forgetting in the heat of the moment just where she was.

Was it her imagination or was he staring rather longer than necessary at the silky length of her dark red hair? It obviously *was* her imagination, Meg acknowledged ruefully, when he began smoothly, 'For your information—'

He broke off suddenly as Meg gave a soft exclamation of concern and, ignoring him, hurried towards her patient, who she could see was looking tired and stressed. But as she did so the arrogant Spaniard who was so determined to hijack their transport stared after her, suddenly exclaiming, to Meg's shock, 'Tia Elena! What on earth…?' at the same time striding past Meg to reach her patient ahead of her.

'Christian,' Elena Salvadores was exclaiming in pleasure as he reached her. 'What a surprise. What are you doing here?'

'I'm just on my way home from a business trip to South America,' Meg heard him answering. 'But what on earth has happened to you?'

'I had an accident in London,' Meg's patient was explaining in Spanish. 'Fortunately nothing too serious, and I am on the mend now, but they would not allow me to return on my own, and since my leg still has to be dressed and bandaged Meg here has accompanied me. She is a trained nurse,' she added, giving Meg a fond smile. 'But I'm afraid she will find it very dull here in Seville with only me for company, especially since it will be Christmas.'

She gave a small sigh.

'I miss my Esteban so much, even though it is over ten years now since he died. Your mother and I were both widowed in the same year, but she has the good fortune to have her children.'

'I'm afraid she does not always consider us to be "good" fortune.'

The rueful smile that illuminated his whole face as he spoke did decidedly dangerous and unwanted things to Meg's heartbeat, things she had no wish to so much as acknowledge, never mind go to the risky lengths of trying to analyse.

So he was good-looking, *very* good-looking. So what? Without realising she was doing so, Meg gave a small toss of her burnished hair, unwittingly causing the object of her thoughts to break off his conversation to look at her. And Meg, although she was too modest to know it herself, was very well worth looking at from a male point of view.

Small, slender, but with a deliciously curvaceous female shape. The harmonious toning of her hair and skin colouring with her caramel clothes allied to the unexpected brilliance of her spectacular eyes set in a soft heart-shaped face, guaranteed to bring out the hunter in even the mildest of men.

Unable to break the contact his gaze was deliberately locking her into, Meg felt her heart start to race whilst tiny flutters of anger-edged nervousness infiltrated her body. It was as though he was silently, subtly taunting her, telling her that of the two of them he had the more power, the power over her as a female, the power to do whatever he wished with her, *to* her.

Abruptly he looked away, breaking the spell, addressing her patient for all the world as though that oh, so male look of domination and power he had just given her had never existed.

'You look tired, Tia Elena,' he said softly, his voice warm with sympathy and concern. 'You shouldn't be waiting out here in the cold like this. Your nurse should—'

Once again he was looking at her, this time with very evident disapproval, Meg recognised wrathfully.

'It isn't Meg's fault,' Elena Salvadores insisted, immediately coming to Meg's rescue. 'We ordered a hire car but so far it hasn't arrived.'

'Allow *me* to give you a lift,' came the swift and firm response, followed by a very sardonic look in Meg's direction before Christian added, 'I have *my* car here.'

Unable to help herself, Meg glared at him. A quick fresh look at the waiting limousine had conveyed to her what she should have recognised much sooner: namely that it was far too expensive and exclusive a vehicle to be anything other than privately owned. However, there was no way she was going to acknowledge her error to *him*! Instead she pointed out grandly, 'This is a public taxi rank, and private cars are not allowed.'

Before she could finish what she was saying Elena was informing her gently, 'Christian has special status, Meg. His diplomatic duties mean that he is allowed to park wherever he wishes.'

His *diplomatic* duties? Meg was struggling not to betray her chagrin, refusing to be impressed even when her patient introduced them formally. So the Spaniard was titled, a member of the Spanish nobility. Don Christian Felipe Martinez, el Duque de Perez!—and her patient's godson. So what?

His suave, 'You may call me Christian,' made Meg's eyes shoot sparks of brilliant angry fire, but somehow she managed to hold her tongue, busying herself instead with ensuring that the chauffeur who was helping her patient did not inadvertently add to Elena's discomfort in any way.

But it wasn't the chauffeur, it was Christian himself who took charge and helped Elena into the car, making sure she was comfortably settled inside it—whilst Meg, who had been about to do exactly that herself, was forced to stand back and look on in helpless indignation. How dared he both pre-empt her and at the same time manage to subtly imply that he didn't trust her ability to take proper care of her patient?

Stiff-backed with growing hostility towards him, Meg allowed the chauffeur to usher her into the car, which had to be the most luxurious she had ever been in—a huge Mercedes with black leather upholstery, and a far cry from her own little compact at home.

For the first ten minutes of their journey Meg listened in silence whilst her patient talked to Christian about his family and various shared friends, but when Elena started to tell him she was concerned that Meg would be lonely and bored in Seville, with only her for company, Meg started to frown.

However, before she could interrupt to remind Elena that the purpose of her being in Seville was for her to nurse Elena, she heard Christian telling the older woman very much the same thing, his voice becoming crisp and rather cool as he looked pointedly at Meg and then away again.

Infuriated by the fact that he dared to disapprove of *her*, Meg did some interrupting of her own, telling him pointedly in Spanish that she could both speak and understand his language.

Instead of recognising that she had been warning him against discussing her, Christian reacted to her interruption by telling her sharply, 'I am relieved to hear it, since Tia Elena does not speak English very well. You should really have told us about your accident.' He turned away from Meg to gently scold Elena. 'I could have come to London myself to bring you home. My mother will be very cross that you did not let us know.'

'I didn't want to bother any of you,' Elena was admitting. 'I know how busy you are, Christian. Your mother told me the last time we met that this charitable work you have taken on for our government is taking more and more of your time.'

Christian was shrugging. 'As my late uncle's representative, it is my duty to ensure that the orphanage he founded in Buenos Aires is properly administered and if, whilst I am there, I can represent the views of our country on certain matters, then it is also my duty to do that as well.'

Unable to stop herself, Meg murmured sardonically under her breath, *'Noblesse oblige.'*

But to her dismay she recognised that Christian had overheard her. 'You think it a matter for mockery that a person should acknowledge a sense of obligation and duty?' he asked her coldly. 'You surprise me, given your choice of career—but then, perhaps I should not be surprised since you obviously choose to sell your services to the highest bidder rather than work in the public services, as so many other nurses do.'

The arrogance and sheer unfairness of his comment took Meg's breath away, but she knew that her hot face and angry eyes betrayed her feelings, even if his comment had been said too softly to reach Elena's ears. Let him think what he liked, Meg decided furiously. There was no way she had any need to justify herself to him, or to explain just why she could only now work as a private nurse.

At her side Elena was saying wistfully, 'I envy your mother so much, Christian. It has always been a deep sadness to me that I never had children, and I especially feel the lack of them at times such as Christmas. You will all be going to the *castillo*, of course. Christian owns a most beautiful estate,' she informed

Meg. 'It was given to his family by King Felipe in the sixteenth century, but Christian can trace his ancestry right back to the Moors.'

'I am sure your nurse does not wish to be bored with the history of my family,' Christian chided Elena, though the smile he gave her and the warmth in his voice robbed his words of any unkindness and instead made Meg feel as though somehow she was the one who was not worthy to receive such information. But Elena was totally oblivious to the underlying note of antipathy and sarcasm in his voice, and was already assuring him innocently, 'Oh, no, Christian, you are wrong. Meg is very much interested in our history and culture, and very knowledgeable about them,' she added, giving Meg an approving smile before continuing fretfully, 'I would have liked to have shown her something of our city whilst she is here, but of course with my knee the way it is that is out of the question.' Her face brightened as she suddenly exclaimed, 'But you are an expert on our local heritage, Christian. Perhaps you—?'

'No.'

Meg's face reddened when both Elena and Christian turned to look at her as she voiced her sharp denial.

'I…I'm here to work,' she pointed out, trying to alleviate the emotional intensity of her exclamation as she saw the bewilderment in Elena's eyes.

Quite what she might see in Christian's eyes if she could bring herself to meet them, she suspected she already knew. It was so unlike her to let a man get so immediately and so dangerously under her skin, but then Christian was no ordinary man. Meg's heart gave a small frantic jump as she recognised the dangerous allure of her thoughts.

Sexy, high-born Spanish aristocrats were not her type, she reminded herself firmly. She liked her men good-humoured, tolerant, compassionate and down to earth, not the embodiment of a female sexual fantasy.

'Ah, here we are.'

Meg jumped guiltily as she realised how little attention she had been paying to her patient whilst she wrestled with her rebellious thoughts. The limousine was pulling up outside an impressive building which Elena had already explained to her had been a grandee's private home prior to its conversion into several large apartments.

'Elena, if you will give me your keys, my chauffeur will go ahead and open the doors for us whilst I escort you inside.'

As Christian handed the keys the older woman gave him over to his chauffeur, he began to frown, his voice taking on its now familiar harshness as he addressed Meg.

'Elena's apartment is on the top floor. There is, of course, a lift, but it is not large. I trust you have checked that it will accommodate her wheelchair.'

'Of course.' Meg was pleased to be able to answer him with crisp efficiency. 'I took the precaution of telephoning the concierge before we left London, to give him the precise measurements of the chair, and he assured me that the lift could accommodate it.'

'I trust you also took the precaution of ensuring that it would accommodate you as well,' was his dulcet response. 'Otherwise my poor godmother will be travelling up and down in the lift, waiting for you to either ascend or descend the stairs.'

Meg took a deep breath, but for once her training deserted her. 'I am not exactly unfamiliar with the necessity of travelling in a lift with my patient, Don Christian,' she informed him with formal hauteur. 'As a theatre sister I once worked in a hospital which had its operating rooms several floors below its wards; I am used not merely to standing in a lift with a patient but also to ensuring that his or her various drips and drains are not dislodged.'

'A theatre sister?'

She could see him starting to frown, but Meg was not interested in whatever it was he was going to say. She had her patient to attend to.

As she had guessed, it was a far more painful process for Elena to get out of the car than it had been for her to get in, and Meg was particularly careful to make the transition to her waiting wheelchair as easy as she could for her.

'It's all right,' she quietly reassured her at one point as the older woman winced and cried out in pain. 'Your leg will have stiffened up during the flight and that's why it's hurting so much now. Once we've got you in your apartment, I'll massage it for you.'

Instinctively Meg touched her own hand. The damaged tendons still caused her a good deal of pain at times, although she was far too professional to say so whilst she was working. She had forgotten, though, just how much those steely obsidian eyes saw, and suddenly Christian was at her side demanding, 'Is something wrong?'

'No, nothing,' Meg fibbed, and to prove it she reached into the boot of the car to remove her medical bag. To her consternation, as she did so it slid from her grasp when her stiff tendons refused to react as quickly as she had wanted.

Christian caught the bag before it reached the ground but it was Elena's sharp exclamation of concern that caused her cheeks to redden as much as her own clumsiness as her patient sympathised,

'Oh dear, is it your hand?' and then, before Meg could say anything, she was telling Christian emotionally, 'Poor Meg has been so brave, Christian. She was attacked in the hospital where she worked by a man with a knife, when she was trying to protect his girlfriend…'

'I was just doing my job,' Meg started to protest. The look Christian was giving her was making her heart bump heavily along the bottom of her ribcage and she fought to regulate her betrayingly unsteady breathing.

'Leave the luggage. I shall see to it,' she heard Christian instructing her sharply as she returned to the boot of the car whilst he manoeuvred the wheelchair.

'I can manage,' Meg insisted, and then gave a gasp of shock as he left Elena to stride towards her, lean brown fingers manacling her wrist as he lifted her hand away from the case she had been reaching for. Turning it over, he studied her palm, his eyebrows snapping together as his gaze absorbed the extent of her scars. But the shock she had felt when she had seen him bearing down on her was nothing compared to what she felt now as his thumb brushed slowly along the length of the scar that disfigured her wrist.

Totally unable to bring herself to meet his eyes, and equally unwilling to suffer the humiliation of an undignified struggle to remove her wrist from his imprisoning grip, she fixed her gaze straight ahead which, unfortunately, meant she was staring at the shirt-covered expanse of a male chest which she could see all too plainly possessed the kind of muscular physique normally only found on a sportsman. Wretched man. Surely there must be *something* about him which she, as a woman, could disdain?

'He must have virtually severed your wrist.'

The quiet words, uttered in a tone of voice that seemed to rumble towards her from the depths of the chest she had just been unwillingly studying, shocked her into lifting her unguarded gaze to meet his.

'No… Well, not… I was lucky in that our hospital had the country's top microsurgical team. They—the surgeon…' She stopped and bit her lip, remembering how shocked she had been when Michael Lord had told her compassionately that he had done everything that he, as a surgeon, could do for her and that the degree of movement she would recover was down to her own determination and, as he had put it, 'the goodwill of the angels'.

She had been lucky, very lucky—due in the main, she was convinced, to his skilled repair work. So far as most things went, she was perfectly able to operate normally, but theatre work was not 'most' things, and the risk that she might be too slow to hand an instrument over to a surgeon or, even worse, might not be able to react at all to instructions, had closed the door on theatre work to her for ever.

'Oh, darling, I'm so very, very sorry,' her mother had tried to comfort her, adding, 'Look, why don't you come and stay with Daddy and me for a while?'

But Meg had refused, signing on instead with the private nursing agency for whom she now worked.

She felt Christian's grip on her wrist slacken and immediately she bent back towards the boot of the car, stubbornly determined to remove her *own* luggage. But Christian moved in the same direction at the same time, so that their heads were close together and he was still holding her wrist.

A sensation of intense awareness and sensitivity to his proximity filled her, making it impossible for her to breathe or think properly. Every protective urge she possessed screamed at her to move away from him, but something deeper, stronger and far more elemental, was refusing to let her do so.

Christian was looking at her mouth and she…she was letting him, feeling her lips moisten and part, feeling too her eyes growing heavy and her breathing becoming unsteady.

What was the *matter* with her? Just because he was totally and undeniably male…just because…just because her head felt dizzy and her legs felt weak and her heart was pounding—*bounding* helplessly from one beat to another like a newborn foal finding its legs—that didn't mean…that didn't…

'Christian, is Meg all right?'

Elena's voice seemed to reach her from a long way away. Like a drowning man, Meg clung to it, forcing herself to remember where she was and why.

If this was a film, right now its audience would be in no doubt at all about what would happen next. But it *wasn't* a film, she reminded herself fiercely as she realised that Christian had released her wrist and she was free to escape from him and the dangerous sorcery of the spell his proximity had woven around her.

Get a grip, for goodness' sake, she berated herself mentally as she hurried towards Elena's wheelchair. It was totally unlike her to react like this and she couldn't understand why she was behaving so idiotically.

CHAPTER TWO

'THERE, how do you feel now?'

'Much better.' Elena thanked Meg gratefully as she finished massaging her patient and smiled at her.

It was less than two hours since their arrival at the apartment, which had proved to be even more luxurious and elegant than Meg had expected.

The bedroom she had been shown to by Elena's elderly housekeeper was more of a small suite than a mere room, complete with its own luxurious marble bathroom and a small sitting room as well, but Meg had been more concerned about her patient than the luxury of her new surroundings, insisting on making Elena comfortable before settling herself in.

The telephone beside the ornately luxurious bed rang just as Meg was slipping the covers back over Elena, and discreetly she left the room to allow Elena to speak to her caller in privacy whilst she made her way back to her suite.

She was, of course, fully familiar with the Spanish

custom of eating late at night, but hunger pangs were now beginning to gnaw faintly at her tummy. It seemed a long time since she had eaten the delicious meal they had been served in the First Class cabin on the plane.

Presumably she would eat her meals in the kitchen with Elena's housekeeper, Anna, whilst Elena herself either dined alone or with friends—or her godson… Meg's heart gave a betraying thump. But, no, he would not be visiting whilst she was here, Meg reassured herself. Hadn't Elena herself mentioned the fact that he and his family would be spending Christmas at his family estate in the country?

His family… Was he married? Her heart gave another sharp thump. Meg guessed that he must be in his early thirties and, although he had made no mention of a wife, a man with a background like his would surely want to have a son to continue the family line.

The intercom telephone on the table next to Meg rang, making her jump. When she answered it, she heard Elena's voice excitedly asking her to come to her room.

When Meg got there, her patient was sitting up in bed, looking pink-cheeked and happy.

'My telephone call was from Luisa, Christian's mother. She has invited us both to spend the Christmas holiday with them. Christian must have told her how concerned I was that you would find it dull here on your own, with just me for company. Oh, I am so pleased. You will love Christian's family, I promise you.'

Valiantly, Meg tried not to show her own consternation. The mere thought of *seeing* Christian again, never mind spending time in his home, was doing the most alarming things to her nervous system. But Meg knew there was no way she could refuse to go. Elena's wound still needed careful cleaning and bandaging, and her surgeon had been insistent that she had to have proper nursing care for at least three weeks after her operation.

Meg had always taken her professional responsibility very seriously and there was no way she was going to stop doing so now, just because of a mere man.

A *mere* man? *Christian?* A delicate hint of pink colour tinged her skin as certain unassailable facts forced themselves in front of her.

Christian bore just about as much resemblance to being a 'mere' male as a medical student did to a senior consultant, which was to say that when it came to quantifying 'maleness' Christian was in a class of his own.

What was *she* doing, boosting the wretched man's already far too high opinion of himself with her foolishly treacherous thoughts?

Anyone would think that she was in danger of finding him attractive—which she most certainly did not, she assured herself vigorously, as Elena started to plan what she was going to need to pack for their visit, suddenly becoming far more animated and happy than Meg had previously seen her.

'This is all Christian's doing. He really is the most thoughtful person. But then all the men in his family have been known for their benevolence to others. Christian's uncle, the one he mentioned, was so affected by the plight of the street children in Buenos Aires that he set up and financed a special home for them and left money in his will for its continued maintenance. Christian's family have had business links with South America for many generations, and now our government has requested his help when it comes to any kind of delicate negotiations.'

It was obvious to Meg just how much Elena admired her godson and how much she was looking forward to spending Christmas with his family. No doubt he was used to women doting on him. Well, *she* certainly wasn't going to become one of his besotted admirers!

'So, if you will wait here with the luggage, Meg, I shall take Tia Elena down to the car in her wheelchair and see her safely installed in it, whilst I send Esteban up to collect the luggage.'

'Oh, but *you* will make sure that the apartment is securely locked up, won't you, Christian.' Elena intervened anxiously.

'Of course,' he told her.

Gritting her teeth, her hackles already rising in antagonistic response to the lordly mantle of control Christian had assumed since his arrival at the apartment ten minutes earlier, Meg tried not to notice how sexually male he looked wearing a pair of casual snug-fitting jeans and a soft cotton shirt, the top couple of buttons of which were unfastened.

Meg was forced to swallow hard against the taut feeling of female awareness threatening to sabotage her determination not to find him in the least bit attractive.

So why on earth was her tummy fluttering, just because as he'd turned towards her patient she had glimpsed the disturbingly male darkness of his body hair where his shirt lay open? And, even more disconcertingly, why was she having to control that upsurge of female wantonness that said so clearly and mortifyingly that it wanted to see more?

Naked male bodies were nothing new to her, as a nurse, so why should the thought of *this* particular male body turn her into a quivering, dithering mass of desire?

Meg had no idea. She was just relieved that Christian was finally wheeling Elena out of the apartment, leaving her to await the arrival of his chauffeur, Esteban.

The amount of luggage Elena deemed it necessary to take with her for a fortnight's stay with friends for what she had told Meg would be a 'family Christmas' had reduced Meg to awed silence as she had watched Anna pack, reverently wrapping everything in layer after layer of tissue paper.

The addition of a large, old-fashioned leather jewellery case had been the final confirmation, if Meg had needed one, that the rich were indeed different.

Everything *she* needed for their two-week stay had taken less than half an hour to repack into her one single case and, indeed, she had spent longer packing her medical bag—not just with everything that she felt Elena would need, but with the basic medical essentials without which she never travelled.

Esteban arrived and then departed with Elena's cases, whilst Meg waited in trepidation for Christian to return to release her to go down to the car with her own luggage, whilst he made sure the apartment was securely locked.

The apartment door opened and Christian strode in, giving Meg an inimical, sweeping glance.

'You have everything?' he asked her, the tone he used to her far more curt and abrasive than the soft affectionate one he used to his godmother, Meg noticed.

Simply nodding her head tersely, she bent to pick up her two cases, intending to make her way to the lift and then down to the waiting car, leaving him to lock the flat on his own.

She was wearing the clothes she had travelled to Spain in, but today she was carrying her jacket over her arm, deeming the soft cashmere sweater she was wearing warm enough for the car journey. Just to be on the safe side, she had also swathed a toning honey-coloured pashmina around herself.

As she leaned forward to pick up her cases, Christian stopped her, telling her, 'I'll carry those.'

It was on the tip of Meg's tongue to remind him

sharply that she was not a sixty-year-old invalid like his godmother, and was more than capable of carrying her own bags, but the truth was that her injured wrist and hand were feeling stiff and painful. She knew that she would have to carry each of her bags out into the hallway individually, and that her medical bag was particularly heavy.

Even so, her eyes smouldered with the feelings caution told her it would be unwise to voice and, for a moment, as their glances clashed, Meg could see in Christian's an answering smoulder daring her to defy him, before it was banished to be replaced by a look of coolly thoughtful consideration.

In silence, he placed her bags outside the apartment door in the elegant hallway, then told her, 'We'll go down in the lift together, if you will just wait until I have secured the apartment.'

Only the fact that she was wary of trying to carry her medical bag prevented Meg from going down to the car on her own. Not that he kept her waiting long... She had barely had time to do more than chide herself for the way she was reacting to him when he was locking the outer door to the apartment and striding past her to summon the lift.

As Meg had already discovered for herself, the lift to the apartments was not exactly generously proportioned. It held Elena's wheelchair with Elena in it and herself—just—which meant that it allowed two fully grown adults, especially if one of them was over six foot in height and with the breadth of shoulder surely more appropriate for a top-scoring polo player than a businessman, just about enough room, provided they did not mind sharing their own personal 'space'.

Even with her two cases in the lift between them, Meg still discovered that her body felt that Christian was standing very intimately close. But that was still no excuse for it to start reacting as though it liked that proximity rather than objected to it.

Determinedly, Meg stared forward, her soft lips clamped tightly closed. There was no way she was going to allow Christian to guess how idiotically her body was behaving. But suddenly the lift jolted to a halt, throwing Meg off balance and into Christian and, of course, it was only natural that he should reach out to steady her. Field her was probably a more appropriate term, Meg recognised, the breath whooshing out of her lungs as she collided with the impressive hardness of his chest.

The lift had stopped and they did not appear to have reached the ground floor, but Meg was only aware of *that* fact with the periphery of her consciousness. Something far, far more important was occupying virtually all her attention.

Pressed up against Christian's body, held there not just by the weight of his arm but also by the dangerous intensity of her own reactions to him, Meg could feel herself starting to tremble, a fine quivering female response to Christian's maleness rocketing through her.

'Don't be afraid. This lift *is* sometimes temperamental,' she heard Christian murmuring, his voice, somewhere close to her temple, a deep rumbling sound she could feel as his chest vibrated against her own.

As she lifted her head to deny that she was afraid the lift moved sharply, causing her to squeak in protest instead and instinctively steady herself again against its unexpected lurch by clinging to the front of Christian's shirt. Now that she had lifted her head she could see his eyes…and his mouth…and, whilst the lift might have stilled, her heart most certainly had not followed suit.

Here it was, the knowledge she had been fighting to reject ever since she had first seen him. Despite everything that her common sense and her instinct for self-protection had told her, right now, more than anything else, what she wanted was…

As though he had somehow tuned into her feelings, Christian started to lower his head, one hand braced against the lift wall behind her and the other resting on her waist so that she felt totally, sensually enclosed by him, totally sensually in thrall—not just to him but to what she herself was feeling.

She could see his knowledge of her feelings in the fiercely male glitter of his eyes, feel it in the aura of power and sexuality that seemed to emanate from him and engulf her.

Helplessly she gave in to it, swaying against him, her head tipping back against the arm he had lifted

from her waist to hold her. The kiss that burned a trail
of life-defining sexuality against her lips was so far
outside her known experience that her eyes opened
briefly in betraying bemusement, hot pools of sensuality, their gaze enmeshing with the heart-rockingly
exciting male danger of his.

As though he had somehow whispered a soft command to them, her lips parted, her eyes closed, and her
body softened in wanton pleasure, her tongue-tip
delicately exploring the alien shape of his mouth. A
small soft sound of female approval purred in her
throat as the sexily hard shape of his lips responded to
the delicate probe of her tongue, opening, daring her
to explore further…deeper…

It took the sudden sharp jerk of the lift as it started
to move to bring her back to reality. Face pink with
mortification, she pulled agitatedly back from Christian.

What on earth was she doing? What on earth was
he doing—or could she guess?

Meg had sensed his arrogant superiority from the
moment they had met and she guessed that this was his
way of underlining it, reinforcing it, of asserting his
sensuality and tormenting her with his knowledge of
just how vulnerable she was to him.

As the lift continued on its journey towards the
ground, Meg tried to convince herself that the shaki-
ness she was experiencing and the breathlessness she
was suffering were the result of being momentarily

trapped in the lift, rather than the effect of being so intimately trapped in her own sensual response to Christian's kiss.

The lift came to a halt; the doors opened. Quickly, Meg hurried out, not daring to allow herself to look at Christian. Anger was beginning to take the place of her original shock and confusion. Anger not just against Christian but against herself as well. No doubt his ego had been extremely pleased by her intense response, but she was in Spain to work, not to fall for some arrogant aristocrat. He was simply amusing himself. Esteban was standing beside Christian's car, holding the front passenger door open for her.

As she hesitated, the Señora informed her from inside the car, 'You are to sit in front with Christian, Meg. He is to drive us to the *castillo* whilst Esteban returns to his family to spend Christmas with them.'

A hundred objections fought for utterance inside Meg's head, but all of them died unspoken as she suddenly heard the totally unexpected sound of two very young male voices from the back seat of the car.

She and the Señora were not to be the limousine's only passengers, she realised, her stomach plunging with icy shock as she studied the two young, boyish faces so similar to those of their father.

Christian was *married*. He had *children*! Now her anger burned white-hot, fuelled not just by her disgust at Christian's behaviour but also by her own guilt. For a second she was tempted to refuse to get in the car, but the discipline of her nurse's training grimly forced her to rethink her emotional reaction. She had a professional duty to remain with her patient and that *must* take priority over her personal feelings, no matter how strong they might be.

Christian and his chauffeur had finished loading the luggage into the boot of the car, and out of the corner of her eye Meg could see Christian heading towards the driver's door.

As he opened it he turned towards Meg, but she refused to make eye contact with him. How *could* he sit there, calmly fastening his seat belt, for all the world as though he had done nothing wrong? But then perhaps to him kissing someone other than his wife was such an everyday occurrence that it didn't bother him at all. It bothered *her* though—and not just because she now felt consumed with guilt, Meg recognised, torn between anger and anguish. From the back seat, one of the boys leaned forward and made a laughing comment to Christian.

'Yes, indeed,' Christian concurred, speaking in Spanish as he turned sideways to give Meg a deliberately speculative look, accompanied by a little curling smile that made her heart start to somersault before she clenched her muscles against such waywardness. 'Meg does have very pretty hair.'

Pretty hair!

Meg could feel the colour creeping up under her skin. Christian had no right to give her that kind of deliberate, explicitly erotic look. No right whatsoever. He was a married man. He had children…a wife… What was *she* like? Meg found herself wondering. Did she *know* how carelessly, how recklessly her husband treated his marriage vows?

For some unfathomable reason, Meg began to feel tears burning the backs of her eyes. Turning in her seat to check on the comfort of her patient, she managed to blink them away. What on earth had she got to cry for? No doubt Christian's poor wife had already had the occasion to shed many tears over him. The occasion and the right.

Another wave of frighteningly strong and totally unwanted anguish rolled over her.

What was the matter with her? Anyone would think she had done something impossible, like falling in love with the man instead of just being stupid and unguarded enough to share a kiss with him. What was a kiss these days, after all?

Nothing!

Nothing and *everything*, a despairing inner voice whispered warningly.

They were clear of the city now. Christian was a good driver, Meg was forced to recognise, his hands controlled and firm on the wheel, his concentration not just on his own driving but on everything and everyone else on the road. He even seemed to know instinctively just when the two boys in the back were going to start play-wrestling just a little bit too fiercely for the Señora's comfort.

A father's instinct. Immediately Meg tried to shut down on her feelings.

The winter-bare countryside they were driving through had a sombre, stately beauty that somehow touched her senses. Seville and its environs were unfamiliar territory to her and she was glad of the Señora's gently informative travelogue, not just because of what she was learning but also because it prevented her from allowing the man seated next to her to dominate her thoughts.

'You're very quiet, Meg,' the Señora suddenly commented from the rear seat. 'I hope you are not feeling unwell with travel sickness…'

'Mama has that,' the younger of Christian's sons suddenly chimed in.

'No, silly,' the older one corrected him immediately, 'Mama is sick because of the baby she is going to have.'

Christian's wife was *pregnant*!

A sharp wave of revulsion attacked Meg, causing her to utter a small sound of distress.

Immediately Christian turned towards her, the car slowing down. He was frowning as he demanded, '*Are* you unwell?'

'No,' Meg denied fiercely.

She couldn't bear to look at him, couldn't endure to be *anywhere* near him. How *could* he have kissed her like that when…when…? Her patient had already told her that Christian had Moorish blood in his veins from the days when that race had ruled this part of Spain. Perhaps it was from those long-ago ancestors that he had inherited his arrogant belief that he had the right to make his own rules, live his life by his own laws.

Meg gave a small shudder and closed her eyes, opening them again as she heard Christian saying sharply, 'You are cold. Why did you not say so?'

Almost immediately the air inside the car grew noticeably warmer, his unwanted attention to her comfort causing Meg's face to crimson with anger. The raw sharpness of the pain she was enduring was far too dangerously intense. Why should she care about Christian's duplicity, his deceitfulness? She cared because, like his wife, she was a woman and because…

They were climbing into the hills now, the terrain around them becoming more rugged and the road decidedly tortuous, narrowing so much in some places that Meg found she was holding her breath and squeezing herself in.

And then one of the boys called out excitedly from the rear of the car, 'There it is. I can see the *castillo*.'

Sure enough, as Meg looked past Christian, she too could see it. Like a fortress it rose magnificently from the rock on which it was built, and the Moorish influence in its architecture was evident in its towers and turrets. The winter sun was burning its stone escarpment rose-gold and Meg stared at it in awed disbelief.

She had expected it to be large, dominating its surroundings in the same way that Christian dominated his, but she had not been prepared for its beauty, like a fairy-tale fantasy.

They were approaching the *castillo*, driving into a large sun-splashed paved courtyard filled with the musical sound of water from its ornate fountain. The car was stationary. Christian was climbing out and going to the assistance of his godmother whilst the two boys scrambled out of their seat and hurried towards an open door, through which a darkly elegant older woman—who Meg guessed must be Christian's mother—was approaching them.

Mindful of her responsibilities, Meg went to help Christian with the Señora. He had already removed her wheelchair from the boot of the car and now, as they gently helped her into it, between them, his fingers brushed against Meg's.

Immediately she gave a small, low cry, snatching her hand away, and the gaze she turned on him was full of reproach and angry disdain.

He was frowning, glancing immediately at her hand as he apologised formally. 'I'm sorry… Is it your hand?'

Her *hand*. Storm signals flashed in Meg's eyes. How dared he pretend not to know why she couldn't bear him to touch her? His poor wife. How sorry Meg felt for her, being married to such a heartless man.

Christian's mother had reached them now, and greetings were being exchanged. Meg watched as mother and son embraced with uninhibited tenderness.

Releasing her son, Christian's mother then embraced her friend with warm affection before turning to welcome Meg herself.

'I have put you in rooms next to one another,' she informed the Señora and Meg as Christian gave discreet orders to the two men who were efficiently removing the luggage from the boot of the car.

'Meg isn't here just to nurse me. I want her to have fun as well,' the Señora was saying firmly, much to Meg's own embarrassment.

'Well, we shall certainly do our best,' Christian's mother laughed, turning away from them to tell her son, 'Juanita is already here, but she is resting. She said to thank you for bringing the boys.'

Meg frowned, indignation clouding her eyes as she listened. Why on earth should Christian's wife have to *thank* him for taking charge of his own sons?

The car was fully unloaded now, and instinctively Meg went to pick up her medical bag, but Christian got there before her, his hand on her arm.

'Don't touch me,' Meg spat fiercely at him.

'Don't *touch* you?'

She could see the angry, almost shocked look in his eyes.

'That's not what your body was saying to me only a very short time ago, *querida*...'

Querida... He had *dared* to call her *that*, when he was married?

Meg had spent enough time on the Spanish resort coast to know what kind of opinion many Spanish men had of British womanhood, those unknowing heedless girls who flocked to the *costas* for two weeks of reckless wanton behaviour, unaware of the reputation they were attracting. If Christian thought that *she* was like that intent on having 'fun'...

'How dare you call me that?' she demanded, white-faced. 'You might be a duke, but to me you are *lower* than the poorest beggar!'

'It was only a kiss, *querida,*' Christian was almost drawling, his voice soft, but his eyes were as cold as sin, promising retribution. 'If you did not want it, then perhaps you should have told those soft, inviting lips of yours so at the time. Instead...'

He paused and then flashed her a long lingering look that made her face and body burn and her toes curl protestingly inside her shoes.

'I don't think I have *ever* kissed a woman whose mouth was more sweet and ripe with promise,' he told her softly.

Meg had had enough.

'You have no right to speak to me like that,' she told him furiously. 'No right at all. And if you do I shall... I shall...' She stopped as her own feelings overwhelmed her.

'Be careful,' she heard Christian warn her savagely.

'When a woman challenges me, I react like any other man, especially when I know she—'

'Christian…'

As his mother appeared round the side of the car Meg made her escape—without her medical bag.

CHAPTER THREE

'DO YOU know something?' the Señora commented conversationally to Meg as Meg helped her into her wheelchair prior to them both going downstairs for dinner.

That the *castillo* was equipped with a lift had been a bonus Meg hadn't been expecting and one she was extremely grateful for.

'I know lots of somethings,' she responded teasingly, starting to push the wheelchair towards the bedroom door.

'You have such a lovely sense of fun, Meg,' the Señora laughed. 'But, no, what I was going to say was that I believe that Christian is *very* attracted to you...'

She said it so approvingly and happily that Meg was glad she was standing behind her and that the Señora couldn't see her own bleakly shocked expression.

'He's a very good-looking man, and so kind and so—'

'—so *married*,' Meg put in sharply, unable to keep back the words any longer.

'Married? Christian?' She could hear the bemusement in the Señora's voice. 'But, no! What on *earth* makes you think that? Christian has no wife.'

'No wife? He *isn't* married?' Meg questioned disbelievingly. 'But what about the boys—his sons?'

'His *what*? They are not *his* sons; they are his nephews—the sons of his sister Juanita and her husband Ramon, who you will meet at dinner tonight.'

Christian's nephews... So he *wasn't* married. He *didn't* have any children. He *didn't* have a wife to be unfaithful to... Dazedly, Meg tried to digest what she had just learned. Christian was completely free to... To what? she asked herself grittily. To flirt with her; to kiss her; to treat her as though...?

That surely wasn't relief and happiness she was feeling—was it? Surely she was far too sensible to mistake a male ego-boosting bit of sexual flirtation with her for something meaningful, wasn't she? Especially when the male in question was the impossibly arrogant Christian.

But she had allowed him to kiss her, and she had... A girl was allowed to enjoy a kiss, wasn't she, in these enlightened days, without having to go into lengthy self-analysis about the whys and wherefores of it?

The lift stopped and she wheeled the Señora out of it and across the hallway towards the room her patient was indicating.

'I am so happy that we have been invited here,' she confided to Meg. 'Christian's mother has been the kindest friend to me.' She gave a small sigh. 'When we are young, we think all that matters is being with the one person we love. My husband was everything to me,' she added quietly. 'But since I have lost him, I have realised how much one needs to be part of a family.'

For some reason, her words touched a sensitive chord in Meg's own emotions.

'At least you and your husband shared love,' she tried to comfort her patient.

They had reached the door now, but before Meg could open it opened for them and Christian was standing there.

'Ah…I was just about to come and find you.'

He was addressing the Señora and not *her*, Meg warned herself. After all, he had not even looked at her.

As he smiled down at his godmother Christian refused to give in to the temptation to look at Meg. From the moment he had set eyes on her at the airport, she had both infuriated and enchanted him. Right now, the temptation to turn his head and drink in the unique combination of physical attributes that made her so dangerously special was overpowering. The way she could turn from being furiously hostile to him one minute to so passionately and sensually responsive another made him feel…made him want…

His mouth compressed in cynical self-judgement as he silently acknowledged just what Meg *was* making him want *and* how fiercely. She had kissed him so passionately in the lift. But throughout their drive to the *castillo* she had virtually ignored him.

Unable to stop himself, he turned his head and looked at her.

What was that look supposed to do? Meg wondered shakily as she felt the hard, silent pressure of Christian's gaze on her. Was he deliberately trying to intimidate her with his power, his sexuality?

Somehow she managed to look away from him, firmly taking charge of the Señora's wheelchair as she pushed her into the salon.

It was a large room, furnished with items that Meg suspected had to be priceless antiques, but in such a way that her first impression of it was that it was a room of immense comfort and warmth. A huge log fire burned in the equally huge grate, and seated on one of the large sofas drawn up close to it were the two boys who had travelled to the *castillo* with them, and a young woman who was quite plainly their mother, Christian's sister.

A man was standing behind the sofa with one hand on her shoulder, and Meg guessed that he must be her husband. The younger man who was engaging the boys in a game Meg could not place, until Christian's mother introduced him to her as her daughter's brother-in-law.

As he bent low over Meg's hand and then raised it to his lips with a theatrical flourish, Meg recognised that Sancho was a practised and expert flirt—and perfectly harmless. He was typical of the many young Spaniards who had frequented the marina her father had run and who had tried, always unsuccessfully, to convince her that their flirting was serious. The feelings he aroused in her were completely different from those she had experienced on meeting Christian.

Sancho might be a very attractive young man, but Meg knew she was in no danger whatsoever of being anything other than amused by the long languorous looks he was giving her, or the way he deliberately kept hold of her hand, only relinquishing it when Christian asked Meg with crisp pointedness, 'Perhaps you might help my godmother to get settled comfortably on the sofa? It will be warmer for her there, out of any draughts.'

Meg could hear the Señora demurring that she was perfectly comfortable in her chair, but neither that nor the knowledge that she was in no way to blame for the manner in which Sancho had kept hold of her hand had the power to stop Meg's face from burning with betraying colour, whilst her eyes flashed storm signals of furious resentment in Christian's direction.

She had no need of *him* to remind her of what her duties were or of her responsibility to her patient.

Seething with fury, she missed the speculative look Christian's sister gave her brother, although she did see the frowning, gentle sympathy in Christian's mother's eyes as she made room on the sofa for her friend.

Having made sure her patient was comfortably settled, Meg was tempted to make her exit, but before she could do so Juanita was inviting her to sit down next to her.

'My sons tell me that you speak Spanish.' She smiled. 'And that you have beautiful hair,' she added with a mischievous laugh.

She was so friendly that Meg couldn't resist cautiously responding to her questions. As she did so she could hear the younger of Juanita's sons demanding excitedly, 'Tio Christian. The tree is here and Pedro is fixing the lights on it. Can we help him decorate it?'

Breaking off from her conversation with Meg, Juanita said firmly, 'Tomaz and Carlos, you are not to go near that tree on your own.' Ruefully, she explained to Meg, raising her voice over her son's protests, 'Every year we have an enormous tree in the drawing room. It is a tradition. Last year, Carlos tried to climb it...' She raised her eyebrows.

'I was very brave. I didn't cry,' Carlos informed Meg importantly.

'*You* may not have done, but Maria nearly did when she saw the mess you had made of her newly cleaned salon,' Christian informed his nephew. 'We shall all decorate the tree together after dinner,' he added, and the warmth of the smile he gave his nephews as they both hurled themselves into his arms made Meg blink three or four times. Not because her emotions had been stirred, she denied. No, it was just...it was just that it was almost Christmas and she was a long way from her *own* family.

In her ear Sancho was murmuring provocatively, 'Decorating a Christmas tree is all very well for children, but I cannot help but feel that it will be very dull and boring for you. If you would permit me, I could drive you into Seville. There is a nightclub there…'

'I don't think—' Meg began, but before she could explain that she had come to Spain to work Christian, whose hearing had to be demonically sharp, was answering for her.

'Meg is not here to visit nightclubs, Sancho,' he said sternly. 'My godmother is employing her to ensure that the wound on her leg is properly cared for.'

'Oh, but surely she is allowed *some* time off?' Sancho was protesting, completely unabashed, whilst Meg writhed inwardly in a fury of righteous anger and discomfort.

'I'm sure she is,' Christian was agreeing scathingly. 'But since she has only just arrived here, I hardly think she is likely to want to make the journey to Seville and back again tonight—and, of course, she will be spending the night *here*, and not in Seville.'

There was no doubt about what he meant, but before she could demand that she be allowed to exercise her own moral judgement—did he really think she was likely to want to spend the night with Sancho? Was his opinion of her really that low?—Sancho himself was responding angrily to Christian's embargo.

'Meg is an adult. She…'

Meg knew she had to defuse the situation. Quietly she told Sancho, 'It's very kind of you to invite me out, but in all honesty I am rather tired.'

To her relief, Sancho took her refusal good-naturedly, waiting until Christian had turned his back to whisper softly to her that there would be other nights, but it was Christian's remark that she could not forgive.

A question from his elder brother, Juanita's husband, drew Sancho away from Meg's side, leaving her free to concentrate on her patient and the gentle conversation of Christian's mother, and to throw a murderously resentful look at Christian's back.

As in all Spanish households, they didn't sit down to dinner until quite late. The elegance of the dining room initially took Meg's breath away.

'There was a Hapsburg connection to the family,' Juanita explained, rolling her eyes in wry amusement. 'A cousin of a cousin of the then ruling family. It was at that time that many renovations were made.'

The dining room did have a distinctly baroque air to it Meg acknowledged.

'We don't normally dine in such style,' Juanita was further explaining with a wide smile. 'This dining room is only used for special occasions.'

Her smile widened even further when she saw the look Meg was giving the dinner service on which their meal was being served.

'It was a wedding present to the Hapsburg bride. It's Sèvres…'

Sèvres and priceless, Meg guessed, swallowing hard, but as though she had guessed what Meg was thinking Juanita told her, 'Christian insists that it is used. He says if it is not then it might as well be placed in a museum. And whilst I agree with him—' she grimaced as she glanced at her sons '—I confess I am always a little nervous that the boys might accidentally break a piece.'

It was impossible not to warm to Christian's sister, Meg acknowledged. And oddly, despite the awesome magnificence of her surroundings, Meg was actually beginning to feel very much at home with the family.

With Christian's family, perhaps, but most certainly not with Christian *himself*.

As they all eventually made their way from the dining room to the room where the huge tree was standing, bedecked with tiny fairy lights and waiting for its final clothing of shiny baubles and decorations, Meg hung back. Bending down, she murmured to the Señora, 'If you are feeling tired, perhaps we should—'

'Tired? No...I am enjoying this *so much*,' she told Meg, her eyes sparkling. 'It reminds me of when I was young—and look, Meg, in the corner of the room, Christian still has the traditional crib display I remember his parents having when *he* was a child.'

Juanita, who had overheard her comments, informed Meg, 'Some families these days do not bother so much with the Christmas crib, but Christian is very much a traditionalist and likes to do things in the old way. Tomorrow night it is Christmas Eve, and then the children will open some of their presents, but as with most Spanish families we shall keep others back for the Night of the Three Kings on the fifth of January.

'We shall celebrate that in Seville, though, where there is the Epiphany Festival. There will be floats in the streets and much merry-making. You will enjoy it. It is a good opportunity for our young people to be allowed to let off steam.'

She broke off her conversation with Meg to shake her head when her younger son urged her to climb the step-ladder and hang some decorations on the tree. 'Perhaps Meg will help you,' she suggested, smiling at Meg as she patted her stomach. 'Whenever I am pregnant I seem to lose my head for heights, along with my waistline.'

Her husband and Christian had left the room a few minutes earlier, Christian taking Ramon to his office so that he could use his computer.

'I am sure that Sancho will be only too pleased to hold the ladder for you,' Juanita gently teased her brother-in-law.

Feeling that it would be churlish of her to refuse, Meg made her way over to the Christmas tree, taking the baubles Tomaz was holding out to her and mounting the ladder.

She had just finished hanging them to his satisfaction when Sancho announced, 'Perhaps we should place Meg at the top of the tree instead of the angel. She is certainly pretty enough,' he added admiringly, giving Meg a long lingering look.

Sancho was obviously determined to flirt with her, but Meg suspected that she was only the focus of his attention because he was bored and she was the only unmarried woman available. Shaking her head reprovingly, she descended the ladder calmly, distancing herself from him to rejoin Juanita. However, her coolness deserted her when she realised that Christian was standing in the doorway and that he was watching her with grim disapproval.

It wasn't her fault that she was here in his family home, where he so plainly did not want her to be, she was thinking indignantly, when suddenly Juanita called out in alarm, 'No, Tomaz, you must not go on the ladder.'

Immediately Meg swung round and started to hurry back to the tree. Tomaz, in the manner of all small boys, was gleefully enjoying himself, unaware of any danger as he tried to reach for the top of the tree.

'I have the star. I will put it at the top,' he was calling out happily, but as he spoke the ladder started to sway a little.

As she heard from behind her Juanita's anxious maternal gasp Meg reacted instinctively, closing the gap between herself and the swaying ladder and reaching out to steady it. But Christian had got there before her, and instead of holding the ladder Meg discovered that it was Christian's body she was embracing as he in turn held the ladder secure and commanded his nephew sternly to come down.

'But I want to put the star at the top of the tree,' Tomaz was insisting stubbornly.

'Tomaz. Come down. You can't reach the top,' Juanita instructed. Eager to prove her wrong, the little boy insisted determinedly, 'Yes, I can. Look…'

Grateful for the diversion he was causing, Meg hoped that no one had noticed her embarrassment as she quickly removed her hands from Christian's torso. Her relief was short-lived, though, when Christian turned his head and looked sharply at her. Unable to drag her gaze away from his, Meg prayed that he wouldn't see in her eyes the shock the action of touching him had given her. He was just a man, flesh and blood, and there was no need, no reason why she should feel so strongly aware of him in a way that was wholly female. Her fingertips were still tingling a little, as though she had received a small electric shock, and…

'Tomaz, that is enough. I shall put the star in place for you.'

The calm firmness in Christian's voice as he turned away from her and back to his nephew had the desired effect on Tomaz's rebellious behaviour, but the effect it was having on her equally rebellious emotions was far from desired, Meg admitted as Christian firmly removed his nephew from the ladder and placed him on the floor, taking the star from him as he did so.

Meg was just about to move away when Christian stopped her, saying quietly, 'If you wouldn't mind holding the ladder for me I shall put the star at the top of the tree so that both it and the ladder can cease to be a cause of further temptation.'

Silently Meg steadied the ladder, waiting for Christian to climb it.

He had only climbed a couple of rungs when he paused, apparently to straighten one of the baubles but in reality to lean down towards her and say in a cool undertone that only Meg could hear, 'It's a pity that there isn't an equally simple way of removing Sancho from his temptation.'

Both his tone and the look he was giving her made it very clear what he meant, and Meg knew that the angry colour sweeping her face was betraying her own reaction to his obvious disapproval of Sancho's interest in her.

What gave him the right to criticise her, to disapprove of her? She longed to say as much to him but she reminded herself, as he continued to climb the ladder and reach out to put the star in place, that she was here under his roof in her professional capacity. This surely should mean that he ought to know she was not in a position to respond to Sancho's flirting, even if she wanted to do—which she most certainly did not.

Refusing to look at him as he descended the ladder, she barely waited until he had reached the floor before relinquishing her steadying hold on it and walking away.

'Meg—a word with you, please.'

Meg paused warily as Christian addressed her. They

were alone in the hallway. Juanita and Ramon had taken the boys upstairs to put them to bed and Meg herself was just on her way back to the salon, having gone upstairs to get Elena's painkillers, sensing that the older lady was in some discomfort.

Christian was frowning, his voice terse, and Meg could feel her body tensing defensively.

'Sancho is a young man who lives a very much more…' He paused and looked at her, and Meg's heart turned over inside her chest before lurching crazily against her ribs, helplessly out of control. 'More modern lifestyle than that of my godmother's and mother's generation. Of course the way he behaves outside my home is no concern of mine, but he is under my roof. My sister claims that I am a traditionalist and old-fashioned, and I suspect she may be right. I am sure you are already worldly-wise enough not to need any warning from *me* about encouraging the attentions of a young man such as Sancho, but whilst you *are* both beneath my roof—'

Meg had heard enough—more than enough.

'What are you trying to say?' she demanded, incensed. 'That if I am not careful Sancho will take advantage of his position and kiss me—perhaps in the lift?'

She knew from the sound of Christian's savagely indrawn breath that he understood what she meant.

'I did *not*—' he began angrily and then stopped, muttering something she could not catch beneath his breath before telling her thickly, 'Just what is it about you that drives me to such insanity? It is *impossible* to reason with you. You are… Perhaps there *is*, after all, only one way for me to deal with you…'

Meg gave a shocked gasp as she was suddenly hauled into his arms and held tightly there, his heart thudding erratically against her body as his mouth took her own captive.

Immediately it was as though somehow, some-where deep inside her, something had thrown a switch. At the touch of his mouth on hers all her an-tagonism left her and in its place she felt the most in-credible sense of piercing longing, aching need, combined with a sense of rightness…of complete-ness, almost.

Without her having any say in what was happening, her body seemed to melt into Christian's. Blindly, Meg opened her mouth to him, wanting to breathe him, sense him, *feel* him within her deepest, most secret places. A shudder ran through him as his hand cupped the back of her head, his fingers stroking and caressing.

She was trembling herself as she recognised what was happening to her—what *had* happened. Helplessly she lifted her hands to draw him closer, and then, as the realisation struck fully home, instead to push him away, fleeing from him when he released her as though he were the devil and not stopping until she had reached the sanctuary of her room.

Once there she stared accusingly at her reflection in the mirror, searching for something—*anything*—

she could see there to explain to her just why she had been so stupid.

She was old enough to know the danger of falling in love with a man like Christian—a man who would never share her feelings. A man who quite obviously regarded her with a mixture of angry contempt and some unfathomable cruel brand of male desire, which he seemed to think he had every right to indulge in whenever he chose.

The Señora's bottle of painkillers was still in her hand. She would have to return downstairs with them. She knew it was going to take every ounce of strength and courage she possessed to get through the next two weeks of their visit to the *castillo* without betraying what had happened to her. Mentally, she prayed that she *would* be able to do so. The humiliation she would suffer if Christian were to guess how she felt about him made her feel physically sick.

But still, heart-achingly, there was a part of her that yearned to relive the sensation of his mouth on hers, the shocking thrill of that heartbeat of time when she had known that she loved him. Her desire to recreate those feelings, to rewrite the whole scene, editing out the harsh realities of it and substituting them instead with her own dangerous fantasy of love and longing was so strong she had to will herself to resist it.

Downstairs in the silent hallway, Christian gritted his teeth. His hand was already on the ornate banister, the urgency of his need to follow Meg a physical pain.

Watching Sancho flirt with her earlier in the evening had made him feel…had made him *want*… The pain that engulfed him was savage and explicit. He considered himself to be a civilised man, but right now there was something very uncivilised about exactly what he wanted to do.

The thought of Meg responding to Sancho's kisses in the way she had to *his*—the thought of her responding like that to *any* other man, in fact—

He *couldn't* go after Meg. He would despise himself if he did, just as he would despise *any* man who attempted to force himself on a woman.

Upstairs in the privacy of their bedroom Juanita smiled at her husband, shaking her head when he asked her if she wanted to go back downstairs.

'Do you know, Ramon?' she commented. 'I think at last that Christian is following our family tradition.'

Ramon's frown told her that he had not followed her quick intuitive thinking. Sighing, she explained, 'You know that it is the tradition in our family for its men to fall immediately and lastingly in love only once in their lives? Up until now, Christian has not done so, but now I think…' She paused. 'I do so like Meg!'

'*Meg*? You think that your brother has fallen in love with *Meg*…' Ramon looked bemused. 'But they have only just met.'

'As had we, when I knew that you were the one for me,' Juanita reminded him lovingly.

'But he is so very cold and formal towards her.'

'Exactly,' Juanita agreed, giving him a secretive female smile.

CHAPTER FOUR

MEG couldn't believe it. It was already two days after Christmas. From her bedroom window she could see Juanita's sons playing in the garden below.

Earlier that morning, Juanita's husband and his brother had had to return to Madrid to attend to some business matters, and Meg suspected that Juanita had been rather relieved to see her brother-in-law go.

Charming though he could be, there was no doubt that Sancho was also extremely irresponsible. For once, Meg had found herself totally in accord with Christian when he had expressed disapproval and anger at the way in which Sancho had encouraged his nephews' excitement and interest in the air rifle he had carelessly brought to the *castillo* with him.

'I like to hunt, and this is the country.' Sancho had shrugged. 'You of all people should surely support such a tradition.'

'Hunting in the days when it was necessary to do so for food was one thing,' Christian had replied curtly.

'But…' His mouth had tightened as he'd looked from Sancho's openly taunting expression to the absorbed faces of his nephews as they had begged to be allowed to handle the gun.

Meg had seen how much Christian wanted to step in and demand that Sancho did not allow them to do so, but she suspected that he, like her, knew that Sancho would enjoy deliberately flouting his authority.

Later, when Juanita had firmly ushered the boys away, quietly reminding Sancho that they were far too young to be allowed to 'play' with something so potentially dangerous, Meg had seen Christian take Sancho on one side, no doubt to remonstrate with him for being so irresponsible.

She was on her own at the *castillo* today, apart from Christian and the boys, Christian's mother having persuaded the Señora, as well as Juanita, to join her on a visit to an elderly relative living some miles away.

At the Señora's insistence, Meg had stayed behind. She deserved to have some time to herself, the Señora had insisted, suggesting that Meg might enjoy walking round the *castillo*'s extensive gardens.

Too much time on her hands wasn't something Meg really wanted, though. It could lead all too easily to the dangerous self-indulgence of thinking about Christian, and from *thinking* about him it was one very easy and short step to remembering the way he had kissed her.

From her bedroom window she could see Christian

walking across the courtyard to join his nephews. Hungrily she studied him. It was a sunny day and the sunshine burnished the darkness of his hair. The small ache which had taken up permanent residence in her heart grew to a tormented yearning. Suddenly Christian turned to look up towards her bedroom window. Flushing, she drew back from it.

She had come upstairs to write a letter to her parents but half an hour later she was still nowhere near finishing it. There was so much that she could *not* tell them, so much that she did not *want* them to read between her lines.

'Meg?'

The totally unexpected sound of Christian's voice calling her name urgently from outside her bedroom door shocked her into wary immediacy. What did he want? Why was he there?

'Meg.'

The sharp, impatient insistence in his voice as he repeated her name made her hurry towards the door.

As she opened it he stepped quickly inside, shouldering the door shut behind him.

Something in his expression told her immediately that something was very wrong.

He had a cloth over his right arm, which he was holding in place with his left hand, and as she glanced at it Meg saw that blood was seeping through it. Instantly her professional training overrode her emotions.

'What's happened?' she demanded as she hurried towards him, focusing her attention on his arm.

'Somehow the boys managed to get hold of Sancho's rifle—I warned him about making sure it was safely locked away. I was afraid there might be an accident and I went to get it from them, but unfortunately…'

He gave a small shrug and then winced in obvious pain as Meg urged him towards her bathroom. The cloth was bright red with blood now. Soon it would be dripping on the bedroom floor, and the no doubt priceless rug that covered it, and besides her medical bag was in the bathroom and she wanted it to hand when she removed that cloth.

'The gun went *off*. You were *hit*?' she demanded sharply.

'Unfortunately, yes,' he agreed. 'The boys are very shocked. Maria is taking care of them.'

Maria was the *castillo*'s housekeeper and Meg nodded her head as she took hold of his arm and removed the cloth.

The pellet from the air rifle had gouged a deep furrow along the length of Christian's forearm and Meg winced as she saw the extent of his wound.

The pellet would have to be removed and the wound cleaned and then stitched, and that was a job for a doctor, not her—a doctor who, she was sure, would immediately prescribe a course of strong antibiotics just in case the wound should become infected.

'You need to see a doctor,' she told Christian quietly.

'It is just a scratch, a flesh wound,' Christian insisted with a small shrug. 'You are a nurse. Surely you can do *something*.'

'*Something*,' Meg agreed. 'But—'

'Then do it,' Christian commanded. 'Unless you would prefer that I attended to it myself?'

He sounded serious enough to have her reaching anxiously for her medical bag. She knew what had to be done, of course, and quickly set about doing it, having first insisted on bringing a chair from her bedroom for Christian to sit on.

'In case I get bored,' he mocked her.

'In case you pass out,' Meg corrected him briskly, starting to sterilise her hands and the area of the wound. The length of the furrow was bad enough, but it was also worryingly deep. Her work as a theatre sister meant that she was thoroughly familiar with the sight of blood, bone and tissue, but even so on this occasion she found she was having to grit her teeth and steel herself as she parted the edges of the wound to inspect the damage and look for the pellet.

Her stomach churned nauseously when she saw it, a small dark object buried into the flesh it had torn and perilously close to a main artery. If she tried to remove it there was a danger she might drive it deeper, to puncture the vein—but if she left it it could move of its own accord and puncture an artery anyway.

'I can see the pellet and I think I can remove it,' she

told Christian, keeping her voice as even as she could. 'But…' She paused.

'But what?' he encouraged her.

'It's very close to a main artery,' she told him honestly.

For a moment they looked at one another. There was something in his eyes, in their expression, that made her heart jolt and her pulse race feverishly. She was imagining it, she told herself sternly. He was already bleeding rather more than she liked, but she was concerned that if she insisted on him sending for a doctor the situation could deteriorate before one could arrive—the *castillo* was, after all, remote.

'It will hurt,' she warned him.

The grim look he gave her made Meg flinch a little. Did he think that she would enjoy hurting him?

'You have—' he began in a clipped voice and then stopped. 'You must do what you have to do,' he continued after a brief pause. Meg could sense his determination not to betray any sign of pain.

Even so she felt him wince as she probed his flesh to remove the pellet.

Fighting back her own nausea, Meg pressed on and then paused as, out of the corner of her eye, she saw Christian beginning to sag. Her hand ached with tension—she prayed it would not let her down.

'Nearly there,' she told him with a determined cheerfulness she was far from feeling. 'Just another few seconds…'

The seconds stretched into minutes as she carefully

worked her way round the pellet, dreading that it might break into pieces before she could safely remove it.

'There…'

She had it. Meg held her breath as she very carefully extracted the pellet, easing it away from the artery. She could feel the trauma of what she was doing sending a small tremor through Christian's arm—and no wonder. Meg was no stranger to physical pain herself, and she knew that her hand would ache badly for days after the strain she had just imposed on it.

The pellet safely removed, she started to clean up the wound. It would have to be stitched and for that he would need to see a doctor.

Christian watched her as she worked, forcing himself to concentrate and not to give in to the nauseating waves of weakness that were breaking over him. She was half turned away from him, her face in profile, intent, professional, her concentration on what she was doing almost a force-field around her. Before attending to his wound she had tied her hair up out of the way, but a few small strands had escaped and he had to fight the impulse to reach out with his uninjured arm to touch them, touch her…

Perhaps his pain had somehow intensified his senses. Could it do so? He didn't know, but for some reason he was acutely aware of everything about her—the soft delicate scent of her skin, the way she was breathing, the tension in her body as she worked and the relief once she had removed the pellet. He had even felt that small second of hesitation before she had started to clean his flesh.

He winced as something suddenly stung the rawness of the wound, his ears buzzing with the intensity of the pain, his vision blurring. He gritted his teeth against the verbal protest his body wanted him to make.

Meg was biting down hard on her own bottom lip, praying silently that Christian wouldn't faint. He had said nothing, made no sound, but her experience told her that his body was in shock. Mindful of her operating theatre experience, she began to talk to him. Having to listen gave a patient something to focus on other than their pain. She spoke quietly, almost hypnotically, her voice soothing and calm.

'I'll bandage your arm but I'm afraid it is going to need stitches and I can't do that—not without a local anaesthetic. It will have to be seen by a doctor, Christian, and you will need a course of antibiotics, just to be sure that no infection has got in—and as soon as possible.'

'Then in that case you will just have to drive me to Seville.' The strength and purposefulness of his voice caught her off guard. He had looked so close to losing consciousness that she had half-expected him either not to reply at all or simply to mumble something, but here he was, speaking as irritatingly authoritatively as normal. In fact, anyone listening to their voices would probably assume that of the two of them *she* was the one in shock.

'I… I can't do that,' she protested. As she spoke she looked towards Christian and immediately wished she hadn't.

Despairingly she recognised that these last few days of telling herself that she was simply not going to allow herself to love him had been a total waste of time.

'I'm afraid you're going to *have* to,' Christian informed her tersely. 'There *is* no one else.'

Meg knew that it was true. Christian's mother, the Señora and Juanita were not due to return until much, much later in the evening and, of course, Christian's chauffeur was with them. Sancho and Ramon were away on business.

There is no one else… Somewhere deep down in her most private and secret emotions, his words touched an aching chord. If only he were saying them to her in another context…an emotional context…as *her* lover, the man who *loved* her, the man for whom there could never be anyone else but her.

Christian frowned as he saw the look of raw anguish in Meg's eyes. Instinctively he started to stand up, wanting to comfort her, but he had forgotten about his arm. A momentary surge of dizziness made him sway slightly. Immediately Meg's professional instinct overturned her private feelings and she was standing beside him, using her body to steady and support him as she placed her arm around him.

'It's all right,' she reassured him gently. 'You've

lost quite a lot of blood and that's bound to make you feel a bit weak…'

Weak?

He was feeling *that*, all right, Christian acknowledged, and not just because of his injury. No, it was *Meg's* proximity that was knocking him off balance, her proximity and the sweetly sensual feel of her body next to his, her arm protectively around him.

He turned his head to tell her that he was all right and caught his breath as he saw that she was looking up at him, her eyes brilliant with concern.

'Oh, Meg.'

He said it so softly that Meg thought she must have misheard the aching note of tenderness in his voice and then, unbelievably, he was lowering his head towards her, brushing his lips against hers in the lightest and sweetest of caresses. Instinctively she reached up to curl her hand around his neck; the skin felt warm and smooth, his hair silky-soft.

'Thank you,' he whispered as he released her mouth.

Desperate to conceal what she was feeling from him, Meg immediately became fussily professional, reminding him sharply, 'You still need to get to see a doctor and—'

'—And the only way I'm going to be able to do that is for you to drive me to Seville,' Christian repeated.

She had released him now and was turning away from him, and he had a sudden violent urge to take her back in his arms and tell her how he felt about her, tell her too about his family's tradition and beg her to give him the opportunity to teach her to share his love.

The last thing Meg wanted to do was to spend several hours alone in the close confines of a car with Christian, but her professionalism and her sense of responsibility and duty insisted that she had no other choice—the *castillo* was so remote that it would probably take just as long to obtain the services of a local doctor as it would to drive Christian to Seville.

Giving a small sigh, she nodded her head in silent acceptance.

Not unnaturally, perhaps, it took Meg rather longer to drive along the tortuous mountain route to Seville than it had done Christian, but unexpectedly Christian did not show any impatience or irritation with her cautious handling of his large four-wheel-drive vehicle. On the contrary, he was calmly reassuring, even taking the trouble to boost her confidence by praising the way she was driving.

They had left Juanita's sons in the charge of the housekeeper—the rifle had, of course, been confiscated and locked away—and Meg had been filled with unwanted admiration for the gentle way in which Christian had handled his nephews' guilt and anxiety over the accident, making light of his injury. Fortunately, both of them were too young to be fully aware of what *could* have happened, although Meg's blood ran cold when she thought of how easily a real tragedy could have overtaken them all.

A brief message had been left with the housekeeper, explaining what had happened, although here again Christian had insisted that Juanita was to be protected from being shocked.

'There was a miscarriage before she conceived this baby,' he had explained quietly to Meg, 'and whilst her pregnancy is past *that* danger point now…'

Meg had nodded her head, immediately understanding and acquiescing with his decision.

And now, here they were, driving into Seville.

As she followed Christian's directions Meg glanced at his arm. The wound was still bleeding, the bandage showing a spreading crimson stain; her heart started to thud anxiously.

'Could we go straight to the hospital?' she asked him. 'Their casualty department will be able to deal with you immediately.'

'If you think that's best,' Christian agreed, deferring to her judgement so easily that her anxiety increased.

She had noticed him holding his bandaged arm surreptitiously whilst she was driving and she knew it must be hurting him. Her own hand was aching with tension, the damaged ligaments tightening. The four-wheel-drive was equipped with power steering and an automatic gear box, but the long winding bends on the mountain road had still taken their toll.

Frowning in concentration, she followed Christian's directions through the city, thankfully relatively empty of traffic. Her shoulders and her chest ached with tension and concentration and she had never been more relieved to see a hospital building.

She parked the vehicle and they both climbed out. Thankfully Christian was perfectly steady on his feet, although he looked a little paler than normal.

It was only a short distance to the Accident and Emergency entrance to the hospital, and they had almost reached it when Christian suddenly reached out with his left hand, stopping Meg from going any further.

'What is it?' she asked him anxiously. 'Are you feeling faint? Sick? Shall I go and get…?'

Christian shook his head, ignoring her anxious questions to demand brusquely instead, 'Your hand— you keep rubbing it. You should have said something. You're obviously in pain!' The brusqueness in his voice deepened. 'I shouldn't have allowed you to drive.'

'There wasn't any other way we could have got here,' Meg reminded him. For some reason, her throat felt constricted with stupid tears. What for? Because, despite his own pain, he had noticed *her* discomfort?

'We could have telephoned for the local doctor to visit, but I know he has a large practice and it seemed unfair to add to his workload, especially at this time of the year.'

'We're here now,' Meg responded. 'My hand will soon recover.'

She was so stoical, so independent, and Christian was furious with himself for being the cause of her discomfort. He wanted to take hold of her hand and wrap it in the warmth of his, to take hold of *her* and wrap her in the protection of his love.

Reluctantly he let her go, falling into step beside her as she hurried towards the hospital entrance.

Angry with herself, Meg blinked away her foolish emotional tears. Just for a second she had been so tempted to fling herself into Christian's arms, to tell him how afraid for him she had been, to feel him hold her and reassure her…to feel him *love* her!

They were inside the hospital now. Bracing her shoulders, Meg reminded herself of her professional responsibility.

CHAPTER FIVE

'MISS SCOTT?'

As she heard her name Meg looked up. A white-coated doctor was hurrying towards her.

'Christian? The Duque?' she began anxiously.

'He is fine,' the doctor assured her. 'My nurse is just finishing bandaging his arm. May I congratulate you on a very neat piece of work? Had you not had the skill to remove the pellet, it could quite easily have become lodged more deeply and dangerously by the time he got here. I understand from the Duque that you trained as a theatre sister.'

'Yes,' Meg admitted, more anxious to discuss Christian's injury than her own past history.

'We have stitched the wound and administered an antibiotic injection, but I should like to see him again in the morning. His temperature is a little raised and he could develop a fever.'

'In the morning?' Meg began. 'But…' She stopped as she saw Christian himself walking towards them.

It was plain that he had overheard the doctor's comment, because before she could say anything he was telling him smoothly, 'That will be no problem. We shall stay overnight at my apartment here in Seville since it isn't feasible to drive back to the *castillo* tonight.' Thanking the doctor for what he had done, he placed his left hand on Meg's arm, gently but determinedly drawing her away.

They had reached the exit before she could manage to speak.

'*Why* isn't it feasible to drive back to the *castillo*?' she demanded. Her heart was racing frantically and she knew that her face must be flushed with the dangerous mixture of excitement and longing that was rushing through her veins.

To spend the evening *alone* with Christian… She didn't think she could bear to, but she knew that she could not bear not to. She was an idiot, storing up even more pain for herself, she told herself fiercely, but it was no good and she could see that Christian was not going to change his mind.

He confirmed this when he said crisply to her, '*I* certainly do not feel up to undergoing the drive back to the *castillo* now, only to have to drive all the way back here again tomorrow morning—even if *you* do. No—' he shook his head decisively '—we will spend the night here in the city at my apartment.'

He paused and looked down into her eyes, his gaze so intense that Meg thought she might suffocate from the tension gripping her own body.

'It seems that I have a great deal to thank you for. The doctor told me that the pellet was perilously close to the main artery and that if you had not removed it…'

Meg couldn't say anything. She knew she would remember for the rest of her life the horror of that sickening second when she had realised how vitally important it was both that she removed the pellet and that she didn't accidentally push it further into the wound in doing so. Never had she regretted so desperately her own injury, never had she prayed more fervently that her hand wouldn't let her down.

Christian's apartment was just as grand in its own way as the *castillo*. A whole floor in a beautiful old building overlooking its own private garden.

The guest room Christian had indicated she was to use was equipped with virtually everything an overnight guest might need.

'I'm afraid we shall have to raid the freezer for something to eat,' Christian had informed her. 'Unless you would prefer to go out?'

Meg had shaken her head. She suspected that once the local anaesthetic wore off the stitches in his arm would make him feel distinctly uncomfortable. The doctor had given her some painkillers for him, in addition to a course of antibiotics to be taken once he was back at the *castillo*.

The long drive had left her feeling gritty-eyed and

slightly grubby, and she looked longingly towards the luxurious marble bathroom attached to her bedroom.

Christian had told her that he intended to ring the *castillo* and explain what had happened. The temptation to indulge in a long luxurious soak was too much for Meg to resist.

Half an hour later she was seated at the dressing table, wrapped in a thick white fluffy towel just finishing blow drying her hair, when the bedroom door opened and Christian walked in.

The shock of seeing him made her drop the hairdryer, and as she made to pick it up so did Christian, apologising as he did so. 'I'm sorry… I did knock but obviously you didn't hear me.'

As he picked up the hairdryer he switched it off and put it down. He was looking at her in a way that made sensual awareness burn along Meg's veins. Unable to stop herself, she moistened her suddenly dry lips with the tip of her tongue, her heart slamming against her chest wall in shock as she saw his reaction to what she was doing in Christian's eyes.

He wanted her… Because she was a *woman*, she fought to remind herself, not because she was *her*. He was a very male man—a very *sexual* man—she already knew that. A man who no doubt was not used to living a celibate life. A man… A man she loved and wanted, and whom she ached and longed to have touch her, stroke her, slide the towel away from her body and slowly and thoroughly caress every inch of her flesh with his hands and then his mouth whilst she—

Yearningly, she stepped towards him, and then stopped as he raised his hand and she saw the bandage on his arm.

She wasn't here because he *loved her*, she reminded herself harshly.

As she stepped determinedly back from him, Christian cursed himself under his breath. This was going to be so much harder than he had imagined and he wasn't sure he had the self-control to keep his distance from her.

'I've checked the freezer,' he told her curtly. 'I hope you like fish.'

'I do,' Meg confirmed. Did her voice sound as shaky and huskily vulnerable to him as it did to her?

'I make a pretty fair paella,' Christian informed her. 'But on this occasion I'm afraid I'm going to need your assistance.' As he spoke he gestured to his arm. 'Are you hungry yet?' he asked, 'Or…'

She *was* hungry, Meg discovered, to her own surprise, but then the last meal she had eaten had been breakfast, and now it was six o'clock in the evening.

'Give me half an hour to freshen up,' Christian began.

'Remember that you have to keep your dressing dry,' Meg warned him, her professionalism coming to the fore, but it wasn't her professionalism that brought a hot surge of colour to her face seconds later as she closed her eyes briefly, trying not to imagine him standing naked beneath the hot wet pulse of a shower. What was she doing to herself, *tormenting* herself like this?

To her relief, Christian hadn't seen her betraying reaction, and was turning away from her and heading towards her bedroom door.

Half an hour. She had half an hour to bring herself back to some semblance of sanity and reality. Then she and Christian would be working together in his kitchen, preparing a meal for themselves, for all the world as though they were a couple, as though they were *lovers…*

Lovers… How tormentingly sweet and dangerous the word sounded, felt…*tasted…* She said it out loud, just for the forbidden pleasure it gave her. Lovers…

The apartment's kitchen was unexpectedly modern and well equipped. Christian was already busily removing items from the freezer when Meg walked in. Unlike her, *he* had been able to get changed. As though he could guess what she was thinking, he told her ruefully, 'I'm sorry. I cannot offer you a change of clothes. The best I can do is to give you one of my shirts, but I'm afraid it would drown you!'

One of his shirts… Was her expression giving her away? Meg wondered. Could he see in her eyes just what the thought of having one of his shirts, impregnated with the unique scent of *him*, to hold and cling on to was doing to her? She prayed not.

To her surprise, it soon became obvious that

Christian was perfectly at home in his role of chef, carefully defrosting the items he had removed from the freezer in the microwave before starting to cook them. However, Meg kept a watchful eye on how much he was using his arm, insisting on taking over when she could sense that it was beginning to hurt him.

A mouthwatering scent of cooking food soon filled the kitchen.

Christian had opened a bottle of wine, pouring them both a glass which he insisted they should drink whilst they were cooking, giving her a rueful look when Meg reminded him that it might not be wise to drink very much whilst he was having antibiotics.

'Always the nurse,' he told her.

'Well, that *is* why I'm here,' she reminded him defensively.

The look he gave her made her curl her toes up inside her shoes. As he turned away from her he muttered something in Spanish that sounded like 'Don't remind me,' but Meg suspected she must have misheard him.

Guiltily Meg smothered a small betraying yawn, but it was too late; Christian had seen her. They had finished their meal and cleaned up after themselves, and at Christian's suggestion they had walked around the elegant nightscape-lit garden. These Spanish gardens had a very special magic that was all their own, Meg had acknowledged, as she paused to admire the fountain at the centre. But now they were back inside and, even though it was still not yet midnight, early by Spanish standards, she was feeling tired.

Christian had refused the painkillers she had offered him earlier in the evening, insisting that he felt fine. He wouldn't need his oral antibiotics until later tomorrow, and she suspected that the doctor at the hospital would give him another intravenous antibiotic when he checked him over in the morning.

'You're tired. Why don't you go to bed?' he was suggesting to Meg now.

Reluctantly Meg got up. He was morally if not technically her patient—in her eyes at least—and her nursing instinct urged her to ensure that he was safely ensconced in *his* bed before she sought her own. But before she could say anything the telephone rang.

As he answered it, Meg heard him say warmly, 'Juanita… No, everything's fine, I promise. A small flesh wound, that's all. No. I promise you, I'm fine… Yes. But that was just a precaution…'

Quietly, Meg headed towards the door, not wanting to eavesdrop on his conversation with his sister.

The huge double bed in her room looked blissfully inviting. Her hand was aching quite badly. She had her own prescription painkillers and she knew she ought to take one. As she padded into the bathroom for a glass of water she realised that she had nothing to sleep in. Her underwear would have to be rinsed and left to dry on the bathroom's heated towel rail. She could, perhaps, wrap herself in a towel, she mused.

Ten minutes later, having showered and brushed her hair, she decided that such modesty was unnecessary, and when she slid into her bed between the cool deliciousness of its pure cotton sheets she was glad she had decided against doing so. There was something almost wickedly sensual about the feel of cool, pure cotton against naked skin.

Wearily she closed her eyes. The events of the day had drained her more than she had recognised. Behind her closed eyelids she kept seeing Christian's arm, the ugly little pellet buried in his torn flesh. For the rest of her life she would remember that moment when she had started to examine the wound and recognised how close it was to his vein, and how careful she would have to be to remove it…

On his way to his own bedroom Christian paused outside Meg's bedroom door. She had tried to hide it from him but he had seen how much pain her hand was causing her earlier. *His* fault… If she hadn't had to drive him here to Seville…

The doctor at the hospital had made it plain to him just how lucky he had been, castigating whoever it was who had been foolish enough to give a young boy an air rifle.

Christian had deliberately played things down when he had spoken to his sister, assuring her that there was nothing for her to worry about and that she would see for herself when he and Meg returned to the *castillo*.

'When will you be back?' she had asked him.

'I'm not sure,' he had told her. 'I have to go to the hospital again in the morning.'

'Again? But why?'

'It is just a precaution…nothing more…' he had soothed her. He had spoken briefly to his mother and to his nephews, both of whom had sounded chastened.

What had happened had not been their fault, and he had said as much to Juanita.

'Thank goodness Meg was there,' she had told him emotionally.

Meg.

Christian realised that he was still standing outside her bedroom door like a lovelorn fool… Meg… He closed his eyes and allowed the pain of what he was feeling to thud through his veins, greater by far than the pain of his injured arm. *That* would heal, fade and be totally forgotten, but what he felt for Meg—that would be with him for the rest of his life.

Somehow there must be a way for him to break down the barriers between them, for him to show her how good things could be between them.

Somehow—but how?

Bleak-eyed, he headed for his own bedroom.

CHAPTER SIX

CHRISTIAN groaned as the pain in his arm intensified. He had been awake for over an hour, his arm throbbing increasingly uncomfortably as the effects of the anaesthetic wore off.

His body felt hot and his head muzzy. He wanted a drink of water and a cooling shower, but more, much more than either of those, he wanted Meg.

Unsteadily he pushed back the duvet and slid his feet to the floor.

Meg had always been a light sleeper, and her eyes were open the moment Christian turned the handle of her door. The sight of him standing inside her room wearing a short robe tied loosely and open to his waist made her heart pound, her stomach cramp with longing.

But then her professional eye saw the hot flush staining his face and recognised the slightly disorientated look in his eyes.

He was clasping his right arm and, even in the dim

light of her bedside lamp, Meg could see how swollen it looked.

'I'm sorry to wake you,' he was telling her. 'Those painkillers—I think I may need one…'

Meg had put them in her bathroom.

'I'll get them for you,' she told him. 'Come and sit down.'

She wanted to take his temperature, which she was sure would be higher than it should be. Even though he had been given antibiotics, there was no guarantee that the wound had not become infected.

As he reached the end of her bed, and slumped rather than sat down on it, she pushed her bedclothes back anxiously and got out—and then realised too late what she had done. She was completely naked, and that Christian was looking at her as though he wanted…as though he felt…

He made a low sound somewhere between a moan and a growl deep in his throat.

'Meg…*querida*…' His voice sounded raw with longing and pain, totally transfixing Meg to where she stood as he came towards her.

Helplessly she felt his arms close around her whilst his mouth sought hers with hungry male determination.

What was happening was wrong and oh, so very, very dangerous, but the touch of his mouth on hers was fulfilling her deepest, sweetest fantasies as he caressed her lips over and over again, stroking them with his tongue, absorbing the taste of her and drawing from her a desire, an urgency to give herself completely to him.

Passionately she returned his kisses, her lips parting, her tongue seeking his, her hand sliding inside his parted robe and spreading possessively across the silky heat of his naked skin. His left hand curled around her neck, holding her a willing captive to his desire. His hand moved, his fingertips tender against her face, before he groaned, bringing his hot face against the soft curve of her throat.

The breath that shuddered from him made her tremble in response, and moan—a soft, acquiescent sound of love. Christian's reaction was immediate, his mouth caressing, devouring the exposed curve of her throat.

As the passion they had both been suppressing exploded into life everything else was forgotten. The pain which had brought Christian into Meg's room no longer existed; the barriers Meg had been so determined to erect against him had totally disintegrated. They were two people being consumed by a need they were powerless to deny.

'*Querida...querida*, you cannot *know* how much I have wanted this...*you*...' Christian was muttering fiercely against her skin as he kissed her.

Meg closed her eyes as she drank in the words whilst her flesh absorbed the sheeting pleasure of his touch. Her whole body felt as though suddenly it had come to life... She ached with him and for him, wanted him with an intensity that was shockingly raw and elemental.

Savagely, her hands pushed aside his robe, her body shuddering in delight as she drank in the fierce dark male beauty of him. Tiny whorls of sweat-dampened body hair lay pressed flat against his torso. In his arms and shoulders she could see the powerful definition of his muscles, the warm gilded beauty of his flesh. Hungrily, her gaze absorbed the physical reality of him.

'You're so beautiful.'

As she whispered the awed words she saw his chest rise and fall with laughter.

'No, *querida*,' he told her softly. '*You* are the one who is that. Here…' he told her, cupping her face with one hand and gently kissing her mouth. 'And here…' His hand dropped to hold her breast, his lips caressing its taut peak slowly savouring its response to him. 'Here…' His voice became deeper, thicker as he dropped to his knees in front of her and placed a small circle of kisses around her navel.

Meg held her breath and tried not to tremble.

His hand was covering her sex, as though he knew how shy she suddenly felt.

'And here,' he told her as he slowly started to caress her, his gaze holding her eyes as his fingers slowly stroked her body, 'you are the most beautiful of all.'

Meg could hear the harsh disjointedness of her own erratic breathing, feel the frantic pounding of her heart, feel too the sweet melting heat that was running through her veins.

She closed her eyes as Christian lifted her onto the

bed. She had been wrong about the feel of cool cotton being the most sensual pleasure she had ever felt. *This*… Christian's hot naked flesh against her own… was what *real* sensual pleasure was all about. She felt…she wanted…

As he touched her she cried out her feelings to him, reaching for him, aching for him.

Somewhere in the tiny corner of her mind that was not wholly consumed with love and longing, a warning registered that the heat coming off Christian's body was not just caused by the sensuality of their lovemaking, but she was too enthralled by what was happening to pay any attention to it.

Christian was kissing her with a ferocity of passion that totally obliterated all the vague, pale beliefs she had previously held about what she wanted from a lover. There was an intensity about the way he was touching her, *loving* her, that made her shudder in semi-shocked pleasure. His hands, his touch on her breasts, her belly, *everywhere*, his kisses, seemed to trigger a thousand tiny bolts of pleasure through her body.

She ached so to have him deep, deep inside her, filling her, taking her to a special place that would be uniquely theirs, completing her and completing the awesome cycle of love they had begun.

Lost, rapt with the intensity of her feelings, Meg cried out her thoughts to him.

Through the hot haze of his own desire Christian heard her, smothering and silencing the words of love his heart was pouring out to her against her mouth as he took it in a kiss of totally elemental possession in exactly the same moment as he filled her with his body—and his love.

The pleasure seemed to last for ever, and yet at the same time it reached its peak so swiftly that Meg felt dizzy and breathless. She cried out and heard the sound of her own fulfilment, a sharp gasped sound, quickly followed by Christian's fierce cry of male triumph.

As she lay trembling with aftershock in his arms, Meg felt Christian gently kiss her closed eyelids and then her mouth. His tenderness brought a hot burn of emotional tears to her eyes and she lifted her hand to touch him. He was burning up with heat, his skin slick with sweat.

Alarm replaced her euphoria. She opened her eyes and turned to look at him. That was surely a febrile feverish glitter in his eyes. Immediately her professional instincts swung into action. She guessed that he had a temperature and a fever, which ominously suggested that, despite the antibiotic shot, his wound had become infected.

'What is it?' he was demanding huskily. 'You look so serious…too serious…' He was reaching for her, obviously intending to take her back in his arms, his lips brushing her temple.

She wasn't imagining it, she was sure; their touch was far, far hotter than it had been before.

'*Querida…*'

Even his voice sounded different, slower, huskier and disorientated. Her anxiety increased. Gently easing herself away from him, she slid out of the bed. She needed to take his temperature, even though instinct and experience told her what she would find when she did.

She was gone less than five minutes—two minutes had been wasted in the bathroom, where she had inadvertently caught sight of her own reflection as she'd opened her medical bag. The face staring back at her from the mirror had indubitably been her own and yet, somehow, the face of a stranger, another Meg who, until tonight—until *Christian*—she had never realised existed. A Meg who looked as though…who looked like a woman who… Pink-cheeked, she had turned away and hurried back to the bedroom.

In the short space of time she had been gone Christian had fallen into a feverish sleep. He was moving restlessly, a hot flush plainly discernible beneath his tan, his body drenched with a fever-induced sweat.

Anxiously, Meg looked at his arm, her heart sinking as she saw how swollen the flesh was around the bandage. There was as yet no tell-tale red line of potential blood-poisoning creeping upwards towards his armpit—thankfully.

Grimly, she knew that at this stage the only thing she could do was to make him as comfortable as possible and hope that the antibiotics he had been given would be able to fight the infection until he was able to see the doctor in the morning.

'Meg?'

The shock of Christian's eyes suddenly opening whilst his lips framed her name held her motionless.

'Oh, you are there…' His eyes had the glazed look of someone not totally fully aware. His voice dropped, becoming softer so that she had to lean closer to him to hear him. 'Closer…'

His command made her instinctively lower her head to catch what he wanted to say, but instead of speaking he curled his left hand round her neck and began to kiss her.

He was her *patient*, Meg tried to remind herself. He wasn't *well*…wasn't even really *aware* of what he was doing. But the aching sweetness of his kiss fired her vulnerable emotions like a match to dry tinder. And yet, somehow, she managed to find the strength of will to pull away from him. Had *any* of what had happened been real for him? Had he *known* who she was when they had made love? Had he really wanted *her*, or…?

He had lapsed into a deeper and less feverish sleep. Mentally, she crossed her fingers, hoping that the antibiotics were now taking effect.

It was three o'clock in the morning. There was no way she was going to spend the rest of the night sleeping in a bed beside him.

Why not? an inner voice tempted her. It's what you *really* want to do, isn't it?

Of course it was, but she couldn't. He wasn't fully aware of his actions.

So where was she going to sleep—in *his* bed?

To her relief, a quiet inspection of the apartment revealed another empty guest room. But, despite the luxurious comfort of its bed, Meg knew she was unlikely to get much sleep in it.

She was right. At six o'clock she had had enough and was up and dressed, a jittery nervousness invading her stomach after she looked in on Christian and ascertained that he was sleeping restfully and apparently fever-free.

As she paced the floor of the apartment's huge reception room she nibbled worriedly at her bottom lip. Would Christian say anything about last night? Would he even *remember*? And, if he did, would he just dismiss what had happened as an unimportant one-night stand?

She swallowed hard. What was the code of behaviour governing such occurrences? She had never… *would* never… To her own disgust, she discovered that she was having to blink hard to keep her eyes free of self-pitying tears.

That's what you get, my girl, she told herself derisively, for giving in to your emotions for a man who doesn't share them.

She would wait until seven o'clock before waking Christian, she told herself, and once he was awake she would not make any reference at all to their lovemaking. If Christian chose to raise the subject…

Agitatedly, she paced even faster. Perhaps if she made herself a cup of tea…

She was in the kitchen, waiting for the kettle to boil, when, to her consternation, Christian suddenly walked in. Engrossed in her thoughts, she hadn't heard him, and the sight of him fully dressed and quite plainly recently shaved—and, she guessed, in full possession of all his faculties—caused her hand to tremble as she held the kettle.

'Careful' Christian warned her.

He was frowning, Meg recognised, and as she turned away from him to busy herself with her tea-making—and, more importantly, so that she wouldn't have to look at him—she could almost *hear* the frown in his voice as he demanded, 'Are you all right?'

'Of course. Why shouldn't I be?'

Confronted by her back and the sharpness of her voice, Christian hesitated. It was quite obvious that she didn't want to talk about what had happened between them. To wake up in the bed that should have been hers but in which he had quite plainly slept alone had told him that, no matter how wonderful the lovemaking they had shared had been to him, Meg did not want him as a permanent feature in her life.

And yet, last night, he could have sworn that she returned his feelings. The way she had touched him, *spoken*…whispering those soft sweet cries of incitement and longing. But although his memories of their lovemaking were sharply etched into his heart, there was a muzzy confusion over just why and when she had left him.

Last night she might have been his lover, his beloved, the embodiment of everything he had ever
wanted or would ever want in a woman, a partner, a
wife. But this morning she was very definitely distancing herself from him.

'You were very feverish in the night,' she was saying to him, her back still to him. 'I was concerned that
an infection might have set in.'

'I remember having a hell of a pounding pain in my
arm,' Christian acknowledged.

'Yes. You came to my bedroom to ask for a painkiller,' Meg confirmed.

She felt sick with nerves as she waited for his response. *Could* he remember anything about what had
happened between them, or had his fever totally obliterated the event?

Behind her back, Christian wondered how she
would react if he were to tell her the blunt truth—
which was that whilst he *might* have gone to her room
seeking a painkiller, what he had really *wanted* had
been her. And he still wanted her—right now…right
here…more than he could find the words to say.

'Meg…'

There was something in his voice that made Meg's
heart thump heavily into her ribcage, but before she
could say anything the telephone started to ring.

Was she imagining it or had Christian started to
make a move towards her before the strident sound of
the telephone had called him away?

What if he had?

He was a man, after all. A man who quite plainly thought nothing of having sex with a woman he didn't love purely to satisfy his own basic sexual needs.

Trying to whip up her own defensive anger against him, Meg felt her lips tremble as she began to drink her tea.

'That was Juanita,' Christian informed Meg as he came back into the kitchen. 'She insists on blaming herself for what happened—totally unnecessarily, as I have already told her. If anyone is to blame it's Sancho,' he added, his voice hardening.

Meg had guessed already that Christian did not have a very high opinion of Juanita's brother-in-law, and she certainly agreed that to show the boys a gun had been totally irresponsible—but for some contrary reason she found herself defending the younger man.

'Oh, of course, I had forgotten that *you* are quite an admirer of him—as he is of you,' Christian replied with ruthless contempt.

In any other man she might almost have suspected that his savage response was motivated by jealousy, Meg decided—but that, of course, was impossible.

No, given Christian's low opinion of Sancho, he probably thought that he and Meg deserved one another.

CHAPTER SEVEN

'I PROMISE you that I am fine and fully recovered,' Christian reassured his assembled family for the umpteenth time since he and Meg had arrived back at the *castillo*, to be greeted by their anxious enquiries.

'We are really sorry, Tio Christian,' Tomaz and Carlos had apologised solemnly.

Kneeling down beside them, Christian hugged them both, telling them gently, 'It was an accident, but now you see what a very dangerous thing a gun can be.'

There was a lump in Meg's throat as she watched this tender little scene.

Before they had left Seville, after their second visit to the hospital, where the doctor had reassured Meg that Christian's wound was healing nicely, Christian had insisted on making a visit to a toy shop, where he had purchased gifts for the two boys.

And today it was New Year's Eve, and the family were celebrating the event with a dinner. To Meg's relief the Señora had not suffered in her absence, and when Meg had suggested diffidently that maybe the family would prefer her not to be there on this occasion the Señora had been horrified.

'But of course you *must* be there... You are a *heroine*, Meg. Christian's mother cannot praise you highly enough, and besides...' She stopped and said nothing. The very promising 'signs' the two old friends had spotted and discussed were, they had agreed by mutual consent, to remain their 'secret' for now.

And so, reluctantly, Meg was now dressing for the special celebration dinner. Juanita's husband Ramon and Sancho had returned from their business trip, arriving just as Meg was crossing the hallway. She had been slightly taken aback to be engulfed in a rather more amorous embrace by Sancho than she had either expected or wanted, but rather than appear rude she had suffered it unresponsively.

'I wish you could have come with us,' he had told Meg, his eyes studying her boldly. 'You would like Madrid...'

'I think my godmother is waiting for you, Meg.'

Christian's voice, cool and sharp, had cut across Sancho's conversation as he'd come down the stairs.

They had hardly spoken to one another since leaving Seville. A part of Meg was glad that he seemed unable to remember what had happened between them, but another part of her felt both furiously angry and desperately hurt that something that had been so precious to her meant so little to him. And the hardest thing of all for her to deal with was that for most of the time her pain far, far outweighed the strength of her anger.

Meg had dressed carefully for the family's New Year's Eve dinner, thankful that she had had the foresight to pack her favourite slinky but simple long black jersey evening dress which, worn with the diamond ear studs her parents had given her for her twenty-first birthday and the gold bangle which had been a present from her brother, looked impressively elegant. Her heart might be breaking but there was no way she was going to allow anyone else to see that.

'Oh, Meg, you look gorgeous.'

The Señora's admiring comment when Meg went to her room to help her downstairs brought a brief smile to Meg's lips.

The Señora too was dressed in black, with diamonds which Meg suspected must be family heirlooms flashing at her throat and ears.

As though she sensed what Meg was thinking, the Señora told her gently, 'My jewellery was a marriage gift from my husband. It had been passed down to him for his bride by his grandmother.' Her eyes became suspiciously over-bright and Meg guessed that she must be thinking of the husband she had lost.

She tried to imagine how she would feel in the Señora's shoes, alone, without the love and support of the husband she had plainly adored, and gave a fierce shudder as she tried and failed to imagine a world without Christian in it.

'There is a pair of matching bracelets, but unfortunately my wrists are so swollen now that I cannot wear them.'

They were the last to arrive in the salon which opened into the *castillo*'s formal dining room.

Immediately they entered the room Meg was conscious of both Christian and Sancho looking at her, and it was obvious that there was still a certain amount of hostility between the two men. An uncomfortable tension pervaded the room and Meg noticed the unhappy looks Juanita and her husband exchanged as Sancho finished his drink and immediately demanded a refill.

When he had finished that and started to pour himself a third, ignoring the concerned frown his brother was giving him, it was left to Christian to say quietly to him, 'I shouldn't, if I were you, Sancho.'

Sancho's reaction was shocking and immediate. Slamming his glass down, he turned on Christian, demanding loudly, 'And who are you to moralise to *me*?' He turned his head to look at Meg, his glance full of drink-fuelled anger that made her feel more alarmed than flattered.

'*You* took Meg to Seville and spent the night alone in your apartment there with her, after you refused to allow her to go to Seville with *me*. You are a man, Christian—and I cannot believe—'

'That is enough.'

It seemed to Meg as though the whole room echoed with the shocked gasp that Sancho's outburst and Christian's tense response aroused.

Juanita was casting her husband an imploring, anguished look, whilst Christian's mother and the Señora looked openly shocked. The young Spaniard who had been serving their drinks blushed to the tips of his ears and Meg knew there was no way she could bring herself to look at Christian. She knew, too, that her own feelings were making her face burn revealingly.

Above the heavy thud of her heartbeat, she could hear Juanita's husband saying his brother's name in a sternly disapproving voice, but it was Christian who cut through the miasma of shock that had choked everyone into silence, his voice cool, crisp, authoritative and totally unemotional as he said icily, 'Your remark is both ill-bred, Sancho, and ill-informed. I am sorry, Mama,' he continued, turning to his mother. 'I had intended to wait until after dinner to make our announcement, but I'm afraid Sancho has forced my hand.'

And then, before Meg could speak or move, he was at her side, holding her hand in his, turning his body protectively towards hers in a pose that said spectacularly plainly just how possessive he felt about her.

'I am proud to tell you all that Meg has consented to become my wife.'

As though he felt her tremor of shock, his grip on her hand tightened warningly.

'As you all know, there is a tradition in this family

that its men fall in love only once in a lifetime, and at first sight. To fall in love very quickly and very passionately—this has always been my fate. And now I can say too—' his voice had started to become lower and softer, like liquid honey, Meg thought dizzily, as her brain tried to cope with what was happening '—that it is also my pleasure…that Meg is my one true love…'

He didn't get any further. Juanita had run towards them and hugged them both, exclaiming tearfully, 'Oh, I am so happy. This is so wonderful…'

And then Ramon was shaking Christian's hand and kissing her formally.

'We can tell you now that we both sensed that this was going to happen,' the Señora exclaimed in delight as both she and Christian's mother kissed Meg warmly.

Meg tried to protest, to destroy the lie before it snowballed totally out of control, but it was already too late.

Christian was holding her so tightly that she couldn't move, and then he bent his head and whispered into her ear in a gesture which was deliberately contrived to look tenderly lover-like to their onlookers, 'Don't argue. If you do I shall be forced to kiss you into silence.'

She dared not allow herself to question whether it was an urge to be honest or her longing to feel his lips against her own that motivated her to try to deny his announcement.

Either way, just the look in his eyes as he focused his gaze on her mouth was enough to make her tremble from head to food and remain silent.

'Very wise,' he murmured to her as he escorted her into the dining room several seconds later.

Very wise? No… What *she* had been and was continuing to be was very foolish, Meg admitted guiltily, as she recognised how easy and how pleasurable it would be to allow herself to believe in the fantasy Christian had so unexpectedly created.

His wife-to-be…the woman he loved… Unable to stop herself, she turned her head to give him a betraying look of misty emotion. For a small heartbeat of time he looked back at her, and Meg had the unnerving impression that not only was he going to sweep her into his arms and kiss her passionately, right there in front of everyone, but that he was also going to sweep her out of the room and—

'I'm so pleased for you both,' Christian's mother began to tell Meg happily as they all took their places at the table.

'You guessed that I had fallen in love with Meg?' Christian questioned his mother.

'We both did,' she replied, smiling at the Señora for corroboration.

In the tidal wave of happy comments and questions that followed Christian's announcement, in some obscure way Meg had actually felt relieved to have him seated next to her, fielding them for her.

'No, we have not set a date for the wedding yet,' he responded to his sister's excited question. 'Meg wanted to speak to her parents before they did that.'

'Yes', he had made arrangements to have his grandmother's engagement ring removed from the bank vault and cleaned for Meg to wear, he confirmed to his mother, whilst Meg's eyes widened at the confident way in which he uttered the blatant lie.

Now that her initial shock had begun to wear off, she felt sick inside, contemplating the problems his fiction of their betrothal and marriage plans would cause. And making her feel even worse than that was the searing sense of pain it gave her to know how cynically Christian was using what, in her opinion, was something that should be treated with tenderness and respect.

The long meal was drawing to a close. The staff had been dismissed to enjoy their own special celebration with their families and soon it would be midnight.

Champagne fizzed and sparkled in heavy priceless flutes, and suddenly Christian, who had been talking to his mother, got up and walked across to a side table on which stood a huge bowl of grapes. Carrying it, he solemnly walked round the table, meticulously cutting off small bunches of twelve grapes for everyone.

Everyone but *her*, Meg noticed in puzzlement as he placed a slightly larger bunch on his own dessert plate, before putting the bowl back on the serving table and coming to sit down again next to her.

'There is a tradition from Madrid that on each stroke of the plaza's clock one eats a grape, one for each stroke, twelve in all…'

'It is a custom I brought to the *castillo* on my marriage,' Christian's mother explained to Meg.

A little bemused, Meg wondered why she had not been given any grapes, but before she could say anything one of the boys cried out excitedly, 'It is midnight…' And, sure enough, they could all hear the first chime of the elegant antique clock on the mantel above the fire.

'Meg.' The soft sound of Christian's voice as he whispered rather than said her name drew Meg's attention to him. 'Open your mouth,' he demanded.

He was holding out a grape to her and, flushing, she did as he was demanding.

As the slight roughness of his fingertips brushed against the sensitive softness of her lips it was *that* sensation, *that* and his taste, that lingered on her lips, rather than the sharp sweet flavour of the grape she was eating as the first stroke of the final hour of the final day of the year started to fade.

'Again,' Christian was insisting and, dizzy with emotion, Meg realised that he intended to feed each and every one of the twelve grapes to her and that, with the eyes of his family on her, there was nothing she could do to stop him.

A sensual wave of reaction shivered over her body every time his fingers brushed against her mouth. What he was doing felt so erotic that she ached to be able to flick her tongue over his skin, to taste the delicious flavour of him, to lick and suck, to… Her eyes widened when—as though by some magical means he had read her most secret thoughts and yearnings—on the last stroke his fingers lingered, his thumb gently rubbing against her bottom lip whilst his index finger rimmed the sexually sensitive flesh her lips protected.

She couldn't help herself. Everything that she was feeling blazed passionately from her eyes as her gaze locked on his.

His hand reached for hers and helplessly she allowed him to take it and hold it, his thumb scrolling delicate secret circles of bitter-sweet pleasure against her palm as he picked up his champagne glass with his free hand.

'A toast,' he announced, 'To Meg, my beautiful bride-to-be…'

'To Meg…'

'Aren't you going to kiss her?' Juanita was asking Christian mischievously.

'Yes,' Christian replied urbanely, giving Meg a long dark-eyed look of sensuality that turned her body liquid with longing. 'But not here!'

They were all laughing, happy for her, happy to accept her into their family, Meg recognised in distress—all of them, that was, apart from Sancho, who, after a few discreet but obviously sharp words from his brother, now left the room.

It was past two o'clock in the morning when the Señora and Christian's mother eventually decided they were ready to go to bed.

Juanita and Ramon had gone up earlier with the boys, and now, when Meg made to go with the Señora, her patient told her firmly,

'No. This is your night, yours and Christian's…' She gave a small wistful sigh, her eyes bright with memories. 'I remember the night of *my* engagement. My parents were very strict, but they allowed us to have an hour alone together…and we made very good use of it!' she added with unexpected forthrightness.

Meg felt too agitated to do anything more than listen. The moment she was sure everyone was out of earshot, she stood up from the elegant brocade sofa where she had been sitting and started to pace the soft-hued Aubusson carpet, for once oblivious to the elegant beauty of her surroundings.

'How *could* you have told them that?' she demanded shakily of Christian. She was almost wringing her hands as her agitation increased.

'I had no option,' Christian informed her. 'I had to refute the slur Sancho was casting on both your reputation and my own…'

Meg tensed. A tight ball of tension was threatening to block her throat, but she had to say what had to be said, no matter how much it would hurt her.

'Surely it's no big thing these days for…for an unmarried couple to spend the night under the same roof? After all…' She paused and then took a deep breath, but Christian was already answering.

'Certain conclusions would naturally have been

drawn by what Sancho had implied, and not just by my family. My family is a very old-fashioned one, Meg… I have a position, a reputation to maintain—not just as its head but as a representative of my country as well. And, besides—'

The haughty arrogance of his profile might at any other time have angered her, but right now…

'—there is no way I want to be judged as the kind of man who indulges in casual, careless sex…'

Meg hated the thought of being anything less than completely truthful, but in *this* instance… After all, Christian seemed either to have genuinely forgotten or had chosen not to acknowledge what had happened between them.

Turning away from him, her voice muffled by her emotions, she said quietly, 'Couldn't we just have told them that nothing happened? After all…that is the truth…'

Her voice had become so low that she could barely hear it herself. 'The truth?'

There was a long pause whilst she held her breath, and then Christian was saying evenly, 'I hardly think *that* would have been a good idea…not given what the "truth" actually is.'

He knew! He had known all along! He *hadn't* forgotten; his memory had never been wiped clean by his fever.

Dismayed, Meg swung round. Her face was paper-white with shock and pain. She heard Christian's sharply indrawn breath, but had no idea what was causing it until he said starkly, 'Have you given *any* thought to the potential consequences of what happened?'

Meg could feel her face starting to burn. This was even worse than the worst possible scenario she could have imagined. Mortified, Meg was forced to tell him with stammering discomfort, 'I… There won't… My doctor prescribed the birth control pill for me for…for other reasons, so…'

She couldn't go on and bit furiously on her bottom lip to stop it from trembling. One of the side-effects on her body of being attacked had been the disruption of her normally regular monthly cycle, and her doctor had advocated she take the birth control pill in order to help re-regulate this.

However, instead of receiving her confidence with the relief she had expected, to her astonishment Christian was actually frowning.

'I wish you hadn't said that we are getting married,' she told him, unable to conceal her anguish.

'Meg…'

She made a small warning sound as he moved towards her and, forgetting his bandaged arm, accidentally knocked it against a heavy table lamp.

Immediately she could see from his expression that the blow had been a painful one, and without thinking she started hurrying towards him. To her chagrin, he immediately stepped back from her.

'For God's sake Meg, can't you see? It isn't you as a *nurse* I want, it's you as a woman—the woman you were in my arms, the woman you were for my body. Do you know what you have done to me?' he demanded thickly. 'Do you care that I lie awake at night longing for you, aching for you? You gave yourself to me with such passion, such emotion, but it meant nothing to you. I thought…I hoped… But…' He stopped and shook his head.

'Have you any idea what it's doing to me, knowing that my love for you, my lovemaking with you, is so repugnant to you that you prefer to pretend that it never happened?'

Speechless, Meg stared at him. What was happening? What was he *saying*?

'You don't love me,' she protested in a small croak. 'You can't!'

'Look at me,' Christian commanded softly.

Reluctantly she did so, sucking in her breath and then slowly releasing it in a series of tiny jolting breaths of disbelief as she saw what was blazing in his eyes.

Christian was looking at her as though—as though—instinctively, she took a small step towards him, and then another and then, 'Christian,' she protested as his arm fastened round her.

'Christian, my darling, my dearly beloved,' he insisted thickly, his mouth so close to hers that she could almost feel his words against her lips. 'Say it,' he urged her rawly. 'Tell me… You can't know how much I need to hear again those sweet words of love you whispered to me in the night, *querida*,' he told her emotionally.

'Why have you been so cold to me?' he demanded passionately. 'So determined to reject me, when every time I look into your eyes I can see there…?'

He stopped, his expression grave, haunted almost, causing Meg's heart to give a funny little bump.

'What? What can you see there…?' she asked him in a choky little voice.

Cupping her face with both hands, Christian looked down into her eyes.

'I can see the woman who lay in my arms and who gave to me the sweetest essence of herself and her love,' he told her rawly. 'And yet that same woman behaves towards me as though she loathes me…'

'Because I felt…because I was afraid that…that you didn't love me,' Meg admitted huskily. 'You've always treated me with such disdain, such *indifference*,' she told him defensively when he said nothing.

'I treated *you* that way?' Christian grimaced. 'Have you thought what it has done to me to have you all passionate intensity in my arms one minute, and all cold rejection the next? When we left my godmother's apartment to drive here—'

'I thought the boys were yours,' Meg defended herself. 'I thought you were married, and then when I discovered that you weren't… When my father ran the marina here in Spain, my parents would often talk about the way that some men regarded the girls who come to Spain on holiday, looking for sex, and I was afraid—'

'You thought I would think that of *you*!' Christian's outrage brought a rueful smile to her mouth. 'Now you *are* insulting me,' he told her. 'And for that you deserve to be punished.'

But his mouth was already slowly caressing hers, as though he was unable to resist its tempting sweetness.

Blissfully, Meg wrapped her arms around his neck and opened her mouth to the hungry insistent probe of his tongue.

A long time later, she opened her heavy-lidded eyes and told him emotionally, 'If *that* was meant to be punishment…'

'Don't look at me like that,' Christian groaned. 'If you do—right now, more than anything else in the world, I want to take you to bed and show you all the ways in which I love you…'

He could feel Meg starting to tremble as she leaned against him.

'Christian,' she whispered.

'No,' he told her regretfully. 'Not until we are married.'

Meg's eyes rounded as she accused, 'That's so old-fashioned.' But secretly a small part of her was pleased.

She suspected that both Christian's mother and the Señora were of the old school, and she knew *she* would not feel comfortable sharing a bed with Christian under the same roof as his family until they were married.

'What is your parents' telephone number?' Christian was asking her. 'There is a very important question I want to ask your father.'

EPILOGUE

'HAPPY?'

Smiling blissfully as she nestled closer to her new husband, Meg nodded her head.

'I don't think I *could* be happier,' she told him breathlessly.

They had just returned to Christian's Seville apartment, having said goodbye to the various members of their families and their wedding guests who were to spend the night at the *castillo* before going their separate ways. They had combined the celebration of their marriage with the excitement of the Seville Epiphany festival, when floats filled the streets and the children received their traditional presents.

Meg had been disbelieving at first, when Christian had announced how quickly he wanted them to be married.

'That's impossible,' she had squeaked but, as he had quickly proved to her, even the impossible could be accomplished by a man passionately in love.

Tomorrow evening they were flying to the Caribbean for their honeymoon, but tonight they were celebrating their marriage and exchanging those most personal of all marriage vows in the very same place— the very same *bed* Christian had teased her—as they had exchanged their bittersweet lovers' vows.

As she raised her head for Christian's kiss, the glitter of the diamond bracelets she was wearing caught Meg's eyes, shiny with emotional tears as she recalled the moment the Señora had presented them to her.

'Christian is my godson, Meg, and in the short time I have known you have become very, very dear to me. These bracelets were a gift of love for me from my own dear husband and I want to pass that gift of love on to you.'

Emotionally, Meg had hugged her as she thanked her.

As he watched her now, Christian knew that the moment he had turned to see her coming down the aisle of Seville's cathedral towards him was something he would remember with intense emotion for the rest of his life.

'And to think that none of this would have happened if I hadn't tried to steal your car,' Meg murmured provocatively.

'You may not have succeeded in stealing my *car*,' Christian responded, 'but you certainly managed to steal my heart.'

'And you mine,' Meg whispered as her eyes darkened with loving passion, a sweet urgency entering her

voice as she begged him, 'Take me to bed, Christian.
I want you so much…'

'No more than I want you,' Christian told her rawly
as he reached for her, holding her tightly against him
with his uninjured arm. The bedroom door was already open and through it Meg could see the bed.

'Christian…Christian…' As she whispered his
name he turned his head to kiss her. This time *both* of
them were burning with fever—the fever of loving
one another, Meg acknowledged, as her body started
to tremble.

A Seasonal
Secret

DIANA HAMILTON

Diana Hamilton is a true romantic and fell in love with her husband at first sight. They still live in the fairytale Tudor house where they raised their three children. Now the idyll is shared with eight rescued cats and a puppy. But, despite an often chaotic lifestyle, ever since she learned to read and write Diana has had her nose in a book – either reading or writing one – and plans to go on doing just that for a very long time to come.

CHAPTER ONE

THE short winter day was drawing to a close as Carl Forsythe cut the Jaguar's speed, slowing right down as he entered the narrow main street of Lower Bewley village.

Shadows were deepening and the ivy that clothed the stone walls of the ancient church looked black, as black as his mood, he recognised drily, his dark grey eyes brooding beneath clenched black brows.

Perhaps it had been a mistake to come back at all. The first visit to Bewley Hall since his uncle had passed away three months ago would be tough, adding to his sense of failure.

But accepting one of the many invitations from the friends who had stayed loyal to him after he and Terrina had split up hadn't seemed like a good idea either. He was no fit company for anyone, especially at Christmas time.

Three days to go before the Big Day and the normally sleepy main street was positively throbbing with expectation. Lights blazed from the bow-fronted windows of the butchers and greengrocers, their displays of turkeys and pheasants, piles of oranges and rosy apples, all decked out with festive sprigs of red-berried holly. And cottage windows were brightly lit, each with its own glittering Christmas tree. People burdened with shopping, buggies and toddlers, bumped into each other, grinning. Everyone was happy, stocking up for the coming festivities.

With a grunt of relief he edged the sleek car past the last straggle of cottages and out onto the winding country lane that led to the Hall.

Reminders of Christmas, family togetherness, he could do without.

Today his divorce had been finalised.

Failure.

Love, or even the pretence of it, had been absent for a long, long time. But when he'd made his marriage vows he'd meant them. For better or for worse. So if everything had so quickly fallen apart was it down to him? If he'd been the husband Terrina had wanted she wouldn't have looked elsewhere.

Or would she? Were his friends right when they said his now ex-wife was a promiscuous tramp? Had he as her husband been the last to know?

Throughout his uncle's long illness he'd kept the true state of his marriage from him. Kept his lip tightly buttoned on the subject when Terrina had demanded a divorce so that she could marry her French lover.

'Pierre knows how to have fun,' she'd told him. 'He knows how to have real fun. He doesn't expect me to have children and ruin my figure or spend dreary weekends in the country keeping a crabby old uncle company!'

So today he had told his executive PA that he was taking two weeks off, had locked up his apartment off Upper Thames Street and headed for his old home in Gloucestershire, where he would spend the so-called festive season sorting through his uncle's personal possessions, and his own which were still in the small suite of rooms that had been his for twenty years—since Marcus has taken him in when his parents had both died in a motorway pile-up when he'd been just seven years old.

His throat clenched as the powerful car snaked along between high, winter-bare hedgerows, the headlights making the bleached, frost-rimmed grass glitter. The next few days promised to be pretty depressing.

The Hall would be empty, unheated. The staff dismissed with generous pensions.

Another failure.

Marcus had never married and had looked to him, Carl, to bring his wife to live there, start a family, carry on the Forsythe dynasty.

The decision to auction the Hall and its contents hadn't been easy. But Carl had no intention of remarrying. Once had been enough. More than enough. So, no wife meant no children, no continuity. Pointless to keep the place on.

Smoky-grey eyes grew stormy. Guilt piled heavily

on top of failure and intensified with a stabbing ferocity as he glimpsed a solitary light in Keeper's
Cottage, beyond the trees that bordered the grounds of
the Hall. Obviously the new owners had moved in.

So where was Beth Hayley now? What had happened
to her? His heart kicked his ribs. If he knew what had
happened to her, knew that she was happy and successful, then maybe he'd finally be able to forget that night—
forget how badly he'd behaved, say goodbye to dreams
that were threaded through with past scenes, like
snatches of a videotape constantly replayed. Her silky
blonde hair, her laughing green eyes, the dress she'd
been wearing, a shimmering deep green silk that had
made her eyes look like emeralds. The way her taut
breasts had felt beneath his touch, the ripe lushness of
her lips. And the deep shame that had come afterwards...

Eight years was a long time for a recurring dream
to last. Too damn long...

In the fading light the sprawling Elizabethan house
looked lonely, almost as if it were an animate thing,
endlessly waiting for light and warmth, the sound of
human voices, laughter.

His mouth tightening, he pushed that thought aside.
It wasn't like him to indulge in flights of fancy. It was
time he pulled himself together and started to do what
he was good at: getting the job done.

Locking the Jaguar, he took the house-key from the
side pocket of his jeans-style cords and mounted the
shallow flight of stone steps to the massive front door.

The main hall was almost pitch-dark, the last feeble rays of light struggling through the tall mullioned windows. Turning on the mains electricity was obviously the first priority. Swinging round to go and fetch the torch he always carried in the glove compartment of the Jag, he froze, his spine prickling.

Laughter, childish laughter, echoed from the upper reaches of the house. Disembodied whispers, a burst of giggles. The shadows of the children his uncle had wanted to see and hear? The new generation of Forsythes that would never be?

Get a grip, he growled inside his head. Failing the uncle who had meant so much to him was making him think irrationally for what was probably the first time in his life!

Young tearaways from the village, he decided grimly, taking the uncarpeted oak stairs two at a time.

The sound of his rapid footfalls had struck terror, judging by the breathy gasp, the sudden, frantic scuffling of feet.

He caught the two of them near the head of the stairs. Boys. Younger than he'd expected.

Keeping a firm but painless grip on their slight shoulders, he demanded sternly, 'What do you think you're doing?'

A beat or two of unhappy silence and then the slimmer, slightly taller of the two said quakily, 'Exploring, sir. Mum said no one lived here any more.'

'So you broke in?'

'Oh, no, sir. We found an open window downstairs. We didn't break anything. Honestly.' It was the shorter, heavier child who spoke now, and Carl's grip relaxed slightly. The boys were well spoken and even called him 'sir'!

'Your names?'

The taller of the two answered first, 'James, sir.'

'Guy.' A sniff. A wobble in the young voice.

Both were probably on the verge of tears, Carl decided sympathetically, remembering some of the scrapes he had got into as a child and the avuncular trouble he'd landed himself in. They obviously hadn't broken in with felonious intent. Just two small boys having an adventure.

'How old are you?' he asked gently, and two quavering voices answered in unison, 'Seven, sir.'

'And where are you from?'

'Keeper's Cottage,' James supplied miserably—no doubt expecting parental wrath, Carl deduced with a flicker of wry amusement followed immediately by an icy feeling, deep inside his heart, which could be translated, when he really thought about it, as a strange sense of loss.

New owners at Keeper's Cottage, the former home of his uncle's head gardener and his wife. A dour couple who had brought up their granddaughter, Beth. None of their dourness had rubbed off on her; she had been all light and laughter, a joy to be with.

During his holidays from boarding school they'd

spent a lot of time together, getting into all kinds of scrapes. Then, in his teens, he'd often brought a schoolfriend home with him and they hadn't wanted a girl tagging along. In a funny sort of way he'd missed her company, although he had seen her around the estate and had found himself red-faced and tongue-tied when they'd actually stopped to talk. Her emerging coltish beauty had made him feel uncharacteristically unsure of himself.

All that had changed on the night of the annual end of summer party Marcus had always given for the estate workers and their families. Eight years ago now, Beth had been seventeen and the loveliest thing he had ever set eyes on. He had been nineteen and should have known better.

New owners at Keeper's Cottage. He would never see her again, never find out what had become of her, and he would never be rid of the memories that had forced themselves into his dreams, where they had no right to be.

Guilt, he decided grittily, and said, 'I'll walk you back home. Go carefully down the stairs.' It was pitch-dark inside the house now, but outside the starlight in the clear, frosty heavens enabled him to see both boys more clearly. Guy was a stocky kid, built a bit like a tank, with floppy blond hair, while James, taller, was wiry, full of grace, with a mop of dark hair. Both seven. Twins, then? Though assuredly not identical.

'We'll walk back through the trees,' he told them as

he fetched the torch from his car and flicked on the powerful beam of light. 'It will be quicker than taking the car round by the road, and your parents will be worried enough as it is.'

And serve them right! he thought starkly. No boy worth the name would pass up the chance to get into mischief. He blamed the parents. If he had seven-year-old sons he would make sure he knew where they were, what they were doing, at all times. Make damn sure they were home before dark! And as it was his house that had been the object of the boys' mischief he had the right to make his opinions known!

Putting that aside, he shepherded the boys along the narrow track and was assailed by a memory so sharp and clear it hurt.

Walking Beth back to the cottage before dawn on the morning after the party. Deeply ashamed of himself and knowing that saying sorry wasn't nearly enough. But he'd said it, anyway, and she'd been—been just Beth. Sweet and considerate. Kind. The way she'd put the palm of her hand gently against the side of his face, the way she'd smiled, the warmth in her voice as she'd told him, 'Don't be. Please don't be sorry,' as if the taking of her virginity hadn't been his fault but hers.

He hadn't taken this four-minute walk since then. Soon after that night he'd left for America, as arranged, to take his place at university to study Economics. He'd written to her shortly after he'd arrived in the

States, asking her to keep in touch, to tell him if there had been any repercussions from that night.

He'd heard nothing. The possibility of pregnancy had all been in his mind, obviously. And as she hadn't replied he'd assumed she'd forgotten everything that had happened, put it out of her mind because it hadn't been important enough to remember.

When he'd finally returned to Bewley, three years later, his marriage to Terrina all planned and ready to take his place in his uncle's bank, old Frank Hayley had died and his widow, apparently, never mentioned her granddaughter, never mind her whereabouts. But then Ellen Hayley had always been close-lipped, dour and grudging. All he had ever been able to ascertain was the fact that Beth had returned to the village briefly to attend her grandfather's funeral.

Chiding himself for thoughts that were beginning to seem much too obsessive—Beth Hayley was the past— Carl pushed open the wicket that led into the back garden. There was a light showing at the kitchen window.

'We can find our way now, sir,' James said with a staunchness that belied his tender age, then spoiled the effect by quavering, 'Mum said we were never to go with strangers. Not ever.'

'Sound reasoning.' Carl swallowed a spurt of amusement at the way the boy had regressed from burgeoning adulthood to just a baby in a split second and pronounced, 'As I found you on my premises I simply assumed responsibility for your safe conduct home.'

He allowed them to swallow that mouthful as he ushered them along the path to the kitchen door, adding with spurious cheerfulness, 'Time to face the music!'

The old solid fuel cooking stove was doing its job just perfectly, Beth thought happily as she removed a batch of cheese scones from the oven and put them on the stout wooden table next to the Christmas cake she and the boys had baked earlier.

Inheriting Keeper's Cottage had been a real surprise, considering that Gran had wanted as little as possible to do with her for the last eight years. Her original intention had been to sell up, invest the money as a nest-egg for James. But since waking this morning another idea had begun to form.

James had kick-started it when he'd asked at breakfast, 'Why don't we live here, Mum? It's brilliant here. Guy would have to stay in horrid London, but he could come for all his holidays, couldn't he?'

St John's Wood didn't really deserve the appellation of 'horrid', far from it, but Beth knew what her son meant. There was precious little freedom there, certainly nothing like the kind of freedom a boy could experience in the countryside. And as for herself, living in someone else's home, no matter how elegant or how kind her employers were, wasn't like having the independence of living under her own roof.

Besides, she had the gut feeling that she would find herself unemployed in the not too distant future.

And living so close to Bewley Hall wouldn't be a problem, she reassured herself as she placed the last of the scones on the cooling tray. Sadly, old Marcus Forsythe had died a few weeks before Gran had succumbed to pneumonia, and she'd learned from Mrs Fraser at the greengrocer's in the village that the Hall was to be sold at auction early in the New Year.

So there was no danger of her or, more importantly, James bumping into Carl Forsythe.

Turning to the deep stone sink, she filled a kettle and put it on the hotplate. Time for tea. Way past time, she thought, her breath catching and a frown appearing between her thickly lashed green eyes.

The boys had wanted to play in the garden, making a den in the ramshackle shed right down at the bottom. 'Just for half an hour,' she'd told them. That had been three o'clock. A glance at her watch told her an hour and a half had passed since she'd watched them scamper down the path between overgrown fruit bushes and rank weeds, then turned back to her baking.

Her anxiety level hitting the roof, Beth cursed herself for being all tied up with working out how she and James could make the cottage their permanent home while time had slipped dangerously by. She snatched a torch from the dresser drawer and dragged open the kitchen door to be met by a blast of freezing air and Carl Forsythe's condemnatory, 'I believe these are yours.'

CHAPTER TWO

GUY put his tousled blond head down and scampered inside, his lower lip trembling, and Carl, the son he didn't know he had still at his side, said 'Beth?' as if he couldn't believe the evidence of his eyes.

'What—what happened?' It was as much as Beth could do to get the words out, her throat was so tight. Her panic, followed immediately by bitter self-castigation because the two boys had been out in the dark and the cold for far longer than she'd realised and coupled with seeing Carl Forsythe again after all this time had sent her into shock.

And he was just staring—glints of piercing light in those sexy, smoky-grey eyes, his mouth a tight line, a muscle contracting at the side of his hard jawline. He was mesmerising her; she couldn't look away. It was James who tentatively broke the stinging silence.

'We were exploring his house, Mum. We really thought no one lived there.' His young voice wobbled as he added, 'He said it was all right to go with a stranger 'cos we were in his house and he had to bring us back home.'

Beth's eyes misted with pride. Her son was being so brave, confessing to his naughtiness, explaining why he had broken the strict rule of never going anywhere with someone unknown to him.

That this particular stranger happened to be his own father was something only she knew. Even so, she would make sure that she explained the rule far more stringently. Her eyes swept from her son's face to Carl's and swiftly back again. They were so alike. She bit her lip. Would Carl see the resemblance? She hoped to heaven he wouldn't!

'I'll speak to you later,' she warned as sternly as she was able, given the panicky emotions that were replacing her initial shock. 'Go to your rooms now, both of you. Get washed and then change into something clean. I've never seen either of you look so grubby.'

As James walked past her he flicked her a look of mute misery which she made herself ignore, and Guy piped up, 'There were spiders in that shed. Massive humungous ones. So we can't make a den until you get them out for us.' As if that explained and excused everything.

He was sitting on the floor, laboriously undoing the laces of the trainers he wouldn't be seen dead without. Beth flattened her mouth to stop the smallest flicker of amusement showing and reiterated firmly, 'Upstairs. Now. Both of you.' And she watched them scuttle up the wooden staircase that led directly up from the kitchen and felt just a little bit safer.

Then she forced herself to give her attention to Carl. She had tried so hard to forget him in the past, but it had proved quite impossible. How could she be expected to forget him when her darling James was so obviously his father's son?

Carl had changed, and yet he hadn't. He was still drop-dead gorgeous, yet his shoulders had widened, and he now wore his thick black hair cropped closely to his head, accentuating the savagely handsome features that were harsher than she remembered. His eyes, the colour of storm clouds, were colder and sharper than they had been before.

Belatedly remembering her manners, she said quickly, 'Thank you for seeing the boys home safely. I can only apologise for their bad behaviour and for wasting your time.'

And then, because it would look mighty suspicious if she continued to treat him as if he were a stranger to whom she was obligated but of whom she wanted to get rid as quickly as possible, she invited, 'Won't you come in?'

She hoped he'd say no.

The lecture on parental responsibility Carl had meant to deliver had disappeared like a footprint covered by a fresh fall of snow. Seeing Beth in the flesh after she'd haunted his dreams on a regular basis had stunned his brain.

Her lovely eyes were wide and troubled, her narrow shoulders tense beneath the soft jade-green sweater she was wearing, and the way she'd scooped her long blonde hair back, coiling it haphazardly on the crown of her head, emphasised the tender hollows beneath her high cheekbones and made her slender neck look achingly young and vulnerable.

How could he lecture her when all he wanted to do was fold her in his arms and comfort her, tell her not to get uptight because boys would be boys as long as the world went round? It was no big deal.

'It's been a long time, Beth,' he remarked softly, and wanted to add, Too long, but didn't. 'You were the last person I expected to see. For all anyone knew you'd disappeared off the face of the earth, so I guess I took it for granted that the cottage had been sold after your grandmother died.'

Moving past her into the warm brightness of the cosy old-fashioned kitchen, he sensed her slender body flinch and his throat clenched painfully. Was his presence so unwelcome? Because she didn't want to be reminded of that one-night stand all those years ago? In this day and age it seemed a bit far-fetched.

Unless, of course, her husband was around—the father of the twins. Knowing Beth and her open nature, she would have confessed her past relationships—if one night of out-of-this-world passion could be called a relationship, he amended drily.

She might be embarrassed at the prospect of having to introduce a past lover to her husband. That could be why she was so uptight.

He wouldn't put her in an awkward position, not for all the gold in Fort Knox, so he'd take himself off, relieve her of his unwanted company. He'd spout a few conventional platitudes first, because it would look weird if he just marched straight back out again, even though she might be hugely thankful if he did just that!

'Are you and your husband spending Christmas here?' he asked as casually as he could when she turned from securing the door. He noted with entirely masculine approval the way her jeans clipped the shapely outline of her long slender legs. 'Keeper's Cottage would make an ideal holiday retreat, and the twins will love the freedom.'

He was simply making idle conversation to make his planned immediate departure seem less precipitate. The thought of returning to that cold, empty house, leaving the warmth, the homely scent of baking, leaving her, leaving all the questions unanswered, was starkly unappealing.

But his seemingly casual question seemed to have thrown her. She looked as if he'd been speaking in Swahili. Her finely drawn brows tugged together and the green of her eyes deepened as she muttered, 'Twins?' and shook her head. 'Do they look like twins? Guy is my employers' son. I've been his nanny since he was six months old. He and James were brought up together.' She relaxed just a little, smiling slightly as she confided, 'Guy's mother is expecting a new arrival any time now. She wants a home birth, so we all thought it best if I brought the boys away and gave them a proper Christmas here. So it's just us. I don't have a husband. James's father and I never married.'

Then she dragged her lower lip between her teeth and bit it. Hard. Why couldn't she keep her big mouth shut? But the tension she'd read in his face had been wiped away, she noted uncomprehendingly. Because of what she'd said? She had no idea.

The trouble was, she had always found him so easy to talk to. Nothing had changed there. She should have had her wits about her—invented a husband—a father for her son—who was working overseas—and put him off the scent. But lying to anyone simply never occurred to her. Never had and never would.

Her eyes wide and troubled, she watched him pull a chair from beneath the old wooden table and sit down, uninvited, one arm hooked over the backrest, his long legs outstretched. He was smiling that slow, utterly disarming smile of his now, and his eyes were as warmly intimate as she'd always remembered them.

He was wearing a soft leather jacket over a dark polo sweater and sleek cord jeans he might just as well have been poured into. If he'd been a film star he'd have had women swooning in the aisles!

Her stomach squirmed and tightened in a sensation she'd almost forgotten it was possible to experience. Raw sexual attraction, she decided, deploring the fact that he could still have this effect on her.

'Tell me more,' he invited smoothly. 'As I said, it's been a long time. You and I have a lot of catching up to do.'

'I—' Aware that all her nerves were standing to attention, her breathing shallow and fast, Beth made a conscious effort to relax. Behaving like a cat on hot bricks would only make him suspicious. She pulled in a slow breath and offered, 'I was just about to make tea. Would you like a cup?'

'Love one. It's been a long day.' His eyes narrowed as he watched her turn away to take the now furiously boiling kettle from the hotplate. The girl who had woven herself into his dreams for so many years had matured into quite a woman. Five feet five inches of seductive, enticingly feminine curves. Why hadn't the father of her son married her? She was lovely to look at and had a nature to match. He couldn't think of a man on the planet who wouldn't be proud to call her his wife.

Unless her lover had been already married.

He would never have put her down as the type to get involved with some other woman's husband. She'd been so sweet, innocent and trusting. Which was why he'd been so ashamed of himself for taking something so rare and precious and sullying it.

He frowned heavily, black brows meeting over darkening eyes. Her son was seven years old. He didn't need a degree in advanced mathematics to work out that she must have jumped out of his bed and straight into another's! Had the air of innocence and openness that had so enthralled him been nothing but a clever act?

Jealousy and a sense of bitter disappointment twisted a sharp knife deep inside him—and that was both warped and ridiculous! For heaven's sake, what had happened was well in the past. He had been married himself in the intervening years; he had no damned right to have any feelings whatsoever about what she might or might not have done with her life!

Oblivious, Beth settled a knitted cosy on the teapot and reached cups and saucers from the dresser, milk from the fridge. In the bedroom overhead she could hear the boys clumping about. From long experience she knew that getting washed and changed could take anything from twenty manic seconds to an eternity.

The latter today, she devoutly hoped. They would surely spin the chore out as long as humanly possible in view of the telling-off they were due to receive the moment they presented themselves downstairs!

Which would give Carl time to drink his tea and her time to make a more normal impression—make something approaching normal conversation. After all, they had been childhood friends. He would think it odd if she didn't make some attempt to do some of the catching up he'd talked about. Not too much, though. She needed him out of here before James reappeared and gave him time to note the almost uncanny resemblance between the two of them.

'I was sorry to hear of your uncle's death,' she said

quietly as she set the tea in front of him. 'I liked him a lot. He always had a kind word for me and apparently a bottomless pocketful of toffees!' Her smile was unforced; she had genuinely happy memories of Marcus Forsythe.

'I miss him,' Carl admitted heavily, his smoky eyes darkening. 'He was one of the best.' He gave her a slight smile. 'I think the fact that we were both without parents drew us together when we were kids. But you drew the short straw. Your grandparents were pretty forbidding.'

'They did what they thought was best,' Beth said defensively, soft colour washing over her cheeks. They had been good to her after their own fashion, and she wouldn't hear a bad word against either of them. In spite of saying she'd washed her hands of her, Gran must have felt something for her. Otherwise, why would she have left this cottage to her? She could have willed it to the church she'd been such a staunch member of, or any number of charities.

Her chin lifting, Beth met Carl's eyes across the table and earnestly explained, 'I think they must have both been born with a strong Puritanical streak—it was in their nature, so they can't be blamed for the way they were. And after what had happened with their only child, my mother, they were doubly strict with me.'

As pain flickered briefly in her lovely eyes Carl instinctively reached over the table and took her hand. 'I remember how upset you were when your gran told you the truth about her,' he said softly.

Home from school for the Easter break, he had found her sobbing her heart out down by the stream, where the wild primroses grew. Gradually she'd blurted it all out. Her mother, a first-year student at a Birmingham college, had got pregnant. The first Beth's grandparents had known about it had been when their daughter had arrived at Keeper's Cottage with a new-born baby. Twenty-four hours later she had walked away and had never been back.

A card—the only one that had ever been sent—had arrived to mark Beth's first birthday, with a note enclosed for Frank and Ellen Hayley saying that their daughter had met and married an Australian and would be going to live in Darwin.

Carl had been fourteen years old to Beth's twelve and he hadn't known what to say to ease her misery, so he'd simply hugged her. And she'd clung to him until she was all cried out. Looking back, that was when his feelings for her had begun to change. Certainly during the next few years he'd felt awkward in her company, increasingly inclined to blush, get tongue-tied and sweaty.

His fingers tightened around hers now, and something sweet coiled around his heart as she responded with increased pressure of her own. 'It was a tough nut to swallow, knowing your mother hadn't wanted you, but it didn't make you bitter and twisted—I admire you for that.'

'Why should it?' Beth's face went pink. She

snatched her hand away from his. What did she think she was doing? Holding hands—and loving it—with a married man! So, OK, she'd had a huge crush on Carl Forsythe for almost as long as she could remember, and he was the father of her son, but that didn't excuse or explain why she should still feel so inescapably drawn to him.

Knotting her hands together in her lap, trying to erase the sheer magic of his touch and bring herself down to earth again, she drew herself up very straight and staunchly defended what her grandparents had regarded as indefensible. 'My mother was very young and probably couldn't face the responsibility of bringing a child up on her own. My grandparents would have given her a hard time. They certainly didn't take the modern, relaxed attitude to single parenthood.'

As she had discovered for herself!

'You did. You shouldered the burden of responsibility,' Carl put in quietly. 'Did Frank and Ellen throw you out?'

'Of course not!' But their disgust and outrage at the way she'd followed in her mother's footsteps and brought shame on them had made it impossible for her to stay. 'And James has never been a burden. I wanted my baby!'

Flushed and flustered, she pushed herself to her feet and cleared away the teacups. Why did talking to him, opening her heart to him, seem so right and natural? She wished he would leave. Any minute now she might say something that would alert him to the true situation. Hadn't Gran always complained that she didn't know how to keep a still tongue in her head?

Rinsing the cups out under a furiously gushing tap, she desperately hoped he'd take the hint and leave. But his hand on her shoulder killed that hope stone-dead, and she could have cried with frustration as he reached over and turned off the tap.

He was too close, far too close. Her breath ached in her lungs. His body heat burned her. They were nearly touching. Almost against her will, but unable to stop herself, she tilted back her head to look up at him.

He had a beautiful mouth. Her eyes lingered on the wide, sensual contours. As if it had been only yesterday she could remember exactly how that mouth had felt as it had plundered hers, so sweetly and gently at first, and then with a passion that had swept her away in a floodtide of feverish longing. And love.

A shiver raced through her as she heard him whisper her name, and her long lashes flickered as she raised her eyes to meet his. There was something in the slow, smoky burn of that intent gaze that made her gasp air into her oxygen-starved lungs.

'Beth—' Lean strong fingers reached out to touch a wildly beating pulse at the side of her lush mouth. 'You don't have to put on a brave face for me. Things must have been tough for you, and I'd like to help for old times' sake. You say you're working as a nanny. I assume that means you and your boy are living under someone else's roof at your employer's beck and call night and day? It shouldn't have to be that way.'

Beth was watching the way his mouth moved, inhaling the fresh masculine scent of him, fighting the insane impulse to wind her arms around his neck and move closer, close enough to be part of him. His words merely grazed the surface of her consciousness, drowned out by the thunder-beats of her heart.

But when he asked gently, his fingers sliding down to briefly caress her delicate jawline, the slender line of her neck, 'Beth, what happened? You didn't marry your boy's father—wouldn't the relationship have worked out?' she was jolted back to stark reality with a vengeance, like the shock of having been suddenly plunged into a pool of icy water.

What in heaven's name did she think she'd been doing? Having lustful thoughts about another woman's husband, her whole body responding to his touch, the seductive velvet stroke of his eyes…

And, just as dangerous, she heard the squeaky hinges of the boys' bedroom door, tentative footsteps on the top of the stairs.

Jerking backwards, she uttered thickly, 'I don't think that's any of your business, do you? Now, if you'll excuse me—' she walked to the door on legs that felt as if they didn't belong to her and dragged it open '—I have a lot to do.'

And she willed him to go, right now, right this minute, before the boys reached the foot of the stairs and he had the time and the leisure to really look at James and begin to wonder...

CHAPTER THREE

'THERE—that should do it.' Beth snipped off one final piece of scarlet-berried holly, added it to the unwieldy bunch she'd already collected, and slipped the secateurs back into one of the capacious side pockets of the cosy fleece she was wearing. For the boys' sake she was doing her level best to be bright and cheerful, to act as if decorating the cottage for Christmas was the only thing on her mind. But inside she was quaking. Did Carl know? Or at the very least strongly suspect that James was his son? Or was her guilty conscience making her imagine things?

'There's loads more over there,' Guy objected.

'You can't take it all,' James countered. 'The birds will be hungry if we have all the berries. Mum,' he added on that reminder, 'I'm hungry now.'

'And me.' Guy put on his pleading face, and Beth hoisted the bundle of holly more securely in her arms, forced her own fears aside and grinned down at them.

The cold wind had whipped rosy colour into their

cheeks, banishing city pallor, and the fresh air had turned what had been often picky appetites into something worthy of a couple of navvies.

Which was just one more reason why the idea that she and James should make Keeper's Cottage their permanent home was becoming more firmly fixed with every hour that had passed since they'd arrived here five days ago.

The village primary school was excellent, and surely she could find a part-time job—cleaning, helping in the village stores—anything that she could fit in around school hours. What she had saved during her years with the Harper-Joneses would keep them while she hunted for something suitable.

'Lunch in an hour,' she promised, marvelling at the way they could be hungry after the piles of pancakes and bacon she'd cooked at breakfast-time. She called after them as they scampered back through the trees to the lane that led down to the village. 'Don't run, and watch out for traffic!' Though very little of that passed this way.

Following more sedately, she watched the two small figures—both dressed identically in bright red anoraks, miniature combat trousers and green wellies—and knew they would miss each other. But their separation was bound to happen, whatever she decided about the cottage. Angela Harper-Jones had dropped several hints since her pregnancy had been confirmed.

Angela and Henry Harper-Jones were both barristers and Guy had been unplanned. At the time of his birth Angela had had no intention of giving up her career, which was why she'd advertised for a full-time nanny, child no objection. The fact that Beth had had a three-month-old son had been viewed as a bonus.

'They will be company for each other,' Angela had said, making Beth view the reasonably paid, live-in position as the godsend it had been.

She hadn't had to farm her precious baby out while she went out to work, and they hadn't had to go on living off the state in a flat in a run down high-rise building the council had provided.

But now Angela was ready to be a full-time mother, and with the resident cook-housekeeper who had been with her throughout her married life she would have no need for a nanny. Beth's days in the Harper-Jones household were numbered.

Scrambling down the last few feet of muddy track to the lane, where the boys were waiting patiently—well, as patiently as seven-year-old boys could be expected to, kicking up the piles of fallen leaves that had gathered at the edge of the band of woodland—she made her mind up.

She and James would move in here when she was made jobless and homeless—he had already told her he wanted to stay for ever. It was a good place to be.

Despite her strict upbringing she had had a wonderfully happy childhood, and she wanted the same for James. The village of Lower Bewley was a close-knit community, rather like an extended family. Her precious son would have so much more freedom than was possible in London, and as for her—well, the Hall would soon be sold, so she wouldn't run the risk of running into Carl and his wife.

Frowning, she tried to empty her mind of thoughts of him. There had been far too many of them. Deeply disturbing thoughts, hinging on the way her body still responded to him, the singing of her pulses, the weakening of her bones, the aching desire to touch and be touched.

It couldn't be love, not after all this time. It simply wasn't feasible. She had long since outgrown the moonstruck state she'd inhabited all through her teens. Of course she had. Lying awake last night, she'd finally managed to convince herself that it was just an inconvenient chemical thing—hormones.

Seeing the only man she'd ever made love with had made her celibate body react alarmingly. Regrettable, but quite natural.

She wouldn't think of him, or his sleek and suitable American wife.

And she'd do her level best to forget the way he'd stood his ground last night. She'd wanted to physically push him right out of that door and bang it shut behind him. But he'd simply stood there, watching as the boys had entered the brightly lit kitchen, saying nothing, his darkening eyes narrowed on James as if he'd been committing the boy's features to memory. It had been a truly frightening situation.

Then, after what had seemed like for ever, he'd turned his attention to her, smoky eyes unveiled by the enviable sweep of thick dark lashes and fixed on hers for several heart-stopping moments, before he'd swung on his heels and walked out.

She'd felt like screaming, her nerves in shreds. Instead she'd lectured the boys on their bad behaviour, explaining that entering someone else's property without their permission was against the law of the land, not to mention the laws of polite behaviour, and had firmly withheld their usual bedtime story session.

And then spent the rest of the evening wondering if Carl suspected that James was his son.

And what he would do if he did.

Nothing, she assured herself now, shepherding the boys along the narrow lane in the teeth of an increasingly bitter wind. He wouldn't want to publicly acknowledge his son. It would mean having to confess to his wife that while he'd been getting engaged to her an eighteen-year-old, back in England, had been giving birth to his child.

He might have his suspicions, strong ones, but she'd bet her bottom dollar that was as far as it would go.

The thought reassured her. She really didn't know what she'd been worrying about. Carl had married his pedigreed American beauty; he wouldn't want to dredge up a spectre from his past in the shape of the humble granddaughter of his uncle's gardener.

Besides, in all probability he had already left the

area, heading back to spend Christmas in some highly sophisticated environment with his perfect wife. His visit to the Hall, the childhood home he had once loved but which was now apparently surplus to his adult and more blasé requirements, would have been a flying one—checking up that there was nothing personal left behind before the public auction of the house and its contents.

Their paths would never cross again.

Good, she thought staunchly, ignoring the sharp pang of loss she hadn't the remotest right to experience as a shriek of delight from James caught her attention.

'Mum—it's snowing! Look!'

Beth lifted her face. A few flakes were falling from a sky that looked heavy with the stuff. She'd been too enmeshed in the tangled web of her thoughts to notice how the clouds had rolled in.

A white Christmas would be story-book perfect, of course. The children would love it. And so would she. All she could hope for was that it would hold off awhile—allow her to drive down to the village after lunch to buy a tree—if any were left. She wouldn't want to risk the car Angela had lent her by making the journey to Bewley.

Then the warning note of an engine approaching from behind focused the whole of her attention on the two small boys. 'Car coming. Keep well into the side.' Her back to the oncoming vehicle, she heard it slowing down. Well, it would have to; the lane was very narrow and full of sharp bends. Drawing level, the car stopped, and only then did she turn to look at it.

'Carl!' She spoke his name without even thinking about it, her stomach turning a series of utterly sickening loops. So much for telling herself he would have already left the area!

Opening the driver's door of the sleek Jaguar, he unfolded all six feet two inches of lean masculinity, planting his feet wide as he instructed, 'Hop in. I'll give you a lift back.'

'There's no need,' Beth countered, feeling the heat in her face and wishing she didn't blush so easily. There was something very different about him this morning. He looked every inch the forceful, intimidating male, and his eyes were as cold as an arctic sea—completely different from the man who had walked back into her life last night.

He looked formidable.

Glancing down at the boys, she saw wide apprehension in both pairs of eyes. They had trespassed on this large and daunting man's property, and although she'd given them both a stern ticking-off they probably thought they were in for more of the same from him. Only worse, judging by his frozen expression.

'We don't have far to go.'

She stated the obvious as firmly as she knew how, only to watch him open the rear door and tell the boys, 'In you get.' Then he turned cold eyes on her. 'You have at least another half-mile to walk and the weather's turning atrocious.'

She'd rather walk a dozen miles than endure his company, Beth thought numbly, her feet dragging reluctantly as she obeyed the imperious movement of his head and joined him at the rear of the car. Lifting the boot, he took the bundle of holly and laid it beside a carton of groceries.

Her heart sank. He wouldn't be stocking up on fresh provisions if he intended to leave the Hall within the next day or two. And this new, bleakly angry mood could only mean one thing: he strongly suspected that James was his son.

Was he about to confront her with his suspicions? And how could she possibly justify what she'd done? she thought guiltily as she slid into the passenger seat and Carl checked that the boys were safely strapped in the rear.

Her stomach was tying itself in knots. She felt nauseous as the worst-case scenario punched itself into her brain: Carl, with his wealth, power and influence, fighting for custody, painting her as feckless and sneaky for denying him the basic right of knowing he had a child, denying that same child all the material and social advantages his father could give him.

But she wouldn't think of that. She would not!

Maybe the sense of guilt she had tried to quash over the years was making her see problems where there weren't any? Perhaps his dark mood was down to something else entirely? A quarrel with his wife? Or having to face a longer stay at the Hall than he'd anticipated? Hence this morning's drive down to the village to collect extra provisions? And the long, searching look he'd given James last night might have been his way of impressing upon him his displeasure at childish naughtiness.

Reacting to his mood wouldn't set her mind at rest, she decided as he slid in beside her and turned the key in the ignition. The only way to discover whether he was angry with her or with some other situation in his life was to pretend everything was normal—do a bit more of the catching up he had expressed an interest in last night.

'I heard through the village grapevine that you intend selling the Hall,' she ventured for starters, wishing her voice hadn't emerged sounding so thin and squeaky. Swallowing hastily, she lowered her tone. 'Marcus might be turning in his grave!'

Not a nice comment, she admitted with immediate regret as she glanced at the harsh perfection of his classical profile and saw his long mouth tighten, a muscle clench at the side of his jaw. But, against the grain of her nature, she'd wanted to hurt him because the way he'd so obviously changed made her heart ache.

The Carl Forsythe she had grown to love with an intensity that had been inversely proportionate to any hope that he might love her in return would never have contemplated disposing of the home that had been in his family for countless generations. Bewley Hall had been in his blood. He'd been so proud of the lovely house and the generations of family history wrapped up within its walls. Now he couldn't wait to get rid of it.

The tough, angular line of his jaw tightened further, and the lean fingers on the steering wheel flexed until his knuckles grew white, but he offered nothing in his own defence.

Her remark had hit home; she could see that very clearly. But the arrogant banker who could trace his ancestry back to the fifteenth century saw no need to explain himself to a nobody like her, Beth thought with deep inner misery, mourning the Carl she had practically grown up around, learned to worship.

The car's wipers were only just coping with the amount of snow that was falling now, but in a thankfully short space of time they drew up in front of her cottage, pulling up behind the car Angela had lent her for the journey.

After helping the two boys out from the rear, Beth walked stiffly to the back of the Jaguar and held out her hands for the bundle of holly Carl had already taken from the boot.

'Thank you for the lift.' She didn't mean it, and the patently insincere words were difficult to frame because her breath was so tight in her throat. She wanted him to go away, yet she wanted to look at him for the rest of her life. Snowflakes were dusting the dark sheen of his hair, settling on the expanse of black leather that sheathed his wide shoulders. She wanted to look away, walk away, but she couldn't.

Pulling herself together took a monumental effort of will, but she did manage it. The holly clutched tightly against her chest, she took an unsteady step away. She couldn't afford to have him around James for one moment longer; it was far too dangerous.

She could have groaned with frustration when James himself prolonged that moment, sliding along the snow-covered ground and thumping to a standstill against the side of Angela's car, piping up, 'Can we go down for the Christmas tree now, Mum? Can we?'

Beth's eyes clouded as she tugged her lower lip between her teeth. She hated to disappoint her son, but taking the car on the three-mile return journey down to the village would be asking for trouble in the worsening weather conditions. And doing the journey on foot with two small boys in tow was out of the question.

Surprisingly, it was Carl who came to her rescue. More surprising still, he had obviously read the situation completely. She was sure she wasn't imagining it—the man who had been positively simmering with some dark internal anger was actually smiling down at James, his eyes soft, his honeyed voice warm and gentle as he vetoed the trip to the village.

'The roads are too slippy to drive on, and in any case I'd guess the best trees have already been sold. How about if I cut one from the estate and bring it round later this evening? I think I can find a box of lights and stuff. I'll bring those too, and maybe we can decorate the tree together in the morning.'

He looked and sounded supremely relaxed, Beth thought on a shiver of bleak anxiety. As if such a toing and froing between their two very different households was as natural as breathing.

James said nothing. He just stood there, a huge grin splitting his attractive, boyish features, until he gave a whoop of joy and turned and wrestled Guy to the ground.

And Beth just stood there too, watching the boys roll around in the snow like a pair of young puppies, squealing and giggling. A release for the excitement that was spiraling as Christmas Day approached.

Crazily, she wished she could join them. Anything to release the dreadful tension that was building inside her.

It was a tension that was in danger of exploding all over the place when Carl, the tightness of banked-down anger back in his face, sharpening his voice, said, 'I need to talk to you, Beth. This evening. About nine. Make sure the boys are in bed. I don't want their holiday spoiled.'

And on that ominous statement he swung abruptly away, getting into the Jaguar without a backward glance and reversing down the track onto the lane that would take him to the Hall—and the wife who would be waiting for the groceries she'd sent him to collect.

He knows!

The thought sent a river of panic through her veins as she stared at the tracks his car had made in the steadily falling snow.

CHAPTER FOUR

AS SOON as the boys were tucked up in bed Beth put a match to the fire she had laid in the small cluttered room Gran had always referred to as 'the parlour' and had only used on rare special occasions, such as when the minister came to tea.

Crammed with an overstuffed three-piece suite of undoubted antiquity, which was starchily protected by stiff linen antimacassars, a forest of Victorian side-tables and whatnots, its walls festooned with gloomy framed prints of dour-looking Highland cattle set in landscapes of ferocious dreariness, the room had a musty, claustrophobic, unused atmosphere.

But if she kept a good fire burning and draped the brightly berried holly all over those depressing pictures then the room would be really cosy and cute, in a quirky kind of way. And the boys could open their presents here on Christmas morning and have fun.

Making plans was a way of taking her mind off what was to come. She'd made no special concessions in preparation for her dreaded confrontation with Carl. She was still wearing the same jeans and comfortable darker blue sweatshirt she'd worn all day, and instead of piling her long hair haphazardly on top of her head to keep it out of the way as she normally did she had scraped it severely back in a ponytail and secured it tightly with a no-nonsense rubber band.

No prinking and preening. Not like that other fateful night, eight years ago, when she'd pulled out all the stops and then some.

Remembering how she'd saved every penny she'd earned helping her grandfather in the gardens of the Hall out of school hours with the precise intention of buying something special for that longed-for evening opened the floodgates, releasing the memories that were as sharp as if they'd happened yesterday.

She didn't need this! She didn't want to relive that night again. But, sitting cross-legged on the hearthrug, watching the flames leap and crackle, she was powerless to hold back the memories she'd hidden away for such a long time.

Early in June, eight years ago. That was when it had really started. Her grandfather had put her to weed the long double herbaceous borders that were such a feature of the Hall's extensive grounds. Hot, back-breaking work, but necessary if she was to pay her way through college after taking her A levels.

If she closed her eyes and concentrated she could still feel the sun burning her bare arms and legs, the way her sleeveless T-shirt and old cotton shorts had stuck to her overheated body, still hear Carl's laughter as she'd almost run him down with the loaded wheelbarrow on her way to the compost heap.

Still feel the punch of sexual awareness that had made her heart tremble and her legs turn to jelly and then almost give way altogether as she'd registered the same awareness in the smouldering charcoal eyes that had held hers with an intensity that had opened up a bone-deep yearning, made her fear she was about to pass out.

There'd been something different about him. She hadn't been able to put her finger on it. For ages he'd seemed to avoid her, had seemed uncomfortable in her company whenever they'd run into each other when he'd been home from boarding school.

She'd really mourned the loss of their earlier close friendship and had sometimes woken at night with tears running down her cheeks, just aching to hear his voice, see his smile, be admitted to the magic circle of his friendship again.

But that day he'd looked delighted to be in her company. He had led her to a bench in the old courtyard, left her in the shade of the walnut tree while he'd fetched iced lemonade from the kitchens in long tall glasses, and their fingers had touched as he'd transferred one of the glasses to her.

Something had shuddered inside her and their eyes had met. Then his had dropped to her mouth and lingered and she'd known he wanted to kiss her. But he hadn't; he'd talked to her instead. And that day, precisely then, she'd fallen headlong in love with him. Looking back, she realised that she had always loved him and falling in love, as a girl on the brink of adulthood, had been a natural progression.

Swamped by an emotion that had transcended anything she had ever experienced in her seventeen years of living, she had barely heard a word of what he was telling her, her huge eyes drinking him in, the sensation of exhilaration making her head spin.

'So you'll be there?'

'Sorry?' She shook her head so hard her hair whipped across her face. She hadn't taken in what he'd been saying. He would think she'd turned into an idiot. But he smiled that gorgeous, heart-stopping smile of his and reached out to sweep her bedraggled hair away from her face. She wanted to capture his wrist, put a kiss in his palm, but didn't have the nerve.

Her eyes widened and her own mouth trembled into a radiant smile as he repeated, 'I'll be back at the end of the summer. You will come to my uncle's party this year, won't you? I'll be looking for you. If you don't turn up I'll come and get you!'

'I wouldn't miss it for worlds!' she vowed, meaning every single word with a vehement passion.

And she spent every waking minute of those waiting months going over every detail of that last meeting. The way he'd looked at her, the way she'd felt.

Holding tightly to the sudden, shattering ecstasy of falling in love for the very first time.

And planning.

At the end of every summer all the household staff, estate workers and their families received an invitation to attend the party Marcus gave for them at the Hall. And every year her grandparents politely declined. They didn't hold with such wasteful and unnecessary goings-on. They would never give her permission to attend, and while she lived under their roof she would do exactly as she was told. That had been drummed into her more times than she cared to remember.

Somehow she was going to go without them finding out.

Thankfully, they always went to bed early, so creeping out of the cottage after they'd retired for the night, wearing her old school coat over the wickedly expensive dress she'd dug deep into her savings to buy in Gloucester was the only option.

When the Hall came into view, all the downstairs windows flooded with light, she almost lost her nerve. She had wasted all her precious savings on frivolous underwear, the green silk dress that was far more daring than anything she'd ever imagined herself wearing, matching silk-covered high heels and a confusing mass of make-up that had demanded hours of secret experimentation before she had been able to achieve the right effect.

All of which would have to be continually hidden

away—because if Gran ever discovered this evidence of what she would call flightiness there would be hell to pay!

And for what?

Just because Carl had asked her if she would be going to his uncle's annual party. Probably because he felt sorry for her, knew she was denied the sort of fun most girls took for granted by over-strict grandparents. And for the sake of old friendship he'd joked about it. 'If you don't turn up I'll come and get you!' Not really meaning it. It was one of those things people said.

Hovering on the edge of the drive, feeling foolish, she suddenly realised what the change in him she'd seen back in June was. It was the patina of sophistication that came naturally to a young adult male with wealth, centuries of breeding behind him, looks to die for and a deeply entrenched certainty about who he was and where he was going.

Carl Forsythe had the world at his feet and he knew it. She might have gone and fallen in love with him, but he would never feel more than moderate friendship for his old playmate—the humble granddaughter of one of his uncle's employees.

A feeling of hopeless misery wrapped itself around her heart as the bright embers of her hopes and dreams crumbled to ashes. Then her sense of self-worth emerged from where it had been hiding, prodding her forward, towards the main door which was flung hospitably wide.

She would go to the party. The money she had spent wouldn't be completely wasted. Besides, she liked the way she looked. And there was little fear of her grandparents discovering her perceived sins.

Grandad never gossiped with his fellow estate workers and Gran never conversed with anyone who wasn't a member of the chapel. A terse nod of acknowledgement was as much as most people got. In any case, she didn't know what she was feeling so strung up about. Carl probably wouldn't be there. He would have better things to do than hob-nob with a crowd of country bumpkins!

But he was there. Entering the huge, raftered inner hall after handing her old coat to the maid who was in charge of the cloakroom she saw him almost immediately. Head and shoulders above the rest, his crisp white dress shirt contrasting sharply with his dark dinner jacket, his strikingly handsome features tanned from a foreign sun, he made her heart stand still.

After a brief murmur of apology to the group he was with he walked towards her, his smile flattering in its sincerity, the sultry gleam of his eyes lingering on her face before dropping to skim her silk-clad body, making her flesh burn as though he was actually touching her…

It was still snowing, Carl noted as he collected the handsome five-foot-tall tree he'd cut earlier and left in the barn. It swirled, a pattern of wildly dancing flakes, in the beam of the powerful torch he carried. And it meant, he decided grimly, that Beth Hayley wouldn't have been able to take the sneaky way out again and drive off, disappearing with his son.

Anger beat at his brain with the harsh insistence of a machine gun. If James wasn't his son he was the Queen of Sheba—he'd stake his life on it!

The dates were right, exactly right, and the boy had his colouring, not his mother's. He had spent an hour tracking down old photograph albums, searching for what he needed. Proof. He'd found it in the last shot that had been taken of him with his parents, only weeks before they'd been in the accident that had claimed both their lives.

The seven-year-old boy grinning at the camera could have been the twin of Beth's son.

His son. He was damn well convinced of it.

His mouth hardened in a line of grim determination as he set out for the cottage. If he was right—and she'd have to come up with some cast-iron reasons why he wasn't—then he'd move heaven and earth to claim rights over his child. How dare she keep his son's existence from him?

He wouldn't have believed the open, sunny-natured, almost painfully innocent girl he had tended to put on a pedestal capable of such duplicity.

Innocent! The word intruded, hammered at his mind. His steps halted as he closed his eyes on the knife-thrust of guilt, letting the snow-laden wind push against him.

That night. That fateful night he'd never been able to get out of his head. The images, the feelings of shame coming back to taunt him when he'd least expected it.

He hadn't meant to seduce her, take away her innocence—he'd swear by everything he held dear that he hadn't. Suggesting—no, demanding that she attend the annual party hadn't been done with any dark ulterior motive. Simply a desire to see her have some fun for once in her sheltered life.

Her upbringing had been severely restricted. Seeing her friends outside school hours strictly forbidden. In case, he guessed, they'd led her astray. Her childhood friendship with him had only been tolerated because her dour grandfather had worked for his uncle.

So he'd believed his insistence that she join them had been motivated by compassion, conveniently forgetting that he'd been sexually attracted to her for some time but had been too young to know what to do about it.

He should have recognised the warning signals when he'd found himself watching for her arrival. He'd put his edginess down to jet-lag. He'd been back at the Hall a mere matter of hours since returning from Mexico, where he'd spent the last three months doing volunteer work for a charity which helped homeless children.

When he'd seen her arrive his heart had lurched, an anguished protectiveness taking him over. She'd looked so lovely standing there, the green dress skimming and flattering those lush curves, and so achingly vulnerable, too.

Her beautiful green eyes had been darkened by an apprehension he had never seen her display before, as if she had no right to be there, and her soft mouth had opened, her hands twisting together in front of her, as her eyes had been drawn to the party decorations that dominated the hall. She'd looked as if she had never seen anything like them in her life.

And the poor kid probably hadn't.

Only she hadn't been a child any longer.

Her heartbreakingly lovely face had lit up when she'd seen him, her huge eyes glowing like emeralds. He'd walked towards her, his heart thumping with pleasure, and they'd been playing a waltz—his uncle on the fiddle, Mrs Griggs the stout old housekeeper pounding the piano, and young Tom the stable boy on the flute.

Taking her in his arms, he had swept her into the dance. Holding her close had been heaven. He'd felt utterly, gloriously complete. They had moved together slowly, her full breasts brushing against him, thighs clinging. His hand had slid further down her back, holding her closer, and when the trio of players had launched enthusiastically into something modern and lively the older couples had left the floor to the youngsters who, he'd noted through eyes that felt decidedly unfocused, were dancing apart.

Compromising, he had rested both hands on her hips, keeping her swaying body against his, unable to relinquish this tormentingly intimate proximity. And Beth, with a tiny sigh, had looped her arms around his neck and pressed closer, so that he had known she must feel the engorged evidence of his desire. Through a dizzying red mist, he had known that she welcomed it. The way she'd tilted the feminine arch of her pelvis against him, parting her thighs just a little to accommodate him, had made his heart pound with suffocating ferocity.

The cessation of the music and his uncle's announcement that supper was waiting in the dining room had come just in time to stop him completely losing it.

Even so, it had taken quite a time to get his body back under control. Loosening his grasp, he had inched them apart a little, just as she'd dropped her arms back to her sides.

His throat had tightened with an emotion he hadn't been able to name as he'd seen her soft mouth tremble. There had been a rosy wash of colour on her cheeks and her eyes had been slumbrous, hazed, the look she'd flicked up at him through thick sweeping lashes oddly shy, uncertain.

'Would you like to eat?' His voice was thick because his breathing was still haywire.

'Not hungry.'

A tiny bead of perspiration nestled in the tantalising cleft between her breasts. He wanted to put his mouth there, take that tiny drop with his tongue. Battling with the almost overwhelming urge, he shuddered convulsively. Both of them were overheated, on a different planet. They needed time out to recover from what had happened.

He pulled himself together. He had to stop behaving like a lust-crazed fool. He'd be leaving for North America in three days' time, and by the time he came back, after his stint at university there, she would almost certainly have flown the uncomfortably rigid family nest and be making her own life. Their paths mightn't cross again for years. If ever.

'Stay right where you are,' he instructed thickly. 'I'll find us something cold to drink.'

People had already begun to emerge from the dining room with heaped plates of fork food when he came back with a bottle of chilled wine and two glasses. 'Let's find somewhere cooler to sit.'

And quieter. He could explain about the degree course in Economics he was due to take, before joining his uncle in the family-owned bank, and find out what she meant to do after leaving school.

Take a friendly interest, nothing more. Show her that their earlier close friendship still counted for something, but dismiss what had happened on the dance floor as a simple aberration by not referring to it at all.

Leaving the heat, the sound of people enjoying

themselves behind, he led her up the wide staircase to the first-floor landing, where a squashy two-seater sofa was placed between an ancient suit of armour belonging to one of his distant ancestors and a low table that carried a bowl of flowers.

His fingers weren't quite steady as he poured out two glasses of the sparkling white wine. The lighting was more subdued here, but he could see the rosy flush that grazed her cheekbones, the slight trembling of her lush pink mouth. She looked adorable, her silvery blonde hair tumbling around her shoulders. The green silk of her dress left her arms and shoulders bare, and the straps that looped around the back of her neck were so delicately fragile they looked as if they would snap if he were to touch them.

Swallowing hard, he carefully placed the bottle and his glass on the polished surface of the low table and turned back to her, her glass in his hand. She bent forward hesitantly to take it and the dip of her neckline revealed the edge of her lacy bra, curving so lovingly against the creamy perfection of her breast.

Whether it was the unsteadiness of his hand or the trembling of her fingers he didn't know, but drops of the liquid spilled on the fine silky fabric that shaped the lush globes of her breasts.

His throat too thick to get an apology out, his heart galloping, he felt in his pocket for a handkerchief. He hadn't got one and, leaning forward, he used his fingers to brush away the offending droplets. Lightly at first, quickly. Until the fingers of both hands took on a will of their own and curved around the breasts that were peaking, spilling into his palms.

She was breathing rapidly, her lips parting, and his blood ran hotly through his veins as his hands shaped her, his fingers playing with the engorged nipples, his head spinning as this thing between them became a wild conflagration.

With a catch in his throat he brought his head down and kissed her, and he heard her low moan of pleasure as she responded with a generosity that made his heart quiver with emotion. Almost without knowing what he was doing, knowing only that this was the most perfect thing that had ever happened to him, something he had been unknowingly waiting for all his life, he swept her up into his arms and carried her to his suite of rooms.

He had never forgotten that night, or the beauty of it, he thought now, his mind jerked back to the present by a vicious gust of icy wind. But how could he reconcile the Beth who had blossomed so generously and sweetly for him on that long-ago night with the woman who had unconcernedly refused to respond to his letter, who had heartlessly deprived him of his own son? he thought with grim cynicism as he strode through the snow towards the lights of the cottage.

Were people never what they seemed to be? Was Beth, like his ex-wife, all sweetness and light on the surface and twisted and devious underneath?

Time to find out, for sure.

Propping the tree up against the side of the porch, he put his thumb on the doorbell. Beth Hayley had a whole load of questions to answer...

CHAPTER FIVE

IN WELCOME contrast to the bitterly cold night air Beth's kitchen was warm, redolent of seasonal baking, mouthwateringly spicy and sweet. Terrina had boasted that she didn't know how to boil an egg. Their sterile, elegant London apartment had been filled with the scent of her sultry perfume and Christmas had come in hampers from Harrods.

But he certainly hadn't come here to mull over his ex-wife's deficiencies in the home-making department, he decided grimly as Beth wordlessly took his ancient, snow-dampened sheepskin coat and hung it on a peg on the back of the kitchen door.

Her features had lost the softly rounded quality of her teenage years, were more finely drawn—even more lovely, he thought, an ache settling in the region of his heart. But she was very pale and her full lips were compressed, unsmiling.

He had kissed those lips. Held her and kissed her until they were both delirious.

Snapping that totally irrelevant thought aside with dark impatience, Carl demanded tersely, 'Are James and Guy in bed?'

Unguardedly, Beth lifted her eyes to the beamed ceiling, and Carl recalled hearing those muffled scuffles and thumps after she'd sent them up to get changed the evening before. Remembered eventually hearing the sounds of their feet on the stairs, the way she'd tried to get him out of the cottage.

Because she hadn't wanted him to get a good clear look at James.

And this morning she'd been on edge, spiky.

She knew he knew.

No wonder she looked pale. The eyes that had thus far refused to meet his own were dark-ringed and haunted.

Guilty conscience. He'd stake his life on it.

The thought that his son was sleeping overhead, unaware of his very existence, made his gut wrench with anger, pushing any compassion he might have felt for her clear out of sight. Controlling it took all his concentration, so he merely followed leadenly when she murmured, 'Through here,' and led him into a time warp.

A smile—unbidden, out of place in view of the fraught circumstances, and most certainly unwanted—curved his lips. The room looked as if it hadn't changed in a hundred years. Pure late Victoriana. Terrina would have wrinkled her aristocratic nose and pulled her mouth down in distaste, while Beth fitted unquestioningly into the old-fashioned surroundings, as she would fit in wherever she happened to find herself.

Catching himself up sharply, he hardened his mouth. He didn't know why he kept comparing her with the cold, grasping creature he had been misguided enough to marry. Despite appearances, and his misplaced long and fond memories of her, Beth was as sneaky and devious as his ex.

Closing the door behind him, he turned to face her. She was standing on the hearthrug, her back to the fire. She looked, he noted grimly, as if she was getting ready to face her own execution.

And she'd be right about that!

He paced forward, moving closer because he needed to be able to read her expression and find the truth.

Since the scales had fallen from his eyes a few short weeks after his marriage he'd become expert at knowing when a woman was telling lies, bending the truth to suit her own selfish ends.

He questioned, slowly and deliberately, so there would be no possible mistake about what he was implying, 'How promiscuous are you?'

For a split second Beth's blood ran cold, then bubbled hotly through her veins. The bone-clenching trepidation that had grown steadily worse while she'd waited for him was swept away in a flash flood of rage.

'How dare you ask such a thing?' Her eyes clashed with his. If she'd had a brick handy she would have thrown it at his head!

Yet Carl looked so coolly controlled, as if he hadn't just asked her the most outrageous question he could think of. And to push the impression home he followed on flatly, 'I got James's birth-date out of him while I was fastening his seat belt this morning. If I'm not his father you must have gone from my bed straight into another's. That would make you promiscuous.'

Beth felt the ground shake beneath her feet. She'd been sure he had strong suspicions, but she hadn't known he'd questioned James about his actual birth-date. That would have made his suspicions a rock-solid certainty. She felt sick. Her hands flew to her mouth, her fingers trembling against her overheated skin.

'Well?' he prodded remorselessly. 'Did your initiation into sex give you a taste for it? So much so that you hawked yourself around to get more of the same?'

His anger was cold, pent-up, dangerous. But hers sprang to answering, blistering life.

Taking two fraught steps towards him, she knotted her hands into fists, to stop herself from actually hitting the loathsome swine. Yet.

But he took the wind from her sails, completely deflating her, as he tacked on softly, 'Or is James my son?'

Beth's heart juddered, all her strength seeming to ebb away. Head and shoulders above her, his powerful body clothed in thigh-moulding jeans and a black roll-necked sweater, he looked terrifyingly intimidating, his hair clinging in damp tendrils to his beautifully shaped skull, his devastatingly handsome features hardened with cruel determination.

What to say? Brand herself as promiscuous or admit the truth? Run the real risk of him trying to take her son from her?

'Been struck dumb, have we?' His velvety voice held a sardonic bite as he took her chin between his thumb and forefinger, forcing her to look at him, to meet his cold, dark eyes. 'Not to worry. A simple DNA test should do the talking for you.'

Beth's throat convulsed. She was living in her worst nightmare. But she would fight to the death to stop him doing anything to upset her son.

James had recently started asking about his father. Guy had a daddy, why didn't he? She'd told him as much of the truth as she felt his tender years fitted him to handle. Explained that his father was a wonderful man and that she'd loved him very much. But that their lives and backgrounds had been too different to allow them to live together, that it was best if she was both mummy and daddy. It was an explanation he had accepted without any further questions.

So no way was she going to allow Carl to upset and confuse him, demand rights in his life, demand to have him with him for weekends or parts of his school holidays. His wife would certainly resent his very existence, and possibly show it.

She would not allow that to happen.

Jerking her head away from his punitive grasp, she

told him fiercely, 'James is mine. I carried him, gave birth to him, cared for him and loved him for every minute of his life. He is everything to me. He is nothing to you—how could he be? Your only input was one night of lust you immediately forgot about!'

Momentarily pain flooded his eyes, the stab of it tightening his mouth, tugging at his breath, and Beth wished she hadn't voiced that last statement. She had wanted to hurt him and had succeeded, but it made her feel ashamed of herself.

She hadn't been a victim. She had wanted him to make love to her—wanted him with a desperation she could still so clearly remember. And he had written to her from America, asking her to keep in touch. She could have told him she was pregnant, but for reasons that had seemed good at the time she hadn't.

She took a step towards him, wishing she could take the wounding words back, her teeth biting into her full lower lip. But Carl, obviously furiously recovered, stated lethally, 'I take it that's your confirmation? James is my son. I have rights. He has rights. He is the new Forsythe generation. He is all Marcus ever wanted.'

Beth wanted to cry but wouldn't let herself. Her voice wobbling, she threw at him, 'Don't drag your uncle into it! You weren't thinking of his wishes when you decided to sell the Hall—he would have hated that!'

She was beginning to wail. She clamped her mouth shut. If he had said James was all he, Carl, had ever wanted then she might have softened, tried to work out a way of him getting to know his son without upsetting the little boy. But he hadn't, and it really, really hurt.

'There wasn't going to be a new generation of Forsythes,' he answered tensely. 'So there seemed no point in keeping the place on. The situation has now changed. I have the heir I never expected to have. The auction will be cancelled.'

Beth sank onto the nearest chair. Her legs were giving way beneath her. She put her hands over her mouth, her fingers flattening her lips.

She could see it now. Obviously his wife couldn't have children and, knowing how he took pride in his lineage, that would have been a dreadful blow. But now he had his heir he would move heaven and earth to claim him, to bring him up as a Forsythe, taking no account whatsoever of her or James's feelings. Then another thought took hold and threatened to shatter her precarious control. If his wife was barren, as he seemed to be implying, then she would resent James even more!

She couldn't let that happen! But how on earth could she stop it?

There was only one way. She took it. Lowering her hands, tears now streaming unashamedly down her pinched face, she pointed out, 'Your wife might not agree with you. I suggest you leave now, go back to the Hall and discuss it with her before you start trying to throw your weight around. And—' she gulped back a throatful of tears '—I have a say in my child's future, too.'

'What say, what rights, did you allow me eight years ago, when you knew you had conceived my child?' he demanded witheringly. 'None. If some quirk of fate hadn't brought us together, now, I would have gone to my grave never knowing I had a son! So don't try to plead your case with me. You don't have one!'

He swung round on his heels and stalked out of the room, and Beth wrapped her arms around her body and tried to pull herself together.

At least he'd done as she'd suggested—gone back to his wife to discuss the matter. Hopefully, she'd talk him out of what Beth was sure was in his mind—having his illegitimate son live with them. That his wife wouldn't be able to talk him out of anything, or would raise no objections, didn't bear thinking about.

Carl Forsythe was a powerful man in the banking world, and centuries of believing that what he wanted was his as of right had been bred into him. How could she hope to fight that?

Despite the roaring fire she was shivering convulsively, cold right through to the centre of her bones, and she leapt out of her skin when Carl walked back through the door. She had been so sure he'd left the cottage.

'Drink this.' He put a mug in her shaking hands. 'Hot, strong tea. You need it; you're in shock.'

For a moment her bewildered eyes met his. The last

thing she'd expected from him was this brusque, rough-edged compassion.

Quelling a shiver, she gripped the mug in both hands to hold it steady. The ache at the back of her throat spread down to her chest. She couldn't blame him for being angry, and she should have remembered that even as a young boy he'd had a caring, compassionate heart.

A sudden memory flashed through her troubled mind, of Carl, probably nine years old at that time, finding a tiny baby frog on the gravel driveway in the full glare of the sun, the careful way he'd picked it up and carried it to the long damp grass which bordered the pool in one of his uncle's meadows, his grin of pleasure as the little creature had hopped away to safety.

So was it so surprising that he should put his anger aside momentarily and have a care for the mother of his child?

Straddle-legged, his back to the fire, he hooked his thumbs in the pockets of his jeans and told her flatly, 'I have no wife to consider. Terrina left me for her current lover, and we're now divorced.'

Every scrap of colour drained from Beth's face. When she'd heard of his engagement, his marriage, she'd been gutted, hair-tearingly jealous. She'd loved him so and had wanted him for herself, even though, deep down inside her, she'd known it could never happen.

But she was older now, and very much wiser.

Except for their son's existence the past was dead and buried. Any residual fondness he might have felt for her had been wiped from his heart by what he had learned.

And he was free, which put her at an even greater disadvantage. No wife's feelings to consider meant he was free to do exactly as he wanted. He'd lost a wife but gained a son. He would do everything within his considerable power to keep him.

'I'm sorry.'

She muttered the expected polite response, wondering if he knew exactly how sorry she was, and why, and inwardly quaked at the harsh bitterness in his voice when he shrugged those impressive shoulders of his and stated, 'Don't be.'

Beth shivered. He seemed to fill the room with his presence, his controlled anger making the air sizzle with tension, and even before he spoke again she knew he would want answers. To her own horror, her defence now seemed unbelievably shaky.

'Why didn't you tell me you were pregnant?' he sliced rawly. 'What did I ever do to make you keep my son's existence from me?'

Guilt swamped her. He sounded so driven. It tore her in two. She had thought at the time that she was doing the right thing, and during her years as a single parent she'd found composure, remained convinced that the decision made so long ago had been the best for all concerned.

And now he would tear her defences into shreds.

She lifted reluctant eyes to his, her heart thudding heavily, then heaved a sigh of cowardly relief as she heard James pattering down the stairs, his voice wobbly as he called for his mummy.

'Darling!' She was out of her chair and opening the door immediately, strength flowing back into her weakened limbs, her only thought now to comfort her child.

Standing on the bottom tread of the staircase in his red and white striped pyjamas, his quivering mouth turned down piteously, the grey eyes beneath a rumpled lock of dark hair flooded with tears, the boisterous seven-year-old had returned to unashamed babyhood.

Her heart swelling with love, Beth hunkered down and held out her arms, murmuring, as he launched himself into her loving embrace, 'Bad dream, darling?' She dropped a kiss on the side of his soft little neck as he nodded wordlessly and took a noisy gulp of air into his heaving chest, burrowing his head into her sweatshirt.

He rarely suffered from nightmares, and she guessed tonight's had been caused by the excitement of the approach of Christmas and the naughtiness of the previous evening. Cuddling him closely, she could feel his slight body shivering. The upstairs rooms were decidedly chilly, and the sooner she got him safely tucked up under his cosy duvet the better.

But first, 'How about a drink of warm milk, poppet?' Feeling his vigorous nod, she got back to her feet and dropped a swift kiss on the top of his head. 'Coming right up.'

She turned and saw Carl's eyes fixed upon them. Dark, brooding eyes, and a line of pain around his mouth, a line of colour along his slanting cheekbones. Her heart turned over. She knew how he was feeling. Seeing his own son in distress, unable to do anything about it.

Whether it was guilt or compassion, she didn't know, but she heard herself calmly suggesting, 'Jamie, why don't you go through and sit by the fire with Mr Forsythe while I heat that milk?'

She held her breath. Would James do that? Or would he remember the ticking-off he'd had for trespassing and hang his head, cling to her, refuse to do any such thing in case the formidable stranger started telling him off all over again?

But James simply nodded and took Carl's outstretched hand, and as they walked back into the sitting room Beth heard, 'Call me Carl. I brought you a Christmas tree. I said I would, remember? I'll come by tomorrow and we'll put it up together.'

And then the door closed and Beth released the breath she hadn't known she was holding. She would have felt utterly, drainingly dreadful if James had refused to have anything to do with his father. Though why she should care about Carl's feelings when she knew his intentions regarding the future of his son—

a future which would see her relegated firmly to the sidelines, a weekend visitor at best, if he had his way—she had no clear idea. And the thought of him coming here tomorrow to help decorate the cottage for Christmas appalled her.

There was too much between them. The past with its lovely bittersweet memories, the future with its threatened dangers, and the spiky tension of the present. She didn't know how she would handle having him around.

She had to get a grip, she told herself fiercely as she poured creamy milk into a pan, slid it onto the hotplate of the Rayburn and reached down a mug.

Her emotions had been going haywire ever since she'd opened the door and found him standing there with the shame-faced little boys. Found the old attraction still alive and kicking and become the unwilling recipient of memories she'd thought she had buried, battling with the fear that he might suspect James was his son, her feelings of horror and helplessness when those fears had been verified.

She just had to start thinking positively, she lectured herself firmly. What court in the land would take a child from its mother and hand him to his father? And if he went ahead and hired the best lawyers in the universe she would fight him.

Never mind if all she had to offer was unstinting maternal love when Carl could offer every advantage known to man that influence, wealth and position could bring. She would still fight him!

Her chin high, she carried the mug of warm milk into the sitting room, only to have her feeble heart melt inside her. They looked so right together, the resemblance truly remarkable.

Carl was sitting on the chair she had used, near to the crackling fire, with James curled up on his lap, his dark head resting against the big man's shoulder. They looked so relaxed, so peaceful. James's tears had dried and his cheeks were flushed with pink, and Carl's eyes were warm, his smile gentle as he helped the little boy sit upright to take the milk, his strong arms anchoring the warm little body.

'Carl was telling me a story about Mole and Ratty and the riverbank,' James announced sleepily. 'His daddy used to read it to him when he was little.' He took a long swallow of milk and came up with a creamy moustache. 'I wish I had a daddy.'

Beth's stomach churned over. James had just unwittingly given Carl even more ammunition. She didn't dare look at him, not even when he put the empty mug down on one of the many little tables and got fluidly to his feet, his son in his arms.

'I'll carry you up and tuck you in,' he was saying in a low, conspiratorial whisper. 'We'll be very quiet, like mice, so we don't wake Guy. And I'll see you in the morning. Say goodnight to Mummy.'

A milky kiss brought tears that stung the backs of her eyes, her skin prickling with goosebumps. She could recognise bonding when she saw it!

And recognise unfairness, too. She had deprived Carl of the first seven years of his son's life, deprived her child of a father.

Pacing the floor, feeling sick, she waited for Carl to reappear. They had to sort something out. He was angry with her, and she could understand that. She would have been spitting tacks, throwing things, had their positions been reversed.

But when he cooled down they should be able to work something out—gently break the news that Carl was James's father, agree on visiting rights. Weekends, certainly, and if, as he'd stated, he would be keeping the Hall on, then maybe James could spend time with him there. It was only a matter of a couple of hundred yards away...

Then her mind went blank as she heard Carl coming down the stairs, his feet quiet on the old oak boards. Her mouth had gone dry and she couldn't stop her fingers twisting together, over and over, as if she were trying to pull the joints out of place.

His face, when she could see it clearly, was unsmiling now. The warmth, the softness that had been there for his son utterly wiped away.

'He went out like a light,' he informed her coolly as he reached for his coat. Shrugging into it, he turned to face her. 'I'll see you first thing in the morning.' He turned the fleecy collar up and took his torch from the kitchen table. 'As I see it, there's only one thing to do in this situation. Marry. As soon as it can be arranged.'

Marry him! Something inside her rose on a rushing tide of tantalising hope. It was all she'd dreamed of at one stage in her life. But the surge of hope died, dropped like a stone.

Her mouth stiff, she parried, 'Don't tell me you've fallen in love with me!' She heard the note of sarcasm in her voice and applauded it. It was the only thing that stopped her from bursting into hysterical tears.

'Of course not.' His voice was flat. 'I want my son. And he wants a father—you heard him. He needs two parents. Full-time. To achieve that we have to live together, marry. I lost both my parents when I was a few months older than he is now. Marcus did his best to replace them, but there was a big hole in my life for a very long time.'

He turned for the door, swung it open, and the bitter wind blew a flurry of snowflakes at his feet. 'You can refuse, of course, but I warn you the consequences won't be pleasant for any of us.' One final look speared contempt into her wide, shell-shocked eyes. 'Don't fight me on this, Beth. You won't win.'

CHAPTER SIX

BETH was woken by muffled thumps and shrill giggles from the room next to hers. The boys were already awake, full of beans and ready to start the day.

Christmas Eve.

She groaned. She didn't want to be awake yet. It was still pitch-dark. And last night she hadn't been able to fall asleep for hours. She felt exhausted.

Marry him!

The reminder of what he'd said just before he'd left the cottage last night, the reason she had paced the floor for absolutely ages and been unable to sleep when she'd finally gone to bed, attacked her brain, brought her fully, stingingly and regretfully awake.

She hadn't wanted to have to think about it. Not again. Not yet. She'd gone over and over it last night and it had got her precisely nowhere.

Her stomach tying itself in increasingly tight knots, she wriggled over and reached for the bedside light. A glance at her watch told her it was barely six o'clock. It wouldn't be light for another two hours!

Pulling a warm woollen robe over her serviceable cotton pyjamas, just as an ominous crash was followed by a breathless silence and then a crescendo of giggles, she heaved an irritated sigh. Obviously her hopes that she could persuade them to go back to sleep were dead in the water. Her opinion consolidated when she opened their door and flicked on the light.

Mayhem. Pillows and feathers everywhere.

James, sitting on the floor beside the upturned night-table, offered spurious innocence, making his eyes seem even bigger than they normally were. 'I fell out of bed, Mum.'

'So I see.' She spoke repressively, but she hadn't the heart to read the riot act. The two small faces were alight with excitement. After all, it was Christmas Eve. Consigning at least another hour of much needed sleep to the dustbin of dashed hopes, she said, 'Get dressed. And tidy this room up before you come down for breakfast. And if you behave yourselves—and only if you do,' she stressed, 'I'll help you make a snowman when it gets light.'

'Wow!'

Guy bounced off the bed and James, grinning from ear to ear, announced, 'Carl can help as well. He's coming to put up the tree. He said so. Where is it, Mum? Is it a big one?'

'Big enough.' She'd seen it propped up in the porch when Carl had let himself out last night. She wished he hadn't promised James that he'd come and set it up.

She didn't want to have to face him again until she'd got her mind sorted out.

Besides, they had nothing to dress it with. Christmas trees and glittery baubles hadn't featured in her grandparents' scheme of things. She'd fully intended to buy some decorations yesterday, when picking up a tree from the village, but the sudden heavy snowfall had put a stop to that.

But that had to be the least of her worries. Leaving the boys' room, she closed the door and leant back wearily against it.

What Carl had suggested was out of the question. How could she marry a man who'd vehemently stated that he didn't love her, who actively and openly despised her?

He had wanted her physically once, briefly, and now he obviously thought she was the pits. That she had loved him, adored him, could safely be relegated to the past. Of course it could.

What she had experienced when they'd been talking after he'd brought the boys back from breaking into his house had been simple animal lust. He had matured into a wickedly attractive male. A woman would have to be blind not to fall victim to his vibrant masculinity.

Marriage would be a form of torture. There had to be another way. But her brain seemed incapable of functioning sensibly.

Using all her will-power, she propelled herself into

the bathroom, shutting her ears to the noises coming from the bedroom where James and Guy were clumping around, hopefully tidying up the mess they'd made.

She needed more time to get her head around Carl's cold insistence on marriage, to work out a compromise that would be acceptable to both of them. She needed a breathing space—but she clearly wasn't going to get one.

Back in her own room again, she pulled on the first things that came to hand. A pair of warm fawn cord trousers, an old navy blue jumper that had stretched in the wash and a pair of suede ankle boots that had seen better days. Dragging a brush through her long hair, she met her eyes in the mirror and groaned at what she saw there. Utter bewilderment.

The brush dropped from her fingers, clattered on the dressing table.

She had never known who her father was, only that he had been a student at the college where her mother had been studying at the time. As a child she had hopelessly daydreamed that both her parents would come and claim her, make her part of a close-knit, loving family. It had never happened, of course.

Had she any right to deny her own son the security of the love and care of both parents? True, he had a mother who loved him, but he needed a father too.

Full-time, as Carl had stated.

Could she handle it? She simply didn't know. Her heart twisting alarmingly, her forehead creased with confusion, she padded downstairs to make a start on breakfast. It was going to be a long, long day.

She already felt like a piece of chewed string and the day had barely started!

Carl found what he'd been looking for at the far end of the attics. The box of Christmas decorations.

In less enlightened times this series of small rooms leading off a narrow corridor had provided sleeping quarters for the servants. But things had changed for the better. Mrs Griggs, his uncle's housekeeper, and her husband Cyril—a cheerful, willing helper around the house and grounds—had occupied a light and comfortable suite of rooms above the kitchen quarters. A phone call early this morning had established the fact that they were only too happy to return.

They would take up their positions immediately after Christmas, hire the extra staff needed and make sure that everything was running like well-oiled clockwork when he took up permanent residence.

With his son.

His heart swelled inside him until he thought it might burst, and he felt strangely light-headed as he lifted the box and walked the length of the corridor to the door at the head of the attic stairs.

He was making decisions. He didn't have to think about it because it came naturally. And he didn't have to think about the possibility of Beth refusing his offer

of marriage. He would make damn sure that the consequences of her refusal would make her blood run cold.

A few days ago remarriage had been out of the
question. But now it was the only option if his son were
to have a permanent place in his life, the privileges he
himself had enjoyed, the security of two loving parents, his heritage and all that entailed.

The Hall was big enough for him and Beth to lead
virtually separate lives—only sharing mealtimes when
James was around, joining forces when the three of
them needed to do things together: celebrating James's
birthday, school sports days, that sort of thing.

He clattered down the narrow staircase. No one had
ever said that such an arrangement would be easy, but
if he could live with that, for their son's sake, then so
could she. That would be the first thing he would make
sure she fully understood. No arguments!

As he passed the small sofa on the first-floor landing his mouth tightened as an unidentifiable pain
clamped around his heart. She had been so sweet, so responsive and loving on that long-ago fateful night. Had
she, even then, been concealing a devious nature, a dis-
regard for anyone's feelings and needs except her own?

He would never forgive her for denying him his
rights as a father.

Outside, the air was crisp and cold. An overnight
frost had hardened the thick layer of snow, just as her
duplicity had hardened the carapace around his heart
where she was concerned.

Once, he had been besotted with her, and if circumstances hadn't removed him he knew he would have pursued her with all the tempestuous ardour of puppy-love. He'd written, asking her to keep in touch, and after weeks and months of waiting for her non-existent reply he'd done what any sane guy would have done—got on with his studies, enjoyed his social life, and forgotten her.

Except in his dreams.

But those erotic, tormenting dreams were a thing of the past. He was no longer a besotted, callow youth, inexperienced in the ways and wiles of women.

Beth was switching off her mobile phone as Carl walked, unannounced, into the kitchen of Keeper's Cottage. She had an arm round Guy's shoulders and her face was pink.

Guilty conscience? Had she been phoning her solicitor? Her current man-friend? Trying to find a way out of the situation she found herself in? Her obvious embarrassment, and the absence of James, certainly pointed that way. If she was thinking along those lines she'd have to damn well think again!

Beth felt her face run with hot colour. She hadn't expected him this early. It was barely eight-thirty. And he looked so dangerously attractive her heart stood still. Gorgeous simply wasn't the word for it. Perfect, very male features, a lean and sexy physique—but cold, killing eyes. He looked as if he hated her.

It was Guy who broke the tension. Beth heard his bright young voice as if it came from a great distance. 'My mummy says the new baby is coming soon, and my daddy says Father Christmas knows where I am. He won't leave my presents at home by mistake.' He squirmed out of Beth's hold and dived over the kitchen floor for his wellingtons. 'My dad says he doesn't mind if the baby gets born a girl or a boy. But I want a boy to play with, 'cos James says he wants to live here for ever and ever.'

'We phone Angela and Henry every day, so Guy can speak to them.' Beth's explanation was shakily delivered, and the hand that placed the mobile on the table was far from steady.

Carl felt the tension ebb from his shoulders. But whether it was because that phone call had been innocent and not what he had suspected, or whether it was because his son apparently seemed keen to stay in the area—relieving him of the worry that he might not want to be uprooted—he couldn't say. A mixture of both, he decided, and he put the bulky cardboard box down on the table just as James came clattering down the stairs.

He was wearing a long woolly scarf round his neck and carrying another, which he bunched into a ball and threw at Guy. His face lit up when he noticed Carl. 'Mum said she'd help us make a snowman. You can help, too.'

'I'd like that, Jamie.' Carl's voice was slightly

husky, warm. The cold, killing look had disappeared. His smile would have melted an iceberg.

Beth shivered. She hugged her arms around her body. What had she done to this man? She'd deprived him of the first formative years of his son's life and turned what had been a fondness for her into implacable hatred.

How could she marry him, knowing that?

How could she live with Carl until their son was of age, making his own way in the world, loving him and knowing that he despised her?

Biting her lower lip until she tasted blood, she made a swift and vehement mental correction. Of course she didn't still love him! It had been the best part of a decade ago, for pity's sake. Love didn't last that long without anything to feed on!

He was helping the boys into their coats, asking them if they'd like to see over his house and look for a hat for the snowman. He was sure they could find something—there were several old trilbys that had belonged to his uncle in the garden room. Marcus wouldn't mind, Carl was explaining, he'd be glad they were making use of something he didn't need now.

As Beth listened to the gentle baritone she felt swamped by lonely bitterness. Of course Marcus wouldn't mind his great-nephew using his cast-offs. The bloodline was all-important to the Forsythes. She felt surplus to requirements. The outsider.

She had never felt that way in those long-gone

happy days when she and Carl had been practically growing up together. But everything had changed. And that was the loneliest feeling in the world.

'Ready?' Carl turned to her, one dark brow gliding upwards. The boys were fidgeting, anxious to get outside. 'You'll need your coat; it's bitterly cold out there.'

He sounded polite, friendly even, Beth thought hollowly. He wouldn't want James to pick up bad vibes. But she wasn't going to jump when he told her to.

'Now you're here to supervise I'll leave you to it,' she came back with a manufactured saccharine-sweetness, an airiness that belied the heaviness of her heart. 'I've got loads to do inside.'

Their eyes clashed for long fraught moments, then his face froze over. Two strides took him to the door. He flung it open and the boys, needing no encouragement, raced out into the pale winter sunshine.

'Sulking, Beth?' he enquired in soft, level tones that sent shivers down her back. 'Grow up, why don't you? You brought this on yourself and it's time you took responsibility for your sins of omission. And by the way—' there was a sharp edge to his tone now '—I'll give the boys lunch at the Hall. It's time James got familiar with the place he'll be calling home. I suggest you use the next few hours to decide when we tell our son who I am and break the news of our forthcoming marriage.' He walked through the door, turned back to her and stated coolly, 'It's going to happen. Just get used to it.'

* * *

It was growing dark when they returned. Beth heard the boyish voices ringing out on the frosty air well before Carl pushed open the kitchen door.

Frantically, she pinched her wan cheeks to coax some colour into them. She didn't want him to see her looking as if she were knocking on death's door. She had more pride than that!

She'd changed into fresh blue denim jeans and a pale aqua silk-knit sweater, brushing her hair until her scalp stung and leaving the soft blonde mass loose around her shoulders. No way would she let him know she'd spent the intervening hours in a state of blind panic at the way he was taking over, keeping James away from her for the greater part of the day without so much as a by-your-leave. Excluding her.

That she could have gone with him if she hadn't stubbornly decided to make a point was something she hadn't contemplated as she'd thrown herself into a mindless whirlwind of cleaning and polishing, baking and ironing, doing anything to stop herself from feeling like a spare wheel, stop herself from thinking.

Now, as the boys rushed past Carl into the warm kitchen, babbling excitedly, their cheeks rosy, their eyes over-bright, she wished she'd been with them and been a part of their fun day.

'The snowman's humungous!' Guy gabbled, kicking off his wellingtons so wildly they flew into a far corner. 'His name's Bert and he fell over, but we builded him up again and gave him a hat and an umbrella.'

'And pelted him with snowballs until he disintegrated again,' Carl put in with a wry smile. 'However, Bert Mark Three is still standing, guarding the approach to the Hall—Guy, be a good chap and pick your boots up and find your slippers—'

'And Carl's house is brilliant, Mum,' James, sitting on the floor and removing his boots more circumspectly, cut in. 'You should see it—millions of rooms and he's lived there since it was built!'

'Which would make me getting on for five hundred years old,' Carl said with a grin that made Beth's heart turn over. She dragged her eyes away from him, her face hidden as she busied herself helping the two boys out of their coats, hanging them up on the back of the door.

Carl in this kinder mood sent a lonely sigh around her heart, where it curled up and stayed right where it was, leaving her feeling bereft because none of this warm gentleness was for her benefit.

How could it be?

'I fed them beans and sausages for lunch,' Carl imparted as James and Guy scampered up to the bathroom to wash their hands, as instructed.

Beth, pulling herself together, but not quite to the point where she could actually turn to look at him and see all that hurtful hating back in his eyes, collected the discarded boots and scarves and told him, 'Thank you. I've made a seafood pie for supper. Will you join us? Or would you rather skip that and come back later? We need to talk.'

She felt calmer then. However unpalatable the facts were, they had to be faced. The fact that she was now willing to do so, and was no longer in denial, had restored some of the sense of self-worth that had been leaching away ever since he'd told her he knew James was his son.

'I'd like that.' Carl knew his voice had come out with an intimate slow huskiness, and felt his eyes soften, grow heavy, as he watched her move around the kitchen. Even putting the diminutive wellington boots in a tidy row at the side of the stove, folding the scarves and placing them in one of the dresser drawers, her movements were sheer grace.

The soft denim fabric moulded the elegant length of her legs, clipping the rounded feminine curve of her hips, just as the sweater she was wearing followed the proud curve of her beautiful breasts. The way she moved had always fascinated him.

And he'd missed her today, he admitted. Wanted her to be with them.

Running out of things to occupy her, she turned and faced him. Her silky blonde hair was tumbling around her face, curving around her slender neck. A faint wash of colour was creeping across the delicate arch of her cheekbones and something deep in the emerald depths of her huge eyes made his stomach clench with a desire that should have died years ago.

The sensation made him want to hit something. His mouth twisted bitterly. He had forgotten what love was, but his body remembered hers.

Lust. That was what it was all about. And lust he could handle simply by ignoring it. He surely hadn't wanted her with them today for any other reason than getting James used to seeing them as a threesome. Sure, he'd like to join her for supper, but only because it would give him the chance to continue the bonding process with his son.

She owed him that much, and a damn sight more!

To hammer that point home, for his own sake as much as for hers, he informed her coolly, 'It's important that Jamie and I spend as much time as possible together before we break our news. And yes, we do need to discuss the timing. Also—' he shrugged out of his coat and hung it with the others '—I promised them we'd decorate the tree.'

The hope that his attitude towards her was softening had been a very faint glow in the darkness of his overt dislike of her, and his coolly delivered words had brutally extinguished it.

No big deal, she told herself staunchly. She would be a fool to hope for anything other than implacable dislike from him.

The thought of that dislike stretching through the years to come, until, when their son was grown, Carl could safely get rid of her, made her feel nauseous. But he wasn't going to see that.

Making herself smile—a thin one, but a smile just the same—she said, 'Then perhaps you could make a start while I see to supper? The boys will come down any time now. I put the tree in a bucket and wedged it firm with split logs. The box of decorations is through in the parlour, too. And while you're in there make up the fire, if it needs it.'

Then, feeling her control begin to slip away, she knelt to bring the seafood pie from the fridge. When she stood up again the parlour door was closing behind him and her eyes filled with tears.

CHAPTER SEVEN

CARL had made coffee while Beth had been settling the boys for the night. The aroma, usually so enticing, turned her stomach.

'Through there.' He lifted the tray and walked into the parlour and Beth had no option but to follow. Crunch-time, she thought, her face paling as her heart-beats threatened to choke her.

The cheerful blaze of the fire drew her. She sank into the chair nearest the hearth to relieve her wobbly legs of the necessity of keeping her upright. Outside, the wind was howling around the little cottage. It sounded like a wild animal. They were in for another snowstorm; she was sure of it.

She felt trapped. By the weather, but mostly, she admitted, by Carl. She shuddered.

'I've decided to set a date for the wedding towards the end of January,' Carl announced unilaterally, his back to her as he poured the coffee. 'It will give time for the banns to be called.' He turned, a mug in each hand, his features expressionless. 'A register office ceremony might be more appropriate, under the circumstances, but traditionally Forsythes have always married in the village church.'

'And we mustn't go against tradition, must we?' Beth was amazed by the strength of her sudden anger, but grateful too. At least the surge of hot, savage emotion injected life back into her wilting spirits. 'This is all about your precious family tradition, isn't it? Did you divorce your wife because the poor woman couldn't produce a Forsythe heir? If you hadn't been the last in the line of your wretched dynasty you wouldn't have given a damn about my son, would you?' she accused heatedly.

Her breasts heaving, she shook her head and crossed her arms over her midriff, refusing to take the coffee he calmly held out to her.

Carl's impressive shoulders lifted in a slight shrug as he put the mug down on the nearest low table within her reach. His voice was as calm as his actions when he countered her blistering accusations.

'Terrina refused to have children—a fact she had neglected to share with me before our marriage. She preferred to take lovers. Her primary aim in life was to look beautiful, spend money, attract men. She had her second husband lined up when she demanded a divorce. I give him six months at best. She has a low boredom threshold.'

He took a mouthful of coffee and, cradling the mug

in his hands, told her forcefully, 'Remarriage was not on my agenda. I decided to sell the Hall because the old house cries out for a family. If I'd been so obsessed with what you choose to call the Forsythe dynasty, I'd have mothballed the place until I could find some fecund young thing willing to marry me and give me an heir. You should think things out before you make judgements.' His face tightened, closing up implacably. 'Now everything's changed. I have a son. Flesh of my flesh. Satisfied?'

Beth caught her lower lip between her teeth. She wished he'd sit down. Looming over her, he made her feel small. She already felt two inches high and shrinking after hearing what he'd had to say.

How any sane woman could even look at another man when she had Carl's love, his wedding band on her finger, she couldn't begin to imagine. He must have been truly, deeply hurt.

But that didn't alter her own unenviable situation. She said, as calmly as her rioting nerve-ends would let her, 'And if I don't agree to be legally tied to a man who loathes me? I could decide to have nothing to do with your crazy ideas!'

His mouth flattened, but there was a thread of danger in his voice as he imparted, 'Then you will regret such a decision for the rest of your life. Be very sure of that.'

He sank into the chair opposite hers while he waited for his words to sink in. He watched the whole gamut of emotions cross her features, like clouds racing over the landscape—saw the pain, the uncertainty in her deep green eyes, and wanted to hold her, kiss the pain away, assure her that he would care for her, always care for her.

Clenching his hands, he reminded himself that she deserved everything he was dishing out, that in her own way she was no better than Terrina. But for some damn fool reason he heard himself qualifying, 'I don't loathe you. I admit I don't want a real marriage—the Hall's big enough for us to rattle around in without having to have much to do with each other—but I don't loathe you. When you opened the door when I brought the boys home that first night, it was like meeting a warm ray of sunshine on a bitter winter's day. That was before—'

He broke off, leaving her to draw her own conclusions. She knew what he meant. Miserable guilt was written all over her pale and lovely face. 'Why didn't you respond to my letter?' he pressed quietly. 'Why didn't you tell me you were expecting my child? I didn't just walk out on you—you knew I was due to leave for the States; I told you.'

Or had he told her? His eyes darkened beneath clenching brows. He knew he'd meant to tell her, had taken her to that secluded place for that reason. He had already known that something pretty monumental was coming to life between them and he'd been trying, for both their sakes, to cool things down.

He'd been nineteen years old, and pretty inarticulate as far as his emotions were concerned, but he'd known he had to make her understand that they had to be adult enough to wait until they'd both finished their education before they took their relationship any further.

But maybe he hadn't actually got around to it. He couldn't clearly remember. His brain had been in a fog ever since he'd started to dance with her. Then the wine had been spilled and events had overtaken them.

She might have seen his disappearance from the scene as desertion...

The slight contemptuous curl of her mouth as she answered his questions confirmed exactly that.

'It was days before I found out why you weren't around. I must have been the last person to know you'd flown to the States directly after that party.'

Even now she could recall exactly how shattered she'd felt at her own naivety. She'd truly believed that he'd made love to her because he loved her. When the truth was he'd simply used her, not even bothering to explain that he was due to leave the country. No wonder he hadn't suggested when they would see each other again.

He'd left the country without a word, leaving her in total ignorance, waiting for him to get in touch, tell her he loved her and wanted to be with her for ever. Fool!

'And then that letter came.' She verbalised her angry thoughts, her rage fuelled by the memory of how eagerly she'd ripped open the airmail letter, how she'd disintegrated after reading the hastily scrawled lines.

Her eyes held emerald scorn. 'Mostly about how well you were settling in at the home of your uncle's banking associate, his charming wife and their daughter Terrina. How welcome they made you feel. And then the really stiff and impersonal bit!' she lashed out. 'You would like me to keep in touch. And contact you if there were any repercussions.' She pushed her hair out of her eyes with impatient fingers, then knotted her hands together in her lap, her voice dry as she recalled, 'It took me until I realised I was pregnant to understand what you'd meant by "repercussions".'

And then she'd been afraid. So afraid.

Her grandparents would have to be told; they'd probably disown her...

'Why didn't you tell me?' He closed his eyes briefly; his face looked drawn.

'After that letter? Get real, Carl! There wasn't one word of affection, the slightest indication of caring. The dreaded "repercussions" had eventuated. You wouldn't have wanted to know—why would you have wanted something like that to mess up your perfect, privileged life? You would have probably sent money for an abortion. I couldn't face your doing that. I wanted my baby. I didn't want to have you spell out that our baby was the last thing you wanted. Do you know something?' she queried witheringly. 'I thought it best for all of us for you to be in happy ignorance!'

There was a beat of heavy silence, then Carl said

wearily, 'I'm sorry if I gave you the wrong impression. When I wrote that letter I was desperately ashamed.'

Ashamed? A vein throbbed at her temples. Her jaw clenched. Her voice shook as she came back at him. 'Of course you were ashamed. The young lord of the manor, heir to a banking empire, having sex with the gardener's granddaughter! Bad form, what?' she taunted, sarcasm dripping from her shaky voice.

Never in her life had she seen anyone move so quickly. Her eyes winged wide open as he left his seat and hunkered down in front of her, taking her hands, loosening her frantic grip, taking each of them into his own. 'That is not what I meant. Then or now. Did I ever give you any reason to believe I didn't think of us as equals? I was ashamed because I'd taken something precious. You were so young and I'd taken your virginity. I'd had no control over my own desire; I'd taken no precautions. I was ashamed of myself, not of you,' he stressed. 'For pity's sake, Beth, I was besotted with you, put you on a pedestal—'

Then, just as quickly, he moved away, standing up, dropping her hands, pacing back. As if he'd suddenly remembered that, far from being besotted with her, he didn't even like her now, not one little bit.

The passion, the vehemence behind what he'd just said rocked her. Had he really felt like that about her? Might everything have been so different? Her eyes swam with sudden tears. The glittery baubles on the Christmas tree shimmered and seemed to lose all substance.

He was standing with his back to her, staring out of the window into the wintry darkness, as if the cluttered room stifled him and he wanted out. Out of the mess they had made of their lives. She could see the tension in the hard, high line of his shoulders, in the taut muscles of his back and long, lean thighs.

Beth blinked, scrubbed the wetness from her cheeks with the back of her hand and forced herself upright, taking a couple of paces towards him, talking to the back of his head. 'I know you'll never forgive me for not telling you about James. But, in my defence, the first time I held our son in my arms I knew I was going to have to. You deserved to know that between us we'd made such a perfect baby. That first time I held him I felt very close to you. It was almost as if you were in that hospital room with me.'

'Really?' His voice was flat. 'Then what stopped you?'

He didn't turn. She could see the reflection of his grim features in the darkened window. She'd been right; he would never forgive her.

But now, while they still had to agree how and when to tell James that Carl was his father, was probably the only chance she'd ever get to put her side of the story. Already he would be regretting having confessed how he had once felt about her, wishing he could take the words back because his youthful emotions had no relevance now.

Her voice unconsciously low and soothing, she told

him, 'As I said, my grandparents didn't ask me to leave. But they made their disapproval so obvious it was the only thing I could do. I found work, a room to live in, and a couple of months before James was born I was given a one-bedroom council flat in a high-rise building that was more than half empty and mostly boarded up because nobody who had any choice wanted to live there—'

'And you took my child to a place like that?' He swung round, and she was sure the hands that were pushed into the pockets of his jeans were bunched into fists. There was a savage glint in the eyes that raked her face.

'What other option did I have?' she demanded rawly. She had hated that flat—the eerie, evil-smelling stair-cases, the lifts that had almost never worked, the wrecked cars in the street outside, the dubious-looking characters who'd inhabited the flats that were occupied. Did he think she'd lived there because she'd wanted to? He knew nothing—nothing about the real world!

'You could have contacted me. You said you were going to, so what stopped you?' he asked icily. 'Stubborn pride or a need to punish me?'

Beth gasped as a tide of anger hit her. Resentment and agonising pain flooded through her as she remembered how she'd felt at that time. She wanted to kill him for always putting her in the wrong! 'You know nothing!' she snapped through gritted teeth. 'Two days before James was born Gran phoned to say Grandad had died. I was admitted to the maternity ward soon after—and the nurses were willing to look after James while I went to his funeral. My baby was three days old then. I'd meant to phone your uncle, to ask for your current address, but as I was going to the funeral I decided to ask him in person.'

Her cheeks burned furiously, her eyes brilliant with rare temper. 'I never got round to it. After the service one of your uncle's outdoor staff told me—in passing, as it were—that you'd just got engaged to some American beauty who could trace her ancestors back to the *Mayflower* and beyond, and your uncle was over the moon about it!'

Unaware that tears of rage and remembered pain were falling in a torrent, she slapped the open palm of her hand against the side of her head. 'So what was I supposed to do? You tell me! Announce that I'd just given birth to your bastard? That would have ruined your engagement, disappointed Marcus—even turned him against his blue-eyed boy!' She was almost sobbing now, her breath catching, her lungs heaving. 'So I held my tongue—for your sake. Not for mine. Not because I was devious or twisted enough to believe I was somehow punishing you.'

She gulped in a long, shuddering breath, oblivious to the sheer anguish in Carl's eyes. 'We managed, James and I. The job with Angela and Henry was a godsend. I must have been with them for around three years when I read an account of your marriage in

Henry's morning paper. A high society affair—and in the photograph you both looked so happy. I knew I'd been right to keep silent.'

He took a step towards her, but she backed away, her body quivering with tension. 'I loved you, Carl, even then. I wanted you to be happy.' Her voice broke. 'Only that!'

'Beth—' His face was drained of colour and he looked bone-weary; only the dark glittering eyes spoke of emotions too raw to articulate. 'I—' Whatever he'd been about to say, he obviously thought better of it. His lips tightened into a long straight line and his voice was flat when he told her, 'I've misjudged you badly. For the first time in my life I've let emotion override logic. You haven't a mean bone in your body. I should have remembered that before dishing out accusations and orders. I take them all back. Unreservedly.'

'Where are you going?' Beth voiced the question even though she already knew the answer as she watched him walk to the door.

Her stomach lurched. Everything he'd said, his insistence that they marry for the sake of their son, had been ruled out of order by his final taut statement. She should have been feeling a rush of happy relief instead of being emotionally gutted.

'Home.' He took his coat from the hook on the back of the kitchen door. 'I've inflicted too much on you for one evening.'

'What about James?' Her voice was high and wild.

She pressed her fingertips to her temples. Was she going mad? He was walking away from them, no doubt thinking he was doing the honourable thing in view of how he'd admitted he'd misjudged her. She'd been praying for just such a scenario ever since he'd guessed that James was his son. So why was she feeling so churned up and desperate because what she'd wished for with all her heart was coming true?

'We'll arrange for access through our solicitors.' He sounded so controlled and sensible she wanted to strangle him. 'There'll be a generous financial settlement. You'll never have to work again, unless you want to, and my demands regarding the time I spend with my son will be reasonable.'

He had the door open. The freezing wind gusted in. Beth watched him walk out, her mouth dry, a sick feeling in her stomach, saw him turn, heard him say, 'I'll leave it to you to judge when and how to tell him he has a father who loves him.' And then she closed the door, nearly wrenching her arms from their sockets in the violent process, shutting him out before he could witness her tearful and utter disintegration.

CHAPTER EIGHT

THERE had been another heavy snowfall during the night. It bowed down the branches of the trees and glittered in the thin winter sunlight.

Beth winced at the noise coming from the parlour. James and Guy were enjoying Christmas morning with a vengeance and it was time to put the chicken in the oven, the pudding on to steam. She passed her fingers over her aching forehead. She hadn't slept last night, but she'd dressed in a figure-hugging cream-coloured cropped sweater and a calf-length swirly scarlet skirt. A heavier hand with her make-up than normal, and her hair falling softly around her face, went some way towards hiding the havoc of lack of sleep.

For the boys' sake she had to pretend she was loving every minute of the day. It wasn't their fault she felt half-dead and more than half-crazy.

She had to be half-crazy to be feeling this way. After she'd met up with Carl again she'd spent all her time wishing he'd disappear, and had been scared witless when he'd insisted on marriage. Yet as soon as that demand had been taken back she'd felt as if half of her life had been sliced away with a very sharp knife.

But she still had James. James was all she had ever wanted.

Not true, she acknowledged as she slid the roasting tin into the oven. She had wanted Carl as well. As a lover, a best friend, her husband, the father of her child.

She still did.

She banged the over door shut, her face flushed. But she couldn't have him. Didn't she know that? She hated herself for thinking like a fool. He had always been out of her league; deep down she'd always known that. If she hadn't she would have contacted him the moment she'd discovered she was pregnant.

Besides, she reminded herself with conscious cruelty, it was just as well he had withdrawn his threat to marry her. Quite rightly, the thought of it had terrified her. Living with the man she still loved—and a plague on her for being such a fool—having him treat her like an only-just-tolerated stranger, would have been torture. She was being a drama queen, pretending to herself that she had lost something wonderfully precious.

It was time to start getting her life back to the way it had been before he had walked in and unsettled it.

Listening to the noise level from the parlour, she wondered whether she could safely leave the boys playing with their new toys for another ten minutes while she prepared the vegetables. She decided to risk it.

As she took potatoes from the vegetable rack the phone rang. She picked the instrument up off the table, stamping firmly on the fluttery hope that it might be Carl. He didn't have her mobile number; the caller couldn't be him.

It wasn't. It was Henry.

'Angela had a little boy just over an hour ago—both of them are fine, but I'm exhausted! We shouldn't have let the housekeeper go to her sister for the holiday; the house is an utter shambles and I spent the whole night making pots of tea for the midwives—'

The outside door opened and Carl walked in. Beth lost the thread of what her employer was saying. Carl's hands were pushed into the pockets of his sheepskin, the upturned collar framing a face that was white with fatigue, the skin stretched tightly over the fabulous bone structure, the eyes deep-set, unsmiling.

Beth's stomach performed a series of somersaults. She hadn't expected him to show his face until everything had been arranged through his solicitor. She felt warm colour steal across her cheeks, her lips curve into an unstoppable smile. She knew she shouldn't read anything into his unexpected arrival, but couldn't help herself hoping...

Holding the phone against her upper chest, she asked softly, 'Carl, would you fetch Guy, please? His father has news for him,' and watched a brief smile touch his gorgeous mouth, a gleam of understanding flicker in his eyes, before he strode past her into the parlour, where the noise was reaching ear-splitting levels.

A pulse was beating madly in her throat as she gave her fractured attention back to Henry, offering sincere congratulations and the information that Guy was having a great time and would talk to him in a moment.

The little boy scampered in, his face flushed with warmth from the fire and happy excitement. Beth gave him the phone, her heart lurching as Carl re-entered the room. Jamie was holding his father's hand.

'I dropped by to wish these two merry Christmas,' he said quietly. 'I'm not stopping.'

Stay! Beth's eyes pleaded, and she could have hugged Jamie when he vocalised the word she hadn't had the courage to force past her lips.

'Stay! Please! I want you to.' Huge eyes shining, the little boy tugged at his father's hand. 'You can play with my train set and have some Christmas dinner! And Guy's got a new football and a Man United away strip. You could be goalie!'

Her mouth running dry, Beth met Carl's eyes. What she read there made her bones go weak. He needed his son and Jamie needed a father. Mums were okay, as far as they went, for kissing sore places better, giving hugs and cuddles, making food. But mums knew zilch about football teams and hadn't got a clue about rolling stock and signals. A boy needed his dad.

'Stay.' She added her own entreaty, making it easier for him by tilting her head towards Guy, who was now capering wildly around the room.

'I got a brother!' he was shouting, over and over, until she felt dizzy.

'I really could do with some help.'

Some of the tension eased out of his hard, handsome face as he conceded, 'So I see,' and his smile was wide and magical as he captured Guy's flying figure with one strong hand and suggested, 'Why don't we go and see how Bert's weathered the snowstorm? If he's okay we could make him a wife for company. A man gets lonely when he's on his own.'

Was she meant to read something into that? Beth wondered hectically, her hand going to her breast, where her heart was pounding violently. She hardly registered Guy's shriek of, 'And make them a baby. A boy baby. If I'd had a soppy sister I'd have given her away!'

As the two boys raced to collect their coats and boots in a competitive jostle Carl said, 'I'll keep them out of your hair for a couple of hours. The fresh air and exercise might calm them down. What time would you like them back for lunch?'

She held his eyes. 'We'll eat at two. You included,' she ordered firmly.

'I didn't intend—'

'I know you didn't.' She cut through the stiff beginning of what she was sure would amount to a stiltedly polite refusal to accept her order. He was used to dishing them out, not taking them. As an inducement he couldn't back away from, she added, 'James would be really disappointed if you didn't share Christmas lunch with us.'

She saw the way his broad chest expanded on a sudden intake of breath, heard the huskiness of his voice as he countered, 'How about you? Would you be disappointed?'

Dragging in a breath just as deep and as ragged as his had been, she answered, 'Very,' and heard the lightening of his tone as he collected the boys and led them outside.

Everything was ready on the stroke of two: the table spread with Gran's best cloth, scarlet crackers by each place-setting, the plump golden-brown chicken surrounded by crisp roast potatoes on a serving dish, vegetables and cranberry sauce, lighted candles and sprigs of holly, glasses of fruit juice for the boys.

And Beth's stomach was being attacked by a plague of butterflies. While she'd been on her own she'd made up her mind to tell Carl how she felt. Exactly how she felt. She had nothing to lose but her pride—and pride didn't count for a row of beans when love was at stake.

She'd managed to convince herself that he did feel something for her. Hadn't he sincerely denied it when she'd accused him of loathing her? Admitted to having been glad to see her again—a warm ray of sunshine on a bitter winter's day? And he'd said he'd been besotted with her all those years ago.

His insistence on marriage—a clinical, in-name-only relationship—had been dropped when he'd realised she had only kept quiet about James for his sake.

If she still felt the same after all these years then maybe he did, too. All she had to do was find out.

But she was tongue-tied, almost paralysed with the fear that she had got her wires crossed.

The boys were upstairs, washing before lunch, and Carl was opening the champagne Henry had given her to wet the new baby's head. This was her opportunity to say something, let him know how she felt. But the words wouldn't come.

The cork popped with a minor explosion and Carl turned to fill the two glasses she'd put ready. He handed her one and their fingers met.

His brilliant eyes shimmered over her flushed face and his voice was low, almost strangely hesitant, for a man who, she was sure, had never suffered a moment's hesitancy in his charmed and privileged life. 'Did you mean it when you said you were in love with me all those years ago?'

Emboldened by the intensity in his dark and beautiful eyes, she answered breathily, 'I was in love with you. I can't remember a time when I wasn't.'

She saw him wince as if he were in pain, and then there was no opportunity to hear what he might have replied because the boys came thundering down the stairs—and no one could have a meaningful and intimate conversation when crowded out by a pair of chattering, hungry, still over-excited seven-year-old boys.

But it was a happy crowd around the table; she had to admit that. Maybe the champagne helped—and the unspoken messages she was receiving from Carl's eyes certainly did. If she was reading them correctly, she amended.

'Why don't you boys go through by the fire and rest up while Beth and I clear the dishes?' Carl suggested after the last scrap of pudding had disappeared, the last cracker had been pulled and the last stale joke read out to gales of childish laughter.

'You could each choose one of your new books to read.' Beth put in her pennyworth, her heart beginning its now familiar skittering again. Did Carl want to continue that earlier interrupted conversation? She had her internal query confirmed when she started to pile up the dishes.

'Leave it.' He caught her hand and a jolt of wicked sensation burned its way right through her. He stood up, facing her, and she wanted to drift her fingers over the lines of his sexy mouth so badly it hurt. There was a moan in her throat and he must have heard it, because every line of his face softened and his voice was a caress that threatened to send her spiralling out of control.

'Do you still love me, Beth? Tell me the truth. There have been far too many misunderstandings already.' He took her other hand and her knees wobbled. She nodded, too choked up to speak. Was he going to laugh at her, or, far worse, tell her he was sorry for her?

His eyes darkened emotionally and then he pulled her into his arms, holding her head against his heavily beating heart for one long delirious moment before he cradled her face between his hands and kissed her.

The wild passion of his mouth as it plundered hers, the fevered touch of his hands on her body, her own abandoned responses to every move he made were just as she'd always remembered them—but better. Far, far better. A million wildfire sensations shot like molten fire through her blood and she could have cried aloud in frustrated need when he eventually held her away, his voice rough-edged as he told her, 'We could have company at any moment, my darling.'

He brought his hands up from the curve of her hips, lightly grazing the narrow span of her waist and then up to brush against the pout of her breasts, making her cry out with the need that was a pulsating fire deep inside her. Silencing her protest with the soft brush of his lips, he murmured against her mouth, 'I have always loved you. Always.'

It took her a little time to recover, to shake her head and remind him, 'You married someone else, remember? Don't tell me what you think I want to hear.'

Carl cupped her cheekbones, his voice rueful. 'I'm telling the truth, Beth. It was something I hadn't fully realised until I saw you again a few days ago. In all those wasted years apart you were often in my thoughts and always in my dreams. Listen, and believe me. When you didn't respond to my letter—and, boy, did I watch the post every day for months on end—I decided that I obviously meant nothing to you, that what we'd shared had meant nothing. I had to stop myself becoming a total wreck, so I worked hard, played hard—and Terrina was there, literally throwing herself at me, vowing she was crazy about me.

'One thing led to another, and that led to an engagement. I wasn't in love with her—I firmly believe the real thing only happens once in a lifetime—but I was fond of her. Marcus, on the one visit he made to the States while I was studying there, thought she was eminently suitable wife material. And she was beautiful. But I didn't love her. I couldn't feel the passion I'd felt for you. I was still in love with you, but I refused to let myself even think about it.'

Beth slid her hands up to his shoulders. Of course she believed him. It had been the same for her. He'd never been far from her thoughts, never vacated that special, secret place in her heart.

'You'll marry me?' His heart beat heavily against hers as she moved closer, her shining eyes alight with love. 'A real, true and lasting marriage? Not merely for our son's sake but for us?'

The parlour door creaked open and James announced, 'Guy's gone to sleep.' He sounded disgusted.

Beth whispered, 'Of course I will—just try to stop me!' and turned to their son.

She took Carl by the hand as the three of them tip-toed back into the parlour, careful not to wake Guy, who was curled up on the sofa, exhausted by the excitement of the day.

The daylight was fading rapidly. Beth closed the curtains and the baubles on the tree glowed in the fire-light. When she turned James was snuggled up on Carl's knee and Carl was saying to him softly, 'I didn't expect to meet up with you, so I didn't have a gift for you this morning. But come the New Year we'll find something special, I promise.'

'Excuse me for contradicting…' Beth knelt with a swirl of scarlet skirts in front of the two dearly loved males in her life. 'But Carl does have a gift for you, Jamie. Carl is your daddy. And very soon now we're going to get married and spend the rest of our lives together.'

There was a heartbeat of silence while Jamie's face went red with sheer happiness, then he wrapped his arms around his father's neck, and when he emerged from the stranglehold he said, 'That's the very best present ever. In the whole wide world!'

Carl caught Beth's hand and brought it to his mouth, and their eyes said to each other, It's been a perfect day.

Outback Christmas

MARGARET WAY

Margaret Way, a definite Leo, was born and raised in the sub-tropical River City of Brisbane, capital of the Sunshine State of Queensland. A Conservatorium-trained pianist, teacher, accompanist and vocal coach, her musical career came to an unexpected end when she took up writing, initially as a fun thing to do. She currently lives in a harbourside apartment at beautiful Raby Bay, a thirty-minute drive from the State capital, where she loves dining alfresco on her plant-filled balcony that overlooks a translucent green marina filled with all manner of pleasure craft, from motor cruisers costing millions of dollars, big graceful yachts with carved masts standing tall against the cloudless blue sky to little bay runabouts. No one and nothing is in a mad rush, so she finds the laid-back village atmosphere very conducive to her writing. With well over one hundred books to her credit she still believes her best is yet to come.

Dear Reader,

Christmas has been special to me from my earliest memories of childhood. The thrill and honour of being allowed to stay up to attend Midnight Mass, a skyful of stars, holding tightly to my father's hand, always wearing one of the beautiful dresses my maternal grandmother, Margaret, used to bring me on her annual visit from Melbourne: a time of great excitement for all of us. Afterward such a supper! But we never did sleep in. Presents had to be opened.

Christmas has even managed to retain its healing magic throughout the sad times that are an inevitable part of life. Christmas is ritual and tradition, family and the annual renewing of the greatest gift that we can offer one another – love. With this in mind, perhaps this Christmas we might commit ourselves to making this great family feast an occasion of paramount importance and show all our loved ones how deeply we care for them.

Marvellous Christmas dinners, carefully chosen and beautifully wrapped presents are fine. They add to the joy and excitement. But in the end what makes us feel absolutely happy is the priceless gift of shared love and peace within the fold. If we've got that, we won't miss much else.

May I take this opportunity to wish you all my sincere good wishes for the forthcoming holiday season with the hope that it will bring more joy and significance than ever before.

Margaret Way

CHAPTER ONE

THE convention hall was almost full when Ronnie arrived ten minutes late and almost out of breath. The Premier was there, along with the Minister for Primary Industries, a visiting Federal senator, representatives of the Cattleman's Union and a good many pastoralists who had flown in from all points of the vast Queensland outback to discuss what was happening within the beef industry. They were there to let the government know of their concerns and hopefully come up with some much needed strategies for the new millennium. As the biggest beef producer in the world, Australia like the other big beef-production countries, was suffering an industry downturn, and conventions like this were being given top priority.

As expected, the print and television media were there to cover the occasion. Ronnie knew all of them. These were her colleagues. Her eyes ranged swiftly over the large crowded room and struggled valiantly to get past a particular tall male figure who seemed to dominate the rest.

Finally she caught sight of two of her pals. There was an empty seat between them almost as though they had been keeping it for her. As indeed they had. And very few people would wonder why. Rowena Warrender was making quite a name for herself in the world of television news. Not exactly a new talent, she had worked for Brisbane's top TV station a couple of years before her much publicised marriage to Kel Warrender. At that time, he was one of the most eligible bachelors in the country and son and heir to Sir Clive Warrender, easily the most colourful and controversial of the country's cattle kings.

Now when her "splendid" marriage was said to be on the rocks, she had returned to her old TV station and been taken on as part of their news team. She was smart, poised, a woman as opposed to the fresh-faced girl she had once been, and she had the excitement of the Warrender name.

As well, she was a good journalist and a skilled interviewer with a natural talent to connect with the people she spoke to. Best of all, she looked marvellous on camera, golden-haired and brown-eyed with a charming speaking voice full of expression. In short, she had the gift for drawing the audience in and, in the process, lifting those all-important ratings. To her bosses at Channel 8, Rowena Warrender was professional magic.

Several yards from her, waiting impatiently for pro-
ceedings to begin, was Owen Humphries, top politi-
cal reporter from *The Courier*. He turned his big,
genial head and caught sight of Ronnie, approaching
nervously. Of course, the husband, Owen thought with
a wave of empathy. He hadn't emerged from the breakdown of his own marriage unscathed. As one of the
State's leading cattle barons, Warrender was bound to
be here and not surprisingly listed as a speaker.

"Hey, Ronnie," he called, patting the seat between
him and Josh Marshall, the well-known TV presenter,
almost consolingly, "a seat here."

Poor girl looked like she was ready to fall into it.
Everyone in the business knew Ronnie's sorrowful
story. The failed marriage that had started out so bril-
liantly in a blaze of publicity. The little girl, Tessa, now
five, apparently so traumatised by her parents' break-up
it was said she had become a selective mute, talking only
to her mother and, of all things, an imaginary friend. Not
that the child wasn't highly intelligent. Owen had seen
her with her mother on several occasions.

Tessa Warrender was a beautiful little girl, but like
her mother, full of a hidden heartache. Owen knew of
the vulnerable person hiding behind Ronnie's glamorous subterfuge.

As ever, she looked great. Every male in the room
turned to look at her. Except Warrender. Owen didn't
wonder why. The separation was said to be tearing
both of them apart.

Guessing painfully at people's speculation, Ronnie moved in her friends' direction sweeping a few strands of her trademark shoulder-length hair from her face. It had been blowing madly outside—typical gusty September day—and she had been delayed overlong talking to Tessa's teacher, a lovely, sympathetic young woman, and the school psychologist, who was on the verge of throwing up her hands at Tessa's determination to remain silent. Everyone was trying so hard to help her little daughter. To no avail. No amount of dedicated efforts could trigger Tessa's voice.

Mercifully her little classmates in the first grade found Tessa's "differentness" exotic. They loved her and made no attempt to tease. Anyway, Tessa was at the top level of her class. She had even won a prize for her exceptional drawing—a beautiful big book with marvellous illustrations of fairies and elves and pixies in their realm of wonder. Tessa, too, lived in her own secret world and it was a source of much worry and anguish to her mother.

Josh was smiling at her, not making any attempt to shift—they both wanted her in the middle like the meat in a sandwich—so she had to struggle past Owen's well-padded knees even though he turned them to one side to accommodate her. Owen was something of a gourmand. Someone, it could even have been her, said he would never make fifty unless he lay off the great quantities of fine food and vintage wines he consumed. Josh, smooth-faced and handsome, was just the opposite, keeping his distance from the dinner table, a slave to staying in great shape and always looking good in front of the ruthless eye of the camera.

"I see your ex is here," Josh warned her, sympathetic and protective. He had been pursuing Ronnie with a passion since her return.

Ronnie squirmed, holding back her pain. "Not my *ex*, Josh, as you very well know."

Josh tightened his well-cut mouth. "It's just a matter of time. Tessa needs a father."

"She has a father, Josh." Ronnie gave him an ironic smile. "He's right over there."

"Hard to miss him," Owen grunted. "A superlative-looking guy. It must be wonderful to look like that and have all the money in the world. Better yet, he's got the kind of brains and energy this country needs. I have to confess I'm eager to hear him speak."

Ronnie smoothed the short skirt of her pinkish beige power suit closer to her knees. "No one better," she said laconically. "One of Kel's great talents is igniting excitement." Kelvin Clive Warrender. One hell of a man and one it paid to keep her distance from. His skin was dark from his life in the blazing Outback sun, and his thick black hair had a deep wave to it. She had always loved it when it grew too long between haircuts. He had extraordinary light eyes that went from silver to slate, hard, high cheekbones, which gave him very definite features although there was a new severity to his commanding handsomeness. Then came the never-ending surprise of his beautiful smile. Like the sunshine coming out from behind a cloud. How many thousand times had he blinded her with that smile?

Even without the extraordinary glamour of his everyday cattleman's gear, the marvellous Akubras, worn at such a rakish angle, the denims, the brilliant bandannas knotted backwards around his neck, the fancy silver-buckled belts and the splendid handmade high boots, he looked incredibly dynamic. Kel was a complete original.

For the conference, he was suited like the rest but never so soberly. He was wearing a beautiful charcoal-grey suit, Australian merino, of that Ronnie was certain, an expensive white shirt with bold blue stripes and a pristine white collar, and an elegant ruby silk tie with some sort of a gold fleck. At six-three, he towered over the group that was standing with him hard in discussion. Every face was lifted to him with attention and respect. Apart from the strength, the acuteness of his intelligence, he was so stunning it was hard for most people to keep from staring. It was like being caught up in some gravitational force-field.

No safe place to hide.

Kelvin Clive Warrender was a man who sparked off passions. Who should know better than her? Once, her own passion for him had been all-consuming. Without boundaries. He had filled her life from day one with the sweetest, wildest joy and excitement. Lord, was it really seven years ago? She had already been launched on a career, a bundle of energy herself in those days, full of the intense curiosity that motivated a good reporter. It was her old boss, Hugh Denton, who had sent her along to try to inveigle an interview out of Sir Clive.

Sir Clive, like his son, always had an eye for a good-looking woman. Both of them, she had found, would use any means short of force to get their way. Not that they would need anything like force. Both the sweetest and, in the end, the most brutal of men, these were ones to steal and imprison a woman's heart.

Ronnie's father-in-law, like her husband, had had a complicated nature. Both of them had strayed. Too often, but maybe that was the fault of their passionate natures. In any event, she had loved both of them. To her cost. Kel had bought her and bound her body, heart and soul. Ronnie's beautiful melting brown eyes began to burn and she turned them away from the sight and the sound of her once adored husband. What was good about Kel, the most difficult of men, was that he loved his little daughter even if he didn't love his wife. What Ronnie had amounted to in the end was a possession.

Her mind went back to their final bitter confrontation when for the first time they had both shown their real feelings—a scene etched forever in her memory.

"Let's get something straight, Rowena," he had warned her in that quiet tone that was infinitely the more chilling for being so still and certain. "I will never, *ever* relinquish my claim to my daughter. She's a

Warrender and she'll take her place in our world. I'll remind you, too, that you're my wife. Talk of a divorce means little to me. You're my *wife*. What I have, I hold."

She nodded in bitter amusement. "Why not, when possession is everything? Don't think I've forgotten you're the big cattle baron, and take your hands off me," she flashed, her body even then confused and reacting.

But his grip had only tightened. "Your decision to leave me is only doing injury to all of us, Rowena." The cold mask of control started to crack. "You're not thinking of Tessa. Are you emotionally blind? These past terrible months have affected her to the point she's withdrawing like a little animal into her shell."

That had turned her to maternal indignation. "You think I don't know that? You think I'm not filled with endless regret? But what's the alternative, Kel? Tell me that. I tolerate your rotten affairs?"

He showed her a face almost shadowed by grief. "My transgression, Rowena." He stared directly into her furious eyes, trying to exert his extraordinary power. "One bloody, loose night when my mood couldn't have been lower. I know it shocked you, but I've tried in every way I know how to make amends. You were giving me hell. You'd turned away from me for no good reason. Nothing was normal."

He tried to wrap her in his arms, but she broke away. "So are you telling me you've got it all out of your system now. No way! You're just like your father." She worked herself up into a fine rage. "Any good-looking woman is fair game."

"Then why do I love *you*?" He grabbed her by the shoulder. "You're so beautiful, but one sanctimonious, judgemental, unforgiving ice goddess. Full of your own sense of righteousness. What happened to the passionate girl I married? Overflowing with love. Limitless, unconditional love. How the hell did you turn into someone else? Now you're so bloody cold you might as well be a nun."

"That's enough!" She fixed him with withering eyes. "Who are you to speak of love? You never loved me. All you ever had for me was *lust*."

He raised his hand then, almost as though he was going to strike her, but even while her heart fluttered, she knew he would never do that. Kel was a very stylish man. He had been raised to behave with perfect courtesy around women and children. Meticulously the gentleman. Anyway, it wasn't true what she said, but that was the extraordinarily bitter position she had reached.

Afterwards she did what Hilary, her sister-in-law, advised her. "Leave him for a bit, Ronnie. I know I would. Kel has always had everything his own way. Make him sit up and take notice. Leave."

So she did. Flying out while Kel was away on business. For all she knew, meeting up with Sasha, the woman who had never really been out of his life. She couldn't even bring herself to leave a note. With be-

trayal raging through her, she had left her home and
the husband she had adored. The harder one was hit,
the heavier one fell.

He saw her the moment she walked in. You'd have to
be blind to miss her. Rowena had always had a glow
about her. The beautiful golden hair, full and swirling,
the soft brilliance of her dark eyes, inherited from her
Italian mother along with the fabulous olive skin, the
graceful body that showed off her stylish clothes so
well, those long, flashing slender legs. The whole spirit
of her, so luminous it imbued her with a kind of radiance. Rowena Warrender. His wife.

She had been moving swiftly, engaged in getting a
seat before the Premier opened the conference, but her
body moved more slowly after she picked up on him.

"Go away. Leave me alone, Kel," it seemed to say.
The truth of it was he would never leave her alone. She
was part of his flesh, sunk deep into him, his self-suf-
ficiency never to be regained. He followed her progress
even when he appeared not to. She was joining Owen
Humphries, one of the State's best-known and respected journalists, and that airhead, Josh Marshall.

He focused on Marshall hard, interested in his body
language. No doubt about it. It didn't need a gut feeling to tell him Marshall was in love with his wife. The
high priestess of sanctity. How unwise to have chosen
Rowena. Rowena had been involved with no man since
the terrible day she had left him. He kept himself ap-

prised of such things. With Rowena, when you did a wrong, you did a wrong. Other women forgave their men. Rowena never would.

"You should never have married her in the first place, Kel," his stepsister, Hilary, had tried to console him in her unintentionally insensitive way. "Don't think I blame you. Ronnie is a very hard girl to pass by. I'm fond of her myself, but she sure knows how to hurt."

Hurt? There had to be another word. So far as he was concerned, he had stumbled into hell. Nights were the hardest. By day he could work himself to the bone. There was even a trancelike aspect to his life. Like now. Here he was holding court with the State's top pastoralists when his mind was in pursuit of Rowena. She knew exactly how to punish him. And what about Tessa, his little princess, golden-haired like her mother but with his grey eyes. Once, they had reflected such joy, such serenity. "Daddy, Daddy, can you make me a tree house?"

To his beautiful little daughter, he had been a magician. He could do anything, make anything, cause wonderful things to happen. Their last Christmas together as a family had been magic. Now another Christmas was coming up.

He hadn't made things easy for Rowena. He had won the right to have his daughter for periods of time. The coming Christmas vacation would take in seven weeks. He couldn't wait for it, though his daughter caught in her trauma never spoke to him. She kissed him, let him cuddle her, put her arms around his neck, but she never spoke. Why? She held him responsible for her strange new life.

It wasn't Rowena manipulating her. Rowena would never do such a thing. She adored their child as much as he did. In recent times, he had seen Rowena cry her heart out when she was pushed beyond endurance. But she had never allowed him to share her grief. In sleeping with Sasha—hell, had he really slept with her or was it one of her fantasies?—he had shattered his wife's trust. But he was damned if he was going to let her get away.

Kel fully intended to waylay her after the morning's meeting broke up. If Rowena loved their daughter as much as she said she did, she'd better agree to coming back to Regina Downs at least for the length of the school vacation. To hell with her job. What was so fulfilling about being a TV reporter? They were parents with a damaged child. Both of them had to find a way out for their little Tessa before she became enmeshed in her world of silence.

A little after one when the meeting broke for lunch, Kel caught up with Rowena as she walked to an exit. The tailor's dummy, Marshall, was with her, more like glued to her side, but Rowena got the message from his eyes.

"I'll see you later, Josh," she murmured hurriedly, making no attempt to introduce them.

"Are you sure?" Marshall seemed ready to defend the fair lady as he rightly should.

"She's sure," Kel clipped.

"I'll catch you later, then, Ronnie," Marshall said, his eyes wavering away from Kel Warrender's diamond-hard stare. Arrogant devil.

"Quite the white knight, isn't he?" Kel murmured in an amused, irritated voice as Josh Marshall moved off.

"He's tried to be a friend."

"As long as he tries nothing else." Kel took her beneath the elbow and steered her through the crowded foyer, ignoring all the speculative glances that were directed their way.

He was so powerful, so seductive, Ronnie felt all the old desire rise in her blood. This happened every time they met and she had to accept she couldn't control it. Hormones, she explained to herself. Hormones raging through her body. Kel had always affected her that way.

"So, have you time for a bite of lunch?" he asked when they were out on the sunlit pavement. He looked so handsome, so vital, so perfect, she relived her loss all over again.

"Kel, haven't you grasped I don't want to be with you?" she said, trying to hold in her emotions.

"We have things to discuss, Rowena." He took her arm urgently. "I'm appalled by your coldness."

Wasn't she herself? "That's unfair," she protested. "It was you after all…."

His eyes sparked. "I wonder if we could get off the

subject of my miserable infidelity and talk about our daughter. I desperately want to see her. Before I go back, if possible."

"Of course you can see her." Ronnie shook her head in dismay. "Have I ever denied you that?"

"You denied me your body often enough." His own bitterness overflowed.

Ronnie looked away. "Maybe my battered pride had something to do with it."

"I guess so," he said wearily. "We can't stand here slugging it out. For what reason I'll never know, people seem to be very curious about us."

"Being in the public eye makes one very vulnerable, Kel. You can't move freely. Neither can I."

"So let's get away." He put up his hand, signalling a passing taxi that immediately pulled into the kerb. Kel had always had that knack. "You can spare an hour. I'm staying at the Sheraton. Their restaurant is pretty good."

Despite her concern, Ronnie found herself in the back seat of the cab as it covered the distance from the Convention Centre to the hotel. Being with Kel was like having a dagger to the throat, she thought theatrically. On no account could you defy him. That's what came of being reared as an Outback prince.

In the hotel restaurant, she looked around, spotted a couple of faces she knew socially, husband and wife, gave them a little wave, which they returned before diplomatically going back to the study of their menu.

"What are you going to have?" Kel asked, taking another glance at her lovely, closed face.

She gave a brittle little laugh. "I don't want much."

"Seafood. Could you manage that?"

"You decide, Kel." She was trying to sound cool, but the slight vibrato in her voice was giving her away.

A young waitress approached and gave Kel an adoring smile. "Nice to see you again, Mr Warrender. Would you and the lady care for a drink?"

"Nothing for me, thank you." Ronnie shook her head. Here was someone at least who didn't watch Channel 8.

Kel sank back into his chair, smiled idly at the girl and ordered a beer. "We'll have the menus, too."

"Certainly, Mr Warrender." She hurried away to oblige, returning within seconds, smiling all the while into Kel's eyes.

A man as sexy and dynamic as Kel Warrender should be registered as a danger to women, Ronnie thought wryly. She, too, sat back trying to conceal all the hurt that was in her. How *should* a wife feel knowing the man she adored was having an affair with another woman?

Never look to Sasha Garland to take a high moral stand. Sasha was the victim of sexual obsession. She'd been Kel's girl since forever. Her father, George Garland, was a prominent pastoralist, a millionaire and a lifelong friend of the late Sir Clive Warrender. Sasha had always been a favourite in the Warrender household and both families apparently had cherished hopes one day Sasha and Kel would marry.

Ronnie had blazed onto the scene, shattering everyone's hopes. Small wonder Sasha had been devastated, but in the end she'd had her vengeance.

Now Kel spread his elegant, long-fingered hands. "And how is my little princess? No worse, I hope."

Ronnie adjusted a piece of silverware, her expression deeply concerned. "I had a meeting with her teacher and the school psychologist this morning. That's why I was late getting to the Convention Centre."

"And?" As usual, he leapt to the point.

"Nothing has changed, Kel. I wish I could tell you differently. Tessa maintains her silence with everyone but me. But astonishingly she's keeping up with her work. She's in the top three in the class and she's doing exceptionally well with her drawing."

"Why wouldn't she be smart?" Kel grated to cover his own pain. "God knows you're bright enough and I managed to pull off a degree or two." In fact, he had an honours degree in commerce and law. "This psychologist can't be any good."

"She's not the only one Tessa sees," Ronnie protested. "I take her to a top professional, Kel."

"Maybe she's trying to teach me a lesson I'll never forget," he said painfully.

"She adores you, Kel. You know that," Ronnie assured him, never mastering her feeling to give him some peace.

"But she won't speak to me. She holds me responsible for our break-up. But I won't accept that entirely." He raised his raven head. "You played your part."

Ronnie let out an anguished sigh. "I had to leave you, Kel. It can't be otherwise."

"The truth is you don't want to front up to your marriage vows," he retorted.

"What if *I'd* been unfaithful, Kel?"

He looked at her, eyes as dazzling as the sun on ice. "I don't think I'll answer that question. But I can tell you this. I'd make short work of the guy involved, but you'd never get away. I loved you passionately. I married you, and I'm going to stick with my vow. Till death us do part."

Baffled, she stared at him. "You don't expect much, do you? I'm twenty-nine. I could have a long life ahead of me. I could fall in love again, marry, have more children. I want them. But first I would need a divorce."

"Over what?" he challenged.

She exhaled deeply. "Over Sasha Garland, Kel. Did you ever get around to breaking the tie?"

He sank back wearily in the chair. "That would be damned near impossible. I've known Sasha all my life. Her dad is my godfather, my own father's best friend. Our mothers were always close. Sasha has been very kind to Hilary. She's shown her a lot of understanding. Lord only knows how Hilary finished up so unattractive."

It *was* a mystery. The parent Kel and Hilary had in common, Sir Clive, had been an outstandingly handsome man. Both Kel and Hilary looked a lot like him, but whereas Kel had turned out stunning, Hilary, six feet tall and well built with features too strong for a woman and a gruff, abrasive manner, seemed terribly disadvantaged. Ronnie had always looked on Kel's stepsister with a good deal of sympathy and tried her best to be friendly, but it had taken a while before Hilary had let her in.

"Don't shift the subject to Hilary," Ronnie warned. "And don't think she's entirely loyal."

His tone showed intense irritation. "What the hell do you mean?"

"Insight, Kel. Insight hard won. Hilary has problems. Most you know about. Some you don't. I know she worships the ground you walk on. But you're bigger, stronger, brighter, than she could ever be. And you're a *man*. You're all-powerful. You were your father's heir. Yet Hilary was his firstborn."

"Hell, Ronnie," he exclaimed, in his anguish using his nickname for her. "Hilary could never run Regina Downs, let alone a cattle empire. Worse, the men don't like her. They show her deference and respect, but that's only because they know they have to."

"Hilary knows how to dish out the arrogance," Ronnie said, witness to it countless times. Hilary trying to match up to her stepbrother. Exert his authority. "She's a woman who desperately needs attention."

"All right, I agree with that, but she's very fond of you."

"Is she?" Ronnie asked quietly, feeling Hilary had somehow betrayed her. "It was Hilary who advised me to leave you after all."

He was visibly shocked. "I don't understand you."

"Then just let it drop."

"How can I?" He set his jaw. "I want to talk."

"That would be fine, only it's all too late."

He stared at her as though trying to see into her soul. "I never heard Hilary say a word against you."

"Are you sure?" Ronnie's eyes flashed bright.

"We agreed you certainly know how to hurt." Faint colour moved under his dark copper skin. "Anyway, Hilary was trying to comfort me. She's devoted to Tessa."

Ronnie nodded. "I know. We're going round in circles. This is solving nothing."

"Then why bring it up?" he challenged her. "I can't believe this! *Hilary* told you to leave me?"

"I'm not lying, Kel." Ronnie lowered her gold head. "I'm sure she didn't mean for long, but she thought you needed teaching a lesson."

"For God's sake!" He shook his head in amazement. "Hilary has gone out of her way to be understanding."

"Maybe she wants to have things the way they were," Ronnie told him bleakly. "You and Sasha, the family choice. As you're Tessa's father and a very influential man with friends in high places, you could get custody of our child. In other words, the whole lot."

His strongly marked brows drew together. "I've never heard anything so stupid in my life."

"Maybe jealousy softens up the brain." She gave a brittle laugh. "I've been reading up a good deal of psychology lately. When I started to put things together, it occurred to me Hilary had some kind of love-hate going where you're concerned. You were the apple of your father's eye. His wonderful son. Your mother idolised you. Sir Clive was always kind to Hilary, but you could see he was trying hard. She has no charm, and you and he had charm galore. Her own mother died when she was a child, which must have been a terrible blow and Hilary and your mother have never really got on, much as Madelaine tries. Such wildly different types. I think, though Hilary appeared to accept me, underneath she may have resented me."

Kel considered a moment, then came to his stepsister's defence. "You want to forget the times she went out of her way to help you? To show you the ropes? What you're saying is absurd."

"I didn't mean to make you angry." She looked away across the beautifully appointed room.

He shook his head. "I *am* angry, Rowena. Believe it. I had a meaningless one-night fling with Sasha I don't much remember. No excuse, but I was very drunk with a demon in me. I shamed myself and I hurt you. I've begged for your forgiveness and I'm not a begging man. But you're going to hang me as though I committed a terrible crime."

"Infidelity is a sin," she pointed out quietly, thinking of its terrible effect on her.

"And I've got my punishment," he said. "I accept that, but I can't have our little daughter punished because of what happened between us."

Wasn't that the truth. "What is it you want me to do, Kel?" she asked in a kind of despair.

"Don't hold me to an impossible standard," he flared. "I've missed you more than I can possibly say. I miss my little girl. I want us to be together forever. Not for it to be like this. Haven't you got any love left for me?"

Above all, she had to keep her head. "Kel, I've grown very self-protective," she tried to explain.

"I can see that." The indomitable Kel Warrender sounded drained. "Is there any chance you can come with Tessa for the Christmas vacation? You must know she needs you there. We have to solve this problem of our daughter together."

"I'm scared to come back, Kel." She felt she could crumble with pain.

"Scared? Not you." His vibrant voice softened.

"I don't want to be seduced all over again."

Hostility bristled. "I thought you treasured our sex life."

"That's right. I treasured it." She tried but didn't quite succeed in holding back a glistening tear. "But I can't take it when you lie to me."

"Lie to you? Hell, woman—" he leaned closer "—didn't I confess right up?"

"You did that *one* time." She shook her head.

"There were *no* other times, Ronnie," he gritted. "I promise you."

Not entirely true. She recalled one occasion when she had caught him withdrawing from Sasha's passionate embrace. She remembered vividly her shock, her sick sensations, the way she had to support herself by clutching a chair. She thought of the number of times Hilary had hushed things up for them but later admitted to the couple's meetings under Ronnie's questioning.

The waitress approached again, glancing from one to the other. "Would you be ready to order now, Mr Warrender?"

Kel nodded absently, staring down at the menu for a moment before ordering the catch of the day, red emperor with French fries and a side salad for two. Neither of them was hungry as it happened. Too many disturbing things on their minds.

They fell silent for a few moments while they waited, then Kel began to ask about her job, listening attentively to the things she told him. He always had been a good listener.

"Is that what you think you really want?" he asked eventually.

"I have to live, Kel. It's all I know," she said defensively.

"When you can have all the money you need." He let out a sardonic laugh.

"Except I don't want to take it from you."

"You're my wife," he reminded her, his expression wrenched.

"I'm also my own woman. And a very successful one."

"I don't mean to diminish your ambition, Rowena. You're very compelling on television. But you're not so very successful at covering up your heartache. It's all there in your beautiful dark eyes."

"None of us can evade pain," she replied.

"But we can *confront* it. I want you back, Ronnie. I'll die before I ever let you down again. And there's more. I want more children. I want them from *you*. I want a son."

Ronnie smiled a little bitterly. "Of course, a man must have a son."

"*I* must have a son, sons, who can take up their heritage," he corrected her. "I adore my daughter, but I would never expect a woman to work a quarter as hard as I do. It's a very physical world, you know that. A dangerous world, too. I love my little Tessa with all my heart. I want the very best for her. That can only happen when her mother and father are together."

It was fruitless trying to defend herself against his powerful charm. "I don't know, Kel. I couldn't bear to go through any more terrible times."

His smile burned. "I'll make it work, Ronnie, I promise."

"Let me think about it," she evaded, shaking her head. "Like you, I'm desperately worried about Tessa, but I have commitments. A contract to honour." In fact her contract was due for renewal with a promised big salary hike.

"You have just over two months left to run." He felt like letting out a great shout of gratitude and triumph. "Surely you can work something out? We'll pay them out if we have to."

What a wonderful thing it was to have lots of money. "It's a pretty big thing to ask, Kel," she said. "I'm promising absolutely nothing beyond accompanying Tessa. She would want me to, much as she loves coming to you."

He groaned, pain in the sound. "And this is the little girl who used to love all my bedtime stories."

"They were so good they used to send her off to sleep." Despite herself she smiled, showing the single dimple in her cheek.

"That's because she was so little. I'm a great storyteller."

"God help you, yes."

"Ronnie, let up," he rasped. "You've already had me on the rack, but enough's enough. My heart, my head and my bed are empty without you."

He was a true magician. She was weakening. "It seems so long...."

"The worst fourteen months of my life. I've been counting." His response was soft and tender.

Unsettled, she asked, "Is Madelaine at the homestead?"

"Not at the moment." His glance was slightly mocking. "My mother comes and goes, but she'll be back as soon as she finds out you and Tessa are coming home."

"Let's take one thing at a time, Kel." She feared her own desire. "Don't get any ideas I'm going to move back into our bedroom, either."

One black eyebrow shot up. "You surprise me, Ronnie. When did I ever force you?"

"A couple of times," she lied. Both of them had been playing games.

He shrugged. "I give you my word." He let his eyes move so slowly over her, Ronnie's pulse began to race. It had been an eternity since he'd made love to her. An eternity. Now just his looking at her was like a free fall in space. She was giddy with sensation but afraid of crashing to earth.

"Should I respect it?" She fixed him with large, liquid eyes.

He leaned forward to grasp her hands. "I can't think of anyone you should trust more."

CHAPTER TWO

BY THE time they parted company, a kind of fragile peace had been established. Ronnie had to meet up with a staff photographer, while Kel had to return to the Convention Centre.

"What time should I turn up to see my daughter?" His silver-grey eyes ate up her lovely face. There was no life without her. None.

"I'm working until around six-thirty," she responded. "Tessa will be staying with Mamma. Why don't you come there?"

Thinking back, he gave a sardonic laugh. "So Bella can tell me yet again what a fool I've been."

"Most likely," she said wryly. "At the same time, you've got a big place in my mother's heart. She lives for the day we're…" She broke off and turned her head so he wouldn't see the expression in her eyes. "Stay for dinner if you like. Tessa will love it."

"What time does she go to bed?"

"That's not a criticism, is it, Kel?"

"It's a simple question." He smiled down at her, that twist-your-heart-in-your-breast smile.

"Generally around half past seven," she answered. "She can stay up a little later. I'm not sending her to school tomorrow. She has an appointment with Dr O'Neill midmorning."

"That's the child psychologist?" There was pain in his eyes.

"Yes," she replied, quietly confronting her own part in their separation.

"Why don't I take her?" he suggested. "Didn't you tell me he wanted to see me anyway?"

"He knows you're an important man and you're only in the city from time to time, Kel."

"So I'll take her tomorrow," he urged. "I can find the time."

"I'll see." She wasn't about to relent. "Anyway, I'd better be getting back."

"Let me find you a cab." Casually he turned, picked one approaching and hailed it. "Until tonight, then, Rowena."

"Fine." She tried to speak lightly despite holding back so much feeling.

And then he kissed her. Caught her chin, turned up her face and lowered his mouth over hers. Her mind's eye glittered with stars. And her emotions heated with helpless fury. Wasn't this the man who had abused her trust? Would she never be free of her own violent longing? It was so humiliating.

As he released her, Ronnie, conscious of the swirling lunchtime crowd and the fact her face was very
well known, smiled up at him with mock sweetness.
"Don't *ever* do that again," she gritted from between
clenched teeth.

"You taste delicious, Ronnie. You always did."

The cab swept next to the kerb. Kel opened the rear
door and waited while Rowena climbed in. Finally he
saluted, ever so gallant, ever so chivalrous, a small
taunting smile etched on his beautiful, seductive mouth.

Kel Warrender, her husband. Ronnie didn't wave.
Didn't look around.

The cab had barely gone a block, moving slowly
through the traffic, before it missed the green light.
Ronnie stared out the window, her mind in a kind of
trance as if a spell had been laid on it. But the spell was
well and truly broken as she found herself staring directly at a woman framed in the doorway of an exclusive boutique. It wasn't simply the fact that the woman
was eye-catching, this woman's features were etched
on Ronnie's memory forever. Early thirties, tall,
poised, model thin, very fashionably dressed, designer
sunglasses hiding those cat's eyes, her short, stylish
bob a lot darker than when Ronnie had last seen it.

Sasha Garland.

Sasha Garland in town. It was all very predictable.
Ronnie swallowed hard on the knot in her throat. What
a rotten start to the afternoon. Get a grip on yourself,
girl, she urged. It could be merely a coincidence. Then

just as swiftly, be your age. Sasha's turning up in town at the same time as the convention was exactly the sort of thing she'd do. Kel hadn't said a word about it. Why would he? Ronnie knew for a fact the Garlands were out of the country. No, Sasha was on the loose. Maybe she was even staying in Kel's hotel suite.

Ronnie mulled that over and felt ill. The calming effect of lunchtime harmony was ruined. This was the woman who had destroyed her marriage. The woman who had never forgiven Ronnie for the terrible injury she had done her. Stolen her man. Only Ronnie had never known a thing about Sasha Garland until weeks after Kel had asked her to marry him. Everyone had kept silent. Including Kel.

Her stomach churning, Ronnie leaned forward and asked the taxidriver to let her out. Perhaps if she spoke to Sasha? Like right now. She and Kel were still married. Sasha must listen. Anger and resolution radiated from heart to brain. Thrusting a five-dollar note at the driver, Ronnie stepped out onto the pavement.

"Keep the change," she called, falsely jaunty.

"Thanks, luv." Women! the cabbie thought wryly. Forever changing their minds.

Several feet from Sasha, Ronnie called her name. She was apprehensive now that Sasha would tell her things she didn't want to know, but she was determined on and in need of some sort of confrontation.

Sasha whirled, laughing though Ronnie had no idea why. "If it isn't the glamorous Rowena Warrender in the flesh," she breathed, her voice full of sarcasm. "What is this—an ambush?"

Ronnie didn't hesitate. She went right up to her. "Surely you're not worried? I saw you. I thought I'd say hello."

"How about the truth?" Sasha challenged.

"What are you doing in town?" Ronnie used her professional on-the-spot voice.

"Loitering with intent." Sasha gave a crooked smile.

"Tell me about it," Ronnie urged. "Tell me about the times you've followed my husband all around the country."

"What if I have, Ronnie?" Sasha said genially. "The thing you can't seem to get is that Kel was mine long before he was yours. Men are to blame for everything. Say, why don't we have a cup of coffee, girls together. Everyone staring at us is hurting my eyes. Tell me, are they staring at you or is it me?"

"I don't know and I don't care," Ronnie said briskly. "I've just had lunch with Kel, but I could manage another coffee." A gallon if she could pin this woman down.

"You're angry, Ronnie." Sasha's smile showed pity. "I can see it in your eyes. What about Nicco's?"

"That'll be fine."

Nicco's at lunchtime was packed with familiar faces, heads swivelling in Ronnie's direction, waves all round. Her good-looking face spelling irritation, Sasha forged ahead, then threw herself into a banquette like an athlete crossing the finish line. A big fish in most ponds, she wasn't used to any other woman catching her waves. As always, it had to be Rowena Warrender.

"So you were telling me you had lunch with Kel?" Sasha lost no time in picking up the conversation, lifting an imperious hand to order espressos for both of them. "Never could kick the habit," she murmured.

Ronnie looked down at her pink polished nails. She wasn't wearing her exquisite diamond engagement ring nor her wedding band, and her hands felt extraordinarily bare. "We may be separated, Sasha, but there are lots of things for us to discuss.

"About Tessa?" Sasha nodded in understanding. "I've been feeling bad about Tessa." She spoke the simple truth.

"I should think you would," Ronnie shot back so sternly Sasha flushed.

"I don't like the idea of hurting her," Sasha said defensively. "She's Kel's daughter after all. But you screwed up your own life, Ronnie," she accused, dark brows puckering.

"How's that?" Ronnie's answer was tight. "We were blissfully happy until you chose to take your vengeance."

"Take my vengeance? God, that sounds melodramatic," Sasha snorted. "It takes two to tango, sweetie. You might have thought you were *it*, but Kel needs a helluva lot of woman to satisfy him."

"You mean someone bigger than both of us," Ronnie retorted sarcastically. "You weren't enough for him, either. He married *me*."

"He was dazzled by you for a while," Sasha said more quietly. "I have to hand it to you, Ronnie. You keep yourself looking great. You're smart, stylish—heck, you're even warm and friendly. I can't help liking you myself, even though what you did to me was horrible. Kel was *my* man. See how you like it now. The thing is, Ronnie, there's no way I'm going to let go. Put it down to my obsessive nature. I grew up believing I was going to marry him. Mumma persevered with it even when you and Kel were standing at the altar. I know it's not a good thing to break up marriages, but I've convinced myself it would never work out. You're an outsider, Ronnie. Hilary and I knew that from day one. It's taken time and I've sent quite a few eligible guys on their way, but they all seem so colourless beside Kel."

"And Kel's so colourful he's dangerous," Ronnie finished wryly. "Listen, I get the picture, Sasha. I even feel sorry for you. But if my husband cares as much about you as you seem to think, why has he never asked me for a divorce?"

Sasha lowered her glossy dark head, then said in a well-thought-out way, "I know his biggest concern is Tessa. He'll do nothing more to upset her at this time. But he's bonded to me."

"You don't feel it's because you're forever hanging around?" Ronnie suggested.

"Maybe." Sasha looked momentarily upset. "But I'll continue to do so, Ronnie, until Kel shuts the door in my face."

Under her professional composure, Ronnie's heart sank. "So tell me, where are you staying while you're in town?"

"The Sheraton, where Kel's staying. What do you think?" Sasha drew back while the waiter set down the two rich dark-roast espressos.

"In a way, you've pilloried the man you confess to love," Ronnie offered in retaliation.

"You expect me to give him up?" For a moment, Sasha's golden-green eyes were quite wild.

Ronnie exhaled sharply. "It's a reasonable appeal from a *wife*. That's if you ever had him in the first place, which I'm beginning to doubt."

Petulance came into Sasha's voice. "You don't believe the rumours? Maybe you'd prefer times and places? Hilary could fill you in."

"That's another thing that's bugging me." Ronnie looked Sasha right in the eye. "Doesn't it disturb you, knowing you're twisting Hilary's mind? You pretend to be her *friend*!"

"Oh, to hell with that!" Sasha tossed off irritably, cheeks reddening. "I get my bad moments like everyone else. Hilary can be incredibly wearing even for me. How can she possibly land a man, which is what she desperately wants and what she tries so desperately to hide, with her dreadful gear and sergeant-major abrupt manner? I've been trying for years to jolly her into changing her image."

There was a grain of truth in it. "Hilary needs someone to love. Someone to love her," Ronnie said, always with a sympathetic slant to her mind.

"You're saying there's someone out there?" Sasha jeered, herself so unhappy with the way things had turned out that sarcasm seemed to spring from her as if from a fountain.

"The thing is I trusted Hilary once." Ronnie stared reflectively across the room. "Now it's dawned on me you were using her to undermine me."

"Got it in one!" Sasha mocked. "But I wasn't lying, Ronnie. No matter whether he married you or not, Kel and I were building a life before you were ever dreamed of. These days, the bond is as strong as ever."

"And it does help if you keep following him around," Ronnie emphasised the point gently. "Hilary, of course, with her confused loyalties, keeps spilling the beans. But get ready for a big surprise. I'll be back on Regina for Tessa's school vacation. Kel has begged me to stay."

It was the last news Sasha wanted to hear; in fact, it upset her deeply, but she made a valiant attempt to rally. "Hey, you are Tessa's mother," she pointed out.

"Indeed I am." Ronnie stood up, her expression one of near serenity. "And you just might remember, I'm still Kel Warrender's wife."

Ronnie arrived at her mother's house some forty minutes before Kel was due. The front door was open and she bent to pat Coco, her mother's King Charles spaniel, who greeted her ecstatically, snagging her right stocking in the process. Tessa followed, smiling at her mother in her heartbreaking fashion, running for the evening ritual of a big hug and kiss.

"Hello, darling, have you been a good girl for Nonna?" Ronnie asked, melting under a torrent of maternal love and protectiveness.

Bella, wearing an apron, appeared in the hallway, a lovely warm smile on her face. "If you can call feeding Coco nearly a packet of Smacko's being good. I'm expecting a grand attack of indigestion later on."

Tessa's lips barely moved. "But don't you think he looks happy, Mummy?" she looked up to whisper, deep in her self-imposed near silence.

Ronnie rested a hand on her little daughter's shining head. "He does indeed, darling." Coco was sitting in front of them, head cocked, tail thumping, the very picture of a contented dog. "But we must look after him and that means sticking to his special diet. Too many treats might make him sick, just as I don't allow you to eat too many sweets. Anyway, good news. Has Nonna told you Daddy is coming for tea tonight?"

Daddy!

Tessa's heart swelled at that infinitely dear name even though Daddy went away and she never saw him again for a long time. Wonderful, wonderful Daddy. Her beautiful, big soulful eyes, so like her father's in shape and colour, conveyed a yes. She would be very, very good so Mummy and Daddy wouldn't fight anymore and the terrible spell on her voice would be broken. She and Mummy would go back to the place she loved more than any other place on earth.

Regina, where the sky was always a vivid, cloudless blue and the endless plains were an extraordinary bright red. And the homestead! The marvellous homestead, so big she couldn't even count the rooms. And the rocking chair Daddy brought down from the attic and put in her bedroom so he could tell her bedtime stories while they rocked back and forth. Regina, the place she called home. The place where she really belonged, the way all the glittering stars belonged in the sky.

"I know you won't feel like going to bed when I tell you…" Mummy was saying sweetly. She never shouted or got cross. "…but you can't stay up too late, sweetheart. Daddy will tuck you in and tell you one of his Dreamtime stories."

Tiny blue pulses beat in Tessa's vulnerable temples. She clasped her hands, drowning in a mixture of excitement and agony. Every morning she woke, it was to a sense of terrible loss. Once, there had been three of them—a family. She remembered climbing over Daddy in the mornings so she could lie between him and Mummy in the big bed, snuggling up. She missed the strong, handsome father she adored, the way he made everyone else look little. Even Mummy felt sad and alone. She just knew it. Though she smiled every night on the television, Tessa knew her mother was missing Daddy terribly. Tessa was sure an evil magician was at work. Just like in her storybooks.

Acutely aware of her small daughter's train of thought, Ronnie stood for a helpless moment staring down at her. Bella had changed the little girl into a very pretty pink dress for the occasion, and dressed her long hair with a cascade of ribbons falling from the crown. Tessa's whole expression was so sweet and poignant Ronnie felt it like a blow. Their marriage break-up had been very hard on everyone. But it had been disastrous for Tessa. She and Kel would have to deal with it as a matter of urgency.

Afterwards, with Tessa sitting expectantly by the window awaiting the arrival of her father, Ronnie grabbed a few moments alone with her mother. Bella was in the kitchen, a professional workplace for the dedicated cook, making final arrangements for dinner. Tonight it would start with the exquisite eggplant ravioli Kel always enjoyed. What made Bella's pasta so special was the fact she kneaded it by hand using the very freshest eggs.

Roast leg of lamb with rosemary and garlic sizzled in the oven, while chunks of vegetables roasted together in a baking dish. Bella usually added a drizzle of balsamic vinegar for the last fifteen minutes of roasting the vegetables, lending them a wonderful caramelised flavour.

When Ronnie's father had been alive—an engineer, he had been killed in a tragic on-site accident a scant

year before Tessa's birth—there had been much entertaining at their house. Her mother had the marvellous
Italian knack of putting wonderful food together, then
setting an exceptional table. Ronnie looked at her now
with great love and admiration. Her mother had been
so brave. Ronnie went to her mother, put her arm
around her trim waist and hugged her.

"How was Tessa, really?" she asked. "Apart from
the incident with Coco."

"I only turned my back for two minutes," Bella said,
laughing. "She's okay. She solved the new jigsaw puzzle I bought her in what I thought was record time. It
said on the box seven to eight years and she's only five."

"She hasn't spoken a word?" Ronnie raised her eyes
to her mother's profile, thinking as always how beautiful she was, how timeless. Isabella was in her mid-
fifties now, hair as dark and abundant as ever, olive skin
unlined, the fine dark eyes Ronnie had inherited full
of warmth and wisdom, her figure full but perfectly
proportioned.

"I'm sorry, my darling," Bella said, herself a mass
of emotion. "It breaks my heart as much as it does
yours. She had a long, whispered conversation with her
little friend."

"Nicholas?"

"I'm not sure if Nicholas isn't her guardian angel,"
Bella suggested. "Have you ever asked her?"

Ronnie sat down in a chair at the long table. "I've
asked her lots of times, but she withdraws on the sub-

ject of Nicholas. He's always there for her. She doesn't know why."

"And Dr O'Neill tomorrow?" Bella checked on the roast.

"Kel wants to take her this time."

"Why don't you let him?" Bella thought it was a particularly good idea. "The doctor's told you he wants to see Tessa's father."

"Tessa's adored father." For a moment, Ronnie's large dark eyes filled with tears almost as though she didn't know what was happening to her.

Bella watched her with deep sympathy. "Kel is one of those men it's very easy to have great affection for."

"Even when he betrayed me, Mamma?"

"Come, come, my darling," Bella went to her daughter and laid a hand on her shoulder. "It seems to me on reflection that perhaps the punishment didn't fit the crime."

"Now, Mamma, you played a part in it," Ronnie protested. "You agreed with me when I left."

Bella's expression grew sad and pensive. "I didn't know it was going to go on this long. I didn't know the effect on my little Tessa. It happened, *cara*. I don't even think Kel knows why. It was one of those accidental things."

"It was planned," Ronnie said, and her voice had a ring to it. "It was planned all along. When I left Kel after lunch, I ran into—"

"Don't tell me. Sasha Garland?" Bella looked agitated.

"She said she's staying at the Sheraton where Kel is this week."

"She would volunteer that information," Bella said with fine scorn.

Ronnie nodded. "She is. I checked."

"How I despise her," Bella groaned. "This is wicked. Did you have it out with her?"

"I managed a few words. She claims Kel is still involved with her. She'll never let go."

Ronnie could see the anger rise through her mother's body. "She's a fool, then. I'll stake my life on it. Kel loves you. It's about time that woman fixated on somebody else. You can't tell me Kel is begging you to come back to him and continuing an affair. I won't have it."

"What am I to do, Mamma?" Ronnie asked in some bewilderment. "He broke my heart."

Bella shook her head, her hair arranged in a classic knot. "You have no life without him, my darling. I know you too well. Tessa is suffering badly. Her world that was so full of sunshine has become dark and menacing. She desperately needs her mother and father to be together."

"So I forgive him now. Is that it?" Ronnie asked in a kind of despair. Pride versus longing.

"What else can you do?" Bella said. "He's human, flesh and blood. He's had his punishment. This Sasha, painful as it is for her to accept, must mean nothing to him. He had plenty of time to marry her and he didn't. He's made no move towards getting a divorce. On the contrary, he has told you many times over he wants a reconciliation."

"So this can happen to me again?" Irritably Ronnie brushed the trace of tears away. "If not with Sasha, someone just like her. Let's face it, Kel is a very sexy man. A rich sex life is very important to him."

"I think, actually, it is to you too. I don't relish saying this, my darling, but you told me yourself you had shut the bedroom door on him."

Ronnie felt chilled by her memories. "That was only after Hilary told me what was going on behind my back."

"Ah, Hilary." Bella gave a deep, ironic laugh. "Sasha and Hilary have been friends for a long, long time. That's just the way it is. These landed people always stick together. Nevertheless, I think now Hilary must have been swallowing Sasha's lies."

Ronnie shrugged darkly. "Except I did see something to confirm it. Something that disturbed me terribly."

"When was this?" Bella stared down at her in consternation.

"It was after a weekend party, a couple of years ago. Kel's team had won the polo cup. I went in search of him, full of pride and love, only to find him in Sasha's arms. It looked like they'd been kissing passionately."

"It was a trick of course!" Bella huffed. "Did you

have it out with them? Did you confront them?" she asked sharply, her eyes very dark.

"I'm not a confrontational person, Mamma. You know that," Ronnie sighed. "Coming on that after all Hilary's hints, I was afraid of my own thoughts. What was I supposed to do? Break up my marriage? Turn the other cheek? I found myself slinking away."

"I don't understand why you didn't tell me." Bella was trying to get it all sorted out.

"You've shed enough tears, Mamma. I'm not a child. I had to work it out for myself."

"So meanwhile, all the tension built up. You became more and more insecure until you finally packed up."

"That's about it." Ronnie shrugged. "I refused Kel my bed as a last resort. Something he bitterly resented. Nothing seemed to add up. Did he really need *two* women? A wife and a mistress?"

"It was Sasha who worked at being the mistress," Bella observed shrewdly. "She's immensely cunning. She may well have seen you coming that night and thrown her arms around Kel. She could easily have made it appear they were kissing. To an insecure young wife, such a thing would be very incriminating. I only know when you first brought Kel to meet your dear father and me, we thought the two of you were made for each other. Both Hilary and Sasha each in their own way have tried very hard to spoil things for you. I don't think you should let them get away with it."

The sound of Tessa's footsteps as she pattered through the parqueted hallway alerted them to Kel's arrival. Even then, the little girl didn't call out, which all three adults desperately hoped for, but her face was wreathed in smiles as Ronnie let Kel through the front door. He was dressed with casual elegance in a double-breasted jacket worn over a soft blue shirt and dress jeans. He was carrying wine, roses, chocolates and a brightly wrapped and beribboned present that was obviously for Tessa. His wonderful vitality flowed from him to his womenfolk.

He picked Tessa up and kissed her until she giggled helplessly with excitement, funny little gasps coming up from her throat as if she was exploding with joy, but no longed-for words. Finally Kel let his eyes rest on his wife, courting her all over again, before Bella came from the kitchen to greet him, her apron removed, arms outstretched.

"Kel, how lovely to see you." It was a gesture of reconciliation and affection.

This resulted in more kisses all round. "Bella, you get more beautiful with every passing day," Kel said so sincerely it filled Bella with pleasure.

"I try to make a life for myself," she said.

"And nothing would delight me more than for you to come to us at Christmas." Kel turned to smile into Tessa's small face, drawing her head onto his shoulder. "Wouldn't you love Nonna to come and stay with us on Regina?"

Hardly daring to breathe, Tessa touched his chest, greatly comforted by the strong thud of his heart.

"Wonderful. Then it's all fixed." Kel spoke warmly, confidently, though he yearned for conversation with his little girl. "Now what about us opening your present, princess?"

"Of course." Ronnie smiled. When he was being good, Kel was utterly irresistible.

Dinner was like the old days, great culinary enjoyment, laughter and good conversation. Later, Kel and Ronnie took Tessa up to bed. It had been decided Ronnie and Tessa would stay with Bella for the night. Kel tucked his daughter in, then sat by her bed telling her one of his store of Aboriginal legends while she drifted off to sleep. He didn't look ruthless, a man without a husbandly conscience; he looked like a deeply devoted father, lingering lovingly at the bedside of his sleeping child.

"I can't believe she's persisting with this silence," he said to Ronnie when they were out in the hallway. "Obviously it's all my fault. One mindless act and I put my whole family at risk. I hate myself, Ronnie." His eyes were as deep as the ocean as he looked at her. She had changed her suit for a short georgette dress in deep blue, a shade he loved on her. Her long blonde hair was tucked behind her ears to show off her lovely diamond-and-pearl earrings. He had given them to her along with a matching necklace when Tessa was born. A beautiful woman who was forcing him to live in celibacy.

"I tried hating you, too. An impossible thing to do."

"So neither of us has escaped our bonds?" He looked into her vulnerable eyes, seeing the aching desire.

"How could we? We have our child." She had a terrible urge to lean forward and rest her head against his chest.

"And we have one another," he exhorted her. "Our marriage is the most important step I've taken in my life. It wasn't just some escapade I engaged in. I married you determined our marriage would last forever. You cut me off, Rowena, long before Sasha flew a thousand miles to turn up at my hotel."

The knowledge made her flare into sudden anger. "I know all about your desires, Kel."

His sparkling eyes roamed every feature of her face. "Yes, I remember. But my desire was all for *you*."

"Yet Sasha is still in your life." She knew she sounded like a tape that wouldn't stop, but she couldn't help it.

He speared long fingers into his raven hair. "I think we'll have to call it arrested development with Sasha," he said, his patience running out. "Mothers don't realise what they do talking marriage from the cradle. At this stage, I couldn't get rid of Sasha with a fire hose."

"Apparently not," Ronnie returned acidly. "She's staying at the Sheraton."

"What the hell! What are you saying?"

"I ran into her a few minutes after I left you. Didn't she tell you?" Ronnie's eyes widened.

"Don't be so stupid, okay?" His voice turned hard. "Sasha's free to stay anywhere she likes. I'll speak to her if I have to, but I'll never fall into her trap again."

Her trap. The words had a terrible ring.

"You're free to divorce me, Kel, any time you like," Ronnie said bleakly.

"For God's sake, haven't you been listening?" He seized her powerfully and drew her towards him. "What is it with you? Some deep-seated insecurity? When are you going to learn I want you. No one else. God knows why when you're treating me so badly."

"Don't do this, Kel," she protested, trying in vain to break free.

"Why not? You're my wife."

Blazing with anger and a desire that fairly crackled, he lowered his head, pressing her against his body so she felt his arousal, kissing her until she was drained of all resistance.

"Let me love you," he muttered. "Let me start all over again." His hand, which trapped her breast and caressed it through the filmy material, became more insistent as the nipple peaked beneath his grazing thumb. "Ronnie, God!" He shaped her arched back, kissing her searchingly, playing her like a violin. "Love, my lover, I want to be deep inside of you," he groaned.

Her resistance, after all, was as fragile as glass. Only the fact they were in her mother's house gave her a vestige of control.

"Kel, you've got to stop," she implored, so full of emotion her voice broke.

"How do I do that?" His deep laugh was edgy.

"Mamma might come." Now he pinned her lower body against his, and for a moment she felt herself in flames, utterly naked.

"Bella never barges in," he told her. "She's too sensitive, too experienced to do such a thing. We can't go on like this, Rowena. We want each other. We always did. Nothing else matters." He began kissing her throat with close urgency. "That's a great dress, but I want it off you. I've never stopped thinking of your beautiful body and how if feels under my hands."

It was as it had always been. He was sweeping her away. "You're dangerous to love, Kel. I've found that to my cost."

"*Forgive me*. That's all I ask. I promise if you come back to me, I'll take great care of you and our child. I'll never allow anyone to come between us again. Promise, Ronnie."

She broke away, gasping. "Kel, stop pressuring me. Moving me about like a pawn. You've always been good at it. I've been through an agonising process of trying to get my life together."

"It's no life for Tessa without her father around," he countered just as urgently.

"Do you think I don't know that?" She looked up at the tall, powerful strength of him. "You're asking me to put my career on hold."

"I'm asking you to abandon it all together," he said flatly.

"When I'm not even at the height of my powers?" she asked with bitter humour. "Not even in my prime?"

"Is that how you see it?" he asked, eyes flashing in the bronze sheen of his face. "Is this your *dream*, Ronnie? To be a passing star on television news?"

Put like that, it didn't sound like much. "I'm good at what I do, Kel," she answered quietly.

He made a little sound of apology. "I know you are, but it's a job another clever, good-looking woman could handle. And there are plenty coming up. Your *unique* job, a job no one else on this earth can do is being Tessa's mother. We hear all the time how children are so resilient. How they can bounce back from anything. I don't feel happy with that. Plenty don't. Most children can't handle the sad breakdown of a family." He stared at her with his silver eyes, his charisma so lavish she felt like buckling at the knees.

"Kel, I know all this," she said numbly. "I know it only too well. But life with you will never be quiet. It's like battling a big surf. The thrill, the excitement, the wonderful exhilaration, then the inevitable crash."

Perversely she never mentioned the countless times he had been so exquisitely gentle and comforting. Kel, the big, powerful cattle baron cosseting her as if she was someone ineffably precious. Kel kissing her face, her throat, every inch of her body. The ecstasy!

"Let's try a period of reconciliation first," she suggested, afraid she would never withstand him once back on Regina.

"I'll try anything you like." He was enormously moved, pulling her to him with quiet, controlled strength. "But don't shut me out, Ronnie. I can't take it again. I bitterly regret my mistake. It was shameful and crazy. I don't have much memory of it." He sighed ruefully as if even he couldn't take it in. "It does me no good to bring this up, but I was really messed up and pretty damned drunk."

"Nice try, Kel, but it won't work." Ronnie shook her blonde head.

"So there's no use my insisting?"

"No." She had heard it all before. His denials. Hilary's admissions. What she had seen with her own eyes.

"Are you going to allow me to take Tessa to the psychologist tomorrow?" he asked in a different, more clipped tone.

"Mamma thinks it's a very good idea."

"Thank God Bella is on my side," he said wryly. "She doesn't want this separation to go on."

"Mamma doesn't believe in divorce."

"Neither do I," he said forcefully. "And neither do *you*, Ronnie, when all's said and done. The only thing I'm asking is for you to give me another chance."

She bit her lip. "I've been very badly hurt by all this, Kel. I'll probably lose my job if I ask for a lot of time off. My contract is up for renewal. Most likely they won't take up the option."

"At this point, Ronnie, our daughter is more important than your contract," he said, his hands closing on her shoulders.

Ronnie nodded but didn't speak for a moment. His hands were warm and hard on her skin and she felt desire cut through her like a knife. She was young. He had taught her everything there was to know about passion. Now this. This barren wilderness.

"I'll come with you tomorrow," she said finally. "Both of us should be there. I never dreamed what happened to us would have such terrible repercussions. Dr O'Neill is treating Tessa's case very seriously."

"I'm sure he is." Kel squared his wide shoulders. "I've checked his credentials. They're beyond reproach, but I feel our being reunited as a family would be far more therapeutic than all the counselling."

He took her hand and began walking with her down the corridor to the central staircase. "So what time?"

"Would it be a problem to pick us up here at ten?" she asked.

"No problem at all." He turned at the top of the stairs then took her slender body all the way into his arms. His blood surged with sensuality. *Bellissima*," he said softly. "You are so lovely. Hair glittering all shades of gold. Eyes like dark velvet. Skin like flowers. Your beautiful breasts just out of sight. I hurt a lot, Rowena. There's the demands of my body but also here inside my head."

He was speaking from the heart, but Ronnie warned

softly, "Don't think I'm going to fall straight into your bed." Pathetic, when her whole body was shaking.

"God forbid I should make you." He was aware of the pulse that beat so frantically in the small hollow of her neck.

"I mean it, Kel. You must respect my wishes."

"I always did. Trust me, darling," he urged. "If you don't, it will kill me." He lowered his head, kissing her very gently at first, then not gently at all, moving his hands hungrily up and down her lower back as her clothes moved and her short skirt rode high.

Finally he put her away from him not a little disoriented, seeing her eyes tightly closed, her mouth trembling, her breath ragged. Their desire still had the same rushing momentum.

"Lord," he breathed onto the top of her head. "It's the same story every time I touch you. I'd better go." His hand grasped the polished newel on the banister. "We've got to be together, Rowena. I give you my solemn promise I won't touch you until you ask me." There was genuine commitment as well as a little smile in his voice.

And I probably will, Ronnie thought. Not ask. *Beg.* The day wouldn't dawn when she would be free of her husband's spell.

CHAPTER THREE

HE ARRIVED back at the hotel, passing but not seeing Sasha tucked into a deep armchair, nursing another nightcap to get up her courage. God knows the multicultural river city of Brisbane was alive with attractive men, Sasha thought, many bearing the dark, striking good looks of their Mediterranean heritage, but as soon as she saw Kel Warrender striding purposefully through the lobby, Sasha felt the same old shock of need through her body. No one could eclipse him. No one. That was her tragedy.

A young woman near her whispered to her friend, "Isn't he a dream?"

"Heck, he's famous." The other woman nudged her companion's arm playfully. "Kel Warrender. You *know*. The cattle baron. Don't you remember he married Rowena Warrender? But the marriage broke up."

"How terrible," the first young woman said, sounding shocked. "I expect another woman got in the way. Who wouldn't try with a guy like that?"

Exactly, Sasha thought grimly. I'm one tough, persistent woman and this is my last-ditch stand. She waited exactly seven minutes, then stood up a little unsteadily and smoothed her short black crepe evening dress with the shoestring satin straps. Kel had always admired her legs. He favoured black, too. It suited her sophisticated looks and the cut was anything but austere. Any article about her in the glossy magazines always mentioned she was one sharp dresser.

Bolstered by the admiring glances that came her way, Sasha made for the lifts aware of the trembling that shook her body. It seemed to her she had always been engaged in some elaborate scheme to get Kel to commit to her. It really was a chronic condition. But for a while there, she'd had him until golden-haired Ronnie had stolen him away. At that time, she and her mother had been counting their chickens before they were hatched. They'd been sure they could pull off an engagement. Women did it all the time. Even married to his precious Ronnie, Kel hadn't actually renounced her.

Kel came to the door of his suite at the second knock. He stared down at her—magnetic, exciting, smouldering blackly.

"Sasha," he said, shaking his head, "keep this up and you can consider yourself a call girl."

"Naughty, darling," she said, wincing. "I live the way I want, Kel. I like to make things happen."

"Tell me about it." He stared past her down the corridor. "Have you brought a photographer with you?"

"Don't be like that," she cajoled, pretty sure he would ease up. "I'd never hurt you or your precious reputation."

He shrugged, bleakly amused. "You exaggerate, of course. One of the things I've learned about you, Sasha, is you don't give a damn who gets hurt."

Her eyes flickered as she felt his mood. "For pity's sake, Kel, after all these years, are you trying to tell me I'm nothing? You allowed me to love you. We were lovers. Now you're telling me I'm no good. Why are you guys so insensitive to a woman's pain? Hell, I love you so much I'd let you carve me up. What happened at the Sandpiper Inn wasn't entirely my fault."

"Especially your fault," he corrected. "You schemed, plotted, planned it."

Her chin shot up. "I had to do it, Kel. I don't care if you are married. Marriage isn't what it used to be."

Kel pitched his voice almost kindly. "Sasha, you must accept this once and for all. I love Rowena. Got it? I love our child. I have not given up on my marriage. I never wanted to hurt you or puncture your pride. I didn't deceive you. You got no talk of marriage out of me no matter how hard you and your mother tried to rope me in. I'm very fond of you. Why wouldn't I be? We grew up together. We share the same roots. But for God's sake, get on with your life and let me get on with mine."

Sasha looked like she had received a body blow. "What a miserable ingrate you are. You can't dismiss me like that. I gave you the best years of my life. Let me in."

Kel's silver eyes turned to slate. "The answer is a great big no. I'm in enough trouble already."

"Scared of doe-eyed Ronnie?" she mocked, slipping her arms playfully around his waist.

"Don't play the fool, Sasha." He drew away. "I'm angry."

Abruptly her confident facade crumpled. "I'm not happy, either. I just want to apologise. Sort this thing out. Life's too short to turn your back on your friends. Please, Kel…" Neatly she bobbed under his arm and entered the suite. "Say, this is great!" she said, looking around.

"Sasha!" he nearly yelled at her, then thought better of it. There was no telling what Sasha would do with a few drinks in her. "I've never ill-treated a woman in my life, but I'm about to throw you out."

"No." She fixed her eyes on him, then threw herself into an armchair, bunking in. "Hang on a sec, Kel. I'm not out to seduce you."

"Really?" His eyebrow shot up. "I thought that was the whole idea."

"Up to now, Kel, you've been my whole existence," Sasha said quietly.

"Then I'm sorry." He couldn't keep the pitying note out of his voice. "But you've been spoiled rotten, Sasha. It's not a case of your never knowing when to give up. You *have* to have what you want. It doesn't matter whose happiness is at stake. I know you're genuinely fond of Tessa, but look what's happened to her since Ronnie and I separated. Doesn't Tessa matter?"

"Of course she matters." Sasha sounded sorely wronged. "I know it's horrendous, but it's not my fault alone. You were with me at the Sandpiper Inn."

"Ah, the Sandpiper Inn," Kel responded flatly. "All I recall is waking up and finding you in my bed. You told me we had one helluva night, but I don't remember a damn thing. All I remember is leaving while you were having a conversation with one of my colleagues."

"Bob Wilding." She nodded. "We were drinking partners."

"I remember telling you to get out of my bed. I also distinctly remember your odd answer. 'I'm on my way.' Is it possible you got into my room via the veranda?" He stared at her so accusingly Sasha began to fidget, then as he came closer, his handsome face positively threatening, she began to radiate guilt.

"Ah, well, you were bound to find out sooner or later," she admitted, suddenly collapsing into confession, her normally strong, clear voice wavering like a child's.

"So I didn't betray Ronnie after all." In the middle of his shock and anger, Kel felt elation.

"Keep your dreams, sweetheart," she said bitterly. "You didn't. You were out of it."

"My God!" He turned way from the sight of her. "The damage that's been done. For what? I don't love you, Sasha. I love Rowena. And both of us have been worried sick about Tessa."

"But, my dear," Sasha gritted, "I thought you could love me with Ronnie out of the way. I pictured it so often I convinced myself it was true." She rose groggily, her eyes huge in her pale face. "I'd better go. I need a drink to ease the pain." She began to walk slowly across the room, starting back a little as the phone shrilled close beside her.

"Don't touch it," Kel warned, alerted by something in her expression. There was a distinct possibility it could be Ronnie with a change of plan. "Sasha…"

Without hesitation, her contrary nature at work, Sasha snatched up the phone and spoke seductively into it, eyeing Kel all the while. "Kel Warrender's suite, Sasha speaking," she added unforgivably.

"Bitch!" Kel breathed, visualising Ronnie's stricken, shocked face at the other end.

"Well, what do you know, no answer!" Sasha crowed, though her pinched expression gave the jauntiness of her tone the lie. Finally, finally, she realised no ploy on earth would ever work. She couldn't make Kel love to order. The bravest thing she could do was take herself off to the other side of the moon.

Kel wanted to believe very much it wasn't Ronnie who had rung, but he knew in his bones his hunch was correct. When he arrived at Bella's, she met him at the door, taking him conspiratorially by the elbow and drawing him into the living room.

"Gosh, I can do without all this, Kel," she said in her rich, beguiling voice. "Rowena isn't here. You'll have to take Tessa by yourself."

"That's no problem, Bella." He turned to stare down at her. "Where in hell *is* Ronnie?"

Bella returned his challenging look fairly and squarely. "Her boss at the station has sent her on a job. He left a message last night. He wants nobody else but Ronnie. She's so good at her job."

"So that's why she rang me at the hotel," he groaned.

Bella swung on him, dark eyes flashing, memories of her daughter's heartache flooding her mind. "Do you think it wise to let that woman into your room, Kel? That brazen Sasha. The woman needs a shrink. She's a terrible troublemaker."

He did his best to keep cool. "Tell me something I don't know. I wasn't entertaining her, Bella. She turned up on my doorstep, ducked under my arm and took up a defensive position in an armchair."

"You didn't throw her out?" Bella asked with blazing eyes. "You so big and strong?"

"I could have," he agreed, "but to tell the truth, I was a bit concerned about bloodcurdling shrieks. Some women are shocking when things don't work out for them."

Bella savoured that for a moment, then asked more mildly, "You're asking me to believe this?"

"I'm not asking. I'm *expecting* you to believe it—and a lot more," Kel answered bluntly. "Sasha's turning up last night might have caused more problems, but it freed me from a lot of heartache. She finally admitted nothing happened that night at the Sandpiper Inn. Absolutely nothing. She suckered me in, damn her. So much suffering, but in the end it was no more than Sasha trying to play Delilah."

"She's prepared to tell Ronnie?" Bella asked hopefully. She had met Sasha Garland enough times to know how far she would go to get what she wanted.

"She doesn't feel *that* bad about it, Bella." His tone was ironic.

"So it's your word against hers?"

"It is, and Ronnie's gone off like a firecracker, right?"

"She was breathing flames," Bella said in confirmation, "and feeling tremendously upset. Can you blame her when that Sasha is taking control of the situation?"

"Why didn't Ronnie speak?" he countered.

"You damned well know why. She's haunted by that woman."

"Not anymore," Kel said grimly. "Ronnie's going to have to trust me."

When Kel and Tessa arrived at Dr O'Neill's, it was to find Rowena unexpectedly waiting for them.

"I thought you had an assignment," Kel said, ignoring her closed expression.

"It'll keep," she answered briefly without looking at him. She bent to kiss Tessa on her small perfect nose. "How are you, darling?"

In answer, Tessa sighed deeply. She had picked up instantly on the vibrations that pulsed between her parents. Little as she was, she could sense what went on behind her mother's soft, tender eyes. She knew exactly how her mother felt and how much she loved Daddy. But she wouldn't let him know about it. The saddest part was that Tessa *knew* Daddy was wonderful. It distressed her terribly that they lived apart, which was one of the reasons why the evil magician had taken her voice. Tessa couldn't remember when it happened. Or even how. She just seemed to stop talking. She knew she would make Mummy cry if she told her all about it. When she saw Daddy, it was like a tight string was wrapped around her tonsils. The magician had done that. She loathed him. Lots of times she felt like talking to Nonna, but the words wouldn't come. Nonna would only tell Mummy.

Mummy and Nonna talked every single minute they spent together. They were the greatest *friends*. Finally Nicholas came to help her. Nicholas, her guiding spirit. Nicholas helped her push away the panic when her voice wouldn't work. It was *so* peculiar.

A few minutes later, Dr O'Neill came to the door smiling, shaking hands with her tall, wonderful daddy before asking her to join him for a little talk. Dr O'Neill was so nice, with sparkly blue eyes and lovely white hair even when he wasn't old. Mummy said he had a great sense of humour. Talk! Wasn't that funny when she was caught in the spell? But the magician couldn't stop her from drawing things for her nice doctor.

While their small daughter with her intense thoughts disappeared into Dr O'Neill's office, Kel took a seat beside his wife on the comfortable leather couch. A collection of beautiful prints all touching on childhood scenes hung on the walls.

"Would you care for coffee?" Judy Richmond, the sweet-faced, rather old-fashioned receptionist, asked, always managing to realise when parents needed a few moments alone together.

"That'd be wonderful." Kel slipped easily into a charming smile.

"I'll be a few minutes," she returned. "You needn't worry about the phone ringing. I'll take it on the extension."

"That was nice of her," Kel murmured after the receptionist had moved into an adjoining room.

"She's a very nice woman," Ronnie confided coolly. "She needs to be since Dr O'Neill works with children."

"What's wrong, Ronnie?" he broached her attitude swiftly. "There's frost coming off you."

She gave a low, brittle laugh. "I'll never warm to *you* again," she said with exquisite contempt.

He nodded, careful to see things from her point of view. "If you give me a moment, I could explain about Sasha last night."

"I doubt if you could explain it even if we had all the time in the world, Kel. What I find difficult to understand is why you *want* to explain."

"It's impossible here," he said, listening to sounds of cups clinking in the next room.

"I'm glad you realise that," Ronnie responded, feeling her own energy absorbed by his.

His rush of anger was quickly followed by a far deeper tide of hurt. "I intend to tell you before I go back," Kel announced, glancing at her set profile.

"Which is when?"

"The conference finishes tomorrow. I flew in in the Beech Baron. I'm due out midafternoon."

"At least the conference has been a success," Ronnie said tonelessly, staring at her ringless hands. "Regina has defied the gloom."

"Not just Regina," he corrected her. "Market prices are at a twelve-month high. We've had the best season in years and the lower dollar gives us a big advantage. We all need something positive after the tough years, or have you forgotten?"

"Cattle are only part of your big portfolio of interests, Kel," she pointed out.

"Maybe." He shrugged. "We've had to diversify, but the cattle business is our life. That's what I am before anything else, Ronnie, a cattleman like my father and my grandfather and his father before him. You assured me it was the life *you* wanted."

"Ah, but I didn't believe then that our marriage could fail." Unable to resist, she gazed briefly into his silvery eyes, seeing them darken.

"It will only fail if you let it, Ronnie."

"Oh, that's good coming from you," she murmured, and closed her eyes.

"Let's sort it out outside," he suggested, badly wanting to pull her into his arms. "What we're both here for is our child. Her welfare comes before our needs. Agreed?"

"Of course I agree." It was the sad truth she had faced. "Whatever happens to us and our relationship appears to be over, our parenthood is not."

His tone was low but his attitude was clear. "*I* don't accept that our relationship is over, Ronnie. You're as much in need of comfort and security as Tessa. I want us to sit down afterwards and discuss this."

She clasped her hands together on her lap. "I have to go back to work, Kel. You appear to want me to accept Sasha Garland as part of your life. I'll never do that."

His striking face tautened by several degrees. "The truth is that Sasha is out of my life."

"Extraordinary way she has of showing it," she snapped back.

"Rowena," he said in an intense undertone, "I've been branded something I'm not. I never did believe it. But I've been made to suffer. That's all over. I want my daughter. The impact of our separation has been disastrous for her. I know you recognise that. I want you back. Make no mistake about that. And take a few minutes to consider the enormous stresses of divorce litigation. You won't take my child from me. I don't intend to be a part-time father. You'd better grasp that."

"So I'm to tolerate your infidelities or battle you for custody?"

Her hands were shaking and he reached for them, holding them firmly. "Don't push me too far, Ronnie, and don't dump infidelities on me. That's just a beat-up. What about that tailor's dummy, Josh Marshall? Isn't he mooning after you?"

"Don't be ridiculous." She pulled her hands away when she craved his touch.

"Hell, Ronnie, I saw the way he was looking at you."

"You don't like the notion of another man looking at me?" Her chin came up.

"They could just get themselves strung up," he drawled, glancing at her with mocking eyes. "I happen to know you've been faithful to me, Ronnie."

Colour stained her lovely skin. "Ah, yes! I bet you even paid someone to keep an eye on me!"

"What do you think," he scoffed, "when you've been talking divorce? Like I said, Ronnie, I'm not cut out to be a part-time father. If you're not going to show me any trust, I'll have to get at you through emotional blackmail. In a few minutes, I expect Dr

O'Neill is going to tell us the answer to our daughter's problem lies squarely with us."

The following morning propelled by their talk with Dr O'Neill, Ronnie decided to take action, requesting a meeting with Channel 8's management. No matter her blossoming career, her daughter's welfare meant far, far more to her. In a quiet tone, she told those sitting around the boardroom table that she would not be renewing her contract at this time, a bombshell that made backs stiffen with shock and dismay. The "personal reasons" she cited didn't appear to cut much ice. People in television tended to be very self-centred, she remembered. Within a highly competitive industry, the number-one priority was ratings.

"That's a pretty heavy thing to spring on us, Ronnie," her immediate boss censured her. "You've got a great future. If it's money…?"

Ronnie shook her head. "I've thought this over very carefully, Joe. Obviously I don't want to let the station down, but my daughter has developed a few problems that must be straightened out."

"Surely we can discuss this," he persisted, mouth drawn down. "There must be other options available."

Basically he was insensitive to her personal problems, she realised. "I'm sorry, Joe," she apologised. "I can give you four full weeks so you can get someone else to replace me. Then it's the Christmas vacation.

Tessa and I will be returning to my husband's property in the Channel Country."

"You mean you've patched things up?" one of the station's top executives questioned, causing Ronnie a momentary flash of resentment.

"To be honest, there's no talk of permanent reconciliation," she answered. "The thing is, both of us are deeply concerned about our daughter."

"Of course, Ronnie," Joe Gannon broke in abruptly. "We understand, but I wish this weren't happening. After all, we've done so much for you."

"And I'm very grateful." Ronnie looked sincerely at each man in turn. "I do mean that. You've been wonderful in promoting me, but I'm a mother before I'm anything else."

She wasn't surprised when she answered the telephone some hours later to be told by Joe they wouldn't need her to stay on until December. Miranda Frost would take over until they found a new "face".

That sounds about right, Ronnie thought wryly. No one is indispensable. She cleared out her desk by mid-afternoon, smiling a little tightly to herself.

"They'll never take you on again, Rowena," a female colleague who had been passed over for Ronnie told her with some satisfaction. "You did a pretty good job, I have to grant you, but they'll find someone better. They always do. Our five minutes of fame is so fleeting."

* * *

She found her mother in the garden planting dozens and dozens of white impatiens along a shady border.

"My darling girl!" Bella looked up in surprise. "I was just thinking about going for Tessa."

"That's okay. I'll go for her, Mamma," Ronnie said, sinking onto the curved white stone bench. "Bit of news. I'm not working for Channel 8 anymore."

Bella's rich, low voice rose to dramatic soprano. "Wh-what!" She shook her dark head, bemused.

"I can't say I'm surprised," Ronnie said philosophically. "They did it to Grant Symons, don't you remember?"

"It's a ruthless business, this television news." Bella straightened up, pulling off her gardening gloves. "What brought it on?" she said sounding outraged.

"I started the ball rolling, Mamma," Ronnie explained. "I told them I wouldn't be renewing my contract. Dr O'Neill didn't mince words yesterday. Tessa's problems reflect the fact we're a dysfunctional family."

Bella looked down at her hands, examining them for wear and tear. "I guess not that many children take refuge in becoming mute," she agreed quietly, sitting down beside her daughter.

Ronnie's velvet eyes stung with tears she wouldn't allow to flow. "Dr O'Neill said such alienation from her family, her peers, teachers and the like must be viewed very seriously."

"As though we don't!" Bella was filled with an overwhelming sense of frustration. A devoted grandmother who had been faced with many problems in life and she couldn't liberate her own little granddaughter.

A strong breeze blew across the garden and Ronnie held her long hair with one hand. "It's reached the stage where I think Tessa is powerless to free herself from this self-imposed sanctuary of silence," she said. "She told me only the other day she 'froze like an ice block' when someone wanted her to talk. It made my heart break. I can't go on like this, Mamma. I'm flooded by anxiety all the time. Tessa is so small and helpless. She adores her father, yet such a confusion of emotions surround her she appears to dread to speak."

Bella drew her daughter to her, pressing her head onto her shoulder. "She'll talk again, *cara mia*, when she feels safe. I know this. I am praying for it. I think maybe we won't let her watch too much television for a while. She's such an imaginative child I'm coming to believe she feels like some little storybook character with a spell on her. One day, she was sitting on the swing with her back to me and murmuring to her invisible friend. She was in tears when she was telling Nicholas about it."

"I'm sure Nicholas isn't hurting her. He's helping her," Ronnie said with certainty. "Invisible friends are important in this world." Like fairies. Or angels.

"She wants her father," Bella said. "She wants her parents together the way it used to be. She demands continuous daily contact with both of you. Another thing she's badly missing is Regina. That's *her* beloved environment. She draws so many pictures of it all the time. The land, the sand hills, the animals, the birds, the wildflowers."

"I know," Ronnie sighed deeply while her mother patted her arm. "It expresses her longing to be back there. She does lots of drawings of the stars and those humanlike spirits Kel tells her all about. She loves the Aboriginal legends. She grew up on them." As Ronnie spoke, so many wonderful memories filtered back to her.

"Both of you are very intelligent, deeply caring people." Bella kissed her daughter's cheek. "I know you can work through to a solution. As for Sasha Garland, she's to be pitied. She's one of those women who can't accept when a love affair is over. But don't let her destroy your marriage, Rowena, I beg of you. Don't cut your husband off from your trust. Allow him to speak to you."

Ronnie gave another deep sigh. "Mamma, Kel can charm the birds from the trees. He could convince you white was black. Whatever happens, both of us have to put aside our conflicts for Tessa's sake. You're coming for Christmas, aren't you?"

"Try to stop me." Bella's beautiful dark eyes flashed and she thumped her breast. "More than that, *cara*, I want Tessa to greet me with a big shout of joy. I believe this will happen as surely as I believe God is in His Heaven."

So the husband who had driven her away now lured Ronnie back to his own private kingdom.

CHAPTER FOUR

I'M HOME, Tessa thought, wanting to shout and shout with joy and excitement, but the evil magician somehow managed to stop her. Instead, she pointed downwards with her hand, down to her proper home, the place where she was born. The enchanted landscape shimmered in the quicksilver heat of mirage. Mirage was a wonderful illusory thing that created phantom billabongs and lakes right in the heart of the desert. Many an explorer had perished following these beautiful but treacherous apparitions, but nothing would happen to her.

Tessa knew and loved her homeland with a passion. Forever, forever the land would be with her. One day she would paint this place, so magical, so old—ancient, Daddy called it. This Timeless Land steeped in Aboriginal legend. She would become very famous for it. People would say, "Ah, yes, Tessa Warrender. She's a member of one of Australia's great pioneering families."

Driven by their vision, her ancestors had taken up this vast, isolated holding in the far south-west of colonial Queensland. In the middle of the great wilderness they had built a splendid house like the home they had left on the other side of the world. They called it Regina after the first English bride. Just eighteen years old but brave enough to confront an overpowering wild landscape, Regina Warrender had aristocratic blood in her veins and eyes like mine, Tessa thought. Eyes like Daddy's. Shining, lake-coloured eyes that had come down through the generations. Regina Warrender was an unforgettable woman. No evil magician could have driven the voice out of her.

It's important I find my voice, Tessa thought, her heart fluttering around in her chest like a wild little budgerigar. Regina was the place it would be found. She was sure of it. But it was too soon for the curse to be lifted. Why else didn't she cry out?

For one heart-stopping moment as they soared over the steep pink-and-orange walls of Jinka Bluff and commenced their descent onto the station's all-weather runway, Ronnie really thought Tessa was about to speak. She could feel the waves of excitement that emanated from her child.

Lord, hear my plea. Let Tessa speak, Ronnie prayed, her eyes glued to her daughter's profile. She crushed her long fingernails into the palms of her hands as Tessa's rosebud mouth opened as if to shout aloud. Her expression was so joyous it was beatific.

This was Tessa's physical and spiritual home. This splendid, untamed *infinity*. Baked red-ochre plains that ran on forever, lightly clothed with golden grasses, spinifex, mulga and mallee under the canopy of a blazing cobalt-blue sky. Painted on the roof of the huge hangar was the station's logo—a magnificent breeding bull, head lowered, tail swishing, beneath the boomerang-shaped caption, Regina Downs.

Tessa's huge silver eyes were stars in her delicate face. She reached for Ronnie's hand, squeezing it. Loving touches were an important part of their communication, as well as lots of hand holding, but for all Tessa's obvious rapture she never uttered a word or breathed a single cry.

Be patient, Ronnie thought. Let this wonderful place heal her. Below them, a long, snaking trail of cattle was being guided to water by stockmen on horseback; clouds of red dust rose from the trampled earth and turned into willy-willies that spiralled like a top over the endless sea of sand.

"Get ready for the big welcome, princess," Kel called to his little daughter, so precious to his heart. "You're *home*!" The fierce joy of his tone gave powerful emphasis to the word. *Home*. But he, too, was aware that Tessa, for all his willing her, hadn't broken her silence. Consternation and frustration were momentarily etched into his strong, handsome features. Surely home was the best treatment in the world. Tessa had a powerful connection to the land. As he did. The land would do its own counselling. Its power was great.

Ronnie, like her daughter was aware of a building excitement deep in her body. It had always been so. This utter fascination with a man and the wild grandeur of his desert home…Kel Warrender and Regina. You couldn't separate one from the other. Fifth generation of a colonial dynasty dedicated to the land. The Warrenders' English ancestors had had this same commitment over many centuries. It was in the blood.

Ronnie knew only too well the extended Warrender family hadn't been overly pleased when Kel had chosen a city girl to be his bride, but Ronnie hadn't just fallen head over heels in love with Kel Warrender. She had fallen completely under the spell of his desert kingdom.

Regina was Channel Country. The home of the cattle kings. A powerful place full of history and legend. This was the best cattle land on the continent, 350,000 square kilometres of Queensland's far south-west, so called because of the great network of braided channels that when fed by monsoonal rains of the tropical north turned the vast area into one magnificent, lush feeding lot.

It was an awesome place, Ronnie thought, this riverine desert, not only for its sheer size and timeless landscape, the terrifying spectacles of drought and flood, but also for its tremendous mystique. This was the most ancient geology on earth, little changed in thousands of years, with little or no intrusion by man. Just to walk over it was to feel it profoundly with all the senses. Then the most sublime factor of all—the coming of the wildflowers. It was a time she and Tessa adored, the beauty and vastness of the floral displays unparalleled on earth. Was it any wonder Tessa felt starved for the sight of her desert home? The city was alien, friendless to her. This was Tessa's world.

On the ground they were greeted by lines of stockmen standing to attention like soldiers on parade. The teacher at the station school, Annie Connelly, without peer at her job, was there with her young charges, children of the station staff, who when they were old enough would be sent off to boarding schools. Ronnie caught sight of Tom and Desley Gibbs. Tom, retired from his job of head stockman after a bad fall, now filled the role of major-domo with his wife, Desley, the long-time station housekeeper. Beside Desley were three of the Aboriginal house girls smiling merrily behind their thin, elegant hands. And last but far from least…Hilary. Hilary with her strong personality but no "give" in her nature. She was dressed as ever in unisex gear. In fact, with her commanding height, her Akubra pulled right down over her dark, short-cropped hair, she could at a distance have been mistaken for a lean young man.

Tessa made no move to run to her aunt, even as a child recognising the eccentricity in her, holding tightly to her mother's hand. But her face was turned like a sunflower's to the station line-up.

I must say hello to them, Tessa thought, with her free hand making rapid little finger signals to them, greetings, like deaf children used to communicate. Of course, the station people recognised her signals immediately, every last one of them. She knew they would, thrilling as they began to respond. Lovely! Some with one hand, others with two, the Aboriginal girls with their marvellous natural talent as dancers and mimers making of their little movements something hauntingly beautiful like a ballet.

She and Mummy loved this impromptu response, but Aunt Hilary strode towards them, the expression on her stern face making her look like she was about to call them all to order like a schoolteacher.

"Rowena, Tessa, welcome home," she said, putting out her hand. She shook Ronnie's resoundingly, then took Tessa's hand in her own. "Well now, you haven't grown much, have you?" she said with a gruffness that still held affection. "I was thinking I might get a great big hello."

The evil magician seized Tessa's throat. "I'm sure she'll speak when she's ready, Hilary," Ronnie said, responding to her little daughter's desperate touch, her tone calm and friendly.

Hilary shrugged. "I guess so." She turned her head, her strongly defined features softening unbelievably as Kel, who had been organising the luggage, moved towards them. "Hi, Bro! What sort of a trip was it?" she asked.

"Smooth. We all love flying." Kel stretched out a

hand and gently tweaked his daughter's long blonde ponytail. "That was a great way to say hello, flower face. You must be able to feel how happy everyone is to have you home. You and Mummy." His gaze caressed Ronnie, her lovely face and her slender body. "Life is going to be more fun, tons more exciting. I promise. Now it's December we're going to get out the Christmas tree and decorate it right up to the ceiling. Would you like that?"

Tessa gave him a great big smile and grasped his hand.

So it was as a family they went forward to greet everyone in turn. Ronnie was reduced to tears by her welcome, touched by the tide of liking and warmth that flowed towards her. It was genuine goodwill and a uniform protectiveness towards Tessa, who smiled very sweetly while tough, weather-beaten stockmen grinned at her encouragingly from ear to ear. Finally Tessa went to stand among the children, who stared at her with a kind of worship. She let Desley exclaim over her, then returned her hug before spontaneously beginning to play a hand-tapping game with the Aboriginal girls, who were always perfectly attuned to her.

It will come, Ronnie thought. It's *got* to come.

"I love them all," Tessa confided to her mother as they drove to the homestead, her small, upturned face so bubbling with joy that Ronnie planted a big kiss on her cheek.

"Speak up, Tessa. Let's all hear," Hilary brusquely urged from the front seat of the Jeep.

"She's okay, Hilary," Kel intervened tersely. "Just leave her alone."

"I'm only trying to help her. I want to do things for her." Hilary frowned. "Get her back to reality. We can't go around cosseting her."

"Just let her relax, Hilary." There was a decided edge of irritation in Kel's voice. "This is Tessa's first day home. The most wonderful Christmas present a father can have."

In the back seat, Tessa, who had lost a little of her exuberance at the sound of her aunt's tone, brightened up again. Her father was *overjoyed* at her return. Christmas was such a lovely time. She had dreamed of this, her mother and father living happily together again. She and Nicholas had prayed together. She glanced off to her left to see if he was still there.

He was. The whole universe was his home.

Ronnie lifted her rapt face to Regina homestead as though it were her first experience. Nothing had changed. It looked as marvellous as ever. A huge house, a proud house by anyone's standards, built substantially of brick rendered and painted white with wings added over the years so it sprawled over a considerable area.

The frontage comprising the original homestead and the major extensions to either side was broken by a series of beautiful bays, the whole structure completely surrounded by deeply shaded verandas. These verandas in turn were decorated by elegant wrought-iron lace, pillars, balustrades, brackets, fretwork, all opening to the verandas by way of French doors with shutters painted midnight-blue.

A creek ran at the homestead's feet, meandering through ten acres of home gardens kept lush and green by the use of bore water. The gardens had been planned in the 1860s by the legendary Regina. It was she who had determined it would bloom and survive in what was then and remained today a great desert wilderness. Masses and masses of scarlet bougainvillea flamed in the sunlight and a flowering jasmine that had been used as ground cover rose above the piers that lifted the single-storey building off the ground and decked the veranda balustrades in great waves of bridal white.

"Beautiful, isn't it?" Ronnie laughed. "Absolutely beautiful. So substantial it could stand for eternity."

Beautiful as you are, her husband thought, his eyes on her in the rear-vision mirror. She wore white linen slacks, a sleeveless linen shirt and a stylish studded belt around her narrow waist. Her long hair, pulled back and tied at the nape with a scarf, gleamed pure gold in a shaft of sunlight. She looked a delicate creature, even fragile. He would have to treat her with kid gloves.

"I'll show them through to their rooms, shall I?" Hilary asked, taking control the moment they were inside the front door.

"No need," her stepbrother answered. "You can see that lunch is ready on time, if you wouldn't mind."

"I've put Tessa across from her mother," Hilary informed him in clipped tones, beginning to move off.

Kel put the luggage down and shot a rapier look at her. "Tessa can sleep wherever she wants."

And what about me? Ronnie thought. Hilary had taken a long time to get used to another woman being mistress of the house. Now it was uncertain how Hilary felt about her being back in the picture. Certainly Hilary was acting as though she and Tessa were guests.

"Don't let her upset you," Kel said quietly, watching Ronnie's expression, the way her long lashes fluttered down onto her cheeks. "She means well. It's just—"

"She's never really wanted me here, Kel," Ronnie answered with simple truth. "Hilary badly needs to be mistress of her own home."

"God help the lucky fellow," Kel murmured in a voice that cracked with laughter. "Where did Tessa scoot off to?"

"She's just saying hello to the house again." Ronnie smiled.

"What about you? How do you feel?" His silver eyes moved intently over her face.

"Hyped up," she said honestly, full of hidden hungers and shadows. "When is Madelaine coming?"

He smiled at her, aware she was marshalling all her defences. "She promised faithfully she'd be here by next week. I told her Bella would be with us for Christmas. In fact, I think we might be crowded out with family. Mabs was delighted. She and Bella always did get on well."

He was right. Despite the great differences in their lifestyles, both women were at ease with one another. Both had suffered the sad fate of losing their husbands in agonising accidents. Sir Clive had died in a light-plane crash when the pilot, who was ferrying him around his various properties, ploughed into an es-carpment during a fierce electrical storm. That had been several years ago, devastating the family. Sir Clive had been such a big, strong, dynamic man that everyone had come to believe he would last forever. Sir Clive's outright approval had been very important to Ronnie. The fact that he had seen her as the right sort of wife for his son had mellowed the entire family.

"Come into the drawing room." Kel reached for her hand. "The house has missed you. I was thinking maybe it could do with a little refurbishment before Christmas."

"Hasn't Hilary arranged that?" she asked quickly, not wanting to cross that strong-willed, abrasive woman. "I don't want to put her out."

"What are we talking about here?" Kel glanced down at her, surprised. "You're my *wife*, Rowena. It's not a position you can put aside. Besides, you have exquisite taste. Decorating isn't Hilary's scene," he added dryly.

"So what do you have in mind?" Though it bothered her greatly, Ronnie didn't pull away. She felt the same old desire rushing to the surface of her skin like the bubbles in champagne. Still, she kept her poise, speaking in an almost professional voice. "It looks very grand as it is. One doesn't interfere with a beautiful historic home too much. Perhaps a few gentle changes. Actually I always did want to get rid of the wallpaper." She smiled wryly. "It's very beautiful in itself, but it's not the best backdrop for the paintings. They're important paintings. The eye shouldn't be distracted by the wallpaper design."

"I agree," Kel said.

It was her turn to be surprised. "But you *never* wanted the wallpaper removed."

"That was then," he said mildly, lifting her hand, looking down at their linked fingers. As usual, his body was responding to her. "Suddenly I can see what you saw all the time. One gets very used to one's home. You looked at it with fresh eyes."

"So I'm to be given free rein?" Pleasure and excitement beat in her blood. She turned her head, her gaze ranging over the long, spacious room with the series of French doors giving on to the veranda. As always, the large, ornately framed portrait of Regina Warrender that hung above the white marble fireplace caught her eye. It was a glorious portrait, the subject's skin so glowing Ronnie felt it would be warm to the touch.

Regina was dressed in a magnificent low-cut, ruby-red ball gown, diamonds and rubies at her throat and ears. She looked what she was—a woman of breeding. She had left her ancestral home in Lincolnshire,

England, to marry her adventure-loving second cousin, who had the outrageous idea he could build his own empire in colonial Australia. As a result, the Warrender family with freehold stations in every mainland State controlled an area as large as the country from whence they had come. The portrait of Regina commissioned by her adoring husband had been painted on a trip "home" when she was in her late thirties and at the height of her beauty. Less than six years later, leaving a husband and six children—four sons and two daughters—she had been laid to rest in the family cemetery some half a mile from the main compound, her death the result of being bitten by a taipan, one of the deadliest snakes in the world. These days, with antivenenes and the Royal Flying Doctor service, she might have survived. Then, such a bite meant certain death.

"How beautiful she was," Ronnie said quietly, staring up at the portrait. "How beautiful and how strong. A gentlewoman despite all she had to endure in a harsh new world. Childbirth in such isolation, deprivation, little female company of her own standing, her husband gone over long periods of time. Drought, flood, fire, illness. The mind boggles at what she had to cope with."

"She had a dream," Kel reminded her. "God knows the English are an indomitable lot. We know from her diaries she shared everything with her husband."

"'One reason why we get on so wonderfully well,'" Ronnie quoted from the diaries. "They were true partners in everything. Remember what she wrote when they wanted to acquire Parinka Run? 'Harry and I talked about it right through the night.'"

Kel gave her a long, speculative look. "I've a feeling they did that in bed."

"Probably. He was a very sexy man." Even saying it, her body began a slow burn.

"Speaking of beds," Kel said blandly, "perhaps we should consider moving back together?"

She closed her eyes and took a deep breath. "Shut up, Kel."

"We could, of course, establish a strict territorial line. Perhaps not quite down the middle. I'm a lot bigger than you."

"*No!*" She wasn't about to be taunted.

"Okay, so what is Tessa going to think?" he asked in a too gentle voice.

Ronnie shook her head. "I don't...I can't..." She felt the tension flowing out of her. When she was in his arms, he was her world.

"Of course, it will be just a front," Kel continued. "There's always the day bed. It's plenty big enough to accommodate little ole you."

"Don't joke," she warned.

"Don't you want to do everything you can to help Tessa?" he asked, genuinely believing the huge demand on his self-control was worth it.

"You know I do." Ronnie's dark eyes skimmed away from him. "But I don't want you jumping me in the dark."

He kept hold of her by one wrist. "You don't, eh? We used to do it all the time."

And I haven't forgotten, she thought. The turbulent clamouring of the senses, the ecstatic release. I'll never lose the memory of you, my lover.

He lifted her fingers to his mouth and kissed them. "Ronnie, I swear to you I will respect your wishes. I know what you've been through." The scent of her light perfume, her own skin, was wrapping itself around him like tendrils. Desire put a sheen on the fine, hard planes and angles of his face.

"You can't," she murmured, mind and heart at war. "Men and women see things differently. I've learned a very painful lesson. I never want to repeat it."

"You choose to continue to believe the worst of me, don't you?" he challenged, responding to her melancholy.

"God, Kel, I loved you so much!" You were all my hopes and dreams.

"You *still* love me." Aroused by her soft cry, he found himself grasping her slender arms and drawing her tight against his hungry body. "Lord, I can feel it."

For a moment, she put up a frenzied little struggle, trying to hold back the gathering momentum, but sensation built and broke over her like a giant wave. "I absolutely hate this," she gritted. Perversity was an extension of passion.

"Shut up." His voice was tight. Once they had been such glorious lovers. That couldn't possibly be lost, he thought. He lowered his head, malelike demanding her submission, his blood running red-hot. Anything was permissable between them. She had been away too long.

Kel wondered how he could contain himself not to catch her up. Carry her through to their beautiful bedroom overlooking the creek, make love so frenetically she would have to plead with him to take her to a place where there was only liberation from all conflict and a rapturous pleasure.

"Ronnie." Space and time receded. He poured every atom of a dynamic persona into the powerful sweetness of his kiss. He wanted to be so gentle with her. He had talked to himself so often about this very thing. Everything depended on it. Yet he needed her so badly just having her near him brought his control to the brink.

Ronnie, too, found herself near sobbing even when she was starved for the magic. Pride. Sometimes she had it. Sometimes she didn't. The trouble was, she loved him with a passion that blinded her.

"I'm sorry, I'm sorry," he crooned over her in contrition, feeling her heart fluttering under his hand like a trapped butterfly. "I want you so badly. You know I can't resist you."

The very air had turned electric. Ronnie felt her body rising to his in waves. His arms wrapped around her as though he would never let her get away. She wondered what would happen, but just then, light skipping footsteps sounded on the parquet of the hallway. The next moment, Tessa rushed into the drawing room, fresh from her exploration. When she saw her parents together, her mother locked in her father's strong arms, Tessa's mouth curved up in a big smile.

They'd been kissing—she knew it! Pure exaltation made her apple-blossom cheeks glow. It had to be all those prayers she and Nicholas were saying. She made a funny little noise in a throat that felt as smooth as honey. Not quite a word but a sound that had her parents smiling. She ran to them and grasped them around the knees, her small face uplifted, her long hair out of its ponytail like a golden flame. As a baby, they called it a group cuddle. She tried desperately to get the familiar request out, wondering if her father heard her. They were a family of three. Her father had to come back to them. Being apart had badly frightened her.

Looking down into his daughter's exquisite little face, Kel felt his heart melt. "My little love." He reached for her and swung her up into his arms. Tessa let her head fall forwards onto his broad shoulders, then snuggled in. It made her so happy to be back on Regina. So happy to see her mother's dark eyes glowing like pansies, safe within her father's arms.

The moment of togetherness warmed Tessa like the glorious Outback sun. It filled her with the brilliant radiance of its light. This was going to be the best Christmas ever. Mummy and Daddy loved each other. They loved her. Like Nicholas promised, she would soon win her voice back from the cruel magician so it would reach everyone's ears.

* * *

Lunch, set up in the breakfast room with its extensive views of the creek and the coolibah trees lining its banks, was surprisingly pleasant. Hilary, after an initial brusqueness, settled down to a more relaxed manner for which Ronnie was very grateful. Afterwards, while Tessa helped Desley, the housekeeper, clear away, Kel took Ronnie by the arm and guided her out the front door. "Look, I'd love to stay but there are a thousand and one things I have to attend to," he apologised, setting his pearl-grey Akubra at a rakish angle.

Ronnie nodded in agreement. "I understand perfectly, Kel." She knew as well as anyone the size of his job.

"About the bedrooms…" He smiled a little, his face handsome, debonair, mocking. "We're agreed on solidarity, right? We're Tessa's parents. That means as far as she's concerned, we sleep in the same bed. We always did."

"Are you considering tying me up?" she asked sarcastically even as her body pulsed. Her husband, her lover, her torment.

"Are we talking wrists to the bedposts?" he quipped, letting his sparkling eyes slide over her.

"No, we're not!"

"Really?" He raised his dark eyebrows. "Wouldn't you like me to tickle you all over with a feather? Make you laugh and cry and tremble and moan?"

He had done that before today, she thought, excitement skittling down her spine. "There's a simple answer," she managed coolly. "No." Then as an afterthought, "You devil!"

One arm snaked out around her narrow waist, pulling her into him. "You used to love me for it."

"Tell me about it." She was helpless against him. Him and his magnetism.

"Move into our bedroom, Ronnie," he urged. "The fact you're going to sleep on the couch can be *our* secret."

God, didn't she want it? Right or wrong, she was the victim of emotional and sexual deprivation. Slowly, aware of how she was giving in to him at every turn, Ronnie began to shake her head. It was then that he kissed her, stealing her will and her breath. He had such hunger, such energy, such passion—the powerful charisma she had fallen in love with. She was probably mad, but she knew Tessa would draw great comfort from seeing her parents together in their old bedroom. Consequently, when Tom came in with the rest of the luggage, she had him put what was hers in the main suite. The rest belonging to Tessa was left in the very pretty bedroom sometimes used as a guestroom almost directly opposite.

It was when she was settling Tessa, who had succumbed to the effects of their journey, for a nap when Hilary reappeared, standing in surprise at the doorway.

"What, no nursery?" she asked. The nursery was where Tessa had always slept.

Ronnie turned her head to smile. "Not anymore. Tessa has always loved this room."

"Well, it *is* pretty," Hilary agreed. "A bit too feminine for my taste. I expect it's the mural."

Eyes heavy, already half-asleep, Tessa nodded her head. Behind the beautifully carved bed that stood on a raised platform were two huge murals of Regina at the time of the wildflowers. They had been painted by a well-known Australian artist who'd often enjoyed hospitality on the station. Fantastic paintings, a touch surreal, they depicted the red plains thickly patterned in the white and gold glory of the everlasting daisies, the pink parakeelya, the scarlet desert peas, the blue gillyflowers, the native hibiscus and many more. It was a wonderful world of colour with the peacock-blue sky adorned with flights of outback birds—the brilliant parrots, the rose-pink galahs, the orange-and-crimson chats and, the phenomenon of the Outback, the flashing green fire of the budgerigar.

"Worth a fortune, those murals," Hilary observed, watching Ronnie walk so gracefully towards her. Ballet lessons, Ronnie always said. Now Hilary wished she had taken a few. She stood back, allowing her sister-in-law the lead, disguising her surprise when Ronnie walked into the main suite and immediately began to tackle the task of unpacking her luggage.

"It's wonderful to be back," Ronnie said diplomatically, watching Hilary subside into an armchair. "Thank you so much, Hilary, for all you've done. The flowers in all the rooms are lovely." She inclined her head towards a huge bowl of pink and cream roses on the circular library table.

"Desley handled all that," Hilary admitted wryly. "She's good at that sort of thing. I'm for the outdoors as you know."

"A splendid horsewoman," Ronnie said sincerely. Hilary had won countless trophies in her youth and up until a few years ago. Dressage, cross-country events, endurance races—you name it. In the right setting, Hilary shone.

"Which reminds me, Tessa must get back to her lessons." Hilary frowned. "Kel bought her the most beautiful pony. Did he tell you?"

"Not as yet." Ronnie felt disappointed and it showed.

"Hell, trust me to spoil the surprise," Hilary groaned. "And it was to be a big surprise."

"I won't let on." Relaxing, Ronnie smiled. "It's easy for these things to slip out." She removed several linen shirts from the case, then walked into the dressing-room for hangers.

"You're always so damned nice," Hilary said, remembering many other times. "I don't deserve it. Look, Ronnie—" she leaned forward "—can we lay things on the table? This is Christmas. A time of peace and goodwill."

"Suits me." Ronnie wondered what was coming.

"You're home for good, I take it?" Hilary asked, preparing to launch into her story.

"Well, we're trying to settle things, Hilary," Ronnie said. "Give it our best shot for Tessa's sake."

Hilary sighed deeply. "I was lied to, Ronnie," she said. "I was lied to and used. I should have acted as a conciliator. Instead, I fell for every last one of Sasha's phoney stories."

Ronnie turned around fully to stare at her. "Hilary, you persuaded me to *leave*, remember? Are you telling me now you lied?"

Hilary put her face down into her hands. Another woman would have cried. "I didn't *lie*, Ronnie. I'm never that bad. I truly believed what Sasha told me. Sasha was my friend. One of us. Lord, Ronnie, if you hadn't come along, Sasha would've been *family*. She and Kel were lovers at one time. I thought he'd gone back to her. She persuaded me of that. But I've since realised Sasha is an accomplished liar. She thought it *funny*, mind you, to use me. You have to remember when Kel went away on his trip, so did Sasha. I've since confirmed she only caught up with him that one time at the Sandpiper, wasn't it? To my endless remorse, I always let her know his exact whereabouts."

Ronnie felt ill. For more than a year… "This is hurting terribly, Hilary," she said. "Kel and I have lost precious time in our lives. Far more serious, look at what's happened to Tessa."

Hilary jumped up in angry despair. "I know, and I want to apologise most abjectly. But I had to tell you *my* side of the story, Ronnie. I was a fool. I was duped. You're everything I'm not, Ronnie. I've always liked you. I couldn't help it, but I was frightfully jealous of you. No man has ever looked at me as Kel looks at you. No man ever will."

Ronnie looked at her with haunted eyes. "You won't *let* anyone reach you, Hilary. I understand how it's been for you. You hide a vulnerable heart behind a brusque manner. If you'd only take a little advice, you could turn yourself into a striking-looking woman overnight. Everything you need is there, but you want a recognised style. I could help you. Mamma could help you."

"Bella?" Hilary's smile was hopeless. "She has offered in the past. I could *never* look like Bella. She's a very beautiful woman."

"I think so." Ronnie sank onto the bed, greatly upset but beyond anger. "You want to get out from under, Hilary. Take complete charge of your own life. You're blessed with looks, splendid health and a lot of money. Why don't you make it work for you?"

"I'm too scared." Hilary finally faced her fear.

"Never! A woman who can do what you can do?"

Hilary shrugged her physical skills off. "I don't have any charm like Kel. He's got it all."

"What you have to do, Hilary, is become more approachable," Ronnie suggested. "Relax and let people in."

Hilary resumed her chair. "Sasha used to laugh

about me behind my back. To my face, for that matter, but I pretended not to see it."

"Maybe I should've pointed that out," Ronnie said wryly. "Have you discussed this with Kel? How Sasha lied to you?"

"Now you're talking really scared." Hilary slumped in her seat, dismay in her eyes. "I adore my brother. He fills the greatest place in my heart, but when he gets going he's as formidable as Dad. He would hate me for wrecking his life."

"There's a chance he might tear a few strips off you," Ronnie had to admit. "But I think it's something you must do, Hilary. For all our sakes."

Hilary met Ronnie's eyes. "I'm *so* sorry." No tears, but her mouth trembled.

"I believe you, Hilary," said Ronnie of the soft heart, "and I accept your apology. It's Christmas, and forgiveness is the order of the day. I'm just wondering, though, how you found out about it."

Hilary gave a strained smile. "Sasha actually had the hide to fly in while Kel was away. She suggested she and Kel had picked up where they'd left off in Brisbane. I knew then for a fact she was lying. I was bitterly upset and angry. Kel never really loved Sasha. I see that now. She was simply *there*. Both families were promoting a match. We had it out, I can tell you. She failed every test. As did I. Every test of loyalty and integrity."

"I didn't behave all that sensibly, either," Ronnie

said. "You sowed the seeds of doubt, I guess, but if I'd used half my brain—"

"Don't lose Kel," Hilary said.

CHAPTER FIVE

THEY had the most wonderful time decorating the tree that evening. It rose in splendour to the beautiful plastered ceiling of the hall, the ceiling's scrollwork delicately picked out in muted tones of gold, ivory and blue. Tom Gibbs had brought the artificial tree in from the storeroom and assembled its many green branches while Tessa enjoyed her afternoon nap. But it was left to the family to decorate the tree.

There were glittering baubles, bells and ornaments galore, all packed away in boxes from year to year. Metres and metres of silver and gold, emerald and ruby roping were unwound to twine around the pendulous branches of the lofty pyramid as the enchanting sound of classic Christmas carols of the world resonated through the rooms. Even Hilary got into the spirit of it, handing sparkling ornaments to Tessa as she ran to and fro.

Finally it was time for Kel to place the Christmas angel at the top of the tree, and Tessa's huge silvery

eyes, so poignant in repose, filled with joy. She sub-
sided to the floor beside her mother, the ankle-length
skirt of her pretty cotton voile dress pooling around her.

"That's Nicholas on top." Tessa leaned in to her
mother confidentially. "Not really Nicholas, of course.
Nicholas is too big. Big as Daddy."

This was news. "Nicholas is big?" Given up to surprise, Ronnie stared into her daughter's eyes. "But I
thought Nicholas was the same size as you. Smaller
even. Elf-sized."

"No, no, Mummy." Tessa shook her head. "He's
tall and so *wonderful*! He's not like us. He's more a
shape. Like a shape inside a light bulb. Only his wings
are very clear. They have feathers like the swans, but
they're all tipped with gold. And they're *big*! They go
up past his shoulders and almost down to the ground."

A child's fantasy, of course. "Such a vivid imagination, my darling." Ronnie hugged her daughter to
her. "How marvellous it is to see with the eyes of a
child."

"But he's right there beside you, Mummy." Tessa
looked matter-of-factly to Ronnie's left.

"*Is* he?" For a few seconds, Ronnie actually felt her
mind reel. It was even the least bit scary.

"Don't worry, Mummy," Tessa said, a gentle, reassuring hand on her mother's shoulder. "Everything
will be all right."

"How's it look, girls?" Kel called, breaking up the
rapt moment and capturing their attention.

Tessa was so excessively happy that Ronnie really thought her daughter might call out an answer, but though she sprang to her feet and clapped her hands in delight, she stopped short of putting her feelings into words.

"Well, that's it. I'm off to bed," Hilary announced, smothering a yawn. "Got to be up at dawn. Where is it tomorrow, Kel?"

By this time, Kel had descended the ladder and snapped it back together. "The Twenty Mile. You don't *have* to come if you don't want to. You might prefer to stay at home. We'll have lots of people flying in from now on. Most folk like to deliver their Christmas greetings in person."

"Don't I know. But I like to be outdoors. Ronnie's here to take care of everything." Hilary rose to her feet, then bestowed on them all a surprisingly warm smile. "We'll have to have a billabong barby soon, Tessa," she suggested. "Remember how great they were?"

Remembering, Tessa started forwards and gave her aunt a big hug, causing Hilary to experience a tremendous rush of affection not unmixed with her many regrets.

"Come on, sweetheart." Kel spoke to Tessa gently, grateful things were going so well. "Time for you to hit the sack. We have wonderful things planned for tomorrow."

Tessa went willingly, holding tightly to her parents' hands. Here on Regina she was no longer uncertain and afraid. God really did love her. He would set her free.

Ronnie spent a long time in the bath, luxuriating in

the scented bubbles even when her mind kept turning over all the events that had almost brought her marriage to the brink. The web of lies and deceit, the different relationships that had caused it, her own inexperience in handling the situation. She should have marched up to Kel and Sasha that night she'd found them withdrawing from an embrace—or *thought* she had. Her mother had probably been right. Sasha had engineered the whole thing. She should have demanded facts not fantasies. She should have confided in her husband when it all began to happen instead of simply accepting the situation.

She had never spoken to Kel about it. She had cloistered her intense fears about the stability of her marriage, feeding her natural jealousy and feelings of betrayal, denying him her body even as she burned with her own fierce desire.

She had known all about Sir Clive's affairs. The terrible mistake she had made was her readiness to condemn Kel simply because he was his father's son. Now remembering, she realised Kel, for all his strong passions, was a far more caring and deeply committed man. A rock to lean on. Pity Hilary when she had to tell him her part in the whole sorry business! But from the misery and remorse locked up in Hilary, she would have to speak out if she wanted to stay fairly sane.

It might help, Ronnie thought, if she asked her mother to bring several outfits with her for Hilary. Bella would love that. She had often spoken sympathetically about Hilary's failure to exploit her potential. Style and design were born in Bella.

Kel had been so sensitive tonight. So sensitive and tender. A magician with Tessa. Why Tessa wouldn't speak to her father when she adored him was the greatest mystery. Maybe Tessa's fears and anxieties had almost literally choked her. And that talk about Nicholas! Tessa had undoubtedly got it all from Ronnie's own beautifully illustrated book on angels through the ages. Tessa had artistic talent. Tessa had great imagination. The two had come together. Even the shape inside the light bulb. That would be the halo of light artists usually employed in their paintings of angels. The radiance. If it wasn't so wonderful, it would be bizarre.

When she finally emerged from the bathroom, her matching peach satin robe over her satin-and-lace nightgown, she could see Kel's tall, lean frame silhouetted against the silvery moonlight that slanted across the veranda.

Despite the fact her bare feet made little sound on the carpet, he turned his head and called to her. "Come on out. It's the most beautiful night. The Southern Cross is right over the house."

How many times had they stood on the same veranda, Kel with his arms wrapped around her, watching the night sky? The stars were breathtakingly beautiful over the desert. They crammed the sky, glittering like great handfuls of diamonds thrown down on black velvet.

"You smell delicious," he said when she came to stand near his shoulder, for a moment closing his eyes in bliss.

"Gardenia."

"And you. I've always loved the woman scent of you." Try to keep it light, he thought desperately as desire knifed into him. The breeze made a little rush for them, whipping Ronnie's blonde hair back over her shoulders. The moonlight pearled her beautiful skin.

"Tessa had a wonderful time tonight," she said with evident gratitude. "Her eyes shone. You're marvellous with her, Kel. You always were."

"So when is she going to speak to me?" he asked resignedly.

"I know she will," Ronnie promised. "She's super sensitive. We have to give her more time. Regina will do its healing."

The certainty of her tone moved him profoundly. "You sound as if you really believe that."

"I do." She stared up at the purple sky, the glorious embroidery of stars. "Regina and her friend Nicholas."

"Ah, Nicholas." He laughed indulgently. "She's always had a wonderful imagination." He was filled with the urge to draw his wife into his arms and take what was his.

"She sees him as an angel," Ronnie was saying as though it was a mystery.

"Then I'm glad of it." He made himself turn towards the bedroom. "The angels are here to help us. You must be tired, Ronnie. It's been a long day."

"I am a bit," she told him while her whole body vibrated for his touch. "Tessa should sleep well. She goes right through the night."

He allowed himself to lightly brush her with his lips. "You're trembling. Please don't. I promised you I'd make no demands on you."

So why don't you? she wanted to cry out in perversity, lacking the right words. "So it's the day bed?" she asked.

"Darling, it *has* to be," he said wryly. "I'm not made of steel. Come into bed with me and I'll totally lose it. You know where my heart lies."

She watched him for a moment, looking so at a loss he thought he would never overcome the doubt in her.

"This is damned ridiculous," he burst out, the bronze skin of his splendid torso gleaming in the light. Once, *she* had worn the top of his pyjamas. "You sleep in the bed. I was only having you on. I have a sleeping-bag tucked away in the dressing-room. I've slept on hard ground countless times."

She put out a hand to stop him. "No, Kel. I'll curl up here. I'm so tired I'll go straight to sleep. You need your rest. You're up at dawn."

Just so he wouldn't argue the point, she lay down on the comfortable day bed and pulled the light rug over her.

"Aren't you going to take off your robe?" he asked her.

"Of course." She threw the rug off and stood up again, letting the luscious garment slip down her arms.

She stood there, slim and lovely in her shimmering nightdress, so lovely he drew in a single ragged breath, his face taut.

"Welcome home, girl. Here, give me that." He all but snatched the robe from her and settled it over a chair. "Good night, Ronnie," he added. "Sleep well." While I take another cold shower, he thought, his frustration boundless.

Ronnie burrowed her head into the pillow, making herself small. What sort of fool was she to shut out love?

She woke up with a wail not unlike Tessa's when she'd had a bad dream.

"Ronnie, sweetheart, what's the matter?" Kel was on his feet immediately, fully alert, guarding the sleeping princess. His wife. He snapped on a lamp, then went down on his haunches and stared at her. "Darling, you're crying." Tears tracked down her cheeks. She appeared to be foundering in grief. "Ronnie!"

On a great wave of love, he hauled her into his arms, feeling her fragility. He carried her to the bed and settled her head against the pillows before sitting down on the side of the bed and taking her hands. "Can't you tell me?"

In the glow from the lamp, her velvety dark eyes were huge, long lashes stuck together in spikes. She looked almost as young as Tessa. Defenceless, vulnerable. He lifted her hands to his mouth and kissed every finger. "Don't you give me a hard time," he groaned.

"I love you, Kel," she said, his very touch making her tremulous. "Yet I've treated you so badly. I should have had more wisdom, more experience. I should have challenged Sasha's claims of an illicit affair. I should have talked the whole thing over with you. Instead, I bottled up all my fears. I was sick at heart I might lose you."

Emotion caught at his throat-a deep understanding of what she had been through. "My darling, that's never going to happen," he answered with compelling fervour. "Don't be so hard on yourself. I made plenty of mistakes. The thing was, we were trying to settle into our marriage after a whirlwind engagement. What should have been so simple—the growth of trust and confidence in one another—was being eroded by deliberate deception."

"I realise that now," Ronnie sighed. "Sasha sabotaged me at every turn. I made it easy for her by letting her play on my insecurities. She fooled Hilary, too. I know Hilary is sorry for that."

His laugh was a little rough. "And so she should be."

"Then I thought I saw you and Sasha together," she finally confessed, her voice low and somewhat hesitant. "Or rather I saw the two of you withdrawing from what I interpreted as a passionate embrace."

His quick, indrawn breath moved her hair. "When was this?" He made no attempt to hide the dismay that overwhelmed him.

She looked into his eyes, finding them very direct

and crystal clear. "I'm going back a few years," she explained. "It was when the Monaro Cup finals were held on Regina. We had a gala weekend, remember?"

"Of course I remember." His black brows knotted. "And you caught me kissing Sasha?" he asked in simple disbelief. It had never happened.

"She was in your arms," Ronnie whispered, leaning forward so her upper body fused with his.

"Sweetheart!" Kel's arms closed strongly around her. "I beg you to believe there was no affair going on behind your back. Goodness, woman, did I ever conceal my love and longing from you? You were and remain the only woman in my life. You're everything I want. As for Sasha, I can't honestly recall anything much about her that weekend. She does as she damned well pleases. Some people are like that. All I can recall is having a wonderful time with you, watching the way you enchanted all my friends. Sasha is one reckless character. Married or not, she'd think nothing of trying to coax a kiss out of a man. That's the way she is. But as far as I'm concerned, you could never have seen me kissing her. It simply didn't happen. What's far more likely is you saw me attempting to maybe cool her ardour. In other words, holding her off.

"You should have kept on coming, Ronnie, instead of steering away. You should have yelled 'Hands off, Sasha. That man is my husband.'" A gentle smile curled up his mouth.

"I suppose." She smiled ruefully at his tone. "But

think for a moment, Kel. They were early days in our marriage. I was trying to establish myself as your wife. I know no one expected you to marry a city girl. Sasha tried to undermine our marriage almost as soon as it began. She manipulated Hilary into helping her."

"I know." For a moment, his striking face looked grim. "She did a lot of unforgivable things, Ronnie. It comes under the heading of obsession. But I'm sure we won't be bothered by Sasha any more. She's done her sorry dash and she knows it. When she tricked her way into my hotel room in Brisbane, she finally confessed she'd been lying about what allegedly happened at the Sandpiper. I've been waiting for the right moment to tell you. To put all your doubts to rest.

"Sasha got into my room then via the veranda that runs around the top suites. In her own words, I was out of it and she took advantage of the situation. Her claim I made love to her wasn't true. It was a cheap, dangerous, ugly lie. I think in her heart of hearts she's ashamed."

Ronnie closed her eyes, feeling the healing power of his love and loyalty. "I can't bring myself to forgive her."

"Not when it caused so much pain," he agreed. "Not when our separation damaged our child. Anyway…" With one smooth, purposeful movement, he was in bed beside her, drawing her trembling body powerfully into his arms. "…we're not going to waste another word on Sasha. She has nothing to do with our life. I want to talk about us."

"Oh, yes!" She turned her face into his bare chest, feeling the delicious tickle of the hair that matted it on her soft cheeks. "We've lost so much time," she groaned, hugging his lean, strong body that had given her so much ecstasy.

"Darling, there's still so much time for us," he reassured her. "Lots of love. Lots of living. I want you, Ronnie, more than I can ever tell you. No one and nothing is ever going to part us again." He lifted her hand and pressed his lips to her palm. "We're together. Alone together. And I'm half mad for you."

"Shall we test that?" she urged huskily.

"My God, yes!" His hands moved to shape her breasts, luxuriating in their sweet, tender weight before locking her closer, half-covering her arching, yearning body with his own. "My wife! My darling heart!" A powerful force was gathering in him, the glorious intensity of the dominant male. "I'm going to love you...love you...!" His blood was glowing, fired by the fuel of his boundless desire.

We can make a baby, Ronnie thought, winding her slender arms around his neck like the tendrils of a vine. The time is just right. She was dazzled by how beautiful the idea seemed. Truly inspired. A son to make their family complete.

She opened her mouth, her heart, her warm woman's body, feeling it pinned by her husband's dynamic strength. The flood of moonlight in the room was like heaven—unutterably beautiful. A miracle. This was truly a miracle.

One of many.

EPILOGUE

THE weeks before Christmas rushed through Ronnie's fingers like the sands of the desert. Family arrived. Madelaine first, laden with presents that she and Tessa set under the tree. Then Bella with her complement of things and a new surprise wardrobe for Hilary that would set her back a few thousand dollars, followed by aunts, uncles, cousins. The huge old homestead embraced them all. People from all over the Outback flew in and out, an annual migration every Christmas to deliver personal greetings.

Desley and her staff were kept busy providing morning and afternoon tea. Magnificent rich Christmas cakes were cut. Toasts drunk. Goodwill and good humour flowed. It was a hectic but a happy time even though the great blessing they all prayed for had been denied them.

Though every last member of the family kissed Tessa and folded her in their arms, she never spoke to them. A tragedy, they thought, the only hope lying in her communications with her mother. Everyone had worried dreadfully that Kel's marriage might be over. Rowena, after all, had walked out, but that little episode was very obviously over. They appeared to be more in love than ever. A few within the circle knew of Sasha's treachery, but they weren't talking. The great thing was that this marriage endured.

Ronnie decided to make Christmas Eve very special. She poured over recipes with Desley, both deciding on a buffet to be served in the long, screened rear terrace overlooking the turquoise swimming pool. The pool was being given lots of use in the Christmas heat. Tessa was allowed to stay up until nine-thirty, but she was made aware she had to be well and truly in bed before Santa Claus made his rounds.

She had been very excited all day, spurred on by the presence of three of her cousins, all a little younger but bundles of joyful energy. The children were to be given adorable, handcrafted teddy bears all dressed up in Christmas finery—white "fur"-trimmed crimson velvet coats and matching bonnets. The wonderful presents would come later on Christmas morning. Tessa went to bed that afternoon for a nap with a singing heart, tears of joy and thankfulness in her eyes. Her imprisoned voice was about to escape.

Ronnie took great care dressing that evening. She wanted to look a dream for her husband. Her final choices narrowed down to two dresses for evening. Pink sequined stretch tulle over an under slip, the other rose-red silk georgette, hand beaded and sequined around the low oval neck and around the sleeveless armholes, the exquisite fabric decorated with sparkling beaded and sequined open scrollwork.

It was Christmas so the red won out. She would wear the South Sea drop pearl earrings Kel had given her, leave her hair out but brushed back over her shoulders. Like Tessa, she was so excited her stomach felt full of shooting stars. It was an extraordinary feeling. One she remembered experiencing before.

Kel came back to their bedroom just as she was putting on her earrings. They had all decided to dress for the party, so he wore a sand-coloured summer suit with a fine quality open-necked blue dress shirt. He looked so vivid, so vital, so handsome and elegant she felt like falling against him in rapture. They were deliriously happy. It was like being transported. They made love all the time, in their bed, twice in the deep green seclusion of Pink Lady Lagoon. They might have been newly married, aching for each other, insatiable.

"Now that's what I call a dress," he said, whistling under his breath. "You look ravishing, Mrs. Warrender."

"All for you." Ronnie twirled.

"I'll remember long after my hair turns white." He went over to her and stood so close their bodies were brushing.

Ronnie put up her hand and touched his mouth very gently with her fingers while he blew softly against them. A tender gesture but incredibly erotic.

"I want you again," he murmured, his tone so lover-like it lit her eyes. They had made love very early that morning when the dove-grey sky was streaked with pink and lemon.

"And you can have me," she replied quietly but emotionally. "Any day. Any time."

"I think I might hold you to that." His hands came up to lightly caress her beautiful breasts. They seemed a little fuller, the nipples swelling like tiny raspberries against his palms. "Ronnie, my love, I love you so much."

She sighed, closing her eyes with rapture. "Do you have any idea what happens when you touch me?"

"I'm good at this sort of thing." He studied her with intense feeling.

"Oh, you *are*!" With a considerable effort, she opened her eyes. Her stomach jabbed her again with those funny shooting stars.

"All right." He was acutely aware of her, the extraordinary sheen on her, the emotional depth of her black-lashed eyes.

"I'm fine." She gave a little bubbling laugh. "Maybe running a bit on full throttle. It's been a very exciting time."

"None better," he agreed fervently, dropping a quick kiss on her brow. "But for now we'd better go join the family. The celebrations are already under way."

It was a wonderful time for all, adults and children. Everyone had their photographs taken in their Christmas finery in front of the tree; the Christmas carols were replaced with other tunes so those who wanted to could dance. Kel with his power and grace was a marvellous partner. He was a born dancer as Ronnie had often told him, but he shrugged that off as a joke. It was at one point when he spun her towards the shadowy end of the terrace that she felt her breath almost leave her, so dizzy only for Kel's support, she would have fallen to her knees. In fact, he had to catch her as she slumped into a faint.

Shocked and dismayed, Kel swept her up into his arms almost unnoticed, then carried her into the library and laid her down on the leather couch. He sank onto his knees, gently slapping her wrists. "Ronnie, Ronnie…" He had seen these faints before and his heart gave a great bound. "Darling, speak to me."

In the next moment, Ronnie rallied, opening her eyes on her husband's face. She had never seen him so pale. "Heavens, did I faint?"

"You sure did. Frightened the hell out of me."

"I'm so sorry."

Tessa raced into the room, anxiety imprinted on every delicate feature of her face and in every line of her small body. What was the matter with Mummy? She had nearly fallen over. Surely all the enchantment she had seen around them wasn't over?

Her father directed a swift look at her. "Stay with Mummy for a moment, sweetheart. She's all right, but I'll get Sam to take a look at her." Sam, Tessa knew, was Daddy's cousin, a doctor.

While her father hurried out of the room, Tessa went to her mother and stared at her with anguished eyes. "Are you sick, Mummy?" Her heart pounded in her chest. "Are they going to take you away?"

This brought Ronnie, who had been lying quietly exploring all the sensations in her body, to her senses. She pulled her little daughter into her arms and kissed her cheek repeatedly. "My precious girl, don't be silly. Mummy's fine." To her astonishment, she found herself adding, "I always faint when I'm pregnant. I did it with you."

Had she really said that? For all her daydreaming, was it true? In an instant, Ronnie accepted its certainty from a great joyous power.

"What?" Looking ecstatic, Tessa laid her hand on her mother's shoulder. "What did you say, Mummy?"

"I'm pregnant, my darling," Ronnie smiled tremulously. "Are you happy?"

Am I happy? Tessa thought. I'm delirious with joy. She kissed her mother's cheek resoundingly, then raced purposefully for the door, her feet sprouting wings, her small body full of vigour.

"Daddy, Daddy," she shouted so loudly it galvanised the small group who were hurrying along the corridor—her father, her two grandmothers and Dr Sam. "Mummy's pregnant!" she announced on a tidal wave of happiness. Her grey eyes sparkled like stars; a lovely big smile curved her mouth. "Did you hear me?" she cried with the same wonderfully animated pitch, launching herself headlong into her father's waiting arms. "Mummy's going to have a baby. A little brother for me. It's wonderful! Nonna, Mabs?" She looked to her grandmothers for confirmation. "I'm going to name him Nicholas. For Christmas."

Kel bowed his head with profound gratitude, kissing his daughter's blonde head. "So you shall, princess," he promised, his vibrant voice thick with emotion. "So you shall."

On the terrace, someone changed the dance tunes back to Christmas carols. Immediately, familiar, heartwarming strains soared through the house, touching them all with magic.

"Joy to the World."

Miracle on Christmas Eve

SANDRA MARTON

Sandra Marton wrote her first novel while she was still in primary school. Her doting parents told her she'd be a writer someday and Sandra believed them. In secondary school and college, she wrote dark poetry nobody but her boyfriend understood, though looking back, she suspects he was just being kind. As a wife and mother, she wrote murky short stories in what little spare time she could manage, but not even her boyfriend-turned-husband could pretend to understand those. Sandra tried her hand at other things, among them teaching and serving on the Board of Education in her home town, but the dream of becoming a writer was always in her heart.

At last, Sandra realised she wanted to write books about what all women hope to find: love with that one special man, love that's rich with fire and passion, love that lasts forever. She wrote a novel, her very first, and sold it to Mills & Boon® Modern™. Since then, she's written more than sixty books, all of them featuring sexy, gorgeous, larger-than-life heroes. A four-time RITA® award finalist, she's also received five *Romantic Times Magazine* awards and has been honoured with RT's Career Achievement Award for Series Romance. Sandra lives with her very own sexy, gorgeous, larger-than-life hero in a sun-filled house on a quiet country lane in the north-eastern United States.

Look for Sandra Marton's latest novel,
Dante: Claiming His Secret Love-Child,
available in December 2009 from
Mills & Boon® Modern™.

Dear Reader,

I remember the Christmases of my childhood with special fondness. I grew up in New York, where chimneys and shingled rooftops were few. Still, on Christmas Eve I hoped to hear sleigh bells and the clip-clop of reindeer hooves.

Santa isn't real. There's no gentleman in a red suit, no sleigh, no goodie-filled sack…but what if there were? What if Santa could reach into that sack and pull out a miracle, just when you needed one?

That's my Christmas wish to you, dear reader. A miracle, just when you need it most.

With love,

Sandra Marton

CHAPTER ONE

NICK BRENNAN figured that Scrooge had gotten it right.

Christmas was definitely the most overrated holiday of the year. He'd had plenty of time to think about it, considering that he'd been stalled in a barely-moving line of traffic for the past forty-five minutes.

A horn blared angrily behind him, setting off an answering chorus from a dozen other cars.

Nick smiled thinly. Right. As if that would change anything. This was New York traffic. Friday afternoon New York traffic, the Friday afternoon before Christmas. Anybody dumb enough to be trapped in it deserved what he got.

Including him.

'Stupid,' Nick muttered, tapping his fingers impatiently against the steering wheel.

That was the only word for it. He'd been living in Manhattan for almost a decade. He knew the score. Even his PA, who was just a few years out of some

Iowa cornfield, knew that leaving New York today wasn't terribly bright.

She'd tried to talk him out of it.

'Why don't you let me phone around, see if I can't book you onto a flight to Vermont?' Ellen had said.

He'd given her a bunch of reasons, all of them logical. Because she'd never find a seat for him at the last minute. Because not even the charter service Brennan Resorts employed would be available at the eleventh hour. Because even if she lucked out, who knew for how much longer anything would be able to take off? The weatherman, as usual, had gotten it wrong. The predicted light snow was about to turn into a major storm.

Nick had told Ellen all those things. The only thing he hadn't told her was the truth. He was driving to North Mountain because he hoped the six hours on the road would give him time to talk himself out of reaching it.

Oh, he'd come up with practical reasons for going. After all, he owned the mountain now, most of it, anyway, the same as he owned the cabin that stood on its crest. And, as soon as the details were settled, his people would bring in the equipment necessary to demolish the cabin and start work on the newest Brennan resort. Nick was a hands-on kind of guy. He always looked a site over before work began. It was, according to Wall Street, one of the reasons for his success.

But nobody was going to bring in any kind of equipment, until the harsh New England winter ended in April, or maybe even May.

No matter how you looked at it, there wasn't a reason in the world to make the trip now.

Nick blew out his breath.

A couple of months ago, he hadn't even known he owned North Mountain. His people had brought him an estate deal that contained several prime parcels of land in New England. Nick had moved fast, as he always did, and quickly given them the okay to make the buy.

He'd had no idea the mountain was part of the package. Not that he'd have cared, if he'd known. The mountain was perfect for development, and no amount of sentimental claptrap would change that. No, it wasn't sentiment that was sending him to Vermont.

Vermont, in December.

Christmas carol time. Horse-drawn sleigh time. Cold, star-studded night time...

Holly time.

Seven years ago come Monday morning, he and Holly had been married. One year later to the day, they'd agreed to a divorce.

And all of it had begun on North Mountain, in a cabin a million miles from anywhere.

The horn behind him blasted Nick into reality. He shot a nasty look into his mirror and inched the Explorer forward.

Okay. So, the realization that he'd bought the mountain, and the cabin, had hit him hard. That had surprised him. He didn't think about his once-upon-a-time marriage anymore. Hell, why would he? Nick's jaw tightened. He'd made a mistake. So what? Life was like that. You made a mistake, you rectified it and moved on. The one thing you never did was look back.

Then, what was he doing, sitting in this God-awful traffic, heading for the place where he'd made his biggest mistake? It made no sense.

Maybe it did. Maybe it would help him get rid of the memories.

Memories of Holly, wearing a flannel nightgown instead of the silky one she'd bought for their honeymoon, because the cabin had been so cold that first night...until he'd slowly stripped her of the gown and warmed her with his body. Memories of Holly, laughing after he'd tumbled her down in the snow, shrieking when he threatened to wash her face in it...her smile fading, turning soft and sexy as she became aware of the sudden pressure of his aroused flesh against hers.

Nick's hands tightened on the steering wheel.

Memories were all they were, foolish shadows of a dead past, and they made no sense because he wasn't in love with the woman in those memories. Not anymore. Not ever, when you came right down to it. Holly, herself, had been an illusion. A fantasy, conjured up by the lonely kid he'd once been.

He needed closure.

Nick almost laughed. Closure. The most popular word in the good old U.S. of A. Every two-bit TV talk show, every tune-in-and-spew-your-guts radio shrink, went on and on about closure. And, yeah, dumb or not, maybe that was what he needed. No point pretending that the seventh anniversary of his failed marriage hadn't affected him. How could he not be affected by the death of a dream?

Nick shifted his long legs. Okay. He'd go to the mountain, spend a few days, and find 'closure.' He'd bury his memories the same way his crew would bury the cabin, once Spring came, once his attorneys got things sorted out. The mountain was Nick's, but there'd been a rider attached to the deed, a 'no commercial construction' clause the owner had tacked on before he'd sold.

No problem. His people would find a way around the stipulation, and he would find a way around the memories. He'd see the cabin, walk the mountain one last time—and then a construction crew would come in, level the place and start building the most luxurious ski resort in New England. It would be the newest, finest Brennan resort in the chain and all the 'closure' a man could possibly want.

And, in the process, he'd have himself a weekend off. Time to unwind, enjoy a break. No boardrooms. No meetings. No desk heaped with memos. Not that he'd be cut off completely. A three-room cabin high on top of a Vermont mountain, no matter how plush, was not an eight-room penthouse, or three floors of office space on Fifth Avenue, but Nick had come prepared. He had his cellular phone in his pocket, his portable computer on the seat beside him, and his wireless fax on the floor.

The guy behind him honked again.

Nick felt his blood pressure zoom. For one sweet moment, he thought about getting out of the Explorer, marching back to the jerk's car, banging on the window and asking the guy if he really, honestly thought things would go any faster with him leaning on his horn…

The breath hissed from his lungs.

Closure was what he needed, all right.

He was angry at Holly, angry at himself, and he had been for six long years because he'd never had the chance to tell her the truth, that he'd never loved her, not really, that she wasn't the only one who'd made a mistake.

Not that he'd ever get the chance to tell her anything. But going to the cabin, to the mountain, would be the next best thing. He'd feel better, afterwards. He wouldn't snarl at Ellen, bark at his staff, sit in traffic with his adrenaline pumping as if he were a boxer waiting for round one to begin.

The tail lights ahead of him winked. Slowly, miraculously, the line of vehicles began moving. Nick downshifted. It was one of the great mysteries in New York, how you'd be creeping along, measuring your success in inches and all of a sudden, the road would open up. It was like life. You'd plod along and then, wham, wings would sprout on your feet and you'd find yourself flying, measuring your success in millions of dollars instead of the twenty bucks still in your pocket after all the bills were paid...

Measuring it alone. Always alone, no matter how many well-wishers crowded around, no matter what the papers said or how many gorgeous women you were with, because the only woman you'd ever wanted to share your success was gone, had been gone for six years, would always be gone...

The horn sounded. Nick shot a look at his mirror and glared at the guy in the Chevy. Then he shot into the fast lane, poured on the gas, and let the Manhattan skyline fade into the fast-gathering darkness of the winter night.

Holly Cabot Brennan figured she'd reach the top of North Mountain in two or three millennia.

She frowned, bit down lightly on her bottom lip, and tried to see through the whirling snow.

At the rate she was going, even that might be too much to expect.

The old guy at the gas station had tried to warn her. He'd looked at her, her rented car and the sullen sky through rheumy eyes and announced that she'd need more than a full tank to get much further.

'Gonna be a bad 'un,' he'd said, in the clipped, Down-East twang she hadn't heard in years.

Holly had smiled politely. 'The weatherman says the storm's not going to hit until after midnight. Besides, I'm not going very far.'

'Weathuhman's wrong,' the old gent replied. 'How far you goin'?'

'Not very,' Holly said, looking over at the battered ice machine that stood beside the gas station office. 'Does that thing work?'

'Aye-up, it works, though why you'd be wantin' ice in the dead of winter is beyond me.'

Holly thought of the big ice chest she'd crammed into the trunk. It was stuffed with shrimp, lobsters, lobster tails, butter, clams, oysters and assorted other goodies. Then she thought of trying to explain all that to the old man.

'I've got some stuff in an ice chest,' she said, leaving off the details. 'And I figure, just in case they forgot to clean out the freezer and turn it on, up in the cabin…'

'Cabin on North Mountain?' The old guy looked at her as if she were certifiably insane. 'Is that where you're goin'?'

'Uh-huh.' Holly popped open the trunk, dropped coins into the ice machine, then marched back to the car with two bags of cubes. 'You just about finished there?'

'Won't have much worry about the freezer bein' on, Missy. Storm like the one that's comin', you won't have no power at all. Assumin' you'll make it to the top, that is, which you most likely won't.'

Holly shut the ice chest, then the trunk, and wiped her gloved hands on her wool slacks.

'Ever a font of good cheer,' she said brightly. 'Okay, how much do I owe you?'

'Chains.'

'I beg your pardon?'

'Chains,' the old guy said. Holly held out a twenty-dollar bill, and he took it from her hand. 'Bettah still, you ought to have a cah with four-wheel drive.'

'I've driven up the mountain before,' Holly replied politely. 'I'll be fine.'

'Aye-up, most times, mebbe.' He cocked an eye towards the sky. ' But there's a storm comin' in.'

'Not really,' she said, even more politely. 'The weather reports say—'

The old man's lip curled. 'Don't care what they say.' Carefully, he plopped Holly's change into her outstretched hand. 'Storm's comin'. Bad one. You at least got them new-fangled brakes in that car?'

What new-fangled brakes? Holly almost said. She hadn't owned a car in years. What was the point, when you lived in the heart of Boston? Besides, she'd spent the past six months in a Tuscan farmhouse, up to her elbows in olive oil, plum tomatoes, and garlic, and the last three weeks on a whirlwind tour across the States, signing copies of *Ciao Down With Holly*, the book that had come out of her stay in Tuscany. She knew all there was to know about the differences between the cuisines of Northern and Southern Italy, but brakes were something else entirely.

Not that it mattered. She'd be at the cabin before the old doomsayer's prophecies came true. So she'd smiled pleasantly and said her brakes were just fine, thanks, and then she'd driven off, watching in her rear-view mirror as he'd stood looking after her, shaking his head mournfully.

'Ridiculous,' Holly had muttered to herself, as she'd made the turn onto the road that led up North Mountain. As if some old man in the middle of no-where could do a better job predicting the weather than the CNN meteorologists…

Halfway up the mountain, the snow started falling.

At first, the flakes were big and lazy. They settled prettily onto the branches of the tall pine trees that clung to the slope on Holly's left while sailing grace-fully off the precipice to her right. But within minutes the wind picked up and the snow went from lazy to fierce, changing direction so that now she was driving headfirst into an impenetrable cloud of white. And there was no way to turn back. The road was too nar-row and far too dangerous for that.

She was driving blind, trapped in the heart of what seemed to be the beginning of a blizzard. All she could do was hunch over the steering wheel, urge the car for-ward inch by slippery inch, and try not to wonder whether or not she had the 'new-fangled' brakes she'd pooh-poohed just half an hour ago.

The old man had been right. She'd been stupid not to have rented a car with four-wheel drive. Who was she kidding? She'd been stupid to have decided to come to the cabin at all.

Everyone had tried to tell her that. Not just the guy

at the gas station. The clerk who'd rented her the car. The traffic cop in Burlington, when she'd asked for directions. Even Belinda, her agent, who knew as much about New England as a vegetarian knew about a pot roast, had blanched when Holly had said she was taking off for a few weeks in Vermont.

'Where?' Belinda had said incredulously—but Belinda figured that civilization ended once you took the Lincoln Tunnel out of Manhattan.

'It's a place called North Mountain,' Holly had replied. 'I've rented a cabin.'

'You're going to spend a few weeks in a cabin?' Belinda repeated, the way someone else might have said, 'You're going to spend a few weeks on the Moon?'

'That's right. It's very luxurious. There's a Jacuzzi, a huge stall shower, a big fireplace in the living room…'

Belinda snorted. 'Try the Waldorf. It's got all that, plus room service.'

Holly did her best to offer a cheerful little laugh.

'I need a change of routine,' she said. ' A real one, before I start on the next book. You know how hard I've been working this year, and there's a whole bunch of ideas I want to try before I begin writing…'

And then she stopped, because she knew she was babbling, because she could tell from the look on Belinda's elegant face that she knew it, too.

'Poor darling,' Belinda crooned. 'You really do sound exhausted.'

'Oh, I am,' Holly said quickly, because it was true. She *was* stressed.

That was what she told herself, at first.

She'd been working hard. She had been for the past seven years—well, six years, ever since she and Nick had been divorced. Her parents had wanted her to come home and pick up her life as if nothing had happened but something *had* happened, and Holly wasn't about to pretend otherwise. The last vestiges of girlhood had fallen away the day she took off her wedding ring. So she'd explained, as gently as possible, that going home just wasn't possible. She'd refused her father's offer of financial support the same as she'd refused Nick's, and set out to create a life for herself.

And she'd done it.

The little column for the *Green Mountain Daily* had blossomed into a monthly feature for *What's Cookin'?* magazine, and it led to the contract for her first cookbook. Holly had found herself on the fast track, and she loved it. She could put in six hours in the kitchen, another two at the computer, tumble into bed and wake up the next morning, eager to start all over again. At least she had, until a couple of weeks ago.

The first time she'd awakened in the middle of the night with a knot in her belly and another in her throat, she'd figured it was a sign she'd put too many capers into the *Putanesca*.

By the fourth time, though, she knew it wasn't a recipe gone wrong that had awakened her.

It was her dreams.

She was dreaming of Nick, which was ridiculous. She hadn't done that in almost six years, hadn't seen him in almost six years, hadn't thought about him in almost six years...

It was a long time. The realization hit at three o'clock on a cold December morning, when she awakened with Nick's name on her lips. That wasn't heartburn she was feeling, it was anger. And why not? She was coming up on the seventh anniversary of what had begun as a marriage and had ended as a disaster.

Holly rose from bed, wrapped herself in her robe and padded out to the living room. She clicked on the TV and surfed through a bunch of movies that had been old before she was born. She zipped past a pair of talking heads that were deep in what she'd thought was a discussion of ghosts, then zipped right back when she realized the 'ghosts' they were discussing weren't spooks at all but memories, unwanted ones, of people in a person's past.

'So, Doctor,' the interviewer chirruped, 'how does one put these memories to rest?'

Holly, with one hand deep in a bowl of leftover gourmet popcorn, paused and stared at the set.

'Yes,' she murmured, 'how?'

'By facing them,' the good doctor replied. He pointed his bearded jaw at the camera, so that his bespectacled eyes seemed to bore straight into Holly's. 'Seek out your ghosts. You know where they lurk. Confront them, and lay them to rest.'

Pieces of nut-and-sugar-encrusted popcorn tumbled, unnoticed, into Holly's lap as she zapped the TV into silence.

'North Mountain,' she'd whispered, and the very next morning she'd phoned her travel agent. Was the cabin on the mountain still available? The answer had taken a while but eventually it had come. The cabin was there, it was for rent, and now here she was, about to face her ghosts…or to turn into one herself, if she didn't make it up this damned mountain.

There! Off to the left, through the trees. Holly could make out the long, narrow gravel driveway. It was still passable, thanks to the sheltering overhang of branches.

The car skidded delicately but the tires held as she made the turn.

She pulled up to the garage, fumbled in the glove compartment for the automatic door opener the realtor had given her. The door slid open. Holly smiled grimly. So much for the old man's predictions about a power outage, and thank goodness for that. Night had fallen over the mountain and for the first time it occurred to her that it wouldn't be terribly pleasant to be marooned here without electricity.

Carefully, she eased the car into the garage. Seconds later, with the door safely closed behind her, she groaned and let her head flop back against the seat rest.

She was safe and sound—but what on earth had she thought she was doing, coming to this cabin? You didn't bury your ghosts by resurrecting them.

'You're an idiot,' she said brusquely, as she pulled her suitcase from the car and made her way into the kitchen.

She switched on the light. There was the stove, where she'd prepared the very first meal she and Nick had shared as husband and wife. There was the silver ice bucket, where he'd chilled the bottle of cheap champagne that was all they'd been able to afford after they'd blown everything on renting this place for their honeymoon. There was the table, where they'd had their first dinner…where they'd almost had it, because just as she'd turned to tell Nick the meal was ready, he'd snatched her up into his arms and they'd ended up making love right there, with her sitting on the edge of the counter and him standing between her thighs, while their burgers burned to a crisp.

The lights flickered. Deep in the basement, the heating system hesitated, then started up again. Holly sighed in gratitude.

What on earth was she doing here? She was an idiot, to have come back to this place.

'Worse than an idiot,' she said, in a voice blurred with tears—not that she was weeping with regret. Why would she? Marrying Nick had been a mistake. Divorcing him had been the right thing to do, and she didn't regret it, she never had. She was crying with anger at herself, at the storm that was going to make it impossible for her to turn around and drive down the mountain…

The lights blinked again. In a moment, the power would go out. She'd never be able to open the garage door without it; the door was old, and far too heavy. The power had gone out for a couple of hours when they'd stayed here years ago, and not even Nick—muscular, gorgeous, virile Nick—had been able to wrestle the door open.

Holly swallowed dryly. She couldn't, she wouldn't, be trapped here, with her memories. She had to get out before that happened, and never mind the raging storm and the treacherous road. She could manage the drive down. She'd be careful. Very careful. Nothing was impossible, when you put your mind to it. Hadn't life taught her that?

'I am out of here,' she said, exactly at the moment the lights went out.

CHAPTER TWO

BY THE time he reached the turn-off for North Mountain, Nick was almost driving blind.

He had the windshield wipers turned up to high but the snow was falling so thick and fast that the wipers could barely keep up.

At least the Explorer was holding the road. That was something to be grateful for. And so was the gas station, just ahead. The last few miles, the needle on the gauge had been hovering dangerously close to empty.

Nick pulled beneath the canopy, stepped from the truck and unscrewed the cover to his gas tank.

'Hey there, Mister, didn't ya see the sign? Station's closed.'

A man had come out of the clapboard house beyond the pumps and jerked his thumb at a hand-lettered sign tacked to the wall. He had the raw-boned look of an old-time New Englander and the accent to match.

'No,' Nick said, 'sorry, I didn't.'

'Well, ya do now.'

'Look, I need some gas. And you're probably the only station open for miles.'

'Ain't open. Told ya, I'm closed.'

Nick flashed his most ingratiating smile.

'My truck's just about running on fumes,' he said. 'I'd really appreciate it if you'd let me fill up.'

'Ain't no need for gas,' the old man said, 'seein' as there's no place to go in a blizzard.'

Oh, hell. Nick took a deep breath and tried again. 'Yeah, well, the weatherman says it's not a blizzard. And by the time it is, I'll be where I'm going, if you'll let me have some gas.'

The old fellow looked him up, then looked him down. Nick found himself wishing he'd taken the time to exchange his black trench coat, charcoal suit and shiny black wingtips for the jeans, scuffed boots and old leather jacket he'd jammed into his suitcase. He'd almost given up hope when the guy shrugged and stomped down the steps to the pump.

'It's your funeral.'

Nick grinned. 'I hope not.'

'Where you headed?'

'Just a few miles north.' Nick peered towards the office. 'You got a couple of five-gallon gasoline cans you could fill for me?'

'Aye-yup.'

'And maybe a couple of bags of sand?'

'That, too.'

'Great.' Nick pulled out his wallet as the old guy

screwed the cover back on the gas tank. 'If you have some candles you'd be interested in selling, I'd be obliged.'

'Well, at least you're not a fool, young man, wantin' to buy ice in Decembah.'

Nick laughed. 'No, sir. No ice. Just the gas, the sand, the candles… Better safe than sorry, isn't that what they say?'

'The smart ones do, anyways. North, ya say. That's where you're goin'?'

'Yes. To North Mountain.'

The old man turned around, a red gasoline can in each hand, and looked at Nick as if he were demented.

'Ain't been a soul come through here in months, headin' for that mountain, and now there's two of you, in one day.'

Nick frowned. 'Somebody went up to the cabin?'

'I suppose. Couldn't tell 'em naught, either. Had the wrong car, wrong tires, wrong everythin'. Didn't have no business on that mountain, I tell you that.'

That was for sure, Nick thought grimly. Vagrants, even damn-fool kids with nothing better to do than go joy-riding, could get into trouble in country this isolated.

On the other hand, vagrants didn't drive cars, and kids around here had more sense than to be out in this kind of weather.

'Hunters, maybe?' he asked.

The old man guffawed. 'Hunters? Naw. I don't think so.'

Nick slid behind the steering wheel of the Explorer. 'How many guys were there?'

'Jest one, but—'

'Thanks,' Nick said. He waved, checked for the non-existent traffic, and pulled out onto the road.

'But it weren't guys a-tall, Mister. It were just this one pretty little woman…'

Too late. The truck had disappeared into the whirling snow.

The old man sighed. Crazy people, these city folk, he thought, and clomped back inside his house.

It took twice as long as it normally would have to make it up the mountain.

The drifting snow had buried the road in many places and at times the visibility was just about non-existent. Nick kept an eye out for another car but there were no signs any had come this way. Of course, with the snow falling so heavily, there wouldn't have been much chance of seeing tire tracks.

Still, when he finally reached the turn-off that led to the cabin, he scanned it carefully for signs of a trespasser, but there was nothing to see.

He pulled up outside the garage and got out to open the door. The snow, and the wind, hit him with enough force to take his breath away but he bent his head against it and grasped the handle of the garage door.

'Damn!'

How could he have forgotten? The door was electric. It wouldn't move an inch no matter how much muscle you applied and, of course, he'd forgotten to have somebody send him the automatic opener.

Well, that was life. He'd have his work cut out for him, digging the truck out from under umpteen inches of snow tomorrow morning. He trudged back to the Explorer, opened the door and stuffed his cellphone and his wireless fax into his pockets, hung his carry-on and his computer case from his shoulders, and hefted a box of supplies into his arms. Steak, potatoes, a couple of onions and a bottle of single-malt Scotch. The basic food groups, enough to hold him through the weekend. He slammed the door shut with his hip, dug the key to the cabin from his pocket, and made his way to the front porch.

Damn, Nick thought as he climbed the wooden steps. He'd forgotten to bring coffee. Well, he'd have to make do with a shot of the Scotch to warm his bones, and then he'd fall straight into bed. It sounded like a mighty fine plan.

He wedged the box against the door, fumbled for the lock and turned the key. The door wouldn't open. He scowled. Was there an unwritten law that said doors had to stick when a man was freezing his ass off on the wrong side of them? Nick grunted, shoved hard, and almost fell into the cabin as the door groaned noisily and swung open on a yawning blackness.

'Idiot,' he muttered.

He had a flashlight, but it was inside the box. And

to put the box down without walking into something, he needed to be able to see.

There had to be a light switch on the wall. He seemed to remember one, to the left…

'Come on,' he said impatiently, as he felt for the switch. 'Where are you hiding? I know you're there.'

Something swished past his face. He sensed it coming just quickly enough to duck before it connected with his skull.

'Hey! What the…?'

A creature flew at him from out of the darkness, shrieking like a banshee. Nick yelled, threw up his arms to ward the thing off, and went down in a heap, box, carry-on, computer and all.

The creature was right on top of him.

Talons dug into his shoulder, went for his eyes. Warm breath hissed onto his face. Was it a bobcat? A lynx? A mountain lion? No, not that. There were no big cats here, weren't supposed to be, anyway. A wolf? Gone for at least a hundred years, but people said…

'Perfume?' Nick whispered.

What kind of cat wore perfume?

The thing began trying to scramble away from him. Nick grunted. His hand closed on something fragile and bony. An ankle? A wrist? Did cats have ankles and wrists?

Perfume. Delicate bones…

Nick's eyes widened against the darkness.

'Bloody hell,' he said. 'You're a woman!'

And then something hit him hard, in the back of the head, and he slipped down and down into deepest, darkest night.

Holly stood over the unconscious intruder and trembled with fear.

Was he dead? Had she killed him?

At first, she'd thought she was dreaming. She'd been lying in bed, still shaking with cold despite wearing her long johns, wool socks, a hat and her New England Patriots sweatshirt, buried to the tip of her nose beneath half a dozen quilts, busily telling herself there was nothing the least bit spooky about being alone on the top of a mountain with no lights and a blizzard raging outside, when she'd heard something.

A sound. An engine.

Good, she'd thought. The snowplows were out.

Snowplows? Back home, in Boston, yes. But here? On the top of this mountain?

Holly'd shot up in bed, her heart pounding. The night was so still. Every sound seemed magnified a hundred times, and each had sent a wave of terror straight through her.

The thud of a car door. The scrunch of footsteps in the snow. The thump of booted feet mounting the steps, crossing the porch. The sound of the front door being battered open.

That was when she'd moved, jerking out a hand for the portable phone on the night table, remembering even as she put it to her ear that the damned thing wouldn't work with the power out. Petrified, almost breathless with fear, she'd looked around desperately for a weapon. Something. Anything.

The phone. It was a weapon. It didn't have as much heft as she'd have liked but she was in no position to be choosy.

Now what? Should she hide and hope the intruder wouldn't find her, or should she tiptoe down the steps, see what he was doing, slip up behind him when he wasn't watching and knock him over the head?

Whatever she did, she'd be quiet. Oh, so quiet. Super quiet, like a little mouse, so that he wouldn't so much as suspect there was a woman in the house. A lone woman…

And right then, just as she was tiptoeing to the top of the stairs, trying to hear herself think over the thud of her heart, the intruder had spoken in a low, angry voice.

'Come on,' he growled. 'Where are you hiding? I know you're here.'

Terror had impelled her, then, terror and the realization that he knew she was here. She'd raced downstairs, tried her damnedest to bash his brains out right away and, when that hadn't worked, she'd screamed the way Belinda had once said she'd been taught to scream in a martial arts class and hurled herself straight at the intruder.

He was huge. Seven feet, for sure. Eight, maybe. Three hundred pounds, no, four hundred, and all of it muscle. And he was strong as an ox. He'd struggled mightily, grunting and shoving and trying to dislodge her, but she hadn't given an inch. Then his hand—a hand the size of a house, and as powerful as a steel trap—had closed around her wrist.

'Perform,' he'd said, in a voice as deep as a bass drum, and just as a hundred terrible explanations for that command swept into Holly's mind his grasp on her wrist had tightened. 'Blood,' he'd snarled, 'you're a human!'

Perform? Blood? Human?

Holly hadn't hesitated. She'd swung the phone again and that time she'd hit him on the top of his miserable head.

Now he lay sprawled at her feet, face-down and motionless.

She poked him with her toe. He didn't move. She poked again. Nothing happened.

Holly's heart was in her throat.

'Oh, God,' she whispered.

Had she killed him? Had she killed this—this escapee from a funny farm? Her teeth banged together, chattering like castanets. What about all that stuff she'd always laughed at? The tabloid headlines that screamed about visitors from outer space? Did an alien lie at her feet, looking to perform some bloody human sacrifice?

Holly forced out a laugh. 'For heaven's sake,' she said shakily, 'get a grip!'

This was no alien. It was a man, and even if he was

a certifiable loony who thought he'd been hatched on Mars, the last thing she wanted was to have his blood on her hands.

She had to turn him over, see if he was alive or dead. And to manage that, she needed light.

There were candles in the kitchen; she'd used one to see her way upstairs an hour or two ago. Was it safe to turn her back, leave the room, leave this—this creature lying here? Suppose he awoke? Suppose he stood up? Suppose…

'Ooooh.'

Holly leaped back. He was moaning. And moving. Very, very slightly, but at least he was alive. She hadn't killed him.

The man groaned again. It was a pitiful sound. Her heart thumped. How badly had she injured him? She couldn't see. Couldn't tell. For all she knew, he might be lying there, bleeding to death.

'Mister?'

There was no response.

'Hey, Mister!'

Holly took a tentative step forward. She poked him with her toe, then poked him again. Carefully, she squatted down beside the still form and jabbed him with a finger.

Nothing happened.

Holly heaved a sigh of relief. Good. He was still unconscious. As for his wounds—that could wait. Right now, she needed to find something to tie him with.

The man groaned and rolled onto his back, one arm thrown over his face. Holly leapt to her feet and scrambled into the shadows.

'Don't move!' she said. Oh, that sounded pathetic! She cleared her throat, dropped her voice to what she hoped was something raspy and threatening. 'Don't move another inch, or so help me I'll...I'll shoot.' And she brandished the portable phone before her.

Move? *Move?*

Nick would have laughed at the idea, if he hadn't been afraid that laughing would make his skull crack open. The last time his head had felt like this was in fourth grade when Eddie Schneider, excited at the prospect of striking out the last guy up, had managed to bean him with a fastball.

'You hear me, Mister? Don't even think about moving.'

It was a boy's voice, young and unsteady. Well, hell. Nick felt pretty unsteady himself. On the other hand, the last thing he wanted to do was lie here, at the mercy of a dangerous kid armed with a gun and some kind of animal that attacked people.

He had to sit up, if he was going to get out of this in one piece.

Nick forced another groan, which wasn't very difficult, all things considered.

'Gotta sit up,' he said thickly. 'My head...' He swallowed. 'If I don't sit up, I'm liable to toss my cookies.'

'No!' The kid's voice cracked. 'I mean...okay. Sit. But no fast moves. You got that?'

Nick nodded. A huge mistake. His head felt as if it might fall off. On the other hand, that might not be such a bad idea.

Carefully, he eased himself up with his back against the wall.

'Damn,' he said, 'what was that thing?'

'What thing?'

'That animal. The cat.'

'Cat?' Holly said. She swallowed dryly. Oh, boy. This was bad. He was hallucinating again. First blood, and humans. Now cats…

'Yeah. You know, the one wearing the perfume.'

Holly took another step back. 'Cats don't wear perfume,' she said carefully.

'This one did, when it attacked me.'

He was crazy, all right. And you didn't argue with a crazy man, you just acted as calmly as you could.

'There's…' Her voice slipped up the scale, and she cleared her throat. 'There's no cat here, Mister.'

'Dog, then. Was it a dog? I hope to hell you've locked it in another room.'

On the other hand, what could it hurt to let him think she had an attack dog by her side?

'It's a, uh, a…' *Think, Holly, think. What kind of dog was big and tough?* All she could come up with was an image of the cocker spaniel that had lived in the house next door, in Tuscany. 'It's, uh, a Rottweilder.'

'A what?'

'A Rottweilder.'

Nick hesitated. 'You mean, a Rottweiler.'

Holly shut her eyes, then opened them again. 'That's what I said. A Rottweiler, and don't you even breathe funny or I'll turn him loose on you.'

What she'd said was Rottweilder. Nick was sure of it. And a very well trained one it must be, for it not to be making a sound, not even a growl or a pant.

'Where is it?'

'Where is what?'

'The dog?'

'It's—it's here, right beside me. You want a close-up look? I'll let go of its collar.'

'No,' Nick said quickly, 'no, that's okay…'

There was no dog beside the kid, not a Rotter or even a poodle. The kid was standing in the shadows but his outline was visible and there was nothing beside him, except for a chair.

Slowly, ever so slowly, Nick brought up one leg and then the other.

'Don't move, I said!'

'I have to. My head's bleeding.'

'Are you sure?'

'Positive.' Nick touched his scalp gingerly, expecting to feel the warm ooze of blood, but all he found was a huge bump. 'Yeah, it's bleeding, all right. Listen, I've got to get to a doctor.'

'No! I mean…' What? What did she mean? 'I mean, I'll get you a compress. After I call the…' *Oh, Lord. She couldn't call anybody. She couldn't even tie the intruder up, without rope. And how was she going to search for rope? Was she going to ask him, politely, to just lie still and wait until she made a circuit of the cabin?*

Nick's eyes narrowed. Call whom? Did the kid have an accomplice?

'Look,' he said carefully, 'I'm willing to forget this, okay?' Slowly, holding his breath, he shifted his weight again. 'I don't know who you are and I don't care. You just turn around, walk out the door, and we'll pretend this never happened.'

'Me? Walk out the door? You must think I'm crazy. I'm not turning my back on you for one second, Mister. And I'm not going out into that blizzard, either.'

'Think it over, kid.' Carefully, ever so slowly, Nick began lifting himself from the floor. How clearly could the guy see him? Not very. He'd have to bet on that. 'I'm willing to give you my word that I won't press charges if you—'

'*You* won't press charges? For what?'

'For breaking and entering. For putting a hole in my skull. For menacing me with a gun.'

'You really are crazy! I didn't break or enter anything. As for menacing…you're the one who's doing the men—'

A scream broke from Holly's throat. The man had come to his feet with a blinding burst of speed. She turned to flee but he was across the room and on her before she'd had the chance to take a step.

'Okay, kid,' he snarled.

The phone went flying as he wrapped his arms around her and lifted her, kicking and screaming, from the floor. They lurched across the darkened living room in a grotesque two-step, crashed against a table and careened into the sofa. The man went down and she went down with him, falling across his body and into his lap.

'The police are coming,' Holly panted. 'I called them, as soon as I heard you breaking in.'

'You didn't call anybody, punk.' Nick wrestled the kid's hands over his head, rolled over and pinned the slight body beneath his. 'And why would you, when you're the one who's done the breaking in?'

'Get off me!' Holly jerked her hips up and tried to wriggle free of the hard body above her. The hard, masculine body that seemed—that seemed strangely familiar...

'Forget it, kid,' Nick growled.

'Get off!' Holly twisted beneath him again.

'Hey.' Nick scowled. 'Don't—don't do that.'

Holly fought harder. Her body brushed his, and a flash of heat shot through her blood, which was not just crazy but sick. 'Get off, dammit,' she yelled, and shoved against him again.

Bloody hell. Nick caught his breath. What was happening here? His anatomy was reacting to the shifting motions of the kid's. That was nuts. Worse than nuts...

...Except, this wasn't a kid trapped under him. And it certainly wasn't a boy. It was—it was...

'Holly?' he whispered.

The body beneath his became rigid. 'Nick?'

'Holly,' he said again. It was all his brain seemed capable of managing.

'Nick,' she murmured, on a rising breath.

'Yeah,' he said. 'It's me.'

And then he did the only thing a man could do, under the circumstances.

He bent his head, breathed in the soft, floral scent of his ex-wife, and kissed her.

CHAPTER THREE

WAS this a dream, or was it real?

Holly couldn't tell.

Nick's arms were around her. His mouth was warm and firm against hers. It felt so good, so familiar, to be in his embrace.

If it was a dream, she wanted it to go on for ever.

Nick groaned softly as he kissed her. It wasn't a sound of pain; it was a sound of pleasure, one she'd heard many, many times during the months of their marriage. Holly's heartbeat quickened in response. She knew what would happen next, how his hands would slip beneath her, how he'd cup her bottom and lift her closer so that she could feel the heat and hardness of his arousal against her belly...

Desire, swift and electric as a flash of lightning, shot through her blood. Her arms rose, wound around his neck. Her fingers tangled in his hair.

'Nick,' she said in a broken whisper.

'Yes,' he said, 'yes, baby, it's me.'

She gave a little moan as he kissed her again, more deeply this time, parting her pliant lips with his. His tongue was hot silk as it slipped into her mouth.

'Oh, Nick,' she whispered, 'Nick…'

His hands slid down her body, cupped her, lifted her, brought her hard against him. Holly gasped at the feel of him. Her body felt liquid, eager and ready for his possession.

'Baby,' he said, against her lips.

Holly arched against him, mindless with pleasure. This was Nick in her arms. Nick, whom she'd always loved, Nick who had once been her husband…

Nick?

Oh my God, she thought, and she slammed her hands against his shoulders at the same instant she bit down on his lip.

Nick yelled, rolled off her and jammed his hand against his mouth.

Holly shot to her feet.

'Light,' she snapped. 'We need light!'

'There's a flashlight in that box,' Nick said sullenly, jerking his head towards the upended carton.

Holly glared at him. Then she stalked to where the box had disgorged its contents and plowed through the stuff until she came up with the flashlight.

'If you had this, why on earth did you come stumbling in here in the dark?'

'Because I didn't expect the lights to be out.'

'You could have used this flashlight.'

'You attacked me before I could get to it. Why didn't *you* turn on the lights?'

'Oh, right,' Holly said coldly. 'I'm supposed to turn on the lights when I hear somebody breaking in? Why not just hold up a flashing neon sign that says "Hey, here I am"?' She switched on the beam and shone it at Nick. 'Anyway, I couldn't. The storm knocked out the power.'

'Hey.' Nick ducked away from the bright light. 'Take it easy, will you? My head hurts enough as it is without you drilling that thing right into my eyes.'

'You—you…' Surely, there was a word that suited the occasion, and the man, but Holly was too angry to think of one.

Nick stood up slowly. He took his hand from his lip and peered at it. There was a blur of something dark on his fingertips, something warm and sticky.

He looked at Holly in disbelief.

'You bit me,' he said.

'You're lucky that's all I did!' Rage bubbled through her, at him, at herself, at whatever unholy combination of forces had brought them together this night. 'You— you sneaky, scheming, miserable, lying, cheating…' She ran out of words but not out of anger. 'I hate you, Nick Brennan,' she yelled, and just to make sure he got the message she kicked him.

'Hey!' Nick danced back out of range. 'What are you, nuts? First you give me a concussion, then you try to bite off my lip, now you're treating my shins as if I'm a soccer ball.'

'Don't make me laugh!' Holly folded her arms over her chest. 'All you've got is a little bump on your head.'

'I'm glad you think it's little!'

'And your lip's still attached to your face.'

'No thanks to you,' he said indignantly. He pulled a handkerchief from his pocket and dabbed at the cut. 'Dammit, I'm bleeding buckets!'

'You aren't…' Holly frowned. 'Where? Let me see.'

'Right there,' he said, pointing to his mouth.

'Where? I can't—'

Nick took her hand. His fingers were warm, the tips calloused, just as she remembered. It surprised her that they would be, after so long. Nick Brennan had made a success of himself. His was the quintessential tale of Boy Makes Good. She saw his name and his photo in the papers, from time to time. Not that she looked; it was just that he was hard to miss. Nick in black tie, at the opera. At charity benefits. At the opening of his newest hotel. No way he'd ever be seen in jeans and workboots again; no way he'd ever wield a jackhammer or drive a big Cat, or work up a sweat…

'Here,' he said softly, and touched her fingertip to his mouth.

It was like touching a hot stove. Heat sizzled through her bones and through her blood. Nick felt it, too. She could hear it in his quick, indrawn breath.

His hand tightened on hers. His lips parted. He drew her hand further across his mouth, until she could feel the whisper of his breath, the softness of his flesh…

Holly snatched her hand back.

'You're fine,' she said briskly. 'There's hardly anything there.'

Nick stuffed his handkerchief back into his pocket. 'Yeah, well, it feels like it's going to be swollen for a week.'

'Good,' Holly said self-righteously. 'What made you figure you could bust in here, scare the life out of me and get away with it?' She pointed at the door. 'You turn around and get out of this house this minute, Nick. You got that?'

'My head hurts.'

'Good. Now, get out!'

'I need a compress. And some aspirin.'

'You need a night in a jail cell,' Holly said coldly.

'For what? Nobody's going to arrest a man for using his key to open his very own door.'

'What do you mean, your very own door?' Holly slapped her hands on her hips. 'Don't tell me that realtor screwed up! I rented this cabin for four weeks of peace and quiet.'

'You couldn't have. This cabin isn't—'

'Isn't what?'

Isn't the realtor's to rent, he'd almost said...but some inner voice warned him that now was not the time to tell her that, or to go into details about his ownership. Besides, there was always the faint possibility he'd screwed up, misread the date on which Brennan Resorts assumed ownership of North Mountain.

'Isn't what?' she demanded again.

Nick shrugged. 'It must be a mix-up,' he said. 'I, ah, I made rental arrangements, too. One of us must have gotten the date wrong.'

Holly stared at him. Nick had decided to spend time at the cabin? But why? She couldn't think of a single reason. Nick Brennan was Brennan Resorts. He had half a dozen of the world's classiest hotels to stay in, if he wanted to get away for a few days.

'My company is thinking of buying property in the area,' he said, as if he'd been reading her mind. 'I decided to come up and take a look around. I figured I might as well arrange to spend the weekend in a place I knew rather than take my chances on some dinky motel.'

'Oh.' His explanation was logical, and yet it disappointed her…not that there was any reason it should have disappointed her. Nick wouldn't be here to bury his ghosts. Why would he, when he didn't have any? Holly smiled coolly. 'Well, that makes sense. I mean, Mr Hotshot Brennan certainly wouldn't want to spend his time in a place that wasn't up to his standards, would he?'

'Cheap shots used to be beneath you, Holly.'

'And pretentiousness used to be beneath you.'

'Oh, for God's sake! What are we arguing about?' Nick stalked across the room, then swung around and faced her. 'Look, there's obviously been some sort of mistake made.'

'You can say that again!' She bent and scooped the portable phone from the floor. 'And you should consider yourself damn lucky. If this stupid thing worked, the sheriff would be here by now, clapping you in leg-irons.'

'Leg-irons?' Nick laughed. 'You've been watching too many bad movies. Besides, the only guy liable to show up here this time of year is going to be riding in a sleigh pulled by eight tiny reindeer.' His grin faded as he took a second look at the thing in her hand. 'A phone? Dammit, Holly. You said you had a gun.'

'What did you expect me to tell a lunatic who breaks into my home in the middle of the night? Stop, or I'll shoot you with my portable?' Holly tossed the telephone onto the sofa. 'You're lucky it wasn't a gun, or you'd be complaining about a lot more than a teeny bump on your head.'

'Yeah, well, you're lucky I didn't decide the only way to take out a guy with a gun was to beat the hell out of him.' Nick put his hand to his head and winced. 'And the bump isn't teeny, it's the size of a grapefruit.'

'That's a pathetic untruth.'

'You're right.' Nick turned and marched away. 'It's really the size of a cantaloupe.'

'Where are you going?' Holly demanded, stalking after him.

'To the kitchen, to get a cold compress for my lip before I bleed to death.'

'Oh, stop being melodramatic. You're not going to bleed to death.'

'And to get some ice for my head.'

'Didn't you hear what I said before? I want you gone!'

'Yeah, yeah,' Nick said wearily. The long, difficult drive, the shock of the confrontation a few minutes ago—hell, the shock of finding Holly here—were all catching up to him.

He paused in the center of the kitchen. The room was dark but he could make out the hulking shapes of the stove, refrigerator and sink. If he remembered right, there was a paper towel holder just above the sink, and he headed for it. What he really needed was a shot of Scotch, assuming the bottle wasn't shattered, but he had the feeling Holly wouldn't appreciate waiting while he went back to the living room to find out.

'I know what you told me,' he said, as he tore a handful of sheets from the roll, folded them into a square and pressed it to his lip. 'But mmf mff mffer.'

Holly snatched the improvised compress from his hand.

'I can't understand a word you're…' She frowned. 'You're bleeding.'

Nick gave a hollow laugh. 'I told you that twenty minutes ago. Heck, baby, that's what tends to happen when you sink your fangs into somebody's face.'

'Don't call me that,' Holly said quickly. She turned on the faucet. It made a gurgling sound, spat out a few drops of water, and went dry.

'Don't call you what?'

'Baby.' She grasped his chin, put the folded paper

towel to her lips to moisten it, and dabbed at the cut on his mouth. 'I don't like it. I never did.'

'Seems to me there was a time you liked it a lot.'

Her gaze flew to his. His eyes were locked on hers, and what she saw in their hazel depths—the shared memory of nights, and days, of breathtaking passion—made her heartbeat stumble.

'Well,' she said, lying through her teeth because he was right, there'd been a time his nickname for her, murmured in that soft, gravelly whisper of his, had been enough to make her melt, 'you were wrong.'

Nick's jaw tightened. 'Yeah.' He jerked the compress from her hand, balled it up and tossed it into the sink. 'I was wrong about a lot of things.' He looked at her again. Even in the near-darkness, she could see the arrogant little smile that tilted across his lips. 'But not about what happened a few minutes ago.'

'That I beat you up, you mean?'

'That you were mighty cooperative for a woman who thought she was in the grip of a guy who'd just broken into her house.'

Holly felt the colour bloom in her cheeks. 'I'm sure you'd like to think so. But I wasn't cooperative, I was shocked.'

'Shocked,' he said, folding his arms.

'Of course. You took me completely by surprise.'

'You're telling me that if a stranger comes along, scares you senseless, then grabs you and kisses you, shock will make you kiss him back?'

'No! Certainly not.' Holly glared up at him. 'I mean, as soon as you kissed me, I knew you weren't a strange…' She stopped and cleared her throat. 'Look, you're twisting this thing around to suit yourself. All I'm saying is that you can't compare a man forcing a woman to kiss him to what happened just now.'

Nick gave an evil chuckle. *Oh, hell.* Holly had all she could do to keep from slugging him again. He'd set her up, and she'd gone for it. She'd walked right into that one.

'Okay,' she said coldly, 'your lip's stopped bleeding. It's time to say goodbye.'

'Goodbye,' he said, and opened the freezer.

'Dammit, Nick—'

'We've only dealt with one wife-inflicted wound. There's still another to go.'

'Ex-wife, if you don't mind.'

'I don't mind at all.' Nick slammed the freezer door shut. 'There's no ice.'

'There's plenty outside,' Holly said sweetly.

He touched his hand to his head, hissing when his fingers came in contact with his scalp.

'What'd you hit me with, anyway? A brick?'

'Did I hit you really hard?'

'Did you…?' Nick gave a sharp laugh. 'No, of course not. I just rolled up my eyes and passed out for kicks.'

Holly felt a tiny twinge of guilt.

'Let me see your head,' she said.

'Why? So you can check the damage and cheer?' He took a step back as she lifted a hand towards him. 'Don't bother. I don't need—'

'Don't be such a coward, Nick. Bend down and—'

'I wasn't a coward.' His hand clamped down on her wrist; his tone was chill and hard. 'It wasn't me who was afraid of change.'

'It wasn't change,' Holly said quietly, 'it was destruction.'

They looked into each other's eyes for a long minute, and then Nick's hand fell from hers.

'Forget the bump,' he said. 'I'll take care of it.'

Holly clucked her tongue. 'Stop being a baby and let me see it.'

'I am not a baby. I am a sensible man who knows better than to offer my skull to the woman who just whacked it.'

'You are a baby.' She rose on her toes. Her fingers moved lightly in his hair, and he held his breath, wondering how in hell the impersonal touch of a woman he hadn't seen in years could be sending chills down his spine. 'Or did you hope I'd forgotten the time you got that tetanus shot and passed out?'

Nick rolled his eyes.

'I don't believe this! A woman takes a couple of isolated incidents, puts her own spin on them and wham, she comes up with her own version of the truth. I was working on that old house—'

'The Shelby place.'

'Yes. And I managed to put a rusty tenpenny nail through my hand.'

'Because you were careless.'

'Because I had the damned flu, and a fever.'

'All the reasons you should have been home, in bed, instead of parading around on a construction site.'

'Oof.'

'Does that hurt?'

'Of course it hurts,' Nick growled. 'And I wasn't "parading around", dammit, I was working because we needed the money.'

'You were working because you were too damned stubborn to let *me* work.' Holly stepped back. 'You'll live. Your Everest-sized bump is no bigger than a *petit pois*.'

'A what?'

'A tiny pea. And the point of my story was that you went out like a light when you got to the emergency room and they gave you that shot.'

'I passed out because of the shock. And the fever. The doctor said so. And because when you came flying into the emergency room you looked as if—'

'As if what?'

As if you couldn't bear it, if something happened to me. As if you really did love me as much as I loved you...

'As if you were afraid you'd barf at the sight of blood,' he said briskly, 'and who could blame you? Well, thanks for the first aid. You're right. I'll be fine.'

'You know, maybe you should put some ice on—'

'I will. I'll follow your advice.' Nick forced a smile

to his lips. 'I'll dump some snow on my head, when I get outside.'

'Oh.' Holly nodded. She ran the tip of her tongue over her lips. 'Well, then…'

'Yeah.' Nick cleared his throat. 'Well…' Merry Christmas. That was the thing people said, this time of year. But he hadn't said those words in six years, and he sure as hell wasn't going to say them now. 'Take care of yourself, Holly.'

'You, too.'

They stood in the darkened kitchen, looking at each other, and then Nick cleared his throat again.

'It was good seeing you.'

Holly nodded. That was all she seemed capable of doing. She wasn't about to risk speaking, not when her throat suddenly felt tight.

Nick raised his hand, as if he might touch her, and then drew it back.

'It's been…interesting.'

'Interesting?' she said, in a croak.

'Uh-huh.' His smile tilted, and he lifted his hand first to his lip, then to his head. 'For lack of a better word.'

'Oh.' Holly gave a quick little laugh. 'I, ah, I'm sorry about that, but—'

'No. No, that's all right, I understand. There you were, figuring you were tucked in bed, safe and sound…' His gaze drifted over her, then returned to her face. 'You *were* in bed, weren't you? When I came in?'

'Yes. Yes, I was.'

'Yeah, well, as I said, it's understandable.'

They stared at each other for another few seconds and then Nick drew a breath.

'Well…'

'Well,' Holly said.

'Goodbye.'

He turned and started towards the door. She followed him in silence, watching as the man she had once loved, the man who had once been her husband, collected the stuff that lay scattered all over the floor and then put his hand on the doorknob.

No, she thought desperately, oh, no…

'Nick!'

He swung around quickly, his eyes on hers.

'Yes?'

The space between them seemed to hum. Holly swallowed dryly; Nick took a step forward.

'Nick,' she said again, this time in a whisper. 'It's—it's late. And the road must be awful. Where…where will you go? How will you find a place to stay? What will you do…?'

Her words trailed away. Nick's eyes burned into hers, and he answered the only question that mattered, the only one she hadn't asked.

'Are you asking me to stay?' he said softly.

Holly stared at him. There was no point in pretending she didn't know what he meant. The kisses they'd shared just a little while ago, the flame that had ignited when he'd taken her in his arms… The memories held within these walls made pretence impossible.

'Holly?'

Nick's voice was husky. Holly could feel the heat of it burning through her skin.

'No,' she said, after a minute. She blinked her eyes against a sudden sting of tears and wrapped her arms around herself. 'No,' she repeated, very softly. 'I'm not.'

He nodded. Then he turned, opened the door, and stepped out into the night.

CHAPTER FOUR

THE moon had risen. It sailed the dark sky like a ghost ship playing hide-and-seek with the clouds.

The wind had died down, leaving the snow in fanciful drifts. The mountain lay cocooned in silent, white radiance.

It was a beautiful scene but a dangerous one. And that, Nick figured, was just as well. It was a lot better to devote his attention to making it down the driveway to the road than to think about whatever it was that had happened back in the cabin. The way he'd felt, seeing Holly. The hunger in the kiss they'd shared, and the question he'd asked her, before he could stop himself from asking it.

He really didn't want to think about any of it. Not tonight.

The snow was deep. Eighteen inches, at least. But the Explorer had four-wheel drive and, by some minor miracle, the wind had almost scoured the driveway clean. Still, it was slow going.

At last, he reached the end of the narrow gravel drive. Ahead, he could see the road that would take him down North Mountain.

The hair rose on the back of his neck.

'Bloody damn,' he whispered.

The road, tortuous on a nice day, was a treacherous white ribbon now. One wrong move, and he'd end up in the yawning blackness of the valley.

Nick cursed and eased to a gentle stop.

What was the matter with him, thinking he could get down this mountain tonight?

He *wasn't* thinking, dammit. That was the problem. Seeing Holly again must have fried his brain.

He glowered out of his windshield. He'd come looking for closure, not for the opportunity to become a statistic.

'Damn,' he whispered, and then he blew out his breath, folded his arms over the steering wheel and laid his forehead against them.

He was behaving like a fool, doing things that made no sense, and all because of an unexpected encounter with a woman who'd ceased to mean anything to him a lifetime ago. It was late. The temperature was probably someplace around zero, there were snowdrifts the size of igloos all around, and what had he been doing?

Heading for a joy ride down Suicide Mountain, for Pete's sake. And Holly had been so glad to get rid of him that she'd never even considered that it might be the last ride he ever took. Nick sat up straight, shifted into re-

verse, backed to a handkerchief-sized space that consti-
tuted a wide spot on the roller-coaster of a road, made
a careful U-turn and headed back the way he'd come.

The cabin was his. Even if there'd been a screw-up,
even if it had been at his end, what did it matter? Not even
Scrooge would send Tiny Tim out on a night like this.

His grip tightened on the steering wheel.

On the other hand, Scrooge had never been faced
with spending the night in a cabin built for two with
his ex. His gorgeous, sexy, desirable ex. The tension
between them, those last couple of minutes, the way
Holly had looked at him...

If he'd gone to her then, taken her in his arms, they'd
have ended up in bed.

Nick squirmed uncomfortably in the leather seat.
Well, so what? All that proved was that the old physical thing was still there, the same as when they were
kids. She'd been eighteen, he'd been twenty. They'd
met at a shopping mall. Not 'met', really; they'd
bumped into each other, and almost the second they'd
looked into each other's eyes the attraction had been...

Attraction? Nick snorted. They'd been hot for each
other's bodies, that was what they'd been, so hot that
nothing else had mattered, and because they'd been
young and naïve, they'd ended up convincing themselves it was love.

But it hadn't been. Holly had come to her senses,
just as her old man had said she would. She'd realized
that sex wasn't, couldn't ever be, love, which was fine

with Nick because *he'd* realized that only a spoiled little rich girl could think that a run-down apartment and second-hand furniture and a mountain of unpaid bills added up to domestic bliss. Twelve months later, they'd done the civilized thing and agreed to a divorce.

End of story.

He'd kissed her tonight. Well, so what? He'd been so damn surprised to see her and yeah, she was still a good-looking woman.

A beautiful woman. But the world, as he'd spent the past years discovering, was filled with beautiful women. Holly was hardly unique. Yes, the old appeal was still there, but they were both adults. They'd have no trouble sharing the cabin for the night. Then, tomorrow, after the sun came up and the snowplow did its job, he'd do the gentlemanly thing and split. And it would be easy to do. He'd come for closure, and now he had it. In spades.

Nick frowned. There was just one thing.

Why had Holly come to the mountain?

She'd said something about needing a few weeks of peace and quiet, but from what? What could be stressful about the life of a rich woman who had everything she wanted? Unless…

His mouth became a thin line.

Unless it had to do with some guy. Unless she was getting over some guy. He couldn't think of any other reason for a woman like Holly to deliberately hide herself away in such an isolated place, where there wouldn't be a servant within calling distance.

Or—or maybe she wasn't going to be alone, all those weeks. For all he knew, a lover could be joining her.

Or a husband.

Nick's hands tightened even more on the steering wheel. Why not a husband? There was no reason Holly wouldn't have married again. She was still young, still beautiful, still everything any man could possibly want.

A muscle bunched in his jaw as he pulled up outside the cabin. He'd made such a fast exit that he hadn't asked any questions. Now, he would.

Gingerly, he touched his mouth and then his head. Damn right, he would.

She at least owed him an explanation.

Holly sat in the middle of the bed, snug under layers of blankets. Her knees were up, her arms were wrapped around them, and she was warm. Well, warm enough. And safe.

Nick was neither. How could she have let him drive that road on a night like this? The snow. The ice. The wind, and the dark.

She shuddered.

Nick was a good driver, sure. He'd been into motorcycle racing when they'd first met but sending him out into a snowstorm, on North Mountain…

'Are you asking me to stay?' he'd asked.

She sighed. If only he hadn't asked it the way he had, in that low voice she remembered all too well, with desire for her etched into every hard plane of his face. She could have said yes, she wanted him to stay, that he could sleep on the sofa because it would be foolhardy for him to risk his neck on the road.

And that *would* have been all she meant...

Wouldn't it?

She sighed, closed her eyes, and let her head droop against her upraised knees.

Absolutely. The invitation would have been an act of kindness, nothing more. They were adults, and adults could surely share three rooms and a bath for one night, especially when whatever it was that had drawn them together years ago was long since dead...

She groaned and fell back against the pillows.

Who was she kidding? She knew exactly what it was that had drawn them together. Sex. Sex, plain and simple. She'd been almost painfully young, and incredibly naïve. No boy had ever done more than kiss her goodnight, before Nick. But, with him, kisses weren't enough. Touching wasn't enough. She'd wanted him, begged him to take her...

It was still embarrassing to remember her abandon. No wonder she'd convinced herself that what she felt for Nick was love, not lust. Nick, in his faded jeans and his black leather motorcycle jacket, with that look of defiance on his gorgeous face...

Holly drew a ragged breath.

The Nick who'd shown up tonight was a different man. The custom-made suit, the pricey trench coat...

She smiled to herself. He'd found what he'd always wanted, and it certainly hadn't been her.

Nick had figured that out first. He'd been out in the world. He'd realized that they'd been wrong for each other, and they'd parted like two civilized people. No accusations, no fights, no regrets, only the bittersweet realization that sex hadn't been enough.

But it was still there. The heat. The excitement. The desire.

Holly shivered, and burrowed deeper into the blankets.

It was probably a good thing he'd left. What was there to worry about? He'd make it down the mountain just fine. Besides, if he'd had any doubts about the road, he'd never have…

What was that?

Holly's head came up sharply. She'd heard something. The throaty growl of an engine.

'Nick?' she said.

She tossed aside the blankets and leaped from the bed. The wind and the cold had rimed the window with snow but…

Yes. Oh, yes. It was Nick.

Had he come back for her?

She put her hand over her breast. Her heart was thumping so hard it felt as if it were going to ram against her ribs.

Nick rummaged inside the Explorer, took out his carry-on bag. When he straightened up, she could see his face clearly in the moonlight. Her heart thumped again. He was so handsome. Big, and masculine, with those hazel eyes that never seemed quite certain if they were green or brown, that proud nose, that wonderful, sexy mouth.

He looked up. Holly knew he couldn't see her but she fell back against the wall anyway. Her breathing quickened. Would he knock? Or—

He used his key. She heard the door open, then slam shut. Heard his footsteps on the stairs.

Holly's knees felt rubbery. Nick was in the house, and he was coming for her. In seconds, he'd be standing before her. There'd be no decisions to make, no weighing of right and wrong. Nick would open the bedroom door, look at her as he had a little while ago, the way he'd always looked at her, and she would run to him, go into his arms.

Footsteps sounded on the steps. Holly trembled. Waited.

The door swung open.

'Nick,' she whispered, 'you came back.'

'Damn right, I came back.' He dropped his carry-on bag to the floor and folded his arms over his chest. 'Get this straight,' he growled. 'No way in hell am I going to drive that road tonight.'

She blinked. 'What?'

'You heard me.' He unbuttoned his trench coat, slipped it off and tossed it on a chair. 'I'm no happier about this arrangement than you are. You, me, this cabin... Believe me, this is not my idea of a good time.'

'No.' She cleared her throat. 'No, it's not mine, either. But you're right.'

'And before you put up a fuss…' Nick frowned. 'I am?'

She nodded as she began stripping half the blankets from the bed and piling them in her arms.

'The storm's bad. And that road must be a nightmare.' She plucked a pillow from the bed, too. With the stuff in her arms piled high enough to almost hide her face, she maneuvered past him. 'It was bad enough when I drove up, hours ago.'

'Well, yeah. I just thought—'

'Do you remember where the linen closet is?'

'No. Yes. I…' *He was right? How could that be? He'd never been right, not where Holly was concerned.*

'It's next to the bathroom. Grab a couple of sheets and bring them down with you.'

He watched, bewildered, as she made her way to the stairs. The bedlinens were piled higher than her head.

'Hey! Holly, wait a second. I'll take that stuff. You can't see…'

'I can manage fine, thanks. You just bring the sheets.'

Holly dumped the blankets on a chair near the sofa. Her hands trembled as she took the throw pillows and tossed them aside.

What on earth had she been thinking? She'd *never* have made love with Nick, not even if he'd begged! She was done with all that, done with wanting him—

'Are these okay?'

She looked up. Nick was holding out a pair of flannel sheets.

'Fine,' she said, and took them from his outstretched hands.

'Can I help?'

She shook her head. 'No,' she said briskly. 'I can manage just fine.'

Nick frowned. He had the feeling she was right: she *could* manage fine. Something about her had changed, but what was it?

Maybe he'd been right, and there was a man in her life. It wasn't his business. It was just that he was curious.

She bent over the sofa and smoothed down the bottom sheet. She was wearing an outlandish outfit—he hadn't really noticed it before but now he took in the details. Sweatshirt, long johns, heavy socks. He'd never seen anything less feminine. No. That was a lie. The sweet curve of her back was—

'Toss me the other sheet, will you?'

His eyes followed her every movement. The heavy sweatshirt disguised her breasts, but he didn't need to see them to remember their conical shape or silken perfection. The rest of her was outlined clearly by the clinging long underwear. Her gently rounded bottom. Her long legs—legs that had once locked around his waist to drive him deeper as they'd made love…

Nick swung away and walked to the fireplace.

'Heck of a thing,' he said gruffly. 'A fieldstone hearth, plenty of kindling and matches...'

'And no firewood. I know. It was the first thing I checked, after the electricity went out. Well, the second thing, after the candles.' She plucked a blanket from the chair, shook it out, then laid it across the improvised bed. 'Too bad. I've gotten really good at building fires.'

'Yeah? I'd have figured it took a small army to get anything started in those walk-in fireplaces at Pinetops.'

'Oh, it pretty much does.' She straightened, blew a strand of wheaten hair out of her eyes. 'I meant in my place, in Boston.'

Nick nodded, his face a perfect blank.

'Nice town, Boston.' He bent down, stared intently into the fireplace. 'Live alone?'

Holly hesitated. The desire to tell him that she lived with a man was almost overpowering, but what was the point? He wouldn't care. Not that she wanted him to.

'Yes. I live alone. And you?' She knew the answer, knew that he hadn't remarried, thanks to the media's interest in him, but why tell him that? 'Do you live in New York?'

'Uh-huh.' Alone, too, he almost said...but she didn't ask. Why didn't she ask?

'I don't know how anybody stands the pace.' Holly added the other blankets, smoothed them neatly and folded back a corner. 'I mean, whenever I fly down to visit Belinda, my agent, or my publisher—'

'Your what?' he said, as if she'd suddenly told him she paid visits to a psychic.

'Belinda, my agent, or my publisher.' She turned towards him, her hands on her hips. The look on his face said it all. He knew nothing about her career. Well, why would he? Just because she knew all about his... 'My publisher,' she said again, with a little smile. 'I write cookbooks.'

Nick's brows lifted. 'You?'

'Me.' Holly folded her arms. 'I know you never figured I could do more than boil water—'

'That's not true. You were great.' He grinned. 'All those ways you came up with to cook hamburgers.'

'Be honest, Nick. You hated every last one of them.'

'That's not true. I just figured—'

'You figured I was playing house.'

'Look, I knew you'd never been inside a kitchen in your life, until we got married. It wasn't fair to ask you to take on—'

'No.' Holly's tone was polite, but her eyes were cool. 'You're right. It wouldn't have been fair to ask. But I didn't need to be asked. I was your wife, Nick. And wives cook. They clean. They iron. Wives do lots of things...but not *your* wife.'

'I don't believe this.' Nick folded his arms over his chest. 'Six years, and it's still the same old thing. Well, you're right. I didn't marry you for free maid service.'

Holly picked up the pillow and hurled it onto the sofa.

'You know something?' She spun towards him again, her eyes dark with anger. 'I never really figured out why you *did* marry me. I used to think it was for sex, but it wasn't that, was it? It didn't have to be, considering that I fell into bed with you days after we met.'

'Are we back to that, too? Listen, baby—'

'*Don't* call me that! I am not your baby. I am not anybody's baby.'

'One argument at a time, okay?' Nick slapped his hands on his hips. 'I married you, dammit, because I loved you! Because I wanted to give you everything you deserved, everything you wanted...'

'Bull! What an incredible ego you have, Nicholas Brennan! How could you possibly have known what I wanted?'

'A man knows, that's all. When he loves a woman—'

'On the other hand,' Holly said coldly, 'what *you* wanted was no secret.'

'Oh, yeah?'

'Yeah.'

'Well, I'm waiting.' Nick's jaw shot forward. 'Tell me what I wanted, since you know so much about it.'

'You wanted success. Recognition.' She threw her arms wide. 'You were determined to show them all that they were wrong!'

Nick laughed. 'Who's this "them"? What in hell are you talking about?'

'You know exactly what I mean, Nick. You wanted

just what you got. Your name in headlines. A fat bank account.'

'Ah, the horror of it all.' He shook his head and put on a mournful face. 'To think of it, that a guy would want to make good in this world. Lord, what a tragedy.'

'Don't laugh at me!' Holly stamped her foot. 'You and that— that monster-sized chip you wore on your shoulder—'

'Chip?' His voice rose as he stomped towards her. 'Hey, baby, I'm not the one with the chip. While I was out there, working my butt off, there you were, just waiting for me to come in the door at night so you could pounce on me and tell me about all the mistakes I was…Holly? Holly!' Holly had turned and was striding away. Nick followed her to the foot of the stairs, watching as she began climbing them. His voice rose, along with his temper. 'Where do you think you're going?'

She swung around and glared at him, cheeks pink with anger.

'I never pounced on you when you came through the door, and you know it!'

'You damn well did. Everything got the Holly Cabot Brennan vote of disapproval. The people I knew. The places I went. The things I did…'

'You know, I used to think we never quarrelled. Even just a little while ago, I was thinking about how—how civilized our divorce had been. Some tears, some polite conversation, and it was over.'

'What's your point?'

'My point,' Holly said bitterly 'is that I lied to myself all these years and never realized it until this minute.'

'Well, you're realizing wrong. We didn't fight. Never.'

'You're the one who's wrong, Nick. We fought. I did, anyway. It's just that I never let the anger out. I kept it all bottled up because I was this—this good little girl who wanted to please you. To make you look at me the way you... Oh, this is stupid! It doesn't matter anymore. The past is dead, and our disaster of a marriage with it.' She turned away, her back rigid. 'And I can't begin to tell you how glad I am for that!'

'Holly, wait a minute—'

'Goodnight, Nick. If we're lucky, and they plow the road during the night, please have the decency to be gone before I get up.' Her voice trembled. 'Actually, if you really had any decency at all, you'd—you'd take those blankets and that pillow and make your bed in a snowbank!' She stormed up the stairs and slammed the bedroom door behind her.

Nick stood there for a long minute, staring blindly at the empty hall and the closed door. Then, very slowly, he made his way to the sofa, sat down, and buried his head in his hands.

CHAPTER FIVE

MAN, it was cold!

And late, too. At least three or four in the morning, Nick figured. No question but that he had to have been tossing and turning for hours, ever since Holly had stormed out of the room.

He lifted his arm and peered at the lighted dial of his wristwatch.

Midnight? It was only midnight?

Nick groaned and fell back against the pillow, except the pillow wasn't there. The arm rest was, and he managed to connect it perfectly with the bump on his head. He winced, mouthed an oath, and rubbed his skull with the tips of his fingers.

'Great,' he muttered. 'Just great.'

What a night this had turned out to be! The laugh of it was that he'd come to North Mountain for a break. Considering how things were going, he'd have found more relaxation if he'd decided to camp out in the middle of Times Square.

And the weekend was only just beginning.

Nick rolled over, picked up the pillow and punched it into shape.

The room lay in total darkness. Not a good sign, he thought sourly. If the clouds had rolled in again, if it snowed...who knew when the road would get plowed? With his luck, he might be marooned here until New Year's.

The thought made him shudder.

No way.

'No way at all,' he said, as he flipped onto his back, folded his arms over his chest and glowered at the ceiling.

Plow or no plow, he was getting out of here at sunup. Holly could keep the cabin and her distorted memories of their marriage all to herself. The way she'd talked, anybody would think he'd been the one who'd screwed up their relationship.

'And it wasn't,' he growled into the silence. 'She knows damn well it wasn't!'

When he'd married Holly, she'd been everything he'd wanted, every dream he'd ever dreamed. She was beautiful. Bright. Kind. Caring. He'd wanted to put down roots, build a marriage, a family, a life they'd both be proud of.

What he hadn't figured was that she'd only wanted to play at being married. Either she still hadn't realized it or she wouldn't admit it, even now. All the self-righteous accusations she'd hurled at him tonight, accusing him of fighting with her and then turning her back on him before he'd had a chance to respond…

Damn, but she'd made him angry!

Angry, hell. He'd been furious. After she'd slammed the bedroom door, he'd paced the living room, muttering to himself, until, finally, he'd run out of steam, peeled down to his shorts and climbed under the blankets on the sofa.

Sofa? Nick grimaced. This wasn't a sofa. It was a slab of concrete, with an occasional steel bar built in for effect. Only an Indian fakir would call it suitable for a night's sleep. It was short and too narrow. His feet dangled over the arm and hung out from under the blankets. And every time he rolled over he risked getting dumped onto the floor.

To top it all, he was freezing. He felt as if he'd curled up on a shelf in a walk-in freezer for the night.

What he needed were his thermals, his wool shirts, sweats and heavy socks, all the stuff still packed in his carry-on, which he'd thoughtlessly left upstairs.

'Another brilliant move in a night of brilliant moves, Brennan,' he muttered in disgust, and dragged the blankets up over his shoulders—a *truly* brilliant idea, since all he accomplished was to leave his shins hanging out in the cold.

Nick sighed.

Amazing, that a fight with a woman who didn't mean a thing to you anymore could be so upsetting.

Holly's rage had caught him off guard. He could

hardly recall her so much as raising her voice, during their marriage. They'd never quarrelled, not even at the end. Sometimes, when he'd found her looking at him with that hurt-little-girl expression, he'd had all he could do to keep from demanding that she tell him what was wrong. He could have dealt with that, with some yelling and anger, even with some flying crockery.

But there'd been none of that. Holly's silence had damn near killed him. That, and the pained look in her eyes.

'What do you want from me?' he'd said to her once. Okay. He hadn't said it, he'd shouted it.

'If you don't know,' she'd said in a broken whisper, 'I can't tell you.'

That was the night he'd finally admitted defeat. He'd packed his things and moved out, and the lawyers had taken it from there. He'd never set eyes on his wife again.

His ex-wife. How come he kept forgetting that?

Now it turned out that Holly had just been waiting for the chance to tell him off. And tell him off she had. The clipped words. The flashing eyes. The regal posture, when she'd walked away.

Holly had changed, all right. Changed a lot.

The Holly he'd married had been a girl who'd spent her life in a world of fairy-tale privilege. And he'd taken her away from all that. Holly the Princess had tied on an apron and become Holly the Housewife.

At first, he'd thought it was sweet. After a while, he'd realized there was nothing sweet about watching his beautiful wife transformed into a drudge, and knowing he was the cause.

She'd baked. She'd cooked. She'd made curtains for their hovel of an apartment. Curtains, by God, when she'd probably never so much as sewn a button on a blouse in her entire life. And the way she'd stood at the door each night, those first few months, breaking into a big smile as he came in filthy and tired and irritable from a day spent building houses for rich people who'd never done a thing in their lives to deserve them, lifting her face for his kiss as if he weren't dirty, and smelly, and her old man's worst dream come true…

Not that her housewife act had lasted. Just about the time he'd finally gotten a handle on how to go from wielding a hammer for the rest of his life to finding the pot of gold at the end of the rainbow, Holly had come to her senses. Instead of smiling when he came in at night, she'd sulked. No. That was the wrong word. She hadn't sulked. She'd seemed…hurt. As if he'd somehow let her down when, dammit, what he'd been doing was working his ass off to give her the life she deserved.

Holly the Princess had become Holly the Silent.

It was anybody's guess who she was now, and none of his business.

Nick sat up, pummelled the pillow a little, jammed

it behind his head and lay down again. He turned on his right side, turned on his left…

And rolled right off the sofa, in a tangle of blankets.

'That's it,' he snarled. He shot to his feet and began pacing.

Sleep was not a possibility. He had to do something or go crazy, but what could you do in a cabin without electricity in the middle of the freaking night, with the temperature someplace around zero and your ex in the bed upstairs…?

Bloody damn!

He came to an abrupt halt. He'd been so busy counting his own miseries that he'd forgotten that Holly had to be freezing, the same as he was. Worse, probably. She'd given him half her supply of blankets. And she'd never dealt well with the cold. He used to tease her about it, when she'd curl up against him at night, those first months of their marriage, with her hand spread across his chest and her thigh over his.

'I don't know what I'm gonna do with you, baby,' he'd say, as he drew her to him, and she'd give a sexy little laugh and say that if he couldn't think of something she certainly could…

'Stop it, Brennan,' Nick growled. What was he trying to do? Drive himself crazier than he already was?

To have come to this cabin in the first place was crazy. To find your ex-wife inside and come back after she all but tossed you out was certifiably loony. Forget the snow. He'd have been better off taking his chances with the road. It couldn't be any more dangerous than where his thoughts were heading but it was only logical to think about waking Holly and suggesting they share the blankets.

Oh, yeah. That was just what he needed, all right. Snuggling down under the blankets with Holly was definitely the way to go.

Nick sighed. He was losing it. What he needed was to do something constructive. Like build a fire in the fireplace, to throw some warmth into the room.

He squatted down before the hearth and looked it over. Somebody had cleaned it, laid out kindling, made sure there were two boxes of safety matches within easy reach—and then forgotten to arrange delivery of firewood.

That didn't make much sense.

There'd been wood waiting, the last time he and Holly had come here. A whole cord of it. Well, no. There'd been some logs stacked here, beside the hearth, but the rest had been neatly stored in a little shed that was built onto the back of the garage…

A grin spread across his face. Hastily, he pulled on his trousers, his shirt and his shoes. Then he made his way through the silent cabin to the kitchen, opened the back door and stepped outside.

Ten minutes later, Nick's soaked clothing was draped over the back of the sofa. And he had a big, beautiful fire glowing on the hearth.

He held his hands out to the flames and smiled with

satisfaction. Then he looked back up the stairs. Holly had all but told him never to darken her doorway again—but she'd change her mind, when she saw the fire.

He ran up the steps, then stood outside her room, listening. At first, he heard nothing but then, after a moment, he thought he could hear something: The sigh of the wind in the eaves, perhaps…

Or the sound of a woman, weeping.

He hesitated, then rapped lightly on the closed door. 'Holly?'

There was no response.

'Holly?' he said, and knocked again.

The noise, whatever it was, stopped.

'Holly? Are you okay?'

Silence. Nick frowned and put his hand on the doorknob.

'Holly, answer me!'

'What do you want?' Holly said, in a muffled voice.

Nick leaned his forehead against the door and heaved a sigh of relief.

'Are you okay in there?'

Holly grabbed a tissue from the box on the nightstand, wiped her eyes and blew her nose.

'I'm fine,' she said. Tears spilled down her cheeks and she rubbed them away with the back of her hand. 'Just—just a little chilly.'

'That's what I want to talk to you about. Can I come in?'

She hesitated. If Nick saw her like this, what would

he think? She'd been crying for so long…her eyes and nose were probably pink and swollen.

'Holly?'

He'd undoubtedly misinterpret her tears and think they were for him. They weren't. She'd done with crying over Nick a long time ago. She'd been crying out of anger, that was all. Anger, plain and simple.

'Dammit, Holly, what's wrong?'

But he couldn't see her, not unless he had the flashlight and he didn't, or she'd have been able to see the beam of its light shining under the door.

'Nothing's wrong,' she said, and sat up. She ran her hands through her hair, fluffing it away from her face. 'Come on in.'

Nick stepped into the room. Holly's face was a pale ivory oval against the pillows.

'Hi,' he said, and cleared his throat.

'Hi,' she said, and smiled.

'I, uh, I…' *What was the matter with him? He'd come upstairs to tell her that he had a fire going in the fireplace, not to stand at the foot of the bed in tongue-tied oblivion.* But it was hard to think straight, when he looked down at the beautiful face of his wife.

'Nick?'

'Yes?'

'You said you wanted to tell me something.'

'Oh. Oh, right. Right…' He frowned. 'Your voice sounds strange. Have you been crying?'

'Crying?' She gave a gay little laugh. 'Me? Of

course not. I mean, it's cold, yes, but I wouldn't cry over that. I, uh, I think I might be catching a cold.'

She'd drawn the blankets to her chin. And there were so many blankets that her body was shapeless beneath them. But his memory supplied all the details. Her graceful throat, with that place just at the juncture of neck and shoulder that always seemed to smell like spring rain. Her silken breasts, and the way they filled his palms...

Nick's body clenched like a fist. That didn't surprise him. What did was the sudden clenching of his heart.

Holly, he thought, baby, where did it all go? What happened to us?

'Nick? Are you okay?'

'Sure.' He smiled. 'Better than okay. That's what I came to tell you.'

He sounded pleased with himself. Not smug. Just pleased, and eager to share the pleasure with her. Holly's heart surged with delight. This was the Nick she remembered. The easy laughter in his voice. The beautiful, tautly-muscled body....

'On second thought, I'd rather surprise you.' He moved to the side of the bed and held out his hand. 'Come on.'

'Come on, where? It's freezing cold—'

'Exactly.'

'It's the middle of the night—'

'Yeah, that's what I thought, too. But it's only...' He lifted his hand, checked his watch. 'It's only twelve-thirty.'

Only twelve-thirty? Her spirits dropped like a stone sinking into a pond, but she kept her tone perky.

'All the more reason for me to stay put.'

Nick sighed. 'Okay,' he said, 'if you're going to be stubborn…'

Holly shrieked as he scooped her into his arms, blankets and all. 'Nick! What on earth are you doing?'

'If Mohammed won't come to the mountain…' He grunted as he rearranged her in his arms. 'Just hang on tight. I don't want to trip over these blankets.'

What choice was there? Holly put her arms around his neck and hung on as he headed for the stairs.

'Really,' she said, 'Nick, this is silly.'

Except, it wasn't. It was wonderful, just like the dreams she'd been having. She was in Nick's arms, where she belonged.

Where she'd once belonged.

She shuddered, and Nick drew her closer. 'Cold?'

'Yes,' she said. What else could she say? Not the truth, that she was engulfed in sensation, almost painfully aware of Nick's masculine scent. The sexy rub of his unshaven jaw against her cheek. The strength of his embrace, and how good it felt to lie, secure, within it.

Her heart was beating like a drum.

'Here we go,' he said, as he carried her into the living room…and she saw the flames, leaping on the hearth.

'Oh, Nick!' Her voice rang with delight. 'You built a fire. But how?'

He gave a wicked chuckle as he sank to the floor before the fireplace and settled her in his lap.

'Well, I was going to tear the sofa apart with my bare hands and feed it to the flames—and then I remembered something.'

Holly knew she ought to move. It was wrong to be here, snug in her ex-husband's arms. But being snug— being warm—was what this was all about, wasn't it? Finding warmth, against the deadly cold of the cabin?

'What did you remember?' she asked.

'Where we found the firewood the last time we were here. It was in the shed, remember?'

'No.' She frowned. 'No, I don't— Oh. Of course! How could I have forgotten? The wood-shed, out behind the garage.'

'That's the place.' He leaned back against the sofa, so that her head lay against his shoulder. 'Do I get a merit badge for this one or not?'

Holly laughed. 'My Eagle Scout,' she said softly.

'Feels good, doesn't it?'

'Wonderful,' she murmured, shutting her eyes and burrowing even closer.

They sat without talking, soothed by the warmth of the fire. Nick dipped his head and inhaled the fragrance of Holly's hair. Her skin. She smelled like a morning meadow, fresh and new and touched with the scent of wildflowers. And she felt—she felt wonderful, here in his arms.

The feel of her was new, and yet it wasn't. How

could it be? Every inch of her body was imprinted on his. He remembered each curve, each sweet line. He knew what would happen if he kissed her throat, where it lay bare. If he breathed against her skin. If he raised her sweatshirt and bit gently at the straining flesh of her breast.

His body turned rock-hard. It was sudden and unexpected, and so unnerving that he shot to his feet while Holly gasped and clung to his neck. He deposited her on the sofa, swung away, grabbed for the poker and stabbed blindly at the burning logs.

'Okay,' he said briskly, 'here's the plan. We'll spread a couple of blankets on the floor, in front of the fire. Then we'll dump the rest of them over us. That ought to keep us warm enough so we can be sure of waking up in the morning with fingers and toes still attached.'

When it was safe to turn around and face her, he saw that her face was flushed with color. Her eyes were dark, almost the color of the night crowding in at the windows. Had she felt the pressure of his arousal? Or was she wary of spending the night lying so close to him?

'It's the only sensible thing to do,' he said softly.

She nodded. 'Yes. I agree.'

'Good.'

She cleared her throat and forced a little smile to her lips. 'It's certainly better than turning into an advertisement for the wonders of cryogenics.' Her smile broadened, and she touched a finger to the tip of her nose. 'Or for freezer burn. I do still have a nose, don't I?'

Nick grinned. 'Definitely.'

'Good. For a while there, I was pretty sure I was going to lose it.'

'That's right. It wasn't just your hands and feet that used to turn icy, it was your nose, too. I remember nights when we'd turn over in our sleep so that you'd end up holding me, and I'd wake up because that cute little ice cube was pressed into my back…'

His words trailed off. Their gazes met, held, then slid away.

'Okay,' Nick said briskly. He plucked some blankets from beside the sofa and laid them before the hearth. 'Ah, the wonders of nature. I don't recall anybody doing this in *The Sound Of Music*, do you?'

Holly laughed. 'No.'

'Yeah, well, maybe they don't have power failures in the Alps.' He grabbed the pillow, placed it at one end of the improvised mattress. 'Ready when you are, Frosty.'

Holly laughed again. She knew what he was doing, making a joke of the fact that they were about to sleep together, but it wasn't helping. Her mouth was dry; her heart was doing a crazed two-step.

'Holly?'

She raised her head and focused on Nick's face. One look told her that he knew what she was thinking.

'You'll have your half of the bed, and I'll have mine. I promise.'

'Of course,' she said, and before she could feel like

too much of an idiot she scooted off the sofa, onto the blankets he'd arranged, and lay down with her head on the pillow.

Nick layered the remaining blankets over her. Then he lifted one corner, edged beneath the stack, and lay down so that no part of his body was touching hers.

'Okay?'

'Fine.'

They lay in silence for a few minutes, and then Nick sighed. 'We should have brought down that other pillow.'

'Here. You can use—'

'No, don't be—'

They rolled against each other, caught their breaths, and instantly pulled apart.

'I'll be fine,' he said gruffly.

'You sure?'

'Positive.'

Silence enveloped them. They lay on their backs, staring at the ceiling, watching the shadows cast by the fire.

All I have to do is reach out my hand, Holly thought...

All I have to do is touch her, Nick thought...

'Nick?'

Holly's whisper was tenuous and soft as a sigh. Nick felt his heartbeat accelerate.

'Yes?'

'I'm sorry for what I said before. About the chip on your shoulder.'

'No, that's okay. You were just being honest.'

'Yes, but…' She sighed again. 'You were a good husband, Nick. It's just that I…'

'You wanted somebody else,' he said, trying not to let the pain show in his words. 'I understand.'

'No! Not somebody else. Some*thing* else. Something I'd thought you—you and I… Never mind. I just wanted you to know that I didn't mean to hurt you.'

'Yeah. Me, too.'

'You, too, what?'

'I'm sorry if I said anything that hurt. All that stuff about the Holly Brennan stamp of approval…it wasn't true. I mean, that's how it sometimes felt, but…' He cleared his throat. 'You were a good wife, Holly. It's just that I—'

'I wasn't the wife you wanted.'

No, he thought, hell, no. It was me. I couldn't measure up. I wanted only you, Holly. I still want…

'Here,' she said, and moved closer. 'The pillow's big enough to share.'

'Are you sure?'

'I'm sure.'

They lay side by side, sharing the improvised bed and the pillow but as far apart as two human beings who'd once shared their lives with each other could possibly be. The moments slipped past and then Nick thought, The hell with it. He reached for Holly's hand and clasped it in his.

'Goodnight,' he whispered.

Holly blinked hard. Tears burned behind her eyelids.

'Goodnight, Nick.'

She shut her eyes. He shut his. The fire burned. The wind sighed.

After a while, Nick murmured in his sleep and rolled to his side. He reached out for Holly. For his wife. Lost in her dreams, Holly went straight into his arms.

CHAPTER SIX

NICK awoke alone, in a heap of blankets that still carried Holly's scent.

His shoulder felt just a little stiff, the way it used to in the mornings when they'd been married. In the days when Holly had still slept the night through with her head tucked just beneath his chin.

That was how she'd slept last night, with her hand splayed over his chest and her leg draped over his...

God, it had felt wonderful.

His smile faded. What good did it do to think such things? She'd probably gone into his arms out of long-remembered habit, nothing more.

He sat up and ran his fingers through his tousled hair. The fire was still burning on the hearth. He'd fed it a couple of times during the night, each time slipping carefully from under the blankets so as not to wake Holly. The last time he'd crept back into their warm bed, he'd yielded to temptation, bent his head and brushed his mouth gently over hers. Holly had sighed and murmured something that might have been his name and he'd drawn her close, tucked her head beneath his chin, and fallen into a deep, peaceful sleep.

Nick glanced at the window. The storm was over. The sun was rising into a cloudless sky.

His heart constricted.

The plows would come through this morning. There'd be no excuse for him to stay. Not that there'd be any use in staying...

'Good morning.'

Nick looked around. Holly was standing halfway between the kitchen and the living room, wearing jeans, hiking boots, and a heavy ski sweater. Her long wheaten hair was pulled back in a French braid, and her face was shiny and as scrubbed as a schoolgirl's.

He smiled. He'd almost forgotten that his wife—his former wife—was a wonderful sight to wake up to.

'Good morning,' he said. 'I seem to have overslept.'

Holly grinned. 'You're a regular lazybones. How about some caffeine to get you started?'

'Caffeine? You mean...' Nick lifted his head and sniffed the air. 'I thought I was hallucinating. Is that really coffee I smell?'

'I was wondering how long it would take you to notice. Just wait there one second...' She disappeared into the kitchen and popped out a minute later with two mugs in her hands. 'You still take it with cream and one sugar?' she asked as she came towards him.

Nick nodded. 'Yeah.'

Holly reached down to the warm ashes in front of the fireplace and removed a grey and white speckled coffee pot.

'Damn,' Nick said with pleasure. 'I never noticed.'

She filled both mugs, smiled, and handed one over. He took it and buried his nose in the fragrant steam.

'A miracle. Thank you.' He took a sip, sighed, and looked at Holly, who'd sat down, cross-legged, opposite him. 'How'd you manage it?'

'Well, I decided to poke through the pantry.'

'And you found a coffee shop?'

Holly laughed. 'I found coffee, and a pot. And we already had the fire...'

'Hey, that's terrific! I've been sitting here, thinking about the stuff I brought with me, wondering if I'd really managed to forget to bring along some coffee.' He winced. 'My stomach kept insisting it wasn't up to starting the day with half-raw steak.'

Holly laughed. 'I remember. You had two ways of grilling steak over an open fire. Burned to a crisp, or raw.'

'Hey, give a guy a break. Call it steak tartare and the price goes up, babe...' Nick shook his head. 'Sorry. I didn't mean to—I know you hate it when I call you—'

'It doesn't matter,' she said quickly.

'It does. There are so many things—'

'Nick.' Holly ran the tip of her tongue over her

lips. 'Let's not do this, okay? The snow's stopped, the sun's out, and before you know it they'll clear the road and you can leave.' A smile seemed to tremble on her lips. 'So why don't we declare a moratorium on the recriminations and apologies for the next couple of hours?' Holly shifted her coffee cup to one hand and extended the other. 'Just two old friends, enjoying breakfast together. How's that sound?'

Impossible, that was how it sounded. They'd been lovers, not friends…

'Nick?'

Friends. It wasn't a bad idea. Maybe that was the way to find closure, once and for all.

Nick clasped Holly's hand in his. 'It sounds fine. Just give me a couple of minutes and I'm all yours.'

He wasn't all hers, not anymore.

Holly stood at the kitchen counter, cracking eggs into a blue ceramic bowl and listening to Nick's footsteps overhead.

What was he doing? Dressing, she hoped. One more look at his bare chest and she'd be lost.

One more minute in his arms, in front of that fire, and she'd have been worse than lost. She'd awakened, when he'd crept out from under the blankets to stoke the fire during the night, stunned to find that she'd been sleeping in his arms. She'd been on the verge of telling him she was awake, that she was going to make a bed for herself on the sofa, but then he'd put his arms around her, given her the most tender of kisses…

It had left her shaken, and silent.

A flush rose in her cheeks. You didn't exorcise the ghost of a dead marriage by sleeping with your ex-husband, no matter how sexy he was. And Nick was sexy, all right. She didn't have to be in love with him anymore to recognize that. Still, it wasn't desire she'd felt last night, lying in his arms. It was much more. Warmth, and comfort, and a sense of rightness and such deep well-being that—

'Hi.'

Holly swung around. Nick was standing in the doorway. Her heart tripped at the sight of him. This was the Nick she remembered, not a sophisticated man in an expensive trench coat and custom-made suit, but a guy who looked like an ad for outdoor living. He was wearing a turtleneck under a worn flannel shirt, faded jeans and leather hiking boots that looked even older than hers. There was a day-old stubble on his jaw, and a beat-up leather jacket hung over his shoulder from his thumb.

It was as if no time had passed. He looked gorgeous and just a little dangerous, the way he'd looked the first Christmas they'd come here…

And the last.

That last Christmas was the one she had to remember, when they'd finally admitted what each had known for months, that their marriage was not dying but dead, and that the only decent thing to do was give it a quick burial.

'Hi,' she said, and flashed a quick smile. 'I made some more coffee and the eggs are ready to go.' She smiled again, even more brightly. 'No bacon, I'm afraid, so you'll just have to make do with whatever I can whip up.'

'Over easy is okay with me.'

'Well, I have some cheese. And some cream. If you're feeling adventuresome…'

'That's right, I almost forgot. Cookbooks, you said.' Nick shrugged. 'What the heck? Surprise me.' He shrugged on his jacket and pulled a toothbrush from his pocket. 'Just give me five minutes to use the facilities…'

Holly laughed. 'You'll be back quicker than that. I've already used the facilities. It's probably ten below zero outside.'

Nick grinned. 'Thanks for the words of warning, but you'll see. This is guy weather. I can handle it.'

'Yeah, yeah, yeah.' Holly grinned. 'That's what they all say.'

He came bursting through the door minutes later, snow sparkling on his hair and on his shoulders, with a pile of wood in his arms.

'You weren't kidding! Ten below is right.'

'Told you so.'

'Let me just dump this wood and then I'll set us up

for breakfast on the coffee table, so we can stay warm beside the… Hey. You already did.'

He dropped the wood, straightened up, and put his hands on his hips. Holly had moved the coffee table so that it stood before the fireplace. She'd set two places, complete with linen napkins. A small basket stood centred between the settings, heaped with…

'Biscuits?' Nick said, looking up at her in amazement.

Holly blushed. 'I brought some leftover stuff, from home.'

'Leftover biscuits?'

'Uh-huh. I've been trying out new recipes, trying to zero in on what I want to do in my next book… Oh, for Pete's sake.' She sat down, cross-legged, before the table. 'Stop looking at me as if I'd just invented penicillin or something. Let's eat, before we both collapse from hunger.'

She served him something that looked like a cheese omelette but tasted like heaven. It was either almost as good as the light-as-air biscuits or maybe the biscuits were almost as good as the egg stuff. Nick couldn't tell and besides, it didn't much matter. The meal was incredible, all the more so because it had been cooked over an open fire by a woman whose only claim to culinary fame had been…

'*A Hundred and One Ways to Cook Hamburger.*' Holly folded her linen napkin and smiled at him. 'That was my very first book.'

'You're joking.'

'Cross my heart. I'd been doing a column for a magazine, and I'd done some pieces on inexpensive meals for couples just starting out—'

'Dining on the Cheapside,' Nick said. 'Wasn't that what we called it?'

Holly laughed. 'Yes. I mentioned that, to my editor, and she really thought it would make a good title, but—'

'But?'

But I knew that I'd never be able to look at the book without thinking of you...

'But I was afraid it would sound too, ah, too flip.' Holly reached for the coffee pot and refilled both their cups. 'So, we went with something more straightforward.'

'And the cookbook was a success?'

She nodded. 'More than we'd expected. They'd done an initial print run of 25,000 and they'd have been happy with a fifty per cent sell-through, but—'

'Wait a minute!' Nick smiled and held up his hand. 'Can you translate that into English?'

'Oh. Sorry. Well, print runs can range from—'

She explained. Print runs. Sell-throughs. Wholesalers, and distribution, and dealers. And he listened. Tried to listen, anyway, but it was tough. This astute woman—this knowledgeable businesswoman—was the same girl who'd never balanced a checkbook in her life, until he'd shown her how.

'I never had a checkbook before,' she'd said, when

he'd almost gone crazy the first time the bank had phoned to say their account was overdrawn.

'That's unbelievable,' he'd snapped. 'How could you never have written a check?'

'I charged things. I mean, I had accounts wherever I needed them.'

That was the first time he'd really understood how different they were. They weren't just a rich girl and a poor boy trying to make a marriage work, they were people from planets at the opposite ends of the galaxy, struggling to find a common language.

'I'm boring you.'

'What?' Nick blinked. 'Boring…? No. Not at all. I'm just fascinated by, you know, how you've changed.'

'I'm not eighteen anymore,' she said quietly.

He nodded. 'Seven years is a long time.'

'A lifetime.'

Nick cleared his throat. 'Are you—are you happy?'

'Yes.' Or, at least, she'd thought she was happy. Until the dreams. Until last night. 'Yes,' she said, and smiled brightly. 'I'm very happy. I love my work. And I love Boston. I've made lots of friends, and I've got this wonderful apartment… What about you? Are you happy?'

Nick hesitated. He hadn't hesitated a month ago, when a reporter on *This Week* had slyly posed him the same question. 'Of course I am,' he'd said.

'Nick? Are you happy?'

'Sure.' He smiled. 'Life's been good to me.'

'I know. I see the Brennan name everywhere. In fact, I stayed in a Brennan hotel the last time I was in Dallas on a book-signing tour.'

He grinned. 'And? Did it win the Holly Cabot seal of approval?'

His smile made it all right; there was no anger to the words this time, the way there'd been last night.

'Absolutely. Fresh flowers in the room, chocolate on my pillow at bedtime. Nothing was missing...'
Except you.

The cup slipped from Holly's hand and clattered against the table. Coffee oozed over the polished wood.

'Here,' Nick said, 'let me—'

'No. That's okay.' She stabbed at the spill with her napkin, then got quickly to her feet. 'Well. I guess it's time to clean up. Why don't you take a pot of water from the kitchen and heat it over the fire so we can do the dishes?'

He nodded. 'Sounds like a good idea.'

He stood up, his gaze following Holly as she walked to the kitchen. There'd been something in her eyes, a moment ago. Regret? Pain? No. He was seeing what he wanted to see—and what did *that* mean, anyway? There was nothing to see, nothing to look for except that which he'd come for in the first place.

Closure. And, thanks to the storm, and the enforced intimacy of the long night, he had that.

He could leave today, knowing he'd made peace with his past, and with Holly.

Holly. Once she'd been his wife, and his lover. Now, at long last, she might just have become his friend.

And that would have to be enough.

'What've you got in this thing, anyway?' Nick grunted as he heaved the ice chest from the trunk of Holly's car. 'Rocks?'

'Supplies,' she said, hurrying ahead of him to open the door. 'Here. Put it on the counter.'

'Supplies, huh?' He groaned as he set the chest down and turned towards her. 'I brought "supplies", too. They didn't weigh enough to give a guy a hernia.'

'Well, I told you, I'm going to be staying a while. And I'm going to be working up some recipes. I've got a new book to write.'

Nick leaned back against the counter and folded his arms. 'One Hundred and One Ways to Cook Chicken?'

Holly laughed. 'More like a hundred and one ways to cook lobster.'

His brows lifted. 'People can dine on the cheap eating lobster?'

'I write for a different crowd now.' Holly wrinkled her nose. 'Two-income households, lots of money but no time to cook during the week, so they go all out on Saturday and Sunday.'

'Ah. Yuppies.'

'Or whatever they're called today. How about you?'

'How about me, what?'

'You said you had some stuff, too. Don't you want to bring it in?'

He shrugged. 'Is isn't much, just a couple of steaks. I left the box in my car. It's cold enough to keep and besides…'

'Besides, you'll be leaving soon.'

They looked at each other for a long moment, and then Nick smiled.

'Remember when we were here before?'

'Which time?'

'The first time,' he said quickly. 'There's nothing about the last time that's worth recalling.'

Holly nodded. 'I remember.'

'It snowed that first time, too.' His smile tilted. 'We had a snowball fight. And you said I cheated.'

'You did! You sneaked up behind me—'

'I hit you, fair and square.'

'Didn't.'

'Did.'

'Didn't! The rules were—'

Nick walked casually to the door and opened it. Holly saw what was coming, shrieked and feinted, but it was too late. He grabbed her, and the handful of snow he'd gathered slid icily down her collar and along her spine.

'That's a declaration of war, Brennan,' she gasped.

'Marquess of Queensberry rules,' he yelled, as they grabbed their jackets and ran outside.

'Street rules,' she yelled back.

'Give me a break, Cabot.' Nick dodged her first snowball. 'What does a poor little rich girl know about the street?'

'Plenty,' Holly said, and set out to prove it.

Half an hour later, they'd fought their way almost to the road.

Nick ducked behind a pine tree. A snowball whizzed by his nose.

'Enough,' he said, laughing. 'I give up, Cabot. You win.'

Holly stalked towards him. 'You'd better not be trying to fool me, Brennan.'

'Me?' he said, eyes wide and innocent.

She bent, scooped up a handful of snow, and kept on coming. 'I haven't forgotten how this started, with you jamming ice down my collar while we were still in the kitchen.'

'It was snow, not ice, and that was different.'

'Different, how?'

'Different, because I saw an opportunity and took it.' Holly yelped as Nick grabbed her and hoisted her up in his arms. 'Like now,' he said, laughing, and they tumbled down into a deep white drift.

She struggled to get away, but he caught her, rolled her on her back and straddled her.

'Give up?' he said, holding her arms above her head with one hand, while he scooped up snow with the other.

Holly gasped. 'No fair,' she sputtered.

'You called it war, Cabot. Anything's fair, in love and in war.'

'You're no gentleman, Nick Brennan.'

'And you're no lady, Holly Cabot.' He leaned forward. 'Say "uncle" or get your face scrubbed with snow.'

'Never!' Holly stuck out her tongue. 'I don't give up that easily.'

'Okay. You asked for it—'

Holly bucked as he leaned towards her. 'Nick. Nick, you rat...'

She laughed, and he laughed...and suddenly they were in each other's arms and their mouths were clinging together.

'Nick,' Holly whispered, 'oh, Nick!'

'Baby,' Nick breathed, 'my sweet, sweet baby.'

He flattened his hands on either side of her flushed, snow-chilled face and kissed her with all the bottled-up passion and desire of the endless years that had separated them. Holly wound her arms around his neck, kissing him back as she had so many times in her dreams.

'Kiss me,' she sighed, against his mouth. 'Kiss me...'

The sound was faint, at first, and had no meaning. It was a distant rumble, but it grew louder and louder.

No, she thought, no, please!

Nick heard it, too. He raised his head, listening. 'What in hell is that?'

Holly tucked her face against his shoulder.

'It's the plow,' she said, in a broken whisper. 'They're clearing the road.'

'No.' The word burst from his throat, harsh with anger and disbelief. He rolled over, sat up, and glared around him. 'I don't—'

'Look. Through those birches. Do you see it?'

Nick's breath left his lungs in one long rush. He saw it, all right. The plow had come, the road was clear.

It was time for him to leave, unless…

Holly reached out and touched her hand to his cheek. 'It's for the best,' she said softly. Her eyes glittered with unshed tears, but she smiled. 'There's no going back, Nick. We both know that.'

The hell we do, he started to say…but she was right. Time machines existed only in the movies, not in real life.

So he nodded, got to his feet and held out his hand. Holly took it and stood up beside him.

'You've got snow in your hair,' she said, and gently brushed it away.

There was a catch in her voice. He knew there'd be one in his, too, if he tried to speak. So he took her hand, instead, and brought her palm to his mouth. Hands clasped, they walked slowly to the cabin.

'I'll get my things,' Nick said.

Holly nodded. 'I'll wait here.'

He reached the top of the porch steps and looked around. Holly's back was to him but he knew she was crying.

'Get it over with,' he muttered, and reached for the door.

What was the sense in prolonging this? She'd spoken the truth. It was too late to go back. Miracles only came around once in a lifetime. They'd had theirs, and they'd tossed it away.

Determination got him through the door and halfway up the stairs to the bedroom—and then he stopped.

How could he leave her? They had just found each other again. Sure, they'd had their miracle, but who said you only got one in a lifetime?

Wasn't Christmas all about miracles?

Nick's jaw tightened. He'd never run from anything in his life, except his marriage. Now, he had a second chance. Okay, maybe it wouldn't work. Maybe by the time the weekend was over he'd be more than ready to admit that what they'd had was really gone for ever.

But how could he know that, if he left now?

He took a deep breath. All he had to do was convince Holly. And, dammit, that was what he was going to do...

'Nick?'

He turned at Holly's whisper. She was standing in the open doorway, looking up at him, her hair wet with snow, her lashes spiky with tears.

'Holly.' He came down the steps slowly, searching for the right words, for the right way to say them.

'Nick,' she said, 'oh, Nick, please, please, don't go!'

And then they were in each other's arms.

CHAPTER SEVEN

A MOMENT ago, Nick had been searching for the words that would convince Holly to let him stay with her.

Now, with her in his arms, words had no meaning.

At the beginning of their marriage, they'd never been able to get enough of each other. Need had fed on need; coming through the door at night, seeing Holly waiting for him, he'd been gripped with such hunger that there'd been times they hadn't even made it to the bed before they were in each other's arms, loving each other.

What he felt now transcended even that.

Desire hammered in his blood and roared in his ears, until the universe was reduced to this moment, and this woman.

His wife.

Nick cupped Holly's face and lifted it to his.

'Do you know what you're asking?' he said, his voice a rough whisper.

Color flew into her cheeks. She slid her arms around

his neck. He felt her fingers curve into the hair at the nape of his neck. She swayed forward, rose towards him, so that they were breast to breast, hip to hip.

'Yes. Yes, I know,' she said, as she kissed him.

The kiss drove away whatever remained of Nick's ability to think. He swung Holly up into his arms, kicked the door shut and carried her through the silent house. Her hands linked behind his head; she buried her face against his neck and kissed his throat, and he told himself to hang on, hang on.

He took her to the blankets that had been their bed throughout the long night. The fire still burned on the hearth; the flames flickered and cast their soft glow over Holly's lovely face as he lowered her to her feet.

'I couldn't have left you,' he whispered, framing her face in his hands.

She caught his hand in hers, turned it to her lips and kissed the palm.

'And I couldn't have let you go.'

Nick bent his head and kissed her mouth. 'It's been so long, baby. And I've been so lonely without you.'

'Tell me.' Her eyes were dark, and deep enough to drown in. She laid her palms against his chest, letting the rapid beat of his heart pulse through the tips of her fingers. 'I need to know that I haven't been the only one—'

He silenced her with a long, deep kiss. She tasted just as he remembered, as sweet as honey, as dazzling as champagne. She made a soft, whimpering sound and pressed herself to him, fitting the soft curves of her body to the hard planes of his. He groaned, slid his hands down the length of her spine and under the waistband of her jeans, under her panties, cupping her warm flesh in his hands.

'Nick,' she whispered, 'Nick, please…' He curved his hands around her, sought and found the heat between her thighs. She gave a broken sob and said his name again.

'Tell me,' he said, because he needed to hear the words. 'Tell me what you want, baby.'

Holly caught her lip between her teeth. He was killing her with the touch of his hands, with the heat of his kisses. She was shimmering, glowing, turning into a flame more radiant than any that blazed on the hearth.

She drew back in his arms and looked up at him. 'Make love to me,' she murmured. 'Touch me. Kiss me, taste me…'

The primitive sexuality of her words shot through him like a pulse of flame. The girl he'd been married to would never have said such a thing. Sex had been incredible between them, but he'd always been the one who'd initiated it, who'd whispered words that had brought a blush to Holly's cheeks. She had been responsive, yes, but she'd never asked for anything.

Instinct warned him that she would not hesitate to ask, now. It made what lay ahead all the more exciting.

He unzipped her ski jacket and slipped it from her shoulders, doing it slowly, dropping his head to kiss her arched throat and brush his mouth over hers. Then he knelt before her and unlaced her boots. He slid them from her feet, one at a time; stripped off her socks; lifted each foot and kissed the tender arch, the delicate toes.

He undid her jeans, and they fell in a rough tangle at her feet. She stepped free of them, and he reached forward and drew her sweater over her head.

Now, she was almost naked.

Almost naked, before a man for the first time in so many years. Holly trembled at the realization. There'd been opportunities, but never the desire. What would Nick say, if he knew she hadn't been with a man since him?

Her own vulnerability terrified her.

Nick was just standing there, looking at her. Why didn't he say something? Do something? Once, he'd never been able to keep from touching her. Had the years wrought so many changes? Was she a disappointment, after all this—?

Her breath caught as he reached out and stroked his hand down her cheek, her throat, her shoulder…her breast.

'Holly,' he whispered. 'Holly, my love.'

Slowly, he opened the front clasp of her bra. Her breasts tumbled free and he saw her reach, automatically, to cover herself.

'No,' he said, and caught her wrists. 'Let me look at you.'

He could look at her for ever, if she'd only let him. She was so beautiful.

Creamy skin. Perfect, rose-tipped breasts. The cambered slope that led to the gentle rise of her belly.

He hooked his thumbs into her panties, slowly slid them down her hips. And he looked at her again, his eyes feasting on her breasts, on the graceful curve of her waist, the roundness of her hips, the golden delta between her thighs.

Need for her raced through him like a flood through a ravine. He whispered her name and gathered her into his arms, lifting her, cradling her, as she put her hands on his shoulders and opened her mouth to the heat of his.

'Yes,' she said, against his lips. 'Nick, please, oh, please…'

He wanted to slow down. For her sake. Hell, for his. It was just the way it was when they were kids, on that hot summer day they'd ridden his old Honda to Gailey's Pond and he'd undressed her, seen her, touched her for the very first time.

This was different. There was no rush…

With a ragged groan, Nick tumbled down to the blankets with Holly in his arms.

'Now,' he said, and his hands and hers fumbled at the zip on his jeans, freed his hot, aching flesh, guided it to hers…

He entered her on one long, hard, heart-stopping thrust.

She cried out and arched against him. His head fell back and he thrust deeper.

And, after so many years of being alone and apart, they were one.

When he figured he had enough energy to stand, Nick got up and took off his clothing.

Holly watched through half-lowered eyelids.

'Mmm,' she said. A smile played across her lips. 'Very nice.'

He flushed. She'd seen him naked a thousand times before. Still, there was the feeling that this was their first time together.

'All testimonials welcome,' he said, with a smile. He came down beside her and took her into his arms. 'You're even more beautiful than I remembered.'

'Thank you.'

She said it so seriously that Nick's brows lifted. 'Thank you?'

'Well…' Holly blushed. 'Six years is a long time. I haven't gotten any younger, you know.'

'Ah. Well, that's true. I suppose a man can't expect too much from an old broad of twenty-five… Hey!' Grinning, he rolled her onto her back and pinned her hands gently over her head. 'You've got sharp elbows, you know that?'

'You haven't gotten any younger, either,' she said indignantly.

'Oh, yeah, I know it. My joints creak, my bones ache…it's a hell of a thing, to be pushing thirty.'

'You won't be pushing it for another three years,' Holly said, trying not to laugh. 'And, if it makes you feel any better you look pretty good for an old codger.'

'Just, "pretty good", huh?'

'Well, not bad.'

'You could try being a little more specific.'

'You're pathetic,' Holly said, lips twitching.

Nick waggled his eyebrows. 'A couple of minutes ago, you were whistling another tune, m'dear.'

'I don't know what you're talking about. For starters, I do not whistle.'

'Whistle, applaud, sigh…what's the difference?' He grinned. 'The point's still the same. You were pretty well pleased a little while ago.'

'What would you like, Nicholas Brennan? Applause? You'll do anything to get me to stroke your ego!'

'Well, you can stroke that, too,' Nick said, with an evil leer.

Holly burst out laughing. 'You're impossible.'

His smile faded. 'And you're so beautiful you make my heart ache,' he said softly, and kissed her again, with sweet deliberation. 'I love you, Holly.'

Holly felt her heart turn over. She clasped his face and brought his mouth down to hers.

'Nicky,' she sighed, 'my Nicky…'

His mouth closed over hers, and the sweetness of

their kisses yielded to the fierce hunger that they'd never forgotten.

'Nick,' she whispered. 'Oh, Nick, how I love you!'

The words, those sweet, sweet words he'd never let himself dare hope to hear again, shot through him like a flame. Nick rolled her beneath him, sheathed himself in her.

'Forever,' he said.

Holly's eyes fixed on his. 'Forever,' she whispered, as he began to move.

How could it be any other way? He was part of her, and she was part of him. That was the way it had been, the way it would always be.

Nothing would ever separate them again.

They slept, awoke long enough to make love again, and slept some more.

When they awoke next, the fire had begun to die. Nick fed it some wood while Holly, dressed in his flannel shirt and her wool socks, made a dash for the kitchen. She raced back, carrying a box of crackers, a jar of peanut butter, and a knife.

'I am freezing!' she squealed, burrowing under the blankets, and proved it by putting her icy feet against Nick's thigh.

'By God, woman, are you trying to freeze me to death?' Nick reached down, caught hold of her feet, and rubbed them briskly. 'I'd almost forgotten that you have no heating system of your own.'

'Complaints, complaints.' Holly bit into a peanut-butter-laden cracker, then held out the remaining half. 'Here. Maybe some food will improve your disposition.'

Nick grinned, bit into the cracker, and chewed. 'You're just trying to keep my energy levels up.'

'Oh, right.' Holly licked peanut butter from her fingertips and flashed him a smug grin. 'As if you have any energy levels left, now that I've had my way with you…' Her smile faded. 'Nick? It's as if the past six years never happened.'

'I know. We must have said these same things to each other a thousand times, and laughed whenever we did.' Nick leaned over and dropped a gentle kiss on Holly's lips. 'We had some good times, babe,' he said softly. 'Didn't we?'

'Yes.' She nodded. 'Yes, we did.'

'I have to be honest and admit that I'd pretty much forgotten the good times.'

'Well, so did I.' Holly shrugged her shoulders. 'I suppose that's only natural. I mean, when two people get a divorce…'

Her voice cracked. Nick frowned, hooked his arm around her neck, and pulled her close.

'That's all behind us,' he said.

'Is it?'

He felt, rather than saw, Holly's sudden hesitancy. 'Damn right it is.' His tone was gruff, almost harsh. 'What kind of question is that to ask?'

'A reasonable one,' she murmured, and looked down at her lap.

'The hell it is!' He clasped her chin. 'Look at me,' he said and, when she finally did, he glowered at her. 'I love you. You love me. What else matters?'

Holly shrugged. 'We loved each other the last time around, too,' she said, after a minute.

'Yeah, but we were young. Just a pair of kids.'

'We had problems, Nick. I don't think they had to do with our being kids.'

'Sweetheart.' Nick reached out and drew her into his arms. 'We got married without your parents' blessing.'

'They didn't try to stop us.' Holly shut her eyes and laid her head against Nick's chest. 'You know that. They even came to the wedding.'

'Yeah.' Nick gave a sharp laugh. 'Some wedding. You and me, standing in the office of a Justice of the Peace, you clutching a bouquet of supermarket flowers—'

'They were beautiful flowers,' she said softly.

'They were the only thing I could afford. Me in my one and only, super-shiny, too-short-in-the-pants, too-tight-in-the-shoulders blue gabardine suit.'

Holly smiled against his chest. 'You looked gorgeous.'

'Oh, yeah. I'll just bet. I know how 'gorgeous' I looked, baby. I could see it reflected in your old man's eyes.'

Holly pulled back and looked into Nick's face. 'My father's approval—'

'His disapproval, you mean.'

'Whatever you want to call it, Nick, that was never a problem for me.'

Nick sighed and drew her close again. 'Look, the bottom line is that everything was stacked against us. We were young, we came from different worlds, I was broke…' He lifted Holly's face and smiled at her. 'Fast-forward seven years. Here we are, young but not wet behind the ears. And I am a long, long way from being broke. As for those different worlds…' He grinned. 'Would you believe I've learned to eat raw clams without turning green?'

Holly smiled. 'I remember that. You were so sick afterwards.'

'Well, sure. Your parents invited us to dinner, your father ordered for us… How could I have told him I'd never in my life seen a clam outside of a can of chowder?'

Holly's smile faded. 'You could have. It wouldn't have mattered.'

'Not to you, maybe.'

'Not to him, either. I admit, he wasn't thrilled when I said I was marrying you—'

'An understatement, if ever I heard one.' Nick's smile was forced. 'Not that I blamed him. President of the biggest bank in town, member of the Chamber of Commerce… Hell, why would a guy like that want to see his daughter hook up with a loser?'

Holly pulled out of Nick's embrace. 'He never called you that,' she said fiercely. 'And I wouldn't have let him! You were never a loser.'

A muscle tightened in Nick's jaw. 'I know what I was then, baby. And I know what I am now.'

'Nick—'

'I know what I want now, too.' In one easy motion, he caught Holly and gently drew her down beside him. 'You, sweetheart, ' he whispered, and kissed her. 'You, in my arms, in my heart, in my life.'

The words were sweet, but all too painfully familiar. Nick had said them before, when he'd proposed all those years ago. Then the words had been filled with dreams and promise.

Where had it all gone wrong? When had the dreams died?

'Nick,' Holly said, 'we need to talk.'

'Later.'

'Nicky. I think—'

'I love it when you say my name that way.' His lips teased hers. His hands moved over her body, cupping her breasts, stroking her skin. 'I used to lie awake at night, after we split up, and sometimes I could swear I'd hear you whispering my name in the dark.'

Holly's breath caught as he bent his head and kissed her breasts. His lips closed around the nipple of one, then the other; his fingers drifted between her thighs.

Don't do this, a voice sighed inside her. Talk about what went wrong, or you'll be right back where you started seven years ago.

But this was Nick. Her husband, as much today as ever, because she had never stopped loving him. And she never would.

CHAPTER EIGHT

HOLLY didn't want to wake up.

The dream—this dream—was too sweet. The comforting weight of Nick's arm around her waist. The heat of his body against hers...

Nick stirred, murmured in his sleep. His arm tightened and he drew her back against him, closer into his embrace.

Holly smiled. She wasn't dreaming. Nick, the man she'd never stopped loving, was real.

Carefully, not wanting to wake him, she turned in his arms and studied his face. Everything about him was just as she remembered. The dark hair, tousled now by sleep. The black lashes, so full that they lay against his cheek. The nose, with its sexy little bend. The high cheekbones, so prominent in the pool of light cast by the lamp on the table beside the sofa...

Holly's eyes rounded. Lamplight? *Lamplight?*

'Nick!' She shot upright in their improvised bed.

'Mmm.' Nick reached up and lightly cupped her breast.

'Nicky. Come on, wake up.'

'I am awake, baby.' He clasped her shoulder and he drew her face down to his. 'Want proof?' he whispered, his voice raspy with sleep and desire.

'You're incorrigible,' she whispered back, but her smile belied her words.

Nick kissed her again, rolled onto his back and drew her close. He caught her hand, guided it to him. 'Is that the medical term for this condition, Doc?'

'Nick.'

'Mmm. That feels nice.'

It did. It felt wonderful. What she was doing to him, what he was doing to her...

'Nick.' Holly pulled free of his embrace, sat up, and gave him the sternest possible look. 'Here you are, fooling around—'

'Another medical term?'

'Fooling around,' she said severely, gently slapping his hand away, 'while I'm trying to give you important news.'

Nick sighed. 'We've landed men on Mars?'

'Nick, for goodness' sakes—'

'The power's back.'

'No! Honestly, you'd think...' Holly blinked. 'You know?'

'Uh-huh.' Nick grinned. 'The heating system went on with a roar about an hour ago.'

'And I slept through it?'

'Yup.' He sat up and threaded one hand lazily into her hair. 'C'mere and give me a kiss.'

'Why didn't you wake me?'

'What for? Besides, I doubt if anything could have wakened you.' He gave her a grin so sexy it made her pulse quicken. 'I can't imagine why, but you were out to the world.'

Holly blushed. 'Exhaustion,' she said primly. 'From that drive through the storm yesterday. You know. Delayed reaction.'

'A likely story.' Suddenly, his smile faded. He swept her hair behind her ears, then captured her face between his hands. 'It was incredible,' he said softly. 'Making love with you again…it was everything I remembered, and more.'

Holly smiled. 'I love you.'

'Again.'

'I love you. I love you. I—'

Nick kissed her. When he drew back, he was smiling. 'Do you remember the first time we made love?'

'How could I forget? We drove up to Cape Cod.'

'It was a moonlit night, in early fall. And the beach was deserted.'

'We went for a walk, down by the water.'

'And then into the dunes.' Nick's voice roughened. 'You said you were cold, and I put my arms around you.'

'You kissed me,' Holly whispered. 'And kissed me again.'

'And you slipped your hands inside my jacket, up under my shirt…'

Holly put her arms around Nick and kissed him. 'I've never forgotten that night.'

'That was the night I told you how much I loved you.' He looked into her eyes and smiled. 'I love you even more now, sweetheart. And I don't want to lose you again.'

'I don't want to lose you, either. But—'

'No "but"s'. We'll make it this time, baby.'

'Will we?' Tears glistened in her eyes. 'I couldn't bear it if we failed again, Nick. I couldn't!'

Nick kissed her mouth, her eyes, her tear-stained cheeks.

'We won't,' he said. 'I promise.'

She knew he meant it, but she knew, too, that a thousand things could go wrong between a promise and reality. They had to talk about what had separated them the first time…

But Nick was touching her, caressing her. After a while, there was nothing to say that couldn't be better said with kisses.

Nick shouldered open the front door. His arms were full of things: the carton of groceries he'd taken back out to his truck, his computer, his cellphone, his wireless fax. He dumped the stuff on the hall table, took off his jacket and ran his fingers through his hair.

It had started snowing again. He wondered if another storm might be rolling in, and smiled. Actually, he didn't much care. What could be better than getting snowed in with Holly? Ellen expected him back at the office first thing Tuesday morning, and yeah, there was business to attend to, but nothing—nothing—would ever be as important as the miracle that had happened here this weekend.

He'd come to North Mountain for closure, and he'd ended up winning back the only woman he'd ever loved.

A grin lit Nick's face. He peeled off his jacket, turned on his computer and set up the fax machine. Then he picked up the carton, and strolled into the kitchen. He had a feeling this wasn't quite what the radio shrinks had in mind when they talked about closure, but it sure as heck was good enough for him. Perfect, if you wanted to be accurate.

He paused in the doorway and looked at Holly. She was standing at the stove, stirring something in a skillet that was sending up clouds of fragrant steam. God, she was lovely.

And she was his.

He put down the carton, propped one hip against the table edge, folded his arms, and happily observed his wife.

She had the same effect on him today as she'd had when he was still a kid. She'd been so sweet and innocent…from the first minute she'd walked into his life, he'd wanted nothing more than to cherish her and protect her.

Now, at least, he could.

He knew why their marriage had failed. It was his inability to accept his guilt over having taken his beautiful Holly from a life where she'd had everything, to one where she'd had nothing. That was why he'd accused her of trying to play house, because it had killed him to see the change in her—a change that was his fault. Her graceful hands, reddened by housework. Her midnight-blue eyes, shadowed by worries over money. Her back, achy after hours spent hunched over the ancient sewing machine she'd rescued from God only knew where.

Oh, yeah. It had damn near killed him, all right, especially since he knew he'd stolen her from the life she deserved, one of grace and beauty and wealth.

It was guilt that had made him work a thousand hours a day, that had driven him to school at night so he could improve himself and improve their lives. It was his fault she'd lost her old friends, and been too weary to make new ones. No wonder she hadn't been as excited as he'd wanted her to be about his successes. What could he possibly have expected the night he came home all excited about winning a contract and she'd said she really didn't give a damn?

He'd thought it meant she didn't give a damn about him.

Nick shook his head. He understood now. What she'd really meant was that he'd neglected her. Well, he'd never neglect her again. Hell, he'd pamper her as she'd never been pampered, fill her life with luxuries, see to it that she had everything she could possibly want.

Love, swift as an avalanche, swept through him.

'Holly,' he said, and when she turned to him, her

face lighting with as much joy as surprise, he was lost. He crossed the room with quick, purposeful steps, took the spoon from her hand and pulled her tightly into his arms. 'I love you,' he whispered, and kissed her.

'Wow,' she said, laughing when he let her breathe again. Her eyes were bright with happiness. It thrilled him to know he'd put that glow on her face. 'What did I do to deserve that?'

Nick grinned. 'It's not you,' he teased, 'it's whatever you're cooking up in that pan.' He leaned past her and took an exaggerated sniff. 'Man, oh, man, what is that? Some secret French sauce?'

'Oh,' Holly said with a coy smile, 'it's just something I whipped up.' She laughed, gently shoved him away, and turned off the gas under the skillet. 'It's drawn butter, you big jerk. For the lobster.'

'Ah.' Nick laughed. 'Well, that's pretty exotic.'

Holly smiled. 'You're right. After all, this is a special occasion.'

'Yeah.' He grabbed her around the waist, spun her towards him, and kissed her again. 'Darned right it is.'

An hour later, Nick stared in amazement at the pile of lobster shell fragments heaped on the plate between them.

'Tell me we didn't eat all that,' he said.

'Okay. We didn't.' Holly grinned. '*You* ate most of it.'

Nick slapped his hand over his heart. 'The woman's trying to hurt my feelings! Me? Eat all that lobster?"

'You liked it, hmm?'

'Liked it? I loved it.' Nick reached for her hand and twined his fingers through hers. "Fess up, babe. That wasn't just plain old butter.'

Her smile broadened. 'You're right.'

'So, what was it?'

'It's a secret.'

He laughed. 'A secret?'

'Uh-huh.' Holly batted her lashes. 'You want to know what it is, you'll have to buy a copy of my next cookbook.'

'Which comes out…?'

'A year from July. Of course, I have to write it first, but—'

'No, you don't.'

'Sure I do.' Holly smiled and lifted Nick's hand to her lips. 'I have a contract that says so.'

'Contracts,' Nick said, dismissively. 'My lawyers will get you out of that.'

Holly's smile grew puzzled. Gently, she disengaged her hand from his and sat back.

'Why would they do that?'

'Because I'll ask them to. You won't have time to do that sort of stuff after we're married.'

'What sort of stuff?' she asked, after a pause.

'You know. This stuff. Mucking around in the kitchen.'

'Mucking around in the…?'

'Yeah.' Nick shoved back his chair, stacked the plates, and rose to his feet. 'I know you didn't do this for the money,' he said, as he scraped the leavings of their meal into the trash. He looked back and flashed her a smile. 'As if there could possibly be much money, playing around with cookbooks.'

Holly folded her hands tightly in her lap. 'Really?' she said, very calmly. 'And how would you know how much money there is, playing around with cookbooks?'

'Well, I don't know. Not exactly. But I figured—'

'You figured wrong,' she said, in that same calm voice, and then told him exactly how wrong he was.

Nick's eyebrows shot towards his hairline. 'Really?' He laughed and shook his head. 'Wow. I had no idea—'

'As for doing it for the money…do you build hotels for the money?'

'I don't build them, baby, I own them.'

'It was a figure of speech.'

'I know, but—'

'Answer the question, please. Do you build them for the money?'

Nick licked his lips. He had the sudden feeling that he was heading into deep water in a leaky rowboat.

'Well, sure. I mean, I like what I do. Hell, I love it. But—'

'But you like being paid, too. Surprise, Nick. So do I.' She smiled tightly. 'And, while we're on the subject, I've always liked what you'd probably call "mucking about" the house. Sewing. Cooking. Fussing.'

'Yes. I know that. I—'

'No. No, you don't know that.' Holly kicked back her chair and got to her feet. 'You never understood that I liked contributing what I could to our marriage.' She grabbed the salt shaker and pepper mill from the table, marched to the counter and slammed them down. 'Not money, but things that I hoped would make our lives more pleasant and take some of the burden, the worry about money, off your shoulders.'

'Sweetheart, that was generous of you. I'm only trying to point out that none of that is necessary any-more.'

Holly swung towards him, eyes flashing. 'I *hate* it when you use that condescending tone with me!'

Nick stared at her. What the hell was happening? 'Holly, baby—'

'My name is not Hollybaby! I might have been young when you married me, but I was a grown woman, not a—a starry-eyed Rapunzel, living in a tower, waiting for a man to come along and rescue me.'

'Hey.' Nick held up his hands. 'How about we take a deep breath and calm down?'

'I hate it even more when you patronize me!'

Holly spun back towards the sink and plunged her hands into the soapy water. Six endless years had gone by but nothing had changed. Oh, they were arguing, yes, instead of sulking in silence, but Nick still saw her as a helpless, spoiled little rich girl. All that was left, if time really was going to spin backwards, was for him to end this scene by saying he had work to do…

'Do you want help with the dishes?' he said, after the silence had become almost unbearable.

'No.'

He sighed. She didn't want anything, not from him. He could read it in the set of her shoulders. Damn if he didn't feel as helpless as he'd felt years ago, wanting to go to Holly and either kiss her or shake her until she understood that all he wanted was her happiness.

The only solution was to get himself out of here before one of them said something they'd regret.

'Fine,' he said. 'In that case…I'm going to get my computer. I have some work to do.'

Holly dumped a pot into the sink. Soapy water sloshed over the edge.

'Important work, I'm sure.'

'Yes. Of course it's—'

'Important. I know. After all, you don't deal in cookbooks.'

'Holy hell,' Nick roared. He stalked to the sink, clasped his wife's rigid shoulders, and spun her towards him. 'You're right. I don't deal in cookbooks. I run a Fortune 500 company, baby, and I'll be damned if I'll apologize for it!'

'Why would you? I'm sure the world turns at your command.'

'You never gave me any credit for what I did, Holly. Well, try this on for size. I've got the biggest deal ever in the works right now.'

'Imagine that,' she said politely. 'I'm just amazed a

man of your importance would have chosen to rent a cabin like this for a weekend.'

'I didn't rent it. I own it.'

He saw, with bitter satisfaction, that that stopped her.

Her eyes widened. 'You own North Mountain?' she said incredulously.

'Damn right I do. I'm going to build a resort right here, where this cabin stands, that'll dwarf anything you've ever imagined.'

'You mean…you mean, you're going to take down this cabin?'

No. Hell, no! He knew it instantly. He wasn't. That was the reason he'd come to the mountain, to admit to himself that he'd never tear the cabin down…

Holly wrenched free of his hands. 'Good. That's wonderful news.'

'Holly, wait—'

'Burn it down, why don't you?' Her heart felt as if it were breaking in pieces, but she'd be damned if she'd let him know that. 'That's the best way I know of to get rid of ghosts.'

'Ghosts?' he said in bewilderment.

'That's why I came here, Nick. Because, lately, I was plagued with memories. I couldn't seem to stop thinking about us. About our marriage.'

'I know. Holly—'

'No. You don't know. You *never* knew.' She spoke quickly, running her words together, despising herself for letting herself think she still loved him, knowing she'd despise herself even more if she let him see her cry. 'Our marriage was a mistake. I always knew that but I guess I just needed reminding.' She lifted her chin and forced a smile to her lips. 'Thank you for providing it.'

Her words knifed through his heart. 'No.' He pulled her into his arms, though her body was stiff and unyielding. 'You don't mean that. Think of how it was between us, just a little while ago. The things we said, the things we did…'

'Sex,' she said. Her voice trembled, but her eyes were steady on his. 'That's what it was, Nick. And it's not enough. It doesn't make up for a lack of love.'

Nick's face whitened. His hands slid from Holly's arms and fell to his sides.

'Closure,' he said softly.

'What?'

He didn't bother answering. What was there to say, when the woman you loved confirmed your most painful suspicions? She'd never said she didn't love him before, not even when they'd agreed to divorce. But he'd always known there'd come a time she'd look at him and realize that their marriage, that *he* had been a mistake.

That time had finally arrived, and there was nothing more to say.

He made his way into the living room, unplugged his computer, snapped it shut and tucked it under his arm. Then he slung on his jacket, stuffed his cellphone and the fax into his pocket and glanced up the stairs.

His suitcase was up there, but he didn't give a damn about something so trivial. A couple of more minutes in this place and, despite his pain, he'd do something stupid, like telling Holly that he still loved her, would always love her, whether or not she'd ever loved him.

He heard Holly's slow footsteps behind him.

'Nick.' Her voice was low and shaky. 'Nick, I'm sorry…'

'Yeah.' He pulled the door open. 'Me, too.'

The door swung shut, and Holly was alone.

CHAPTER NINE

NICK took a hard right as he came down off the mountain and swung into the gas station with tyres squealing.

The station looked deserted. He got out of the Explorer and put his hands on his hips.

'What kind of a place is this?' he growled. 'You can't sell much gas if you're never open for business.'

A bell jingled behind him. Nick spun around and his mouth dropped open. An old man was coming down the steps from the office. But it wasn't the owner of the station. Hell, no. This bozo had white hair down to his shoulders, a big moustache and a bushy white beard. His red cap was trimmed with a perky white tassel; he had on shiny black boots and a bright red suit.

'Santa Claus?' Nick said, with an I-don't-believe-it laugh.

'Aye-up.' The old guy swaggered towards Nick. 'It's Christmas Eve, you know.'

'Is it?' Nick shrugged. 'I guess I forgot.' He looked the old man over from head to toe. Just went to prove that you could never trust anything. Who'd have figured this character would go in for Christmas hype? 'What's with the outfit?'

'Been doin' it for near onto twenty years. You want this thing filled up?'

'No, the gas is fine. But I've got a long drive ahead of me and the light on my dash says my oil's running low.'

'Don't want that to happen, especially with a new storm comin' in.'

'Yeah, that's what I thought.'

Santa cocked an eye skyward as he opened the hood of the Explorer.

'Storm'll be here late tonight. Good thing you came down from the mountain or you'd have been snowbound for a week.'

'Yes, I know. I…' Nick frowned. 'You remember me?'

'Oh, aye-up. Remember you well. Bought extra gas, some bags of sand…didn't need any of it, I take it.'

'No. No, the road was passable.'

'And you decided not to stay, hmm?'

'That's right. I…' Nick looked at the old guy. 'I never said I was going to stay.'

'Aye-up, that's true enough. Let's see…you're a quart down. Regular, or the extra-expensive stuff?'

'The extra-ex…' Nick laughed. 'Regular. Regular's fine.' He tucked his hands into his pockets. 'So, you put on this outfit every Christmas?'

'Just about.'

Nick smiled. 'And does it sell extra gas?'

'Does it…?' Santa shook his head. 'Don't do it for that. I'm headin' over to the home down on East Main. Been turnin' up there every Christmas Eve for the past—'

'Twenty years,' Nick said slowly. 'You mean the Hunter Home for Boys, right?'

'Aye-up, that's it.'

'Man, but it's a small world! I grew up there. You used to show up at Christmas and give us each a toy.'

'Uh-huh.'

Nick smiled. 'Wow. You were the best thing that happened to me all year.'

Santa shut the hood of the vehicle and wiped his hands on a bright red rag. 'Thought as much, from the way you climbed up on my knee one time when you were maybe five or six, and whispered your one wish in my ear.'

Nick blanched. 'You couldn't remember that… Oh. Oh, of course. It's what all the kids did, right?'

'"Give me somebody to love,"' you said. Remember?'

There were a couple of seconds of silence, and then Nick gave a little laugh. 'Amazing,' he said, 'that we'd all have made that same wish.'

'Then, when you got too big to climb on my lap, you said you had another wish.'

Nick's smile faded. 'I suppose you remember that, too.'

'"I want to make lots of money when I grow up,"'

you said.' The old man looked into Nick's eyes. 'Well,' he said softly, 'your wishes came true, son. I just hope you managed to figure out that money can't buy happiness but it sure as heck can get in the way of it.'

Nick stared into Santa's blue eyes. They'd seemed faded with age yesterday but now—now they were bright, and clear, and bottomless.

'I found happiness,' Nick said in a choked voice. 'But I lost it.'

'Lost it, or misplaced it? There's a big difference.'

Nick shook his head. 'Lost it. I was a damn fool. I let the woman I loved—the only woman I'll ever love—think that my becoming successful was the most important thing in the world.'

'Wasn't it?' Santa asked softly.

'No! Hell, no. She was the most important thing. She still is. She'll always be. It's just that…' He swallowed dryly. 'I wanted to give her everything she'd given up, to marry me. It killed me to see her doing things she'd never had to do in her life, scrimping, sweating, counting pennies just to keep us going…'

'Ah. I see.' Santa nodded thoughtfully. 'So, while she was supposed to be grateful you were knocking yourself out to give her everything, she was also supposed to understand that you didn't want her to give you anything in return.'

'You don't understand. I'm not talking about turning away her gifts. I'm talking about not wanting to watch her work. She sewed, she cooked, she cleaned…'

'She made you a home,' Santa said quietly. 'And you didn't want it.'

'No!' Nick's hands knotted into fists at his sides. 'God, no! Of course I wanted it. I wanted her. I wanted…I wanted…'

And suddenly, after all the years and the sorrow, he saw it all. How Holly had tried to give him tangible proof of her love and how his own stiff-necked pride, his damnable ego, had made him blind to those tokens of the heart. How he had rejected her offerings again and again…

How he'd rejected them tonight.

Nick whisked his wallet out of his pocket and peeled off a bill. He pressed it into Santa's mittened hand.

'Does that cover the oil?'

Santa looked down at the bill and his bushy brows lifted. 'Ten times over. Just wait a minute while I get change.'

'No. I don't want change. In fact…' Nick opened his wallet again, pulled out half a dozen bills, and stuffed them into Santa's hand, too. 'Buy some more toys for the Boys' Home. How's that sound?'

Santa grinned. 'Sounds just fine.'

'Good. Great. Terrific.' Nick grinned, too. Then he patted the old man awkwardly on the back. 'Thank you,' he said, as he slid behind the wheel of his Explorer. 'For everything.'

'You're welcome.' Smiling, Santa watched as Nick pulled out onto the dark, deserted road. His smile broadened when the vehicle suddenly stopped, then roared into reverse.

Nick put down his window. 'Santa?'

'Yes?'

Nick smiled. 'Merry Christmas.'

The old man chuckled. 'Merry Christmas to you, too, son. And to that sweet young woman you left up on North Mountain.'

Nick's brow furrowed. 'How did you…?'

'Got to get goin',' the old man said, and just at that moment a sudden snow flurry swept through the station, obliterating everything in a whirl of white. When it had passed, the old man was gone, and the station lights had winked out.

Nick stared at the darkened gas pumps. Then he took a deep breath and swung the Explorer across the highway, back towards North Mountain.

Holly sat, cross-legged, in the middle of the bed.

The wind was howling wildly around the cabin; snow pattered against the windows. It was the kind of night to curl up by the fire, to lie in the arms of your lover…

She blinked back her tears.

What an idiot she'd been, to have thought she and Nick might have had a chance at being happy. He was so full of himself, of his plans, his successes…

She jumped at the sudden, piercing shrill of the telephone, then stared at it as it rang again. Who'd call her here, especially tonight?

Her heart thumped and she snatched up the phone.

'Nick?' she said.

'Holly?' It wasn't Nick. The voice was too deep. 'Holly,' it said again, and then the instrument went dead.

Great. This was just what she needed. Another storm building, a telephone that wouldn't work...

The phone rang again.

'Hello?' Holly said, jamming it against her ear.

A chorus of metallic shrieks and whistles poured through the receiver. Holly winced and held the thing away from her ear.

'Is anybody there?' she shouted. 'You'll have to speak up, whoever you are. I can hardly hear you.'

'Holly? It's...linda.'

'Who?'

'It's me. Bel...'

'Belinda?' Holly frowned and switched the phone to her other ear. 'I don't think this connection's going to last. Why are you calling? Is there a problem?'

'No. No prob...' Static crackled like lightning. '...hello. And to tell you...idea.'

'An idea? What kind of idea? Listen, this phone's going to die any second. If you called for a reason, you'd better get to it.'

'I just...wonderful new recipes yet?'

'No. But I will.' Holly frowned. 'Belinda? Your voice is so deep. Are you okay?'

'I'm fine. Just...flu. There's...going around.'

'Well, you sound awful. Not at all like yourself. You ought to make yourself a toddy. Hot, buttered rum is—'

'Holly. Listen to me. I've had…book.'

'What?' Holly shouted. 'I can't hear you.'

'I said, I have an idea for your next book.'

Holly blinked. That was certainly unusual. Belinda didn't know a thing about cooking, or cookbooks. The success of their relationship had to do with Holly's talent and Belinda's contacts, not her expertise. But then, this entire conversation was unusual. The static. The howling wind. The surprising depth of Belinda's voice.

The faint hint of a New England accent?

Holly swung her legs to the floor and sat up straight. 'Belinda? Belinda, is that really—?'

'…book for…marrieds.'

'Marrieds? What does that mean?'

'…cookbook. For…newly-weds.'

A cookbook. For newly-weds? Holly rolled her eyes. Of course, this was Belinda on the phone. Who else would come up with an idea that had been done to death?

'There are a hundred books like that,' she said. 'One-dish meals, quick meals, easy meals… I really don't think there's a market there.'

'…with advice. Know what I mean?'

'No, I don't know what you mean.' Holly's frown deepened. 'You really should see a doctor. Your voice is so strange, it's, well, almost masculine. It's kind of spooky.'

'Holly. About the book—'

'Belinda.' Holly pinched the bridge of her nose and took a deep breath. 'Look, it isn't that I don't appreciate your efforts. It's just that I've had a long day. It snowed up here, and—and you were right, I shouldn't have come at all, and—'

'A recipe on one page, a bit of advice on the other,' Belinda said.

Holly sighed. 'What kind of advice?' she said wearily, because it was becoming obvious she'd never get Belinda off the phone until she heard her out.

'Are you sure you can hear me clearly now, Holly? I want to make sure you get all of this.'

'Yes. Actually, for some reason, you're suddenly coming through just fine.'

'Good. As for the sort of advice you could offer—how's this? You'd ask your readers, "Is your husband working longer hours than you think he should? Is he less appreciative of the things you do around the house than you think he should be?"'

'Honestly, Belinda…'

'"If he is, perhaps you need to consider things from his viewpoint. If he grew up poor, and you grew up rich, he probably feels guilty about taking you away from that lifestyle."'

Holly got off the bed. 'Belinda? What is this?'

'"Maybe he's overcompensating. Maybe he's working harder than he should to try and give you the things he thinks you deserve."'

'Wait a minute. Wait just a darned minute! Who is this?'

'"Maybe, when he sees you sewing curtains, and cooking hamburger in a zillion different ways, he sees only that he's condemned you to a life of drudgery."'

'Who *is* this? I know it isn't Belin—'

'Aye-up, maybe he's behaved badly, Holly, but if he has, it's only because that boy loves you with all his heart.'

There was a gentle click, and then a buzz, and Belinda's voice—someone's voice—was gone.

Holly stared at the phone and then, very carefully, put it down. Who could have known so much about her? About Nick?

Her throat constricted.

Who could have been so right?

Why hadn't she seen it? It wasn't that Nick was self-centered, it was that he blamed himself for not having been able to give her the things she'd grown up with.

'Things,' Holly said bitterly. As if 'things' mattered, as if Nick weren't the only thing that mattered, the only man, the only love of her life.

'Holly?'

Holly's head came up. 'Nick?' she whispered.

It couldn't be. She had to have imagined his voice.

'Holly. Where are you? Holly, sweetheart…'

She raced from the bedroom and through the hall. Oh, it was true! It was Nick, coming up the stairs.

'Nick,' she said, and when he looked up and saw the joy on her face he knew everything would be all right.

'Holly,' he whispered, and a second later they were in each other's arms.

A little before midnight, the snow stopped. The stars came out, burning fiercely against the blackness of the sky, and a big white moon hung over North Mountain.

Holly, snug in her husband's arms, turned her face to his.

'I love you, Nicholas Brennan,' she said.

Nick kissed her. 'And I love you, Mrs. Brennan. For richer, for poorer, in sickness and in health…'

'Forever,' Holly whispered, and they kissed again. After a moment, she put her head on his shoulder. 'Will it bother you? My career, I mean.'

'Bother me? Sweetheart, I'm proud of you. I can't wait to tell everybody I know that my wife writes cookbooks.' He grinned. 'I might even buy a couple, and learn how to cook—if you'll agree to give me private lessons.'

Holly laughed softly. 'Absolutely—if you'll take me along on some of your business trips.'

'Come with me on all of them—although there won't be so many, now. I've got some damn good people working for me. I don't have to be involved in every detail of running Brennan Resorts.' His arms tightened around her. 'I don't want to be, baby…I mean, sweetheart. Not anymore.'

'Actually,' Holly said dreamily, 'I love it when you call me "baby".' She touched her fingers to his lips. 'It's sexy. And it makes me feel protected.' She snuggled against him, and then she cleared her throat. 'Nick?'

'Hmm?'

'I know this sounds weird, but—did you call me on your cellphone this evening? Before you got here?'

Nick shook his head. 'I tried. I wanted to tell you how much I loved you, and what an idiot I've been…'

'What idiots we've both been,' Holly interrupted.

'But your line was busy.' He sighed. 'It's probably just as well. I might have said the wrong thing and you'd have told me not to bother showing my face.'

'No. I'd never have told you that. Not after I spoke with— with…'

'With whom?'

Holly frowned. It was a good question. Who'd telephoned her tonight? Belinda? In her heart, she didn't think so. But if it hadn't been Belinda or Nick…

'Somebody who gave me some good advice,' she said.

'I had a conversation I'm grateful for, too.' Nick laughed. 'You'll never believe it, but this old guy was all dressed up as--'

'Nick! Nick, look!'

Holly and Nick turned towards the window. Something was moving across the face of the moon. Figures. Tiny figures. One, two, three, four…

'…five, six, seven, eight,' Nick said in hushed tones.

Holly stared, transfixed. 'And that,' she whispered, 'that looks like a sleigh. Nick, do you see it? And—and there's someone driving it. He's waving to us...'

A cloud swept in, obscuring the moon. When it passed, the silhouette was gone.

Nick gave a shaky laugh. 'Snow geese. That's what it probably was. Snow geese, flying across the night sky.'

'Snow geese,' Holly said, letting out her breath. 'Definitely.'

Nick smiled. 'Merry Christmas, wife.'

Holly smiled, too, as she went into his arms. 'Merry Christmas, husband.'

'Aye-up,' the wind whispered, as it curled around the snug little cabin. Off in the distance, the sweet, haunting sound of sleighbells rang out across the mountain.

JANE PORTER

Jane Porter grew up on a diet of Mills & Boon®
romances, reading late at night under the covers
so her mother wouldn't see! She wrote her first
book at age eight and spent many of her school
and college years living abroad, immersing herself
in other cultures and continuing to read vora-
ciously. Now Jane has settled down in rugged
Seattle, Washington, with her gorgeous two sons.
Jane loves to hear from her readers. You can write
to her at PO Box 524, Bellevue, WA 98009, USA.
Or visit her website at www.janeporter.com

CHAPTER ONE

"YOU can't arrest me." Emily Pelosi's voice betrayed none of the icy cold she felt on the inside. "I've done nothing wrong."

"Step aside, *mademoiselle*," the uniformed customs agent repeated tonelessly, destroying the effect of his lilting Caribbean accent.

Emily worked to keep her irritation from showing. She wasn't easily intimidated, had never been timid, and after five years of fighting fire with fire she held her ground now, hanging on to what had been written up once in the *Times* as "her remarkable cool." "Can you legally detain me?"

The customs agent looked at her as if she were stupid. "Yes."

Emily's brain raced, trying to absorb facts. Clearly she was in trouble, and clearly it wouldn't do to alienate the customs agent further. "I understand. But if someone could just get my friend…she's outside, waiting?"

"She'll just have to wait."

Emily looked away, swallowed, the long veil of her chestnut hair half hiding her face, cloaking her frustration. *Be cool, stay calm. Annelise will eventually return to the terminal and we'll get this whole thing straightened out.*

Head throbbing, eyes dry and gritty after the red-eye flight from Heathrow, she scanned the small island terminal. The squat cement building was virtually deserted, leaving just her and the customs agent alone.

She wished for the first time she'd taken something to make her sleep, like Annelise had, instead of working. But Emily had made herself work through the night. Just as she always worked these days. Emily Pelosi. Workaholic.

For a moment Emily had a strange view of her life—a life lived in international airport terminals and foreign hotels, with business meetings conducted over pots of green tea.

She didn't live, she thought wearily, she existed. To attack. To plunder. To destroy. But now she had to focus on more practical matters—like that of Annelise outside, waiting. "I understand you're not interested in my friend, but if someone could just let her know what's happening?"

"Your friend has already been advised that she can't return to the terminal." The customs agent crossed his arms over his chest. "And you must wait until the detectives arrive."

Detectives? Detectives from where? Emily had

been flying into Anguilla for years, *en route* to St. Matt's, and she'd never been stopped before, never been hassled about anything. "You have a warrant, then?" she asked, feeling as if she were piecing together a puzzle in the dark.

"Yes, *mademoiselle*. We have a warrant issued by a member of the EU." The uniformed officer spoke with the heavily accented English of the Eastern Caribbean. Most of the islands close to South America were multi-lingual—French, Dutch, English, Spanish—and many of the smaller islands, like St. Matt's, were privately owned.

"But this isn't part of the European Union."

"We're working more closely with US and EU Customs to control piracy."

Piracy. International smuggling. And suddenly Emily suddenly understood. "Which member of the EU?"

"Italy. More specifically, a group called the Altagamma."

The Altagamma. Her lips nearly curved in a small, bitter, brutal smile. Of course. It was all beginning to make sense.

The Altagamma was an association that represented quality Italian goods for national and international markets. Some forty brands comprised the Altagamma, with sales in excess of eleven billion dollars—most of which came from exports. And Tristano Ferre was the new president of the Altagamma.

Tristano Ferre.

Emily felt a shaft of ice pierce through her chest.

Tristano Ferre. This was his doing.

For a moment her head buzzed with white noise, the kind of empty static that drowned out other sound. There were few people she knew as well as Tristano. Few people she hated as much. Tristano had taken over from his father, Briano, a number of years ago, and if Briano had been hard, tough, ruthless, Tristano was a thousand times worse.

"Ah." The guard exhaled with relief. "They've arrived. The detectives are coming now."

She heard a metallic clang, and when she turned around Emily saw the doors at the far end of the small terminal part. Three men entered the building—two uniformed, one in plain clothes—and Emily realized her war on Ferre Design was just about to get interesting.

Two hours later the detectives had gone, and for a moment Emily sat alone in a small room that had probably never served any purpose in all the years the little island terminal had existed. She'd flown in and out of Anguilla so many times, and had never known about the little room before.

Tired, hungry—she'd been offered nothing to eat or drink—she glanced down at her hands, flexed her fingers. As always, her fingers were bare, her nails unpolished, filed smooth and short. She had practical hands, and yet it was an impractical life.

Her trips to China, her meetings with manufacturers. What had once been merely a stab at Ferre had become a deep-rooted commitment to Asia itself. She'd learned that many of the Chinese were great capitalists—creative, driven, dedicated to perfecting technology—and she'd respected that drive to succeed, admired the fact that everyone she'd met in China wanted the opportunity to work for himself, everyone had a dream of being an entrepreneur.

The door opened quietly, and yet Emily heard it. Her head lifted.

Tristano stood in the doorway. His thick dark brown hair was neatly combed, and yet even dressed in elegant clothes there was still something fiercely masculine about him. He was very tall, and very broad-shouldered. Rugged. Like a Tuscan farmer instead of one of the richest design manufacturers in Italy.

"*Buongiorno*, Emily." His voice, so deep, whispered across her skin.

Her jaw clenched, and for the first time she actually felt sick.

She'd wondered when he'd appear, had expected to see him once the customs agent had said the Altagamma was involved, but somehow seeing him here, face to face, was worse than she'd expected. She hated Tristano. Hated him so much she wanted blood.

"You can't escape me this time," he continued genially, as if they were two friends meeting in the middle of a sunny public square.

But of course he hadn't given up. He'd never give

up. Not until he'd removed her as a threat to his company. It might have been two years since his last lawsuit, but he had kept going. And that second one should have been a clear warning.

"Really?"

He entered the room, gently closed the door behind him, and yet she flinched at the click of metal on metal.

Tristano approached and she longed to look away, avert her head, but she wouldn't let him have the upper hand.

"More interrogation?" she mocked, calmly crossing her leg above her knee, hands folded in her lap.

His eyes, the darkest blue, held hers. "This is serious, Emily."

She felt a sizzle of alarm as he continued to approach, the fabric of his slacks hugging his thighs, the muscles taut, honed, visible. "I'm sure it is." He was bigger than she remembered. Harder. But she was stronger, harder, too. Her lips curved in a cool challenge. "You're losing money."

"I have lost money, yes, but the association is losing, too. You're not just hurting me. You're hurting many, many Italians."

"I'm only reproducing Pelosi designs."

"Ferre designs," he corrected.

"But they're not your designs. They're mine. Emily Pelosi Designs."

He stood over her, the table between them, his eyes

narrowed as he gazed down at her. "So why are your handbags and luggage lines exact replicas of ours?"

She shrugged. "It's as I told the detectives. The bags are generic lookalikes, which is legal."

"Not generic. Your luxury line infringes on our company trademarks, and when you sell the bags they're marketed as Ferre & Pelosi, like our original line."

Another cool shift of her shoulders. "I label nothing. If retailers choose to market a bag as such, how can I stop them? I'm in London, not Chicago or San Francisco."

He leaned across the table, looked her in the eye. His voice dropped low, so low she had to strain to hear. "What you're doing, *cara*, is illegal."

Cara. Cara. She'd once been his *cara*, but she'd been young and innocent. Trusting. He'd taken that trust, along with everything else. So she said nothing, just held his gaze, staring up at him furiously, defiantly, grateful in some respects that their battle was finally taking place face to face.

Her silence succeeded in provoking him. His features tightened. "Where are your ethics?" he snapped, leaning further across the table, moving so close she could smell a whiff of the spice of his subtle fragrance, see the grooves paralleling his mouth.

"Where are yours?" she countered.

"Everything I do is legal. While you...you're a pirate."

A pirate? She nearly smiled. He was right. She felt like a pirate, a buccaneer, one of the many outlaws that settled in the Caribbean in the middle of the 1600s.

"You weren't raised like this," he continued tersely.

"Leave my education out of this. I'm doing what needs to be done."

"Despite the consequences?"

"I'm not afraid."

"Just foolish," he concluded, with a faint shake of his head, watching her, seeing how her blue-green eyes flashed fire, seeing how determined she was to bring him down.

Everything in her was bent on destruction. Specifically, destroying him. But she hadn't been reckless, she'd been smart. Very smart, and remarkably careful. Only he'd been just as smart, and even more careful, because this time he was going to make sure the charges stuck.

This time Emily Pelosi would be held accountable.

"The detectives have a plane waiting," he said, sitting down on the corner of the table, close to her, invading her space, making his presence known.

He saw her lips compress. She didn't like to be crowded, especially not by him. Too bad. This time Emily wasn't going to get what she wanted. This time it was his way.

Her head tipped back, long hair spilling down her back. "Put me on it."

Tristano had to admire her. She had guts, he thought, enjoying the hot spark in her eyes. But then, she'd never been afraid of a fight. He wouldn't call her a tomboy, but she'd always believed so fiercely in things, had loved her family passionately, loved her friends, too. Growing up, he'd never thought of her as English…British…but Italian through and through. And yet now she wasn't a girl but a woman, and she was the epitome of tough. Cool.

"The detectives will take you to Puerto Rico, where the investigation is based."

"Fine."

"They will toss you in jail." His lips curved, firmed, and there was bite in his words. "With all the other thieves, smugglers and criminals waiting prosecution."

She shifted, one leg crossed high above the other knee, without putting a single wrinkle in her impeccably white pinstriped linen trousers. She'd paired the expensive trousers with a black halter-top which revealed her slim pale gold shoulders, and the pale gold column of her throat. "Great. Let them know I'm ready."

"You don't mind going to jail?"

"No."

"You'll be locked up with dangerous people—people without any regard for human life—"

"Fine," she interrupted. Her chin lifted. "You've no regard for human life either, and, frankly, I'd rather be there than here with you."

Maledizione. She *was* a pirate. A rogue beauty— brave, foolish, swaggering, cunning, vain. If she'd lived during the seventeenth Century he was certain she would have followed in the footsteps of famous women pirates, like Grace O'Malley, Anne Bonny and Mary Read.

Instead she was here, alone with him, beautiful, proud, intelligent, fierce.

And he wanted her. He felt like a bounty-hunter, because he'd been working for a long time to rein her in, bring some control back to his life and Ferre Design. But, unlike a bounty-hunter, he didn't want her shackled in jail. He wanted her shackled in his bed. He wasn't about to turn her over to the authorities.

But he wasn't going to tell her that. Let her think she'd be handed over to the detectives and customs officers. Let her think she had a choice when really she had none.

It was time Emily Pelosi faced facts, and this time she was going to face them. Alone with him.

"So what happens now?" she asked, and she sounded almost bored. Definitely complacent.

"After deportation, or after time in jail?"

Her expression didn't change. "I was thinking more in terms of my friend Annelise. What happens to her?"

"She's already taken a plane back to London."

Tristano saw a flicker of emotion cross Emily's flawless face. Worry? Dread? Regret? And then the expression disappeared, leaving her perfect oval-shaped face serene again.

"Going to jail doesn't scare you?" he asked, trying to understand her, wanting to understand how she'd changed so much in the years since they'd been close friends. Although friends wasn't an adequate description. They'd been more than friends, they'd been lovers, too, and for a couple of weeks one August they'd been together every moment possible.

He tried to remember the last time he'd seen her. It couldn't have been all that long ago. She'd once moved in similar circles. They both came from affluent Italian families, had both grown up in the same inner circle, with big houses in Milan and rambling estates in the Tuscan hills, estates where vines covered acres and orchards of olive trees covered more. But the problems with her father had resulted in a deep break between the families, and the Pelosis had left Italy to return to England, where Emily's mother was from.

And even with half of Europe stretching between them he had bumped into Emily more often than one would have thought. They had both attended a party in Sienna a year or two ago, and then there'd been the passing at the airport. Her flight had just landed and his had been about to depart. They hadn't spoken either time. They'd simply looked at each other and moved on.

It had been clear to him then she had nothing to say, and he hadn't been sure what he wanted to say to her.

Well, that wasn't entirely true. He'd wanted to tell her to stop with the counterfeiting, tell her he was cracking down, that he had to get serious. But he couldn't breach the divide, couldn't reason with her when she looked at him with so much ice and hatred in her eyes.

Emily.

He was only four years older, but right now he felt vastly her senior, knowing that the charges leveled against her this time would stick, that his director of security had gathered enough evidence, enough samples, enough of everything to cost her…everything.

"You don't want to go to jail," he said roughly, knowing she wasn't going to listen. If a week alone with him couldn't persuade her to change course, then he'd go the legal route. Punish her to the fullest extent of the law. But he wanted a week first. Christmas together.

"There's a lot of things I don't want to happen that do," she answered, and she glanced at her wristwatch, as if she had some pressing engagement to go to. Again he marveled at her cool, at her incredible calm.

"You do have other choices," he said.

Emily drew a slow breath and exhaled just as slowly. She was tired. She knew she couldn't fight forever. But she also knew she wouldn't go down until she'd brought him to ruin, too. "I'm not giving up."

The corner of his mouth tugged, but his dark blue eyes were hard, void of all compassion. "I don't expect you to."

"So what are my choices? How do I avoid arrest?"

"You don't avoid arrest—that's happened—but it's up to you where you spend your Christmas holiday." He paused and she stared at him, waiting for him to finish. "You can," he continued tonelessly, "get on that plane to Puerto Rico, or you can come home with me."

"Home with you?"

"St. Matt's."

"St. Matt's isn't your home."

His eyebrows lifted and Emily bit down on the inside of her lip hard. *What the hell?* A dozen questions welled up inside her but she wouldn't ask one. She had to stay cool, collected, had to hang on to whatever dignity remained. There was no way she'd let Tristano see how much he disturbed her. And he did disturb her. Not as an adversary, but as a man.

And that made him the most dangerous adversary of all.

"Let me see if I understand you correctly," she said rising from the table, sidestepping Tristano's powerful frame.

In the past five years she'd been confronted by tremendous difficulties—more problems and controversy than she'd ever imagined—and yet she'd survived every crisis by staying cool, keeping her wits about her. But right now her wits felt scattered. Lost. Instead of thinking her way out of the problem, she kept thinking about *him.* "I'm still under arrest, but I won't be deported if I agree to accompany you to your house on St. Matt's?"

Tristano nodded his confirmation.

"How convenient for you," she drawled coolly, shooting him an icy look.

"I'd say inconvenient—but why mince words?"

"Indeed." Her voice dripped sarcasm and she stared

at him a long moment, then looked away, her lips curving in a hard smile. If this was war—and it had been war for several years now—he had just won a major battle. But he hadn't won the game yet. He hadn't stopped her.

Still smiling that small, faint smile, she glanced back at him. "Maybe I'd rather go to Puerto Rico."

"I wouldn't be surprised, dearest Em. You've always preferred doing everything the hard way."

She bit down, working her teeth, her jaw tight. "Can you please use Emily, not Em?" She hated being called Em. Her father was the only other person who'd ever called her Em, and to have Tristano use the same intimate form of her name hurt.

Tristano had helped destroy her father. He'd taken her father's strength…stripped him of his power, his pride, that inherent male dignity…leaving him empty. Dead.

"Whatever makes you happy, *cara*."

"What do you want, Tristano?"

He stood up, approached her, towering over her. "You know what I want. The question is, are you ready to work with me?"

"But you don't mean work with you. What you intend to do is shut down my company—"

"Your company isn't a company!" His voice rose, his anger palpable. "Your entire company is based on undercutting mine."

"I'm merely offering consumers a comparable

product at a lower cost, and that's called commerce. Capitalism. Something even *you* should understand."

His eyes narrowed, creases forming at the corners, and his frustration became tangible. He was losing patience. "It would be fair commerce if you were truly offering a comparable product. But you're not. You're offering our line, reproducing virtually our entire line, flooding the market with counterfeit leather goods, destroying market value."

"How terrible." But she thought it anything but terrible.

If he'd been there Christmas morning, struggling to revive her father, struggling to save him before Mother saw. If he'd been there, stretched out over someone he loved dearly, trying to force air into his lungs, trying to bring him back to life, he'd know what she felt and he'd know this wasn't about leather goods. It was about justice. It was about fairness.

It was about revenge.

She'd have her revenge, too. She'd find a way to bring peace to her poor father's soul.

And maybe, somehow, peace to her own.

"As I said earlier, this is serious, Em."

Her eyes burned, her heart just as hot, and the pain washed through her. The picture of her father sprawled on the bathroom floor was too vivid still, the picture forever burnt into her memory. "Yes, it is."

"I'll prosecute."

"I'm sure you will." And then she smiled, if only to

keep the tears from forming, to shift her muscles, the tension, the need, the loss. "You see, the only reason you're going after me is because I'm successful. I've hurt your business. I'm doing something well—so well that it's forcing you to stop me, try to recoup your losses."

He said nothing, but she saw from his expression, the fixedness at his mouth, the hardness in his eyes, that she was right. She'd been good. Her business model—much to Ferre's consternation—was very good. But of course it would be. She'd taken Tristano's principles of commerce, taken everything he'd done well, and applied it to her own company.

Tristano's business model was brilliant. He'd make her a very wealthy woman. A year ago she'd made her first million. This year she looked to make two.

"It'll get ugly when this goes to court," he said now.

"It won't hold up in court."

"It will. I'm pressing charges in the United States first, and the US courts will recognize your designs as the legal property of Ferre Design."

"Even though the Ferres haven't a designing bone in their greedy, manipulative bodies?"

"Article I of the US Constitution gives inventors exclusive rights to their discoveries."

"*Father's* discoveries."

He crossed his arms. "The legal fees alone will ruin you."

She thought back on her hard-won financial security, thought back on the years when she and her mother had struggled, especially right after her father's suicide. "I'm prepared."

"Emily."

"You know the truth," she said bitterly, stepping toward him, fury sweeping through her. Did he think she was afraid of him? Did he think he could do anything to her that hadn't already been done? "You destroyed us, Tristano. You and your father. So don't think I have it in my heart to forgive. Because I'm not that big. I'm not. I can't forgive, and I can't forget. So here we are."

Tristano sucked in air, held his breath, his lungs hot, explosive. She pushed his control, tested his willpower. He wanted to touch her, wanted to take her in his arms, cover her lips, plunder her mouth the way she'd plundered his company, but he held himself still.

"You're the one who doesn't know the truth," he said softly, staring at her mouth, at her lips, wide, full, incredibly lush. She had the mouth of an Italian film star, and yet her eyes were the stunning blue-green of great English beauties. "And if this goes to court you'll hear the truth. Along with thousands of strangers."

Dusky pink color suffused her cheeks. "I can handle it."

Emily, Emily. He shook his head. "I don't think you can."

"You don't know—"

"No," he interrupted curtly, his deep voice crackling with anger and impatience. *"You* don't know. And

if you think you can handle this on the front page of the paper, or on the evening news, then think about your mother. Can she? Is this what she needs? Is this what's best for her?"

Emily stared up at him, onyx flecks in the blue-green of her eyes. He could see her hatred there, could see the violence of her emotion, but she turned her head away, averting her face. "She'll be fine," she said hoarsely. "She's been through a lot."

Tristano laughed hollowly. "Then bring it on, *cara*. Let her suffer some more."

He moved to the door and knocked once, indicating he was through. The door opened. The green-uniformed customs agent appeared. "Is she ready?" the agent asked, nodding at Emily.

Tristano shot her a glance through narrowed eyes. "She's ready. She's looking forward to Christmas in San Juan. Right, Em?"

Emily felt too hot, too alive, and with a wretched sinking in her stomach she found herself turning to Tristano and smiling a preternaturally calm smile. "Right."

He stood there a moment, staring at her. "You kill me, *carissima*."

Sometimes she killed herself.

Somehow she'd become this fierce.

Suddenly Emily didn't want to be so tough, so strong, but she couldn't let go of the past, couldn't forgive or forget. Not when her family had been crushed, reduced to bits of agony. "This is about Ferre Designs," she said, her voice breaking, her bitterness slicing through the room. "Not about me."

He looked at her. A muscle pulled in his jaw. "Are you sure?" When she didn't answer, he shrugged. "She's all yours," Tristano said to the agent, and then to Emily, "Have a good Christmas, Emily. See you in court."

"And when will that be?"

"January? February? Depends on the hearing date." He hesitated. "I'll call your mother—let her know the name and number of the prison in San Juan—"

"Don't, Tristano."

"She'd want to know."

"Tristano—"

"She's your mother, Em. She deserves the truth."

And he walked out, leaving her alone with the customs agent.

The truth? Emily silently repeated. But it wasn't the truth! The truth was that Briano and Tristano Ferre had destroyed her father and grown rich at his expense! *That* was the truth.

"If you'll put your hands out, *mademoiselle*."

The custom agent's voice brought her back to the moment, and the small dismal room where she'd been interrogated.

She blinked, eyes focusing, and felt her blood drain as she saw him draw out handcuffs. "You're going to handcuff me?"

"If you'll put your hands out?"

She really was going to be deported, sent to San Juan to who knew what kind of conditions. And while she wasn't afraid for herself, she was very afraid for her mother. She wasn't well, hadn't been well in years, and Emily knew she couldn't handle this—not now… definitely not after the last six months of agonizing pain. Her mother's arthritis had become so bad, completely debilitating. She didn't need anything else to hurt her.

"Get him," Emily said tersely, coming to a swift decision. "Get Tristano Ferre before he leaves."

CHAPTER TWO

TRISTANO had known the mother card would work with Emily—because he knew Emily.

She might think he didn't understand her, but he understood more than he let on. And maybe it hadn't been fair to dangle her mother like bait on a hook, but what was fair in love and war?

He watched now as she was escorted from the terminal into the bright afternoon light. She'd been inside the terminal for nearly three and a half hours. He knew she hadn't eaten since arriving, knew she hadn't been offered anything to drink, and her flight had been an all-nighter.

Yet as Emily walked toward him she looked stunning, her white pinstriped suit jacket still crisp as it dangled casually over one bare shoulder, long hair gleaming in the sunlight, high heels emphasizing her confident stride.

She could have modeled professionally, had been sought after late in her teens by several big Italian agencies, but she'd passed, devoted to school and apprenticing at the company.

For a moment his gut burned. Not guilt, he told himself, but a rare flicker of remorse.

She'd loved the company.

She'd loved Ferre & Pelosi as much as he had, but she'd been cut out when her father had been written off. It must have hurt her. He suppressed the thought, knowing her father had nearly ruined the company, robbed the company blind. His father, Briano, hadn't had a choice.

"Changed your mind?" he said as Emily reached his side.

Her jaw compressed, eyes sparking defiance. "Do you really own a house on St. Matt's?"

"Yes."

She stared at him disbelievingly. "The Flemmings sold to you?"

"Five years ago."

"I can't believe they'd do that."

"Why not?"

"They…the Flemmings…promised they wouldn't."

"Did you ever meet them? The Flemmings?"

Emily's eyes narrowed as she studied Tristano's hard but handsome face. His dark blue eyes were almost too perfect with his thick dark hair and dark brown eyebrows. "No. But I talked to them on the phone many times."

"Mmm," Tristano said, his expression bland.

Emily battled her temper. For twenty years her family had owned St. Matt's; for twenty years it had been her second home… Every Christmas holiday had been spent on the tiny island, and when her father had been forced to sell St. Matt's he'd sold to John Flemming, a wealthy American.

John Flemming had been wonderful about keeping in touch, letting them know when the island house would be free in the event that the Pelosis wanted to visit.

But they hadn't visited. Not after Father's death. Even though it had been tradition to escape London's chilly dampness for the Caribbean sunshine. It would have been too painful returning to St. Matt's, too painful facing what they'd all loved and lost.

Tristano held the door open to the waiting limousine. "Maybe you should have done a little more research."

Emily shot him a dark look as she slid into the back of the limo. "What does that mean?"

He climbed in after her. "It means there are no Flemmings." He shut the door and the car set off, heading for the water, where an anchored yacht would take them to St. Matt's. "Let me clarify myself. There *is* a John Flemming, but he doesn't own the island. He never did."

Confused, Emily stared at Tristano blankly. "I don't understand."

"John Flemming worked for me," Tristano continued blithely. "Represented me during the purchase of St. Matt's."

A wave of nausea swept Emily and blindly she reached for the door handle, as if to throw herself out of the moving car.

Tristano reached over her lap, covered her hand with his and held tight. "Don't do it. You'd break a leg…or worse…and then you'd be dependent on me for far more than you'd like."

His hand felt hard, warm, and far too personal. She flashed back to that summer years ago, when all she'd wanted was his hands on her body, covering her breasts, clasping her face, and him kissing her until she couldn't breathe or think.

Disgusted, Emily jerked her hand out from beneath his. He arched an eyebrow at her reaction and she shuddered, pulling as far from him as possible. "Don't touch me."

"You're scared of me."

"I'm not." She fought panic, realizing how she'd put herself in his care, handed herself into his keeping. Not good, she thought, glancing nervously out the tinted car window. Not good for body or mind.

"So why do you flinch whenever I get near you?"

She laughed, low and harsh. "Because I hate you."

"Hate?"

She laughed again, and the sound felt as raw in her chest as it sounded. Her insides were hot with emotion, bubbling with the acid pain that never went away. "Hate." Her gaze met his and she let him look into her eyes, let him see what she felt, let him see the anger burning there. "I will never forgive you for what you've done."

"You hate me because I let you believe the Flemmings owned St. Matt's?"

"No. I hate you because of what you did to Father. What you did to the company. What you did to my family."

"I'll take the blame for the purchase of the island, but the rest of it—" He shrugged, leaned forward to retrieve a chilled bottle of water from the limousine's mini refrigerator. "That was your father's doing."

She closed her eyes, held the pain in, holding tightly to what was left of her control.

But it was worse with her eyes closed. With her eyes closed her senses were sharper, more acute, and she felt even more aware of Tristano sitting so close. She could feel his warmth, his immovable presence, could feel his smug arrogance, too.

He was awful. Despicable. And she'd bring him down. All the way down. She'd fight to destroy him and his father, just the way they'd destroyed the Pelosis.

She heard Tristano twist the plastic cap off the bottle and swallow.

"Want a drink?" he offered.

She opened her eyes, saw he was holding the bottle out to her. "No."

"Are you certain? You're looking quite pale, *cara*."

"It's just the sound of your voice making me ill,

Tristano." And she closed her eyes again, tipped her head back and prayed for deliverance. But even with her eyes closed she could feel his gaze on her, feel *him*—his size, his strength, the heat from his impossibly solid, muscular body. And now St. Matt's was just one more thing Tristano Ferre had taken from her family.

The car rolled to a stop, and as Tristano opened the back door Emily avoided his hand. She reached into the trunk of the car to retrieve her own luggage and walked quickly toward the waiting yacht.

They boarded the yacht in tense silence. The trip from Anguilla to St. Matt's would take less than ninety minutes. Fifteen if they'd flown.

As the yacht left Anguilla's harbor Tristano sprawled on a padded lounger, basking in the golden sunlight, while Emily stood stiffly at the railing, staring out across the endlessly blue water.

"Why did you buy the island?" she asked as they reached open water.

He folded his arms behind his head, sunglasses shielding his eyes. "I wanted it."

"Why?" she persisted, turning to face him, the warm wind lifting her hair.

"Memories."

She couldn't imagine how he could have such good memories of a place that had nearly broken her. Emily looked away and bit the inside of her cheek, feeling far more alone than she liked. She'd only felt able to make this trip this year because Annelise had offered to accompany her. Otherwise there was no way she'd have been able to return, much less for Christmas. She hadn't been back since Father's death, and yet she knew it was time.

Father wasn't coming back.

He was gone. His name wiped first from the famous Italian leather design company, Ferre & Pelosi, and now his memory wiped away by pain.

She couldn't bear to think of him. Couldn't bear to think what had been done to him. Couldn't bear to think what he'd done to himself.

Emily swallowed the raw grief, her sorrow rising like a strong tide, threatening to engulf her.

"It was your choice to sell," Tristano said, and she steeled herself, resisting him, his voice, his reasonable tone. "We never came to you," he continued. "Never asked, encouraged or pushed. You chose to sell."

"To the *Flemmings*." She turned her head, eyes hot, furious, and shook her head. "You knew I'd never sell to you. You knew you'd be the last person I'd want to own it."

"I did." And he smiled, white teeth bared. With his strong jaw shadowed with the hint of a day's beard and the warm wind blowing through his hair he looked as if he could have been a privateer. "I kept wondering when you'd discover that we'd actually bought the island, that the Flemmings were just a cover, but it seems you were too busy…" he hesitated, considering his next words "…trying to stay one step ahead of the law."

"The *law*?" She spat the words back at him. "Just because you hold a law degree doesn't mean you know anything about justice."

"Someday you'll know the truth and you'll apologize."

"*Assolutamente no!* No way. Never."

He studied her a long moment, his dark blue eyes creasing at the corners and deep grooves forming next to his mouth. "You've always been welcome to return. I know Mr. Flemming always let you know the main house was available to you anytime you wanted to visit."

She shook her head, still stunned. "All those talks I had with him…all those things I shared…?"

"You didn't share that much, but, yes, whatever you told him, he told me."

Emily couldn't believe it. She'd liked John Flemming—had found him so open, so friendly, so…American. And all this time he'd been just a front, a cover for Tristano.

Wearily, Emily rubbed her temples, her head pounding. The sleepless night was catching her up, as well as the realization that all these years her house, her beloved plantation, had been Tristano's. It was laughable. Horrible. Tristano just kept on winning, didn't he?

The rocking motion of the yacht should have lulled her, relaxed her. Instead the surging sea rocked her, maddened her, each crashing wave seeming to chant *Tristano Ferre, Tristano Ferre* as it broke against the ship's hull.

A half-hour into their voyage the steward appeared with lightly toasted Club sandwiches and wedges of fresh fruit. Emily was too hungry to refuse food. She was proud, but not completely stupid. Hunger was hunger. She needed to eat. But that didn't mean she had to share a table with Tristano.

When Tristano sat down at the table she moved to the padded lounge chairs and balanced her plate on her lap. When Tristano silently rose, leaving his place at the table to sit next to her on a lounger, she tried to rise to return to the table. But Tristano put an arm out, clasped her wrist and pulled her back down on the chair next to him.

"Stay put, *cara*, or I'll pull you onto my lap and hand-feed you."

Color flared in her cheeks. "I'd bite your fingers."

"What about your tongue?"

Her cheeks darkened to a crimson red. "What about it?"

He shrugged. "Just asking."

She ducked her head, her toasted sandwich clasped tightly in her fingers. Suddenly her appetite was gone. How could he do this to her? How could he make her feel so…unhinged? Like a derailed train?

She heard the soft pop of a cork and moments later Tristano was placing a glass of wine at her feet. "Drink it," he said dryly. "You need it. You're so uptight you're about to explode."

That was it. She'd had enough. More than enough. Flinging back her head, she opened her mouth to give him hell—and discovered Tristano's mocking smile. He was just waiting for it. He wanted her upset.

What was happening to her? Her famous calm was deserting her right when she needed it most. Emily drew a slow, deep breath and lifted her sandwich to her mouth, forced herself to eat. One bite, and then another. He wanted a fight? Fine. She'd give it to him.

She'd fight him to the end.

Fight him until she had no air left to breathe.

Swallowing the sandwich with difficulty, Emily reached for her wine glass and downed half the wine in one gulp. Courage, she reminded herself. Courage and control.

She was glad now she'd decided to go with him to St. Matt's. In jail on San Juan she could have accomplished nothing, but alone with Tristano she could make him feel, make him aware, make him know what it was like to be obsessed. Possessed. Alive with pain, and anger, and the burning need for revenge.

Revenge. She savored the word, watched Tristano refill her wine glass. She'd get even. She'd make him pay if it was the last thing she did.

Halfway through lunch St. Matt's appeared on the horizon, just a speck of green.

Riveted, Emily's gaze clung to the distant island.

Slowly she set her wine glass down, her heart leaping to her throat as her right hand clenched and unclenched the linen napkin spread across her lap. St. Matt's. St. Matthew's. Her home away from home.

After a few minutes she was aware of Tristano's gaze resting on her, his expression closed but watchful. He said nothing, but she was certain he knew what she was thinking. She might hate him, but it wouldn't change the shared history between them.

Emily forced herself to turn her head and look at Tristano, who still sat far too close to her. "Exactly how does house arrest work, Tristano?"

"Like this. I stay close. I keep you under constant watch."

"No guards?"

"Just myself."

They were speeding along the water, growing ever closer to the island. Little by little the steep green sloping hillsides took color and shape, rugged with buttonwood, coconut and sea grape. The island had been landscaped years ago, a mutual project between a prominent English landscaper and her father—her father who'd loved the island terrain nearly as much as he'd loved the Tuscan landscape.

"And that will be enough?"

"You want more?"

"No. I'm just surprised you don't feel the need for stronger measures."

"Like handcuffs?" he asked, his dark blue eyes the

color of the deepest part of the ocean. "Because I'm sure I could get some. If you prefer."

"I don't prefer."

"Well, if you change your mind…" He let his voice drift off, and his speculative gaze slowly, leisurely swept over her, from the top of her head to the tips of her high leather heels.

Emily made a rude sound in the back of her throat. "You probably prefer your women locked up."

"Just how many women do I have?"

"Hundreds."

He smiled lazily and slipped his sunglasses back on, hiding his eyes. The sun glinted off the dark sunglasses. "That's right. I'd hate to forget."

"You are a playboy."

"Whatever you want to believe, *cara*." He stood up, pushed his chair back and left her to finish her lunch on her own.

The yacht was able to pull directly up to a long pier built from an island cove. No car was necessary to transport them to the house, as it was just a short walk up from the beach.

From the water the plantation house had looked the same, but as Emily climbed the old stone stairs she heard the grunt and whine of big machinery. As she rounded the side of the house, its façade came into view, the entry hidden behind new lumber and extensive scaffolding.

Her house was being destroyed.

She stood frozen, her horrified gaze fixed to what had once been elegant weathered stone. "What... what's happening?"

A massive concrete mixer pulled out just then, lumbering over what was left of the green lawn and the neatly bordered hibiscus beds.

Hot tears spiked her eyes and she turned her head, briefly closing her lids.

This couldn't be.

It was cruel—bringing her to this, confronting her with this. She and her father had both loved the house, the gardens, the island history. How could Tristano destroy so much so thoughtlessly?

As staff dealt with their luggage Tristano headed up the front steps, the stone arch above the front door now invisible beneath the scaffolding.

"Hurricane Francis," Tristano said, gesturing for her to follow. But she couldn't move. "Once we'd started renovations, one thing led to another."

Literally, she thought, and discovered that the former sugar plantation had been enlarged, with new guest wings built on either end of the main house. From the front porch she glimpsed a new terrace fronting the ocean.

Emily felt a catch in her chest. "It's not the same house."

"It'll be beautiful when it's done."

"It won't be the same," she repeated.

"More people will visit now."

Who? His mother? His father? His incredibly stylish sisters? Impossible. They'd never leave their ritzy Mediterranean resorts, preferring their chic condos in Monte Carlo or larger, posher villas on the Italian Riviera.

"How many bedrooms did you add?" she asked, fighting to keep the bitterness from her voice.

She'd loved the house the way it was—loved the old hardwood floors with their scratches and nicks, loved the weathered floor-to-ceiling wooden shutters that had framed the five French doors facing the ocean. The house had felt so permanent to her in a sea of impermanence.

Now it was all new paint, new trim, new gloss.

"Seven. Three bedroom suites in the new right wing; four on the left."

She moved through the hall to the great room, and even here the ceiling was different, its beams refinished to the line of French doors overlooking the small protected cove.

At least the beach was the same. The water still the same dazzling azure blue, the strip of sand soft, powdery, an inviting white.

"I thought it'd be good for the family," Tristano said, and she laughed—because he had to know he'd never get his sisters here.

The house was lovely—new fixtures, new furniture, new everything—but it wasn't Cannes or St. Tropez. There were no beautiful people here, no parties, no glamour, no excitement. Just the warm sun, the dazzling sea, and the fragile coral reef just beyond the mouth of the cove.

She turned, looked back at Tristano, anger building inside of her. "Has the new house wooed them?"

"Not yet."

"So they're not spending Christmas here?"

"No. They're remaining in Italy."

"Of course."

He shot her a narrowed glance before setting off, leaving the great room with its cathedral ceiling to head to one of the new guest wings. Emily followed, hating that the house was so different, that it wasn't her house anymore but his.

Tristano stopped outside a bedroom near the end of the long hall. "You'll sleep here," he said, indicating a lavish bedroom. "I'm here—across the hall."

"So how are you going to watch me from across the hall?" Her hands were on her hips. "Or do you have hidden cameras recording me?"

"Sorry, Em. I've nothing hidden here. No cameras, no listening devices. Just you. Just me."

"And your staff of…?"

"Six." He entered her room and pushed open one of the massive plantation shutters, flooding the limestone tiled room with warm light. The walls were glazed the palest blue, the silk bed coverlet a darker blue, with plump pillows covered in fine white linen, edged with white lace. "Before I forget—I'm expecting visitors later. I'm not sure how many will be coming. Pay them no attention."

"Are you having a party?"

"No. It's business. An estate agent is coming with clients. They've been pre-qualified. Apparently they're serious buyers, or I wouldn't have them visiting now, so close to Christmas."

His words were like a hammer in her head, and she flinched as she realized what he was saying. "You're selling the island?"

"I've been approached by a British hotelier with visions of turning St. Matt's into the next St. Bart's." Tristano paused, rubbed the back of his neck. "I thought that before I made a decision I should find out what the island's value would be in today's market—who else might be interested in buying."

Emily heard him talking, heard the words, but she couldn't move past the word "hotel". She couldn't believe he'd just said that he was thinking of selling St. Matt's—and to a hotelier. A *hotelier*. Her heart constricted. Did he really mean it? Would he really do it? Turn the island into a tourist spot? A place for pampered, self-indulged playboys and It Girls?

"And the house?" she whispered, dry-mouthed.

"Mr. Viders has promised to contain the traffic. Try to preserve the island's character."

Viders. Tony Viders. She knew the name well. Tony Viders was Mr. London himself. He owned numerous chic hotels all over the world—places that catered exclusively to the rich and beautiful—and even if he promised to preserve the island's character, the plantation house would quickly become nothing but a pit-stop for those with more money than common sense.

"Sell to me," she said desperately, unable to contemplate the lovely old house littered with sandy high heels, half-empty bottles of suntan lotion and dirty cocktail glasses.

"You couldn't afford it."

"I could get a loan."

"Not for that much money."

"How much, Tristano?"

He walked out, heading for his room, but paused in the corridor. "I've poured cash—a couple million—into the renovations alone. I've been told the island would sell for twenty, maybe thirty million today."

"Tristano." Her voice came out strangled. "Please."

"No."

"But—"

"You can't afford it, so forget it. And why would I sell to you, Emily," he persisted coolly, unkindly, "when you've declared me the enemy?"

He waited, silent, knowing full well that he'd made a salient point and she had no defense—nothing she could say.

He was right.

She'd declared war on him for the past five years—had challenged him, mocked him, virtually humiliated him with her flood of knock-offs. Why would he give her what she wanted? Why should he care?

In her room, Emily opened her gorgeous luggage—a matched set of her own Pelosi design, of course—locating her shampoo and bath gel. She showered and changed into a long black chiffon skirt and a sheer black top over her white bikini.

Her head was pounding—jet lag—but she'd learned early on in her travels to shift time zones immediately, to fight fatigue and to push through. And that was what she'd do now. Dressed, she gathered her business papers, left her room and wandered through the house, eventually bumping into a housemaid who told her that Signor Ferre had gone down to the sea for a swim, and did the *Signorina* know her way to the beach?

It was all Emily could do to smile politely. Yes, she knew. It had once been her beach. And, no, she didn't wish to join him.

Instead Emily carried her briefcase outside to the terrace, where she sat beneath an umbrella reading charts and graphs until she thought her eyes would fall out.

Business was good. Profits were high. The forecast for the next year was brilliant. But even making good money—big money—didn't answer the horrendous anger burning inside her.

Mum was still sick. Father was still gone. And Tristano was still CEO at Ferre Design.

Ferre Design. Just thinking of the name "Ferre" without "Pelosi" made her see red. It wasn't ever supposed to be just Ferre. The Ferres had never designed anything—much less come up with an original idea. Her father had been the creative genius, and it was her father's brilliant leather goods—handbags, suitcases, belts, shoes—that she faithfully reproduced today, manufacturing and selling them for a fraction of what the Ferre Design charged.

Call it counterfeit if you want. She called it fair.

Emily heard car doors slam and the distant murmur of voices—female voices. Tristano's visitors had arrived.

Disgusted, she slouched deeper in her chair, drew her papers higher, and forced herself to focus on the numbers in front of her. But the voices were loud, and they carried.

"The view is worth thirty million alone."

"I'm not that crazy about the house, though."

The voices soon reached Emily where she sat.

"Darling, you can always replace the house."

"Bulldoze it down?"

"Of course. Everybody does it these days."

There was a pause, and Emily squeezed her eyes shut. It was torture being here, torture hearing this. She wished now she had gone down to the beach. Sitting next to Tristano would be painful, but it would be better than this.

"How much do you think it'd cost to knock it down?" The women were still discussing demolishing the plantation house—a house that had stood on St. Matt's for hundreds of years, a house that had history…mystery…secrets.

"Fifty thousand? A hundred? No more than a hundred thousand, not even with all these stone walls. Bulldozers are amazing. One day here, the next gone. Whoosh. And think what you'd gain—all-new construction, the best of everything, top-line technology. You could even put in your media room here."

Abruptly Emily sat up, anxious to flee. But her haste sent her paperwork flying. On her knees, she scrambled to gather the graphs and reports even as the women's voices echoed in her head. *The view is worth thirty million alone…you can always replace the house…bulldoze it down…no more than one hundred thousand…you could even put in your media room here…*

Two sleek, well-preserved blondes, with shiny gold hair and expensive jewelry, appeared in the doorway overlooking the terrace. "Oh!" one exclaimed. "I didn't know anyone was here."

Hands shaking, Emily shoved the crumpled pages into her open briefcase. "Yes—I'm here."

The woman marched over to Emily, hand outstretched. "Di Perkins, Lux Estates. I'm showing the property to my client."

Emily awkwardly rose. "I'm not the owner."

"Oh." The women looked disappointed.

"I used to be," Emily added, thinking that maybe she could say something about the house, and its history, that would give it value…respect. "St. Matt's is a wonderful island—it has a fantastic history—"

"I'm not really into history." The second woman's

nose wrinkled. "I just want a great beach, a bay deep enough for my husband's yacht, and privacy. We don't get enough of that in the States."

"It is private. You don't get visitors here. Not unless they're invited." Emily fought to hide her irritation. "It's said that Blackbeard hid here for a month one December—"

"Blackbeard? Ugh." The second woman shuddered. "Didn't he kill a lot of people?"

Not enough, Emily thought, smiling so hard her eyes watered. "Excuse me." She nodded and, leaving her briefcase on the table, practically ran down the stone steps heading for the beach.

She found him stretched out on a lounge chair on the sand, his arms extended over his head, his eyes closed, his long nearly black hair combed back from his face.

Either he hadn't heard her approach or he was ignoring her.

"You can't sell the island," she said flatly, not bothering with pleasantries. "Not like this—not to these kinds of people. The island's special. Beautiful. You can't let people without taste destroy it."

His eyes slowly opened. He looked up at her, his arms folded behind his head. Deep blue eyes met her own. *"Ciao, bella."*

"Did you hear me?"

He held her gaze.

"Did you hear me?"

Damn him.

He still thought he ruled the universe. Things hadn't changed. But then in the Ferre world why should anything change? The gods divided up the pie and gave the Ferres everything, leaving everyone else with crumbs.

"Those people want to tear down the house. Just bulldoze it." She held his gaze. She wasn't afraid of him, didn't need him, didn't give a flying fig what he thought of her. But the house, the island, the history—that she loved.

"It's their prerogative if they buy it," he answered, stretching a little, lifting his face higher to the sun. "That's the privilege of ownership. Something you lost when you sold."

"You know we didn't want to sell. You know we sold only because we had to."

"I'm sorry."

"You're not." It crossed her mind that the estate agent's visit wasn't coincidence, but rather something Tristano had arranged. He'd wanted Emily to see the future of St. Matt's. He'd meant for her to meet the prospective buyers. "You set me up," she said softly.

"Set you up?" He grinned, and his teeth flashed white. A small dimple appeared briefly in his carved cheek. "Intriguing deduction."

"And a correct one. You planned all this. The Flemmings…the arrest. You intended for me to come here, remain here. You've spent a great deal of time orchestrating this."

"I did hunt you down, yes." His smile had faded and his dark blue eyes burned intensely. "And, yes, I've deliberately brought us together. You're stranded here on St. Matt's, alone with me. And you're going to listen—work—co-operate with me."

"Never."

"Careful, *cara*. Never is a very long time."

CHAPTER THREE

"Why are you doing this?" she demanded, her head spinning a little. She'd flown all night, hadn't slept. This had become a day that seemed as if it would never end.

"You know the answer, Em. Just look inside your heart—or your bank account—and you'll see the answer there."

She shook her head. "You could call them off, you know." She fought to keep the fury from her voice, fought for the control she so desperately needed. "Since you arranged this whole thing you can end it, too."

"Yes, I know." He'd closed his eyes again, and, exhaling, relaxed his tanned upper body into the chair. "But I won't." The warm sun gleamed on his bronzed skin, on one burnished highlights in his dark hair. "*Cara*, could you just move over a foot or two? You're blocking my sun."

Blocking his sun? She felt a bubble of hysteria form in her chest. She was standing here, pleading for her freedom, and he was worried about his *sun*?

"Sorry about that." Her voice dripped venom.

"No problem."

For a moment she remained rooted to the spot, frozen in anger and indecision, and then she moved. But not in the direction he expected. Emily knelt down and buried her hands in the sand, grabbing great handfuls of the fine warm grains, and before she could think twice she stood up again and poured the sand on top of his head.

Tristano sputtered, coughed, then gave his head a sharp shake, sending sand flying.

Emily planted her feet, hands on her hip. "How's that? Better?"

"Oh, yes." But Tristano clasped her by the forearm and with a tidy twist flipped her down on her back in the sand. He left his lounge chair and straddled her hips. "How's that?"

The sun shone in her eyes, blinding her. Tristano's body was heavy, hard and warm—very warm—and Emily felt stunningly aware of the size of him, the fierceness of him, the sensual nature he'd never tried to conceal.

"Off," she demanded hoarsely, her voice nearly breaking, betraying her rising anxiety. Maybe for Tristano this was nothing, but she was incredibly uncomfortable, almost paralyzed by the intimate contact.

Tristano Ferre had had more girlfriends than twenty Italian playboys put together. For him it had always been new week, new woman. It had galled her back then, when she had still been part of his life, and it galled her now. She shouldn't care who he was with, or what he did with whom, but somehow she did. She told herself it was anger, hatred, but the intensity of her feelings made her wonder.

"Not until we get a few things squared away," he answered, and suddenly he was stretched out over her, his hands still wrapped snugly around her wrists, his body extended over hers until his chest pressed to her breast, his hip rested on hers, his thigh parted her thighs. And even though she was wearing the silky skirt and shirt, the sheer chiffon fabric allowed her to feel all of him.

"What do you think you're doing?" she breathed, ineffectively pushing up against his grasp.

"What you've been dying for me to do ever since last time."

"Screw you!"

"We already did that, *carissima*, or do you not remember?"

Her body grew tellingly warm, and blood rushed to her cheeks. Embarrassed, Emily struggled to drive her knee up, straight into his groin, but he knew, because he knew her, and he shifted, immobilizing her legs, his hips gouging into her.

Emily drew a short breath. Tristano lay heavily on her, pinning her down, pinning her legs, and the friction of skin on skin made her conscious of the hardness of his hips, the hair on his legs, the heat of his chest.

"I hate you," she choked, emotion filling her, sweeping through her, hot, so hot, and full of anger.

"You lie, *cara*." His head dipped, his lips traveling over hers in a brief tortuous caress. "You love me."

And his head dropped again. But this time his lips covered hers, completely, firmly, and he kissed her the way she'd remembered all these years. His lips slowly moved across hers, parting so slowly that she wondered if it was her encouraging him or the other way around.

This was the kiss that had driven her mad all those years ago, when she'd thought she'd tasted real life, real love, real passion.

And then she'd discovered it wasn't anything. It was just Tristano practicing his craft. Tristano the expert. The seducer. Tristano the Ferre sinner.

Eyes burning, she tried to hold back, pull back, tried to forget that his lips were making her shiver, that the flick of his tongue made her want to open herself up to him, that the feel of his hands against her neck made her want those hands everywhere, against everything.

This was how she'd given herself to him last time.

Innocently. Naively. Sweetly.

She'd never be so stupid again.

Fighting tears, Emily sank her teeth into Tristano's lower lip and he cursed, rolled partially away, to gaze down at her.

Her heart was racing and she struggled to catch her breath, struggled to get a grip on the emotions that were flying all over the place.

He was right. She had loved him once.

And he'd broken her heart into a thousand pieces—broken her heart along with her trust.

Then his father had done the unthinkable—sold her father out, seized the company—and the Pelosis had suddenly become cast offs.

And Tristano hadn't just watched it all happen. He'd helped. He'd stood at his father's side and made sure with his fancy law degree that the Pelosis were stripped of everything.

"I never loved you," she said now, her voice deep, husky with the hunger she hadn't quite contained. "It was lust. You had the goods, and I wanted them."

His eyebrow arched. "Is that so?"

"Yes."

"And is that how you explain yourself this time?" He touched her soft lip with the tip of his finger. "Your mouth quivered. It wanted my kiss. It welcomed my kiss."

"Lust is lust."

"So I still have the goods?"

She thought of the company he'd helped seize, the company he'd torn apart, and the island she'd loved and lost. Her throat ached. "In more ways than one."

His smile grew, and yet it was the smile of a pirate, the smile of one taking exactly what he chose without fear, without worry, without conscience. She had to leave, had to escape before she did something criminal.

She fled back to the house, running up the steep steps, the stones weathered and worn smooth, and into the cool semi-dark house. She heard Tristano following close behind and ran faster, through the great room, where the big dark plantation shutters had been closed against the brightness of the afternoon sun, down the corridor toward her room. But before she could slam her door shut Tristano caught her, trapping her against the wall.

"I have the goods," he said, his voice deep, his hand closing around her wrist.

"And you love that, don't you?"

"Is that what you're thinking?"

"I don't know." She couldn't focus, too aware of the warmth of his skin against hers, his bare chest against her chiffon top, the salty spiced fragrance of him, the pulse pounding in her own veins.

"What *do* you know?"

Emily drew a shaky breath. "Don't ask. You don't want that kind of honesty."

"I wouldn't have brought you here if I didn't."

She stared up at him, her emotions barely contained, her pulse pounding wildly. It was all she could do not to faint. Everything about Tristano was huge. Significant. Like his treachery. His ability to detach and destroy.

"I trusted you." The words were torn from her, flung in his face. She hadn't meant to say them, hadn't even known she was going to say them, and she felt as if she were sailing straight into the eye of a storm. This was bad, so very bad, and there was no one—again—to help her.

Tristano leaned closer, his chest hard against hers, his knee brushing the inside of her thigh. "You know why you're in trouble now? You've confused objectivity with subjectivity—taken something that had nothing to do with us—"

"Nothing to do with us?" she interrupted roughly. "*Tristano*. We *were* them. We were—are—what they made."

"But that was your mistake, *cara*. We have always been different. We are different people, a different generation. We've always had different dreams. After your father left—"

"Left?" She laughed, feeling hysterical. "He didn't *leave*. You shoved him out. Tied him to a speedboat and dragged him out to sea."

Tristano abruptly reached for her, touched her cheek with the back of his fingers. "Is this the story you tell yourself? No wonder you hang on to such hate—"

"Don't touch me." Flinching, she closed her eyes, steeling herself against all response. The enemy, she whispered silently, reminding herself. He is and always will be…

Drawing a quick breath, she opened her eyes, his expression clear, cool again. "This isn't a story, Tristano. You know what you did—you and your father."

"Yes, I know what we did. But do you know what *he* did? Your father?" The cool shadows of the hall made his voice sound deeper, his accent warmer.

They were both fluent in English and Italian, and

they switched back and forth between the two, comfortably, easily, neither noticing when the language changed.

She wanted to escape, but she couldn't move, squashed between Tristano and the wall. "He did nothing."

His head dropped, his voice lowering. *"Em."*

She heard the warning in his voice, and it sent a ripple of fear through her. He'd never hurt her. Not physically. But emotionally…he was as dangerous as hell.

"Unlike you, Tristano, Father was a good man—a principled man. He didn't do anything wrong. I'd have known it if he had. Mother would have told me. Father would have told me. But there was nothing for him to confess—" Emily broke off at the sound of voices echoing down the hall.

Tristano heard the voices, too. The realtor and the buyer. They were discussing the buyer's dream house. Pool pavilion here. Sculpture garden there.

Tristano saw Emily pale, one smooth line of her jaw tightening. He straightened, giving her a little space—but not much. He wasn't going to let her go. There was no escaping him this time. The course they were on was nothing short of madness. It would lead to nowhere good. He had to put a stop to the insanity before it destroyed her—him—all of them.

The two women disappeared into a bedroom and Tristano turned his attention back on Em. They were still standing close but he felt her resistance, saw the mutinous set of her mouth. She wasn't ready or willing to learn the truth. Her family had done her a disservice, keeping the truth from her, letting her father's flaws and weakness poison her life like that.

She was so different from the Emily he'd once known, the Emily he'd made his lover all those years ago.

That Emily had been so warm, so sunny, so open. She'd been passionate, earnest, hopeful, strong.

This Emily was strong, too. But it was strength born of bitterness. Hatred.

"What would it take to get you to cease and desist?" he asked, surprising even himself with the question.

But she wasn't ready to talk. There was still no negotiation. "Nothing."

"Nothing?" His eyebrows lifted. "Not even this… island?"

He saw her eyes widen, heard the soft catch in her breath. For a moment she looked hopeful, endearingly young as she stared up at him, torn between wonder and worry. He realized then how vulnerable she was— how vulnerable she'd been. And then the hope died in her eyes and her features hardened, freezing into the cool don't-touch-me mask she always wore these days.

"Nothing," she repeated, her voice low, brittle.

Emily squashed the rise and fall of emotion in her chest, squashed that flicker of hope—because really her only hope was removing Tristano from Ferre Design, taking Ferre Design apart, bit by bit, just the way they'd dismantled her father.

And remembering her father made her stronger, fiercer. Hurt was replaced by old rage. She wanted to take Tristano down, take him to the mat like the Greco-Roman wrestlers had, and beat him mercilessly. Show him what the Pelosis were really about. Show Tristano that he and his father had gotten it all wrong.

Integrity, she told herself. Truth. Determination. This was everything.

"I won't be bought," she said, her spine pressed flat against the wall, her whole body rigid with years of heartbreak and hatred. "There's only one thing I want from you." She paused, held her breath a moment, lungs bursting, and then she exhaled. "I want you to fail."

Emily looked up into his eyes, such a dark blue, a lovely blue, if you loved sapphire and the sky close to midnight.

"I want you to fail so badly you lose everything."

She saw a small muscle jump in his jaw, but his voice was gentle when he spoke. "Everything?"

She didn't know why she wanted to cry—she who didn't cry, she who didn't feel anything, was feeling far too much. "Everything. Your house, your cars, your wealth, this island—all of it. I want you to know what it was like being me."

The women emerged from one of the guest bedrooms and Emily used the opportunity to duck beneath his arm and escape into her room, locking the door behind her. And as the women stopped outside her door to speak to Tristano Emily heard the strangest noise—a muffled cry somewhere between a mouse's squeak and the scream of a bird. She sat down on the foot of her bed and realized the agonized sound had come from her. She was crying. Huge tears, hot wet tears. Even though she hadn't cried in years.

Later, a knock on her door roused her. She'd fallen asleep fully dressed on her bed, and groggily she pushed herself into a sitting position. "Yes?"

It was one of the young Caribbean housemaids outside her door. "Dinner in an hour, *mademoiselle*. Drinks in a half-hour."

Emily didn't want dinner—not if it meant joining Tristano—but she wasn't the type to sulk and hide. All her life she'd been a fighter, and she'd continue fighting now.

Washing her face, Emily pulled herself together. She combed her long hair smooth, adding a little concealer to hide her under-eye circles, and a little blush to give color to her pale cheeks. She wasn't beaten. Not by a long shot.

Dressed in a white Spandex cap-sleeve top and a long black sequin-beaded skirt, Emily headed toward the great room—only to be told that dinner was being served outside, by the pool. Indeed, she could hear the faint strains of calypso—odd here, on the quiet, remote St. Matt's.

Turning a corner, she caught a glimpse of a slender, fashionably chic woman with long chestnut hair, wide somber eyes. Emily paused, puzzled by the woman's lonely expression, and then realized with a discomforting flash that it was her—her reflection in a mirror. She was seeing herself, seeing her own unhappiness, and it unnerved her.

She didn't even recognize herself anymore.

Emily started to move on, and then glanced back over her shoulder into the mirror one last time. The same face looked back at her.

Funny—she saw her father in her, her mother as well, and for a moment she saw a timeline to the past. She saw her father dressing for dinner—he'd always dressed, he'd been Italian and gorgeous: a Latin Cary Grant, her mother used to say. She saw her mother, too—her mother's blue eyes, her mother's porcelain rose complexion, a hint of her mother's sweetness.

Her parents had met when her father had been in London on business. Mum had worked as a receptionist for a London textile exporter and her father had stopped by to meet one of the owners. They'd met and, despite Father being nearly fifteen years older than Mum, they'd fallen in love. They'd married and had soon moved to Milan. They'd had a good life together, too, until Mum's illness had progressed and Father...

She suppressed the rest of the thought, knowing she didn't need to go there. She knew the history too well. She'd been tortured by it for years.

Reaching the pool, Emily stopped in the courtyard doorway, greeted not by the simple old pool but an entirely new landscape. The new pool was surrounded by buff limestone pavers, softly lit and lined by young native palms. A splashing fountain shot up from the middle of the illuminated pool and dozens of candles shone around the perimeter of the courtyard. More candles gleamed on the staircase leading to the new guest wing.

As she stood there, taking it all in, she gradually became aware of being watched intently.

Turning her head slightly, she scanned the exterior until she saw him—Tristano—standing in the shadows, too.

He was wearing pressed green linen slacks and an off-white linen long-sleeve shirt, cuffs rolled back. He looked elegant, distant, a stranger.

Here they were, Ferre and Pelosi, together as they'd once been. Lives so entwined that in nearly every good memory Emily had—like the shiny new bike or the white Vespa scooter—Tristano was also there, riding alongside her, racing her to who knows where. And yet even though they were together, they were poles apart.

Tristano stepped out of the shadows. "You look beautiful," he said, moving slowly toward her.

She didn't feel beautiful, and suddenly she couldn't leave the security of one door, overwhelmed by all the changes on the island. This visit had been about coming home…making peace with her past…but nothing felt peaceful. In fact, she felt even less settled than before.

"I've noticed you only wear black and white," he

said, his gaze roaming leisurely over her slim-fitting beaded skirt and the snug Spandex top that hugged her breasts and emphasized her small waist.

"It's easy to co-ordinate pieces for travel."

"As well as being stark. Hard. Controlled." Hands in his pockets, he crossed close behind her—so close she felt energy ripple between them, heat and awareness, and her lower back tingled, suddenly unbearably sensitive.

Her stomach clenched in a knot of anxiety, trepidation. "Is that how you see me?"

"Isn't that how you see yourself?" He stood behind her, still—too still—and Emily's skin prickled, her muscles coiling.

She had to turn her head slightly to see him, and looking at him over her shoulder she felt very vulnerable, her throat, breasts and body open, exposed.

"What—?" And then her voice failed her, the air blocked in her throat as Tristano suddenly touched her low on her back, his fingers trailing across the small dip in her spine.

His touch felt like fire and ice, and she couldn't move, frozen in place. Eyes closed, hands knotted, she nearly cried out when he trailed his hand lightly up the length of her spine. How could she feel so much? How could she feel like this? Because it was huge, hot, sharp—it was as if life had expanded, so powerful, so sensual that it stopped the air in her lungs.

"Breathe," he murmured from behind her, and she

shivered, feeling him, feeling him everywhere, even though he only touched her back. She felt his strength, and the shape of his chest and thighs, knowing he was hard, knowing he was responding to her just as much as she to him.

"Breathe," he repeated, fingers sliding up from her shoulderblades to the back of her neck.

And she did—only because black spots had fluttered before her eyes and she couldn't think, couldn't see.

His hand moved beneath her hair, his fingertips brushing the skin at her neck, circling her nape and then up into her hair so that she felt weak. Helpless. Boneless.

"You're killing me," she whispered, her voice faint as air.

"You're killing yourself," he answered, and his hand slid up, against her scalp, before clasping a handful of her hair, twisting the silky length around his hand. "Emily…my own little freebooter," he said, his voice dropping as he leaned forward to place a kiss on her nape.

She shivered, and balled her hands more tightly into fists, digging her nails hard into her palms. "You're not playing fair."

"No," he answered with mock gravity, turning her around to face him. "But when have you?"

Slowly she looked up, dragging her gaze first to his mouth—he had gorgeous lips—and then to his eyes. The intensity in his gaze stole her breath. His words were light, almost teasing, but she saw the fire in his eyes, saw the strength of his will.

His intensity touched her, teased her senses, stroked her nerves awake until she felt heat rise and shimmer between them. She was hot, too hot beneath her skin, hot and molten, like chocolate melted down to the warmest, sweetest, darkest liquid.

Her lips moved, tried to shape words. But nothing came to her—no sound, no thought. Instead she just *felt*. Emotion. Passion. Desire. All the things she shouldn't feel, all the things she didn't want to feel.

"No." The word slipped from her in soft, low protest.

"No what?" he asked, reaching out to touch her ear-lobe, and then the hollow beneath her ear. And all the while he touched her she looked up at him, fascinated, appalled.

If there was hell on earth, she'd found it. What he stirred within her was so strong, so raw and carnal, that the sensation threatened to pull her down—pull her under. It was, she thought, staring into his midnight-blue eyes, an agony being here. An agony feeling so much.

It crossed her mind as his palm cupped her collarbone, fingers lightly stroking her skin, that this was how it had always been between them. This was how she'd fallen so hard, so fast for him. This was how friendship—close, familial ties—had turned into wild, fierce emotion. His touch turned her inside out. His touch blew her mind.

There could never be anything platonic between them. Could never be anything but the fiercest love and the fiercest hate.

And she hated him. Didn't she?

Her heart seemed to slow, pounding harder, yet less steadily as she searched his eyes and then his face.

He'd aged in the past five years, but it was the kind of maturity that suited his hard, strong face, carving beauty into his jaw, whittling the broad cheekbones, putting the finest lines at his eyes and near his mouth. His dark hair was as thick as ever, and yet there was caution, wisdom in his eyes

Yes, he was a little older, but she was older too, and somehow the chemistry was so much stronger. Or was this how all women felt when Tristano touched them? Looked at them?

The thought knifed her, a cut in the chest, between the ribs, and she drew in a short breath, trying to discount the pain. She didn't care, she told herself. His life, his women…they meant nothing to her. Not after what he'd done to her father.

The reminder of his role in her father's humiliation should have chilled her, frozen her in place, but she wasn't frozen—just confused. His touch felt good. Right. And yet he represented everything wrong with the world, everything selfish and hurtful in human beings.

"You're torturing me, you know." Emily tried to smile, to make it a joke, but she couldn't pull it off.

"If only it were that simple." He leaned forward to pluck a tendril of hair that clung to her lashes, lifting the tendril and smoothing it behind her ear. His lips curved but he wasn't smiling. He looked piratical.

"Torture isn't to be taken lightly. Proper torture requires effort. Planning. It's an art form."

"Father died here."

"I know."

"Christmas morning."

"I heard."

Tears scalded the backs of her eyes but she didn't let them fall. "Did you hear how?"

"A tragic fall."

"No." And the word whispered out—soft, stealthy, speaking of a heartbreak that few people would ever know about. "It was tragic, but it wasn't a fall."

Tristano said nothing, asking no questions, and Emily offered no more information. There were some things, she thought, too cruel, too ugly, too unbelievable to ever reveal.

Dinner was beautiful, the meal cooked perfectly. Tristano's chefs had trained on the Continent, and had prepared fresh seafood in the best French and Mediterranean styles.

Sitting at the table, with candlelight flickering and the torches around the pool burning, Emily saw light everywhere—the pale ivory taper candles, the stainless steel torches, and the nearly full moon reflected whitely in the pool. She didn't remember the island this way, didn't know the house like this, either, and she felt off-balance all over again, felt the strangeness of everything, the strangeness of her own emotions. She'd been so determined for so long, and yet she wasn't sure of anything right now—certainly wasn't sure of herself.

As coffee was served she turned to examine the pool courtyard again, dazzled by the perfectly matched palm trees and sophisticated lighting. It was all so pretty, but almost too perfect—like a designer set waiting to be photographed.

"Is this for your hotelier?" she said, and she'd meant to sound tough. Instead her voice had cracked.

"The new pool? No. It's for me. The family."

"So why sell?"

"To get your attention."

Emily sat very still, her hands resting in her lap, aware of the steam rising from her coffee cup but unable to reach for it. "You're selling something I desperately love to get my attention?

"Yes, *carissima*. And it's working, isn't it?"

CHAPTER FOUR

SHE stared at him, disgusted, appalled.

They were older. But no wiser. Everything with Tristano boiled down to a deal. Sell. Buy. Bargain. He was all about money. Power. He'd had it. She'd wanted it. Amazing how little had changed in five years.

And suddenly the source of her real hurt surged through her—a scorching memory. Their families had been as one.

"We were a family business," she said, forgetting the island, the house and the history in the Caribbean and returning to Italy, where it had all begun. "And I thought family business was about pooling strengths, everyone helping one another." She sat very still, and yet her voice blistered with fury. "Obviously I was wrong."

"The difficulty was between them, not us."

"No, we were like a family. We were always together. Your family, my family—we were what I thought a real family felt like. But I was wrong. Your father wanted more, and he cut us out. Not just Father. He cut me, Mum—"

"It was a business decision. You're making it personal."

"And it's *not* personal? It's not about giving everything to the Ferres and taking everything from the Pelosis?"

"Our fathers had differences in opinion."

"So how did your father get everything and mine get nothing?"

"My father always was the practical one. He knew the business—"

"While my father was just the genius, the creative mind, and therefore dispensable?"

"Emily."

"No, Tristano. I shall never forgive your father, and I shall never forget how you've allowed—encouraged—this injustice to continue. You yourself have grown rich from my father's designs. You have built your own empire on his back."

His dark blue eyes looked nearly black in the candlelight and his expression was taut. "And it's my empire you hate most. Not my father's. But mine. That which I've done."

"Yes! You're perpetuating a sin."

"A sin?" he demanded, rising.

She left her own chair, moved toward him, conscious of the height difference between them, conscious of the fact that he would always be bigger, larger, more dominant. At least physically.

Mentally she was his equal, though.

Emotionally she'd hold her own.

Maybe her father had cracked in the face of such ostracism, maybe he hadn't been able to endure the shame, but she felt no shame.

She loved her name. Loved what her father had accomplished. And just because he wasn't around to fight for himself anymore that didn't mean she wouldn't continue the fight herself.

"A sin. A wrong. A tragedy." She met Tristano's narrowed gaze and lifted her chin in outright defiance. "You can arrest me. You can throw me in jail. Take me to court. But I won't cease and desist. I won't. I will fight you forever. Understand? I will not give up. I will not forget."

"Fighting words," Tristano said softly, watching her face every bit as intently as she'd watched his.

She saw the curiosity in his expression, the blatant interest, and it wasn't innocent, either. He looked very male just now, very much engaged in the hunt.

What on earth was this anyway? What had brought them on this collision course?

They'd once played together as children, behaved like brother and sister…cousins…

Hadn't they?

Or had there always been this edge of anger? This vein of emotion that went deep, so much deeper than anything Emily had ever felt for anyone else?

"Marry me and this stress—this fear—will disappear." Tristano's voice sounded soft, persuasive.

His soft, smooth voice had temptation buried in it, its deep tone compelling, soothing, as if he had a power greater than she knew—as if he could put everything right, as if he were the answer to all her problems…

But he had created all her problems.

"Marry?" She said the word just as softly, but there was no give in her voice, no persuasion. She was angry, deeply angry. "Marry you? Never. Ever."

"Aren't you tired of worrying so much? Tired of the pressure? The weight of caring for your mother?"

Her head lifted and her hot gaze met his. "I love my mother. It's a joy to care for her." A lump filled her throat. The pain of his betrayal was fresh all over again. "And if we have worries, if we're bowed by pressure—"

She broke off, pressed a knuckled fist to her mouth to contain the sound of heartbreak. She fought for control. "You were supposed to be the good guy," she said finally, and the words were wrenched from her, practically a confession.

He laughed once, a low, mocking sound that made their differences all the more obvious. "But, Emily, I was never the hero. Maybe that's what you wanted, but I've never wanted to be the good guy, and you shouldn't have been surprised. We were once close…at least close enough that you should have seen the truth. You should have known that my family would come first, that the business would always be important. Essential."

But I didn't think you'd put the business before me.

There—the truth. Only she hadn't admitted it to him, just herself, and that was bad enough.

Hours later, lying in bed, with the windows open to let in the fresh air and the dull roar of the sea, Emily tried to sleep. But the day played like an endless movie in her weary mind, scene after scene, discussion after discussion, every nuance and inflection slowed, repeated, her life on rewind.

The arrest on Anguilla.

The never-ending confrontations with Tristano.

Dinner and his absurd proposal, the realization that she still responded to him, that she didn't know how not to respond to him…

She shouldn't be here. She should have stayed home, celebrated Christmas with Mum like she always did, instead of making this crazy trip with Annelise. Well, Annelise was gone, and she was trapped here on St. Matt's—her former home—under house arrest.

The only small mercy was the fact that her mother didn't know. Her mother would be protected from the chaos and indignity of it all.

Another hour passed, and Emily flipped from her back onto her stomach and back again. The sheets were hot, the Egyptian cotton clinging limply to her skin. She couldn't stop thinking, couldn't shut off her mind. But it wasn't just being here. She simply couldn't sleep anymore. For the past couple years she'd take forever to fall asleep, and then once asleep would wake repeatedly in the night, thoughts racing, muscles twitching, her body unable to shut down long enough to let her rest.

She'd gone to her doctor about it, asked for help so she could start sleeping properly again, and though the doctor had said he could prescribe pills, he'd thought she needed more than pills. She needed a change of lifestyle. Too much stress, he'd said. If she wasn't careful, he'd added, not knowing the details of her father's death, Emily would end up just like him...

Emily had left the doctor's without getting a prescription for sleeping pills and returned to work, to her small office, and the stress had continued—just as had her sleepless nights. But her sleep deprivation was getting worse. Soon she'd have to do something about the insomnia. Soon she'd have to give her body a break, before her body broke her.

Hopelessly wide awake, Emily left her bed, put on shorts and a cotton top and headed outside, away from the plantation house, down the worn stone steps to the cove.

It was late, well past midnight, but the night air wasn't cold. She walked along the edge of the surf, her feet wet, waves splashing and breaking against her calves. The water was warmer than the night air.

The heaviness on her chest didn't ease, and the heaviness in her gut just grew worse, as if she'd taken to eating bricks.

When had everything gotten so hard? She looked up

at the sky, at the nearly full moon obscured by a sil-ver-plated cloud. When had she'd become this tired, flat version of herself?

She didn't need to ask the question. She already knew the answer, knew exactly how and when. So the issue wasn't what was wrong, but how to deal with it. How to fix it—because something had to give. Something had to go. But what?

And somewhere from inside her she heard the answer. *Let go of Father.*

Let him go.

And Emily's eyes, which never watered, never felt anything, burned again, burned for the second time in one day. Before she could fall apart, dissolve into tears, she stripped her shirt off, pulled off her shorts and dove naked into the water, swimming out, swimming far, as far as she could. Then, turning onto her back, she floated, looking up at the sky. In the clouds that slowly covered and uncovered the moon she felt her tiredness, felt the endless weight of battle, the fatigue of never being able to rest, never being able to find peace.

But how to let go of her father?

She flipped over, began swimming again, parallel to the cove, trying somehow to outrun her thoughts. And yet before she'd swum far she understood why Tristano had brought her here, trapped her on St. Matt's alone with him. He was going to force a confrontation with the past even if it killed her…him…them.

Feeling a prickle of awareness, the same awareness

she'd felt earlier at the pool, she knew she wasn't alone in the cove anymore. Tristano had arrived. She couldn't see him, but she knew he was on the sand somewhere. Watching.

Slowly she swam back to the shore. As she neared the beach Emily lifted her head and caught sight of him. He stood close to the surf, dressed in faded jeans and a dark T-shirt. He was watching her, waiting for her, and she let herself sink deeper into the water, trepidation weighting her limbs. She couldn't do this again. Couldn't argue so soon, not when their confrontation at dinner still troubled her so much.

It wasn't fun fighting with Tristano. At least there was no fun in it now, when she was close enough to see his face, feel his warmth and intense energy. She'd once been part of his inner circle, and yet now she stood on the outside, bayonet in hand.

As she walked out of the water she kept her chin high, making no apology for her nudity. Tristano dropped a towel around her shoulders, lightly buffed her skin. "You shouldn't swim alone at night," he said.

She took the towel away and wrapped it around her torso, cinching it tightly over her breasts. "I've always swum at night."

"That doesn't make it right. It's dangerous—"

"My career is dangerous," she interrupted impatiently, wringing water from her hair.

Shipping merchandise from China into the States wasn't without traps. She'd learned all the different methods for avoiding customs—trans-shipping, selling the goods first to a country not associated with counterfeiting and then importing from there, or smuggling the merchandise in containers filled with legal goods—but the pressure was intense, the fear of being caught always there at the back of her mind.

He looked away, muttered something unintelligible, then glanced back down at her. "What happened to you?"

Even in the dark she could see his face clearly and she held his gaze. "I learned from you."

"Oh, *cara*—"

"It's true." She reached up to comb wet hair back from her forehead. "You were my role model. Whatever you did, I wanted to do." The corners of her mouth tipped. "Just better."

"I don't recall stooping so low as to make cheap, knock-off merchandise."

"My handbags and suitcases aren't cheap, and they're not knock-offs. They're exact Pelosi design. And maybe you don't have to go to Asia to get your merchandise made, but I vow if you can make a thousand bags, I can make ten thousand. If you can produce a gorgeous leather, I can do it one better. And that's been my goal—not to just match you, but beat you."

"Beat me?"

"Yes."

"What a terrible waste of your life."

"I've no regrets."

When he said nothing, she smiled, but she hated

how she felt on the inside—so cold, so tired. It felt as if she'd been carrying this enormous burden on her shoulders forever, and she felt exhausted by the weight of it—the weight of worrying, the weight of hating. She'd vowed to make the Ferres pay, and yet she saw now she'd been the one who just continued to suffer.

She could have sworn he knew, that he was thinking the same thing, and he shook his head, his jaw pulling. "You would have been better off focusing your considerable energy into making Ferre Designs succeed."

"I would never help Ferre Designs."

"Not even if it benefited you?" he asked softly.

"The only way I could benefit is if Ferre Designs fails."

"That won't happen."

"You sound awfully confident."

"I am. I know our revenue." The corner of his mouth lifted in a faint smile. "You're the one backed into a corner, *carissima*. You're facing not just jail time but financial ruin."

Furious, she squeezed her wet hair again. "I'm prepared."

"Are you?"

Her chin inched higher. "Yes."

His gaze never left her face, his blue eyes searching hers intently. "And your mother? Is she prepared?"

For a moment Emily heard—saw—felt nothing, and then the implication of his words hit. "You wouldn't go after Mum."

His blue eyes were hard, cool. "I already have."

Emily let his words seep through her, let the stunning pain go on and on, until she was certain she could speak without her voice betraying her. "What have you done?"

Tristano tipped his head. His expression appeared to gentle, but it was deceptive—nothing about him had gentled. She knew him too well for that.

"Tristano." She said his name, low and sharp.

His lips curved. His blue eyes flashed. He intended to destroy her. "You weren't the only one arrested."

Her jaw dropped, eyes widening in horror. "You didn't?"

"*Cara*, you don't listen. You didn't heed my warnings. I tried—"

"Not Mum."

"She's a Pelosi, too."

Emily felt wild on the inside. She couldn't breathe, couldn't seem to get air inside her despite the fact that her head had begun to swim.

Mum didn't deserve this. She hadn't been well. She hadn't been well for years. But it was worse now…her arthritis so crippling she needed help doing the most basic things, like bathing and dressing. Emily had hired a nurse to stay with her mother so she could make this trip.

"Mum's not well," she said quietly, unable to even look at Tristano.

"The officers told me."

Panic welled fresh. "Officers?"

"The two that arrested her."

Emily's legs nearly went out beneath her, and she sank slowly down into the sand, chilled. "You've had my mother arrested?"

"She's on the company letterhead."

"That's just paper."

"And she shares ownership in your company stock."

"Where is she now?"

"Being looked after."

Her fingers curled into her palms.

Silence stretched, lengthening, and Emily felt as though the sweeping indigo night sky was smothering her, suffocating her. She'd come to St. Matt's and left her mother at home, helpless and vulnerable. She should never have left at all, but Mum had insisted...had agreed with Annelise that Emily needed a break... Oh, no...

"This isn't that difficult." Tristano broke the silence. "You should count yourself lucky—"

"Lucky?" Emily scrambled to her feet, sand flying. She marched on Tristano, trembling with shock and anger. "You killed my father. You killed him, and you think I should feel lucky? That I should welcome marriage because it will what? Stop me from infringing on your copyrighted designs?"

She was poking him in the chest, each furious word accompanied by a stab of her finger, and Tristano gazed down into her flushed face. The moon was reflected in her green eyes, lit with flecks of blue, bright and intense, like the Caribbean waters surrounding the island.

He took her anger, let her fury wash over him. He could handle it. He'd been her first lover, and in some ways he knew her better than himself.

"I want my mother home for Christmas," she said, her finger still jabbing against his sternum. "She should be home—"

"Marry me, and she will be."

Emily gasped, fell back a step. "You didn't just say that."

"I did. Marry me and we'll start over. A fresh start—"

"For Ferre Design!"

"For both of us. Correction, for all three of us. Because your mother will benefit, too. As the mother of my wife, I'd make sure she was surrounded by every comfort conceivable."

Emily took another step backward. Her expression was stricken. "That's blackmail."

"If you look at it like that."

He moved toward her, settled his hands on her bare damp shoulders and felt a shiver race through her. Her shiver should have moved him, but it didn't. He felt cold and hard on the inside, and he wasn't going to back off. He knew exactly what he was going to do. Make Emily his. Make her a Ferre, make her family—his family—and nullify the threat to his business and his sanity.

She tried to squirm away. "And how do *you* look at it, Tristano?"

"Business."

Her eyes flashed daggers. She hated him. He knew she hated him. But she was still attracted to him, still responded when he touched her, and for now it was enough.

"Merger and acquisition," he said lightly, carelessly, his fingers tightening against her shoulders. He was rewarded with fresh fire in her eyes, the blue-green irises hot, stormy, like the sea churned by wind and rain.

"I don't want to be merged or acquired."

Her voice sounded like brittle bits of glass, and he smiled—because he knew what this was costing her— knew she was fighting for control, for calm—knew that Emily loved a good fight. But he'd taken all her weapons away and she was virtually cornered. Trapped. His favorite place for his favorite Pelosi.

"You should have thought of that before you devoted the last five years of your life to counterfeiting Ferre Designs."

"They aren't your designs—"

"Legally they are."

"Morally they're not."

"But law isn't about morality, is it?" One hand stroked upward, along her neck, to cup her cheek while the other tangled in her long wet hair, keeping her still so she couldn't escape. "Which is why I can make you mine without any pangs of conscience."

He forced her head up, forced her to see the desire, the determination in his eyes. "But it's not as if you've no choice, Em. You don't *have* to become Signora Ferre."

"No, I can just let my mother rot in jail."

"I'm certain the courts would be lenient with her."

He saw the fury sweep through her, and as she opened her lips to speak he covered her mouth with his and drank her breath and warmth and anger into him.

His lips moved across hers and he could taste salt water, taste the cool ocean on her tongue, and as he sucked the tip of her tongue into his mouth she shuddered, this time with pleasure.

Tristano reached between their bodies, grasped the towel and tugged it off Emily, drawing her naked body into his arms. She arched as she came into contact with his hips, her body instinctively pressing against his. He loved how her breasts felt crushed to his chest, her nipples peaking hard and tight, and as he pressed a hand to her bottom she moaned deep in her throat.

He was hard, and his jeans barely restrained him. It would be so easy to lay her down on the sand here, so easy to put his hand between her legs and feel her softness and warmth. But he kept his desire in check, concentrating instead on the satin texture of her skin and the sweet gentle curve of hip and breast.

She was so responsive to his touch, her slender body rippling with pleasure, and he parted her mouth wider, his tongue teasing her inner lip. Emily tasted of honey and spice. He wanted her, all of her, loved the feel of her body against his, the cool, damp taste of her mouth.

He remembered how sweet she'd tasted when he'd kissed her years ago. As her first lover, he'd taught her his favorite pleasures, showed her how exciting, how erotic lovemaking could be with the right partner. He'd been with plenty of women since that summer, but he'd never forgotten the way she'd felt in his arms, beneath his body. Nor had he forgotten kissing her intimately, tasting her wetness, feeling her shudder against him as she broke in waves of sensation.

He'd discovered everything he could about her that August, discovered she was curious and open, trusting, sensitive. He'd discovered she welcomed his hands, his mouth, his body, his touch. He'd discovered she enjoyed lovemaking—sex—as much as he did, and they'd spent hours alone—hours wrapped in nothing but each other's skin.

Tristano had waited a long time to reclaim her, but he'd known all along that eventually he would. She didn't even know that the lawsuits, the counterfeiting, had just played into his hands, giving him power over her.

His hands shaped her hips, held her firmly against him, and she quivered when he curved his palms across the firm contours of her bare bottom, molding her even more closely to him.

"Tristano…" She choked against his mouth and she shook, her whole body trembling.

He lifted his head and gazed down, uncertain what he'd find in her eyes. They were wide, wet with tears.

"You will make me hate you," she said, her voice breaking, her control smashed.

"But you already do," he reminded her, stroking her soft, warm cheek before tracing the swollen contours of her mouth.

Blindly Emily pushed against his chest, pushing to be free, and his arms fell away. He was the one who stepped back and retrieved her towel, draping her body again.

Emily clutched the edges of the towel. "I'm not afraid of you, Tristano."

"No, you're just afraid of yourself."

Sick with self-loathing, Emily stumbled back to her bedroom. She headed straight for the bathroom and turned on the shower.

What had she done?

But she didn't have to try hard to remember…didn't have to try at all to see herself in Tristano's arms, her body fitted to his, her desire spiraling higher and hotter, threatening to spiral right out of control.

Despite it being three-thirty in the morning, she was desperate to get clean, to rinse the sea and sand and Tristano's touch away. But even after scrubbing, even after toweling off and climbing back into bed, she still felt his hands, his mouth, his hard body against hers. In his arms she'd lost all control. She'd been completely gone—reason and rationality swept away in the face of her tremendous physical need.

Maybe that was what made her feel so sick right now. The fact that she'd wanted him so much. The fact that she'd turned her conscience off, turned down the volume on her voice of self-respect and given herself over to Tristano's touch, given in to hedonistic pleasure.

Worse, she still wanted his touch. Wanted more of what they'd started. But it wasn't right. She knew who he was, what he represented...how could she just hand herself over to Tristano like that?

Yet thinking back to the beach, remembering the feel of him against her body, the shape of him, the strength and hard warmth of him, she knew it had been natural.

The attraction hadn't died over the years. If anything, it was stronger, more real than ever before. Desire had just flared, shooting to life, superseding everything else. Including self-preservation.

Marry Tristano? She might as well put her head on the chopping block.

CHAPTER FIVE

"WE'RE heading out for the day," Tristano said the next morning, appearing on the terrace, lazily ruffling his still damp hair. He'd obviously just showered, for his jaw was freshly shaven and his shirt hadn't been buttoned yet, the linen fabric hanging open over tanned, honed muscle.

He looked too good, Emily thought resentfully, not knowing where to look—at his clean, smooth jaw or the lean hard muscle of his torso.

Her gaze skimmed his face—the intense blue eyes, the deep groves etched on either side of his mouth, his mouth itself. She'd always loved Tristano's mouth. He had lips that were real. Firm. Full. Wide enough to smile, sensitive enough to kiss properly. But then her gaze dropped down, to the sinewy plane of his chest, and then lower still, lingering appreciatively on his flat stomach with its tight, rippling abs.

It wasn't right that a man in love with his company, a man married to his work, should have a body like this. Tristano's large frame, with its abundance of smooth, hard muscle made her crave skin. His skin.

"I didn't think I could leave the island," she said, feeling absurdly primal.

"We're just going out on the water. We won't be heading ashore."

She pictured a day of sunbathing in skimpy swimsuits. A day of bare, gleaming skin. A day of heated bodies fragrant with coconut oil. It wasn't what she needed right now. "I'm to spend all day on a boat with you?"

The corners of his mouth lifted in a faint, challenging smile. "You make it sound miserable."

"It will be. If I'm trapped with you."

"Trapped." His smile grew fractionally. "Trapped. Hunted. Bagged. Caught." He said each word slowly, as if savoring the syllables. "Interesting words. Particularly when applied to you. And, yes, *cara*, I suppose you're right. You are trapped. At least until after the holidays. And then…"

She knew what he meant. "Jail."

"It's up to you."

"And I wouldn't go to jail if I married you?" The muscles between her shoulderblades tightened. He was treating her as someone very dangerous…a threat to be eliminated. Permanently.

"There are worse things."

"I can't think of any."

"You've clearly led a sheltered life."

Emily shot him a poisonous glance. She shouldn't

have come back to St. Matt's—should have stayed away. Mum had stayed away, and Mum was the smart one. Good. Sensible. But then Emily was neither good nor sensible. She'd thought she could handle the return, thought she was ready to face the ghosts of Christmas past. But the ghosts were bigger than she'd thought.

The ghosts of the past owned her. Body and soul.

Tristano leaned over, brushed hair from her eyes before straightening. "You need me."

"I don't."

"You do. You need someone to watch over you, keep you from harm, keep you from ruining your life."

A lump filled her throat, and as she looked up into Tristano's face the lump grew bigger.

He regarded her steadily, and as he gazed at her she felt a current of energy, a sizzle of light, and for a moment all she saw was possibility. For a moment she thought life could be anything she wanted it to be, that not everything had been predetermined. Her father's failure and shame had run its course; the future could hold something good and beautiful for her after all.

For a moment she could feel Tristano's warmth, feel it deep inside her, where she'd once kept everything she held dear. She could focus on all the good things again. Think about that which gave meaning, contentment, pleasure.

No more feuding, no more anger, no more conflict and no more revenge.

She could let go the burden, the dead weight she'd been dragging around, and she'd be free.

Then she glanced past his shoulder to the beach, and she saw the girl she'd once been running down the sand, laughing. And then she saw the woman she'd become, bent over her father, battling to pump air into lungs that had stopped working.

She'd grown up that Christmas on St. Matt's, and she might want to be young and innocent again but she knew who she was. Knew who Tristano was. The realist in her took over.

She couldn't kid herself. Tristano might find her physically attractive—might desire her body and be willing to bed her—but the attraction would end there. She'd be a temporary distraction, a woman to bed, but once the challenge was gone...so would she be.

"So full of mistrust," he said softly.

She turned back to him. It was on the tip of her tongue to say that he didn't know what she was thinking, that he didn't know her, but he probably knew her just as well as she knew him. "Too deeply engrained now."

He said nothing for a moment, just studied her, and Emily felt the heat between them grow. His eyes said all the things he wasn't speaking aloud: he wanted her. And the attraction was mutual.

They'd always had something raw and physical between them, a slow simmer on a low heat, with the potential to boil over. The heat wasn't definable, wasn't entirely physical, and wasn't based on externals, either.

They'd always had this peculiar competition between them, sparked by admiration and a hunger for challenge. They'd spent years dueling in unwritten one-up-manship. Who could best the other?

And yet this wasn't a contest. This was real life, serious life, and there were unholy consequences.

She tried to break the hold he had over her, reminding herself about the past. Hell had broken loose once. He'd broken it open, too. How could she forget? How could she ever let him close after what had happened?

Life was hard. Savage. She had to be hard and savage, too.

"Why can't you let the past be the past?" he asked.

She could never tell him what she'd given up to exact her revenge, never admit that she'd given up her own life, her own dreams, to bring justice to her father's name.

Tristano, standing so close, his body strong, hard, taut with honed muscle, was nothing short of sexual—physical, gorgeous. And his maleness did something to her. It made her see the world as suddenly bigger, made her realize how small and puny she was. She could fight for her father all she wanted, but his time had come and gone and now she was taking her life, taking her energy and her heart and her hope, and pouring it all into something that would never truly reap a just reward.

Because nothing she did, nothing she could ever do, would bring her father back.

And no matter how hard she fought, how long she battled, he would always have died the way he did.

By his own hand. Broken by his own despair.

So he'd never be truly avenged and she'd be—what? Alone and bitter? Bitterly lonely?

As it was, she'd given up love. Companionship. Nearly all her friendships. There'd been no time or energy for relationships, no emotion for love or even a love affair.

How could she love when she was so angry, so hard, so intent on destroying the Ferres?

All this time she'd thought she was breaking down the Ferres peace of mind, and yet it had been her own.

She'd destroyed herself, crushed what she'd needed, and for what?

She didn't like the answer—didn't want to face it. She knew herself well enough to see that if she admitted the futility of her pursuit it would negate everything she'd done these past five years. And then what would her life mean? What about all the grief? All the heartache?

"Nothing in life will ever be fair," Tristano said, and he reached for her, took her by the arm and pulled her against his bare chest, into the circle of his arms.

She resisted the tug, but he was stronger, and he was determined. She knew she couldn't want this, but at the same time she needed his arms and his mouth and his kiss.

She needed someone who would hold her, keep her. Someone who knew her and still…loved her.

But Tristano wasn't talking love. He was talking conquest. Ownership. Possession.

Entirely different than love.

She shivered at the press of his body, suddenly sensitive all over, aware of him from the hardness of his thighs to the muscular planes of his chest. He felt even better than he had down on the beach, and she was beginning to want this contact, crave the closeness.

"Stop fighting me, *carissima*," he said, and he tipped her head up and kissed the corner of her mouth so lightly that her nape tingled. "It's a useless fight," he added, and she knew he was speaking on several levels.

He wanted her to stop attacking Ferre with her counterfeit goods, and he wanted her to stop fighting the physical attraction between them. But in all honesty it would be easier for her to drop her attack on Ferre than it would be to drop her defenses with regard to him.

Tristano had been the bad guy for so long she didn't know how to think of him otherwise. And even if she stopped manufacturing her leather goods she'd still remember how Tristano had buried her father with so many legal threats that he'd had no choice but to leave the company with nothing but the shirt on his back.

She'd always remember. She had to remember. Because if Tristano could do that to her father, he could do that to her. Maybe not now, maybe not this year or next. But sooner or later he'd harden whatever it was inside him—and it wasn't a heart, she knew that much: he had no heart—and she'd be lost.

Twice broken.

Twice stricken.

And she couldn't do it. She was too proud, had too much self-respect. You could play her for a fool once, but you couldn't twice.

"Don't," she whispered, her voice tremulous as he widened his stance and drew her into even more intimate contact with his body. He was touching her everywhere, his hips cradling hers, his arms encircling her waist, hands resting low on her back, shaping her firmly against him.

"Why not?" he asked, kissing the side of her neck.

She burned at his touch, nerves tightening, skin prickling, her heart leaping to her throat. She wanted him, so wanted him, but she couldn't give in to the desire. Desire was passing, fleeting—oh, hell, desire would just complicate an already impossible situation.

"Because I haven't said I'd marry you and I don't want a cheap fling."

"It wouldn't be a cheap fling, and you *will* marry me. You're mine already. You just haven't admitted it."

Heat flooded her, heat and hunger, weakening her limbs. "Not yours."

He lowered his head, whispered against her cheekbone. "Yes, mine. And mine for the taking."

Emily closed her eyes, felt her heart race, felt everything collide. He was tormenting her, creating twin strands of excitement and fear. She couldn't allow this to happen. She couldn't seem to stop this—him— much less her response, because she wanted his touch, felt positively frantic for more him, more power, more of everything.

"Where's the protest?" he murmured, his breath warm against her heated skin.

Her lips parted to answer, but before she could speak his hands encircled her waist, his fingers splayed, spanning the width of her, fingers touching from hipbone to lower ribs. He seemed to know the right way to hold her, to silence the stream of words, the empty, frantic thoughts. She had felt lost—yes, lost—and suddenly she was found.

He was big and hard and powerful. He was strong.

He was everything she wasn't.

She repeated the last words in her head, repeating them so this time she heard, understood. He was everything she wasn't.

He was Ferre. She Pelosi. He was brain. She was heart. He was strong. She soft.

This would never work, never do.

One of his hands brushed the swell of her breast and she shuddered. "Tristano…" She'd meant to sound a warning but instead his name had come out a husky whisper.

His hands wrapped beneath her ribs, his fingers brushing the undersides of her breasts, and sensation rushed through her, nipples peaking, hardening, her body responding.

"Not going to let you go," he said, his head dropping lower, his mouth nearing hers, and she froze, waiting, heart hammering. And when his lips finally covered hers she exhaled, tension dissolving, her body sinking into him.

He tasted like the sun and the sea, like life and intensity, and as his lips moved across hers she wanted to feel more, wanted to capture what had been lost between them.

His mouth firmed, his lips parting hers, and what had been light, teasing, quickly became searching. Insistent. He demanded a response from her, his lips drawing so much more than she wanted to give—but hadn't that always been the way?

He won. He had to win because he was the conqueror. The victor. And she, despite all, gave in to him.

His thumbs stroked the outer swell of her breasts and she stiffened, sensation, fierce sensation, running rampant through her. He stroked again and, arching against him, she groaned.

He seized advantage, finding her tongue with his, using everything he knew, everything he could, to destroy, to ravish her senses. His hands caressed. His lips sucked and nipped. His body heated hers all the way through, warming her, melting the last of her resistance. She clung to him, resistance gone, thoughts silenced, leaving her warm and willing.

Tristano's lips briefly left hers and he whispered at her ear. "I told you that you were mine. And if you stopped thinking about yourself for a moment you'd realize that your mother doesn't need a nasty trial."

It was like ice water being thrown in her face. Emily jerked, hands rising to cover herself. "What?"

"Your mother doesn't need your father's problems— or his poor decisions—made public knowledge—"

"My father did nothing wrong." Her head still spun, her senses reeling, and it was a struggle to put together an argument.

"If this goes to court, there will be endless public scrutiny," he continued, as if she'd never spoken. "The media will follow the trial closely. You'll be besieged by snooping reporters, sleazy photographers, trying to get close, to get unflattering photos of your mother as she enters and exits court."

"That's enough." Her voice shook. She felt sick all the way through.

Tristano's dark blue eyes narrowed, gleamed dangerously. "*Cara*, the pressure hasn't even begun."

She took an unsteady step backwards. "How can you do this? You know Mum. You *know* her. She's not part of the business—never has been, never will be. How can you punish her like this?"

"You're the one punishing her. You're punishing her because you can't let go of the past."

Trapped. Hunted. Caught. The words circled wildly inside her head. She did feel trapped. Caught. "I can't let go of the past because my father died tragically and yours is alive and well."

"Quite well, yes," he agreed.

"Rich, too."

"That's true. My father was able to retire comfortably. But we are not our fathers—"

"No. We're not. I don't have a father anymore. I don't have his love or his advice. I don't have his laughter or his sense of humor. I just have pain." Her hands balled, fingernails digging into her palms. "And that's why I can't let go of the past. Because the hurt, the suffering, makes me desperate for justice."

"Justice?"

"Revenge," she clarified. "It's all I think about. Making you suffer." She closed her eyes, pressed a hand to her eyes, seeing red—all red—the red of heartbreak, the red of heartache.

After a moment she looked at him, numb, exhausted. "I've lived to destroy you." Ice-cold adrenaline shot through her and her voice sounded faint, eerily disjointed. "I've wanted to destroy you just the way you destroyed my father. An eye for an eye, a tooth for a tooth."

"One life for another?"

Tears filled her eyes. "Yes."

"And you'll be satisfied when you've taken my life from me?"

"I hope so. Because you're right. I hate living this way. I hate who I've become. But it's too late to go back. I am who I am, and I don't know how to change."

"Em—"

"No." She moved away from his outstretched hand, needing to keep her distance, needing to keep her heart surrounded in thick, impenetrable ice. "I'm not your Em. And you're not my Tristano. We're nothing to each other— understand?"

His expression didn't change. "I don't accept it."

"You'll have to."

"No, I don't. And as long as you're here, under my roof, I'm not going to give up on you. You need more, even if you say you don't."

Wearily she stared at him, her words used up. He didn't understand. He'd never truly understand.

"We might be nothing to each other," Tristano continued calmly, "but that doesn't change our plans. We're still heading out for the day. So pack a bag with your swimsuit, a change of clothes, and something for the evening. I'll meet you at the dock in a half-hour."

Emily threw her swimsuit and clothes into a small travel bag and headed down to the dock with time to spare. The yacht was already moored, waiting for them, and as she approached she drew a deep, rough breath, her emotions wildly chaotic.

Tristano was confusing her, knocking her off-balance with his arguments, his lovemaking, his not-so-subtle pressure and persuasion. She hated Tristano. She did.

So why did she want the old days back? Why did

she want everything the way it had once been between them, before the families had split apart, before Tristano had fallen off his pedestal?

Standing on the dock, Emily breathed in the tangy salt air and looked out across the shimmering ocean. The turquoise and lapis waters sparkled beneath the incandescent Caribbean sun. It had looked this way on the Christmas morning she'd found Father, too. Stunning. Beautiful. Unforgettable. That Hollywood kind of lovely, where the beaches are all smooth white sand, blooming hibiscus and fragrant orchid blossoms.

Tristano was late. Nearly a half-hour late. And when he arrived down on the dock he looked tense. Distracted. Not at all Tristano's usual unflappable calm.

"Sorry to make you wait," he apologized, giving her a hand and assisting her onto the sleek white yacht. "I had a call come in. It was important I took it."

She felt the warmth of his fingers around hers as she stepped onto the yacht, caught a whiff of his cologne as she moved past him. Her skin prickled with awareness, her nerves stretched taut. You hate him, she told herself harshly. Don't lose focus.

"It's fine."

He joined her on the deck. "Another offer from Tony Viders came in just as I was leaving, and it was a good offer. Clean. I couldn't ignore it."

And just like that her icy reserve shattered. "An offer for St. Matt's?"

"A very good offer."

"You accepted?"

"We'll probably counter."

Emily gripped her travel bag by the handles. "What does your estate agent think?

"That it's an incredibly generous offer. She thinks we should accept and sign today."

Sign today. *Today.* Her stomach rose up, high in her throat, and she nearly gagged. The island could be gone by the end of today. "Don't sell," she choked. "Please don't sell."

"I don't need it, Em."

No, but I do.

The yacht was pulling away from the pier in a slow, steady hum of sound and motion. But Emily couldn't feel the engine's hum—not when everything inside her was squeezing tight, choking her. Battling tears, she turned to look at the island, the green slopes emerald in the sun, the beach a blinding white. Home, she thought. This was home. Not London. Not China.

Her gaze fixed on the plantation house, nestled among lush palms. The history of St. Matt's was nearly as colorful and violent as that of the bloodthirsty pirates who'd once taken shelter in and among the islands. As a child she'd made up stories about pirates and life on the old sugar plantation. Her stories had been dramatic, rich, and her father had used to pinch her cheek and tease her—"My baby has an imagination, *si*?"

It had made him proud, her imagination. "You'll be the next generation," he'd say, pinching her cheek again. "You'll make us all so proud."

Half-laughing, half-crying, she'd beg him to stop pinching so hard, beg him to leave her alone, give her space. And now she had all the space in the world.

"You don't really want to turn St. Matt's into a tourist destination, do you?" The anguish in her voice was palpable. "You don't."

He shifted his weight, looked at her. "I can't take care of the island anymore. It takes a lot of time—time I don't have now, between managing the Altagamma and trying to control the damage you're inflicting on my business."

"So this is *my* fault?"

"It's been war, Em. You've turned my life into a living hell and it's got to stop."

He was right. But stop how? Just let him—the Ferres—win? *Again?*

"Marry me and the island is yours." His voice reached her, deep, placating. "Marry me and you'll have St. Matt's in the family forever."

He knew she'd spent every important holiday here on St. Matt's, knew all her early family memories were here. Even her favorite gifts had been given to her here. Like the shiny aqua-green bike she'd been given when she was seven. Her father had hand-painted flowers on the shiny frame, added a straw basket to the handlebars, and she'd loved the bike, ridden it everywhere. The white Vespa scooter when she was sixteen…

Her lips curved in a small, painful smile. "Marry you. How? I don't even like you."

"You could like me again. If you wanted to."

He was right. She could like him. She could like him a great deal. In fact, if she carved away the hate and anger, she'd find the love she'd felt for him all those years ago…

But there was Father, and there was pride. There was fear and problems of faith. As well as trust.

Or maybe it was just pride.

She reached up, pressed a knuckle to her brow bone, trying to ease the pressure building. "There's got to be another way to make this work, Tristano. What if we merge companies—?"

"I don't need or want your company."

"Then hire me. Put me on your staff. Let me prove that I'm valuable, that I can help Ferre's bottom line."

"I want a wife, not a business partner. And it's children I need, not another member on my board."

His bluntness sent blood rushing to her cheeks, her skin burning with shame. "Ironically, I don't need a husband. Now, I wouldn't mind sex, but I don't need someone checking up on me and asking me where I'm going and what I'm going to do."

"So what do you suggest? That I make you my mistress instead of my wife?"

The thought hadn't crossed her mind, but now that

he'd mention it, yes. Being his mistress would be a whole lot more palatable. "It's an arrangement I could live with."

He made a rude sound in his throat. "I couldn't."

She relished his expression. He looked like a dog about to lose his steak bone. "I could get an apartment in Milan. We could…*see*…each other regularly. You'd have access to me, you'd know what I was doing, and you wouldn't worry about my activities."

"What about children? How do you raise children in different households?"

"But we're not talking children—"

"I am." He caught her chin in his hand and lifted her face to his, his blue gaze hot. Possessive. "I'm Italian. And traditional. I want family, a wife. I want *you*. In my home. In my bed. Not in some apartment across town."

"You'd sleep better if I were across town."

"Probably. But the children wouldn't—"

"I don't want children."

"You always wanted children. You used to say you'd have two or three—"

"That was before." She wrenched away, moved as far from him as possible, her skin scalded from his touch, her pulse racing like mad.

"Before?" And then his expression cleared. "Before everything," he added quietly, and those two words did indeed say everything. She'd been a different person once. "But you'd be a wonderful mother."

"I'm sure I could get them fed and dressed." She

smiled, but her eyes felt dry, cold, like her heart, which had been on ice ever since Father had taken his life. "But the rest? No. Can't protect them, Tristano. They'd be hurt, they'd feel things they should never have to feel, and I can't do it…can't bring children into the world and let them be hurt like that."

"Everyone gets hurt."

"Some less than others."

"But that's life."

"Exactly my point."

She felt his hard gaze, felt his disapproval. "It's not right. You're Italian."

"Half."

"And one hundred percent devoted to your family."

She couldn't argue that. Look at how she'd spent the past five years. Look at how she'd picked up her father's cross and followed him into battle.

"I do love Mum," she said after a moment, walking away from him, moving to the other side of the deck. "But…" Emily shook her head, long hair rippling. "Can't have more. Can't risk more. There's not enough of me left." She smiled almost wistfully. "I'm sorry, Tristano. I'm sorry I've turned out the way I have. But I am what I am, and you can't change me."

His expression was surprisingly gentle as he stared back at her. "No, I don't suppose I can."

A little later the yacht slowed, circled once in the middle of the ocean, and then dropped anchor. "Where are we?" Emily asked, emerging from one of the guest bedrooms where she'd changed into her two-piece black swimsuit.

"Fifteen miles off the coast of St. Bart's."

She smoothed the straps of her suit flat. "Hassel Ledge?" she guessed, naming a famous diving spot— a ledge nearly seventy feet down—home to some of the most unusual coral in the Caribbean.

"You've been here before?" he asked.

"Long time ago." She'd only dove here once before, and it had been years ago. She'd been considerably younger—probably sixteen, maybe seventeen—and the seas had been rough that day, the water cloudy. Today the sea was calm, the sky a gorgeous blue, with not even a cloud overhead. But even with the calm seas they'd want wetsuits since they were going down so deep.

They tugged on neoprene suits, Emily drawing hers snug over the shoulder and zipping the front closed. The suit fit tightly, which was good.

Once dressed, Tristano and Emily crouched on deck, checking their equipment—the air, the gauges on the tank, the tubes. The procedures were both familiar and discomfiting. She'd gone diving with Tristano before, when there'd been a group of them one holiday, but her usual dive partner had been her father. She hadn't been down since.

Emily felt the weight of Tristano's gaze. "You okay?" he asked.

His concern felt genuine, and for the first time since

arriving she felt a flicker of their old friendship, the deep ties that had once made her love Tristano more than anyone.

"I'll be fine."

They hit the water slowly, leisurely swam down. Despite the depth they were going to, the clarity of the water was stunning. The world was so still beneath the surface of the ocean, and Emily relaxed, her tension leaving her.

For awhile they swam together, and then, as Tristano slowed to inspect a crevice harboring an eel, Emily swam on, following the intricate beds of coral, fascinated by the vivid schools of tropical fish.

Gradually she became aware of the time—she'd been under nearly thirty minutes, and she'd swum a considerable distance, following the exquisite coral reef.

She checked her gauges. She still had oxygen. Enough for another ten, fifteen minutes, but she ought to head back—return to the boat. The last thing she needed now was Tristano worrying. He already thought she didn't know how to manage her own life.

She took her time surfacing, aware of the dangers of rising too fast, and as she broke the surface of the water lifted her mask, removing her mouthpiece and swimming to the side of the boat.

One of the stewards was standing on the deck of the yacht. "Signor Ferre?" she asked, gesturing to the deck, assuming Tristano had already gone aboard.

The steward shook his head. "No. He hasn't returned yet."

Emily trod water. "He hasn't surfaced at all?"

"No. Haven't seen him since you both went down."

She glanced at her watch again. Thirty-five minutes since she and Tristano dove deep. Tristano didn't have that much in his tank. He shouldn't push it this close.

He never pushed it this close.

Emily felt a knot in her chest. Her belly did an icy flip. She didn't like this. She'd used to be a really good diver, but it had been years since she'd spent a lot of time in the water and her skills were rusty. Tristano was the more experienced scuba diver now, and he ought to be here at the moment. On the surface. At the boat. His tank was nearly empty.

So where the hell was he?

CHAPTER SIX

STILL treading water, fighting the curl of icy panic in the pit of her stomach, Emily glanced at her own gauges. Not much air left.

"I need another tank," she said to the steward. "Quickly."

"I'll get the captain."

"Where is he?"

"I'm not certain."

Time had come alive. Emily felt it breathing down her neck, showing teeth. She couldn't afford to wait for the steward to hunt down the captain, or locate another tank. Time was precious now. Fleeting.

"I'm going back down." Filled with resolve, Emily knew it was now a matter of doing what needed to be done. There'd be no fruitless discussion, no worrying. "Let the captain know there could be a problem."

"Mademoiselle—"

Emily barely heard the steward's protest. She was already swimming away from the yacht, popping the mouthpiece back between her lips and pulling the mask over her eyes.

Everything was fine, she told herself. Stay calm. Panicking will only use up more oxygen and more energy.

This time as she submerged she could hear her heart pounding in her head, hear the frantic beating of her heart echo in her ears. The water now seemed too still. The ocean less clear.

It's your imagination, she told herself, swimming deep, knowing she was a strong swimmer, capable, knowing that if anyone could help Tristano she could.

Emily knew she had just minutes left on her own tank. The pressure gauge had dropped to nothing. She had to swim fast, be smart, and not give in to fear.

Reaching Hassel Ledge, she was confronted by the immense size of the coral reef. When they'd first begun to explore the reef earlier she'd been thrilled to be under water again, and she hadn't felt anything but excitement.

But now, facing the huge, delicate reef, she realized she'd forgotten the numerous nooks and crannies, the hollows where the coral formed beautiful caves large enough for a person to swim through. Where to even start looking for Tristano?

Emily did her best to retrace her path even as her gaze swept the coral, side to side, searching for a glimpse of Tristano's midnight-blue wetsuit, or a flipper. Near the edge of the ledge she peered over and down. The sea shelf gave way to nothing but deep, bottomless ocean.

Her heart contracted. What if something had happened and he'd fallen down there?

No. Not possible. Tristano wasn't a risk-taker. Not like that. She was the risk-taker. Tristano played according to the rules.

And the rules meant he'd stay on the ledge, he'd swim close to the coral, he'd—

And then she saw him. Floating face-down above the coral, his body oddly twisted.

Bullets of ice shot through her, one after the other, until she felt nothing. Why was he floating like that? Why wasn't he moving?

She swam to Tristano's side, tried to lift him— couldn't budge him. He was stuck. She looked into his face. His eyes were closed, and yet as she touched him his lashes fluttered open and he looked at her, recognition briefly darkening his eyes before his lashes dropped again.

Propping him up she checked his gauges. Empty. The tank was empty.

How long had his tank been empty?

She removed her mouthpiece, put it to his lips and pressed an arm around him, gratified when he took a short, rough breath. Good. She slipped her tank off her shoulders, put it on his. There wasn't much left in her tank, a minute maybe, and she had to get him dislodged before it ran out.

Holding her breath, Emily ran her hands down his legs and discovered his right flipper deeply wedged in a coral crevice. She tugged on his foot. It wouldn't move.

Swimming lower, she took a closer look at his flipper. He'd obviously been struggling to free himself. His ankle looked shredded, his flipper punctured near the instep. She couldn't reach his toes.

Slipping her hands into a different crevice, Emily felt around the bottom, trying to discover what was holding Tristano prisoner. Her fingers scraped sharp rock, traced it until it ended at Tristano's flipper.

The coral rock had broken, a piece caving in on his foot.

Without tools she wasn't going to be able to get him out. And she didn't have enough air to reach the top and get the necessary tools.

Hot emotion filled her, tears burning at the backs of her eyes. This was bad. So bad. She didn't know what to do.

And then she heard her father's voice in her head. *Be calm, Emily. Stay calm. Everything's okay.*

The fear lessened—just enough. Just enough to know she needed a breath, air, time to figure this out.

She could do this. She'd find a way. She always did.

Emily swam up a little, took the mouthpiece from Tristano and drew a breath, before replacing it between his lips. The gauges had fallen. The tank had to be virtually empty. That would be her last breath, she knew. Whatever was left was Tristano's.

As she replaced the mouthpiece between Tristano's

lips his lashes fluttered open again and he looked at her, his expression puzzled, and then he shook his head, once. He tried to lift his arm, point, but he was too weak.

She put her hands on his chest. I'm not leaving you, she answered silently, defiantly. I'm going to get you out.

She could do it, she told herself. Her father believed in her. Her mother believed in her. Tristano had to believe in her, too.

With air bottled in her lungs, she dug around in the coral again, jamming her hands into the rock, pounding away with another piece of broken coral. Her head grew light. Specks drifted before her eyes. She shook her head, trying to focus. She had to free him. She *had* to.

Her father's voice whispered in her head again. *A life for a life…*

No, she answered, uncertain now if it was her father's voice or her own. *Not Tristano's life. I don't want his life. I want him happy.*

But you said…

She knew what she had said, knew far too well, and remorse washed over her. Remorse, regret, sorrow. What had she done? To him? To them? Everything about the past five years was wrong.

The sea seemed to rush at her, enclose her, and in turn she reached for Tristano. She didn't feel strong anymore. Didn't think she could hold on.

At least she was with him. She was scared, but she wouldn't want Tristano to be alone.

She loved him.

Her arms wrapped around his chest, she held tight, exhaled—and then suddenly Tristano was free. Moving. They were both moving—floating up.

Emily's lungs burned, bursting for air. Her head bobbed forward against Tristano's chest. She needed air, needed air, needed—

A mouthpiece was roughly shoved into her mouth. She gasped, gulping in air and then spluttering at her greediness. She breathed deeply, desperately, and arms wrested Tristano from her grip. She tried to protest, didn't want to let him go, and then lifting her head, she realized that help—members of Tristano's crew—had arrived.

Tristano was safe.

Two days later Tristano was home from the hospital after observation, and he was fine. At least physically. Mentally, emotionally…that was another story.

He burst through Emily's bedroom door, stalked across the room to where she sat at the writing desk.

"Don't you ever do anything so stupid again," he said roughly, his throat raw, his voice hoarse. "What you did was stupid—stupid, stupid."

She'd jumped when the door flew open, but the moment she realized it was Tristano, home safe from the hospital on St. Thomas, she smiled. "Welcome home."

His brow darkened. He practically growled at her. "Don't you dare smile, Emily Pelosi. What you did on Hassel Ledge was insane."

"Stupidaggine!" Emily flashed in Italian, rising from the desk to face him.

She'd spent two days worried sick about Tristano—unable to now sleep despite the fact the doctors had assured her that Tristano was fine—and now finally she had proof he was well. He must be well. He was certainly in a foul enough temper.

"That's rubbish," she repeated, switching to English. "I was not going to let you die, or drown. Besides, you're always taught to share oxygen during certification—"

"We weren't sharing," he interrupted grimly. "You gave up your oxygen for me. You had nothing."

"I was fine."

"Emily!" He tried to roar a protest, but it came out a guttural groan. "You don't do things like that. You can't."

"I do." She jammed her hands on her hips and attempted to stare him down, but she couldn't quite keep a straight face. He was back. He was safe. He was fine. He might be madder than hell, but this was her Tristano. Tough. Arrogant. Opinionated. "I can't help it. I am who I am. I fight for my family and I fight for those I—" She broke off and blood surged to her cheeks.

Tristano's gaze narrowed. "For those you…?" he demanded softly.

Her face burned. She felt exposed. It was one thing to try and protect Tristano. It was another to declare love. "For those I am loyal to," she concluded awkwardly.

"Loyal?"

"Yes."

"And that's why you'd die for me? Because of your *loyalty*?"

She said nothing, her lips compressing, and Tristano took another step closer. "Two days ago," he said quietly, leaning toward her, his tone conversational, "you hated me."

She swallowed, picked her words with care. "I didn't actually *hate* you."

"No?" One black eyebrow lifted. He seemed to wait in anticipation of what she'd say next.

"No."

"But your feeling now has to be pretty strong if you'd be willing to give up your oxygen for me."

"You're making a big deal out of nothing." She gestured breezily, attempting bravado. "You're fine. I'm fine. Can we just move on to other issues?"

Tristano made a hoarse sound before grinding his teeth. "You can't escape me forever."

"I'm not trying to escape. I'm trying to put a nearly tragic situation behind us and concentrate on what's before us."

"Like…?"

"Dinner."

"And…?"

"Christmas."

"Ah." He studied her face for a long moment, his gaze resting on her eyes and then her lips. "It is

Christmas, isn't it?" He suddenly reached out, stroked her cheek with the pad of his thumb. "Doesn't feel much like Christmas. We've no tree, no ornaments, no tinsel—nothing festive."

Her eyes burned and she swallowed hard, hating the lump filling her throat. "I don't need ornaments and tinsel. You're safe. You're healthy. And now you're back home. That's all I wanted this year, all I asked for."

His jaw pulled, a muscle working. "I think the lack of oxygen down there did something to you."

He was right. It had scared her witless, made her realize everything she was about to lose—time, life, love. Tristano.

Emily tried to smile but her chest constricted, the muscles tight. Her emotions were hot and painfully chaotic. "It just brought me to my senses. I realized I was everything you said I was—bitter, hard, selfish—"

Tristano abruptly leaned forward, pulling her into his arms, firmly against his body, and silenced her words with a long kiss.

"I never said that," he said much later, when he finally lifted his head. "I know you're not hard or bitter. You just miss your father. And I don't blame you. I never have."

"You hated him."

"I didn't. As you said, we were practically family. Nothing about this situation has been easy." Gently he smoothed a tendril of hair from her cheek and then lightly caressed the curve of her cheekbone with the tip of his finger. "And losing your father the way you did would tear anyone's heart to pieces."

The lump in her throat seemed to swell. She gulped air, dizzy, feeling submerged all over again.

"I know," Tristano added, tracing the shape of her mouth. "I know how he died. I've known for years. I just never knew what to say or do."

She couldn't speak. She tried to smile, but she couldn't do that either.

"Emily, an eye for an eye—"

"No." She shook her head fiercely.

"A tooth for a tooth."

"No, Tristano. I don't want your life. I don't want this to continue. I can't anymore. It's wrong. Wrong of me. I'm ashamed. Ashamed that I wanted to hurt you that way—"

He touched her mouth with the tip of his finger to silence the stream of words. "But you have my life. I give you myself. Completely. Freely."

"No," she whispered against his finger, even as her emotions rioted inside her. She wanted to say yes, wanted to throw her arms around him, hold him, feel his warmth and strength all the way through. But she was scared.

"Emily, everything's changing—and you better get used to it."

Everything's changing...

Tristano's words echoed in her head as Emily

dressed for dinner. Everything *was* changing, and she wasn't sure where the changes would lead…or what the changes would entail. Setting her hairbrush down, she turned toward the bathroom window, gazed out over the turquoise ocean. The sun had begun to drop in the sky, painting the horizon bronze and orange.

She wanted a different life, was ready for more out of life. And if Tristano proposed again would she accept?

She cared for Tristano—cared deeply, passionately—but in her mind marriage could never be a business relationship. Marriage wasn't about contracts or deals, terms or power. It was love. Plain and simple.

Finished dressing, Emily checked her reflection in the mirror twice, nervous. She was wearing all black tonight—a black lace halter top by one of Italy's top designers paired with slim black silk pants and black leather criss-cross wooden mules. At the last moment she'd swept her hair up, pinning it in a loose chignon, and the only jewelry she wore was a wide sterling silver bangle on her wrist.

Now or never, she told herself, leaving her room to meet Tristano.

He stood on the terrace, facing the ocean, waiting for her. The sun's orange rays cast long golden fingers of light in every direction. He looked amazing. So strong, so male, so important in her world.

His head turned and he looked at her. The reddish-gold light played off his striking cheekbones, bronzing his dark hair. *"Bella,"* he murmured. "You look beautiful."

"Grazie."

Dinner was served in the formal dining room with the expansive windows overlooking the ocean. The table had been covered in a red linen cloth, the flowers were white orchids with dark green, and the red linen napkins had been tied scroll-like, with a pearly seashell on a white satin ribbon.

But seated at the table, directly opposite Tristano, Emily could barely get the appetizer down. Food was the last thing on her mind. Her appetite wanted something entirely different from what the chef was preparing in the shiny stainless steel kitchen.

Tristano knew, too. She looked up from her little plate of canapés and her gaze locked with his. He was smiling, but his expression was intense, his dark blue eyes hiding nothing, and she knew something was going to happen soon.

She'd been waiting for that something ever since she'd arrived. She wanted him. Wanted to be seduced. Loved.

"Let's go somewhere a little more private," he said, pushing away from the table.

She could only nod. She wanted to go somewhere more private. She wanted him to strip off her clothes— the black lace halter, the silk trousers, the heels. She wanted his mouth where her lace and silk had been. She wanted his hands everywhere.

Wordlessly she followed him from the dining room, through the mahogany great room to Tristano's bedroom suite. She'd never been there, and when he pushed open the door she knew it was most definitely his room. The walls were painted a rich chocolate, the cream raw silk drapes were drawn for the night, and the large iron lamps had been turned down low. The bed was covered in the same rich silk as the windows and the top cover had been pulled back to reveal paler ivory sheets.

Tristano stood in the middle of the bedroom. "Close the door," he commanded quietly, and she did.

"Lock it," he directed.

She locked it.

"Look at me."

Heart racing, she forced herself to turn and meet Tristano's gaze. He looked hard, determined, fire blazing in his dark blue eyes. His navy shirt was open at the throat, exposing the upper planes of his bronze chest where the muscle was dense and smooth.

As she watched he began unbuttoning his shirt, one button at a time. His shirt unbuttoned, he held out a hand. "Come to me."

She suddenly felt fear.

"I'm afraid," she confessed, skin heating, blushing. "Of me?"

"No. Of…this." She could see he didn't understand. She wasn't sure she could explain, but she tried. "I think I've forgotten how."

His brow knit. "Has it been that long since you've made love?"

Years, she thought. Her desire had been killed along

with her dreams. But the desire was returning, and she wanted Tristano so much she didn't know if she could handle the fierceness of her emotions. "Yes."

"Nervous?"

"Very." That much she could admit.

"I'll come to you, then." His gaze was possessive as he walked toward her. At her side, he drew her against him, cupped the back of her head and kissed her.

She felt his fingers in her hair, felt the press of his hand against her head, felt her mouth quiver beneath his.

He deepened the kiss, and as he kissed her he slid a hand up her ribcage, beneath her flimsy lace halter top, to cup one breast. She gasped as he brushed the fullness of her breast, his fingers catching, tugging on her hardening nipple.

She couldn't silence her husky groan of pleasure, couldn't keep from pressing closer to him. She needed more from him, needed all of him.

Funny how she could go years without contact and yet just one touch from Tristano and she couldn't survive twenty-four hours without more. Without everything.

She felt his hands at her neck as he unhooked the top, peeling the delicate black lace down over her bare breasts. "Stand still," he said, stepping back to better appreciate the fullness of her breasts, the taut tips aching to be touched. "I want to look at you."

But she didn't want to be looked at. She wanted touch, and she wanted it now. Emily reached for

Tristano, clasped his arms, pulled him back to her. "You can look at me later. Now I want you. I want us."

Her clothes seemed to fall away as he laid her on the bed, his hands caressing her skin, his mouth following the path of his hands, sucking, kissing, tasting her breast, her hip, her inner thigh. Emily shifted impatiently against Tristano's body. She loved the feel of his hands and mouth on her heated skin, but she wanted more of him—the more that could only be answered with him inside her.

He moved between her knees, poised between her thighs, and she reached out, stroked the hard length of him. His erection strained against her, and her body was very warm and willing.

Gazing up at Tristano's face, she thought he'd never looked more gorgeous or sensual as he lightly stroked between her thighs, his fingers finding every sensitive nerve. She felt the warm slickness of his finger against her, slick because of her, and it aroused her even more, her readiness for him. He'd been her first lover and no one had ever replaced him in her heart or her affections.

She trembled as he stroked her again, the pad of his finger teasing the delicate hooded nub, and she lifted her hips, trying to find satisfaction. And then he was on his knees, between her thighs, and she felt him press against her. Her body was tight, she was nervous as well as excited, and Tristano leaned over her, kissed her, teasing her with his lips and tongue.

He slid in slowly, deeply filling her. The moment

he'd buried himself all the way inside her she dug her fingers into his shoulders, overwhelmed by the incredible sensation of him with her, of him in her. He was warm and hard and her body gripped his, holding fast. For the first time in years Emily felt safe, secure. It was as if she'd stumbled her way home.

And then he moved, a long, slow thrust that made her hold him tighter, closer, as helpless tears burned the back of her eyes. She was here, with Tristano, and she knew even if he'd never said the words that he loved her. He had to love her. No one else had ever touched her like this, held her so.

As he thrust again she rose up to meet him, overwhelmed by an emotion she'd never thought she'd feel again. Tristano was supposed to be the enemy, but he actually was the hero. He'd rescued her, saved her from herself.

His body filled her, pressing more deeply, and she opened her arms, opened her heart, needing him, needing to give herself over to him. There had been so much anger, so much hurt and resentment, and suddenly she needed only that which was good, that which was life-giving.

Together they made love, their bodies moving smoothly, seamlessly, both silent, needing no words at this time. But his thrusts were stronger, deeper, and she felt the muscles deep in her belly begin to tighten. Hot emotion rose, waves of love and waves of need.

Her father had left, but Tristano remained. An eye

for an eye, a tooth for a tooth, a life for a life. She would have given her life for Tristano's. She loved him more than she could ever say. Her lips found his, clung, trying to tell him that he was right, she needed him—needed him not just now but always, forever. She needed his love and his strength, his courage, his stability. But most of all she needed him to spend her life with.

Suddenly the pleasure was too hot, too bright, the sensation too intense. She reached for his hands, found his wrists and gripped him tightly as the pleasure surged to a blinding peak.

"Tristano," she whispered urgently, her nails biting into his skin, his body both familiar and tantalizingly new. It was like being hit by a tidal wave, a rush of brilliant green and blue. The sun seemed to glint whitely in her eyes and she was gone, sucked under, pulled in, her body rippling beneath his.

He sucked her breath from her as his orgasm hit hard, strong.

"Bella," he murmured against her mouth as his body emptied into her. "I want children," he said, kissing her. "Many, many children—with you."

CHAPTER SEVEN

LATE the next morning Tristano stood in his silk boxers on the balcony overlooking the water, knowing things were about to get exciting.

He wasn't sure how Emily would react to what he had to tell her, and, lifting the small porcelain cup, he took another sip of strong black coffee. It had been an incredible night, a night stretching into morning, the morning stretching into midday.

Just remembering the hours of lovemaking, the erotic pleasure he'd found in Emily's smooth, satin skin, in her softness, in her willingness to meet him where he was made him hard all over again.

It had been years since he'd felt desire like that— years since ardor hadn't been just an idea but a tangible thing. And desire…hunger…made him feel young, alive, strong.

The corner of his mouth lifted in a small self-mocking smile. Rather ironic that the two best lovers he'd ever known had been Emily the Innocent and Emily the Woman. There was just something about the way she felt…about the way she fit his body, fit his life.

She belonged in his life. Maybe it was fairness, justice, or maybe it was the fact that he loved her, understood her. He knew she belonged with him.

Now if he could only convince her of the fact before the wedding began…

He returned to the bedroom where Emily still slept the deep sleep of one who has earned her rest. Her long brown hair was a silky gloss against the pale ivory cotton pillowcases. Beautiful Emily.

He leaned over and kissed her cheek, near her ear, smelling the hint of perfumed bodywash from their shower some hours before, when they'd wandered from bed to shower and back to bed again. They'd been like teenagers…insatiable…the night had been unforgettable.

"Wake up, *carissima*," he whispered, brushing his lips across her cheek a second time. "Time to get up."

Emily's lashes fluttered. She stretched and rolled over onto her back to get a look at Tristano. Her blue-green eyes were still cloudy with the unfocused gaze of lingering sleep. "What time is it?"

He lifted a long tendril of hair from her cheek, smoothing it back. "Time to wake up and dress."

"Why?"

"Your mother will be here in an hour."

She struggled into a sitting position, sheet haphazardly clutched to her breasts. "*My* mother?"

"The very one."

Emily blinked up at Tristano and dragged a hand through her tangled hair, trying to clear her head. "Why is Mum coming here?"

"It's Christmas."

Recognition dawned. "It is! Oh, Tristano, lovely. Really—that's lovely of you. I'll be with Mum for Christmas."

"Annelise, too."

She was blinking again, her brow wrinkled anew. "Annelise?"

"Yes. They're arriving quite soon."

"But why Annelise?"

Tristano kept his expression carefully neutral. "She didn't want to miss the wedding, and I thought you'd want her as a witness—"

"Wedding?" Emily interrupted, the sheet creasing in her fists. "Is that what you just said?"

"Yes."

Emily's mouth dried. Frowning, she touched her tongue to her upper lip. Her mouth was like cotton, her lips chapped from a night of kissing.

Tristano glanced down at her, his expression kind, considerate. "Should I send for coffee, *cara*? Might help clear the head a little."

"Yes." Her head definitely needed clearing, because she could have sworn that Tristano had said Mum was on her way to St. Matt's for their wedding and Annelise would be a witness. "I don't remember any plans for a wedding," she said, leaving the bed, accepting the white silk robe Tristano was holding out to her.

"We've discussed it many times these past few days."

Emily cinched the silky sash tightly around her waist. "And I always said no."

"But you didn't mean no."

She couldn't believe it. She'd only spent one night in his bed and he was already making decisions for her, acting as if she didn't have a mind of her own.

"Tristano, I'm not marrying you." She crossed her arms over her chest, the cool silk fabric shaping her full, firm breasts. "It may be Christmas, and you may have my mother flying in, but there's no wedding today and no wedding tomorrow. We're lovers. Nothing more."

He grimaced. "You explain that to your mother."

"I will."

"Because she's thrilled. She's like a kid at Christmas—" He broke off. "An English cliché, but you get the picture."

Unfortunately Emily did. She headed for the bathroom, then turned in a circle, faced Tristano again, her head spinning. "I'm not a puppet or a doll—some little plaything you can manipulate."

"I know."

She couldn't believe he was doing this—couldn't believe he was controlling her like this, shifting her as if she had strings attached to her arms. Little wooden marionette girl.

There was a discreet knock on the door and Tristano opened it. One of the young French Caribbean housemaids carried a silver tray into the bedroom, setting up the coffee service on the round mahogany table—an antique piece sent over as a wedding gift to the daughter of the original plantation owners from England.

Emily waited for the young maid to leave, doors quietly closing behind her, before facing Tristano. Heart hammering, her eyes searched his. She needed to understand, needed the truth. "Why would you tell my mother we're getting married?"

"Because I thought it'd make her happy—"

"You don't tell people things like that… You don't get their hopes up…"

"And I love you."

Emily's lips parted and then closed. She stared at Tristano, not knowing what to say now.

"We're meant to be together, Emily. Ferre & Pelosi. It's the way it always was. It's the way it should always be."

"But you don't want a business associate."

"No, I want a lover. A best friend. A wife." He reached out, stroked her cheek, smiled down into her eyes clouding with tears. "And I do want you back in the business. I want you on my side, working with me, to make Ferre & Pelosi the best it can be."

"Your father doesn't want Ferre & Pelosi—"

"But he does." Tristano's voice dropped and his expression grew sober. "My father and I have discussed the mistakes we made—both then and now. We were both wrong. We acted rashly, my father and I. My father was angry, and I was determined to do what was right. But what I did wasn't right. And I ask you to forgive us...forgive me..."

"I forgive you. But your father..." Her voice drifted away and she gazed across the bedroom, seeing not the painted walls or the view of the water but the morning she had discovered her father, the anguish of losing so much so quickly. "Your father prospered while my father died."

"But my father didn't prosper. My father went to hell, too." He crouched before her, his hands on her thighs. "You don't know how he suffered, Emily. How your father's death broke him. My father loved your father. As you said, they were like brothers. It's been a nightmare for the Ferres, too."

But her father's name had been blackened; her father's shame had crushed them.

Turning her head, she looked at Tristano, and her self-righteous anger died. Because she saw now the suffering in Tristano's face, saw the haunted expression in his eyes. Tristano had hurt, too. And Tristano was a man of his word. If he said his father, Briano, had suffered, regretted his actions, then Emily believed him.

Reaching up, she touched Tristano's face, his hard cheekbone, the square cut of his jaw. "My father was just borrowing that money," she said softly, needing to clear his name one last time. "It was a loan...he'd written a letter, had it notarized. He was going to pay the money back." She blinked, looked into Tristano's eyes. "Father wasn't a thief."

"I know. My father knows." He hesitated. "My father isn't the way you remember him. He's quite ill, Emily. Very frail. He's grieved terribly…and I don't think he'll ever recover. But know this: my father did love your father. We all did."

Emily blinked again and a tear slipped free, sliding from the corner of her eye. "What now? How do we move forward?"

"We just do." Tristano's lips curved but his smile was hard, fierce. "We learn from our mistakes, we accept what we've lost and we decide we deserve happiness. We make a new life, together."

"Again," she whispered.

"Ferre & Pelosi."

"Ferre & Pelosi," she echoed, before biting her lower lip to keep the tears from falling.

The corner of his mouth lifted. "Has a nice ring to it."

"Yes."

His eyes searched hers. "So you'll marry me? You'll come live with me, share a life with me, my own Emily?"

She couldn't look away from his lovely blue eyes—the blue of the sky before midnight, blue like the sapphire waters surrounding St. Matt's, blue she loved better than any shade in the world. St. Matt's was like a precious emerald surrounded by sapphire and gold, and yet it was nothing…meant nothing… compared to the love she felt for him. Tristano. Her treasure.

"Yes." She smiled at him, heart full, aching. "I'll marry you, live with you, share a life with you."

He kissed her, her lips trembling beneath his. She reached for him, hanging on to his forearms, needing his strength. The kiss stole her breath, weakened her knees, and warmed her soul all the way through.

She moved even closer to him, slipping into his arms, and the strength of his body comforted and teased. They'd made love for hours last night, and yet she hungered for him again.

"Make love to me," she urged, shuddering as his hands slid beneath her robe, settling on her naked satin skin.

It was too sweet an invitation for him to resist.

Later, sated, their bodies still warm and damp, Tristano cupped her face in his hands and kissed her again, more lightly but no less tenderly.

"Merry Christmas, Em," he murmured, his voice still husky. "I hope we can spend every Christmas here."

"Together, you mean," she corrected lazily, her palm pressed to his abdomen, loving the feel of sleek sinewy muscle beneath golden skin.

"Together, yes, but specifically here."

"Here?"

"St. Matt's."

It took her a moment to understand, her mind as languid as her limbs, and then with a prickle of heat and another prickle of joy she pushed up on her elbow to gaze down at him. "You're not selling the island?"

"I can't." He reached up, drew her down to him, kissed her deeply.

She could hardly breathe. "Why not?"

His eyes glinted at her for a moment and then, tossing back the covers, he leaned out of bed, opened a drawer on the nightstand and pulled out an envelope. "Open it," he said.

Hands shaking, she tore the back of the rich cream envelope open and drew out a Christmas card. She read the sentiment on the front, opened the card and read the verse printed inside. It was romantic, emotional, but it was what he'd written below, in his own strong, firm handwriting that brought tears to her eyes.

To commemorate our first Christmas together, I deed the island of St. Matthew's to you, Emily Pelosi.

She looked up at him, eyes burning, tears not far off. But she'd had enough tears, didn't want to cry.

She shook her head, struggled to speak, words nearly impossible. "You're giving the island back to me?"

"It should be yours. No one will ever love St. Matt's like you do."

And despite her best efforts the tears fell. It was impossible to hold such fierce, hot emotion in.

Wrapping her arms around Tristano, Emily held

him tightly, afraid to let go. This wasn't a dream, was it? This wasn't a wonderful dream that would disappear when she woke?

"Tell me you're real."

"I'm real."

"Tell me I'm awake."

"You're awake."

But it wasn't enough. Her heart burned, bursting, and she needed him more than she could ever say. "I love you, Tristano," she whispered against his neck, where his skin was warm and fragrant and everything she loved best. "You've no idea how much I love you."

He reached up to cup the back of her head. "But I do. That's just it, Em. I do." His deep voice broke and he drew her even closer, holding her within his arms, holding tight, as if to protect her from every gust of wind and storm. "A life for a life, Emily, and you have mine."

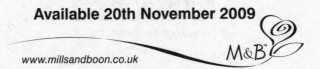